PATRICIA D. CORNWELL

Body of Evidence

WARNER BOOKS

A *Warner* Book

First published in Great Britain in 1991 by
Macdonald & Co (Publishers) Ltd
This edition published by Warner Books in 1992

A CIP catalogue record for this book is available from the British Library.

ISBN 0 7088 5327 7

Printed and bound in Great Britain by
BPCC Hazells Ltd
Member of BPCC Ltd

Warner Books
A Division of
Little, Brown and Company (UK) Limited
165 Great Dover Street
London SE1 4YA

For Ed,
Special Agent and Special Friend

PROLOGUE

August 13
KEY WEST

Dear M,

Thirty days have passed in measured shades of sunlit color and changes in the wind. I think too much and do not dream.

Most afternoons I'm at Louie's writing on the porch and looking out at the sea. The water is mottled emerald green over the mosaic of sandbars, and aqua as it deepens. The sky goes on forever, clouds white puffs always moving like smoke. A constant breeze washes out the sounds of people swimming and sailboats anchoring just beyond the reef. The porch is covered and when a sudden storm whips up, as it often does late afternoon, I stay at my table smelling the rain and watching it turn the water nappy like fur rubbed the wrong way. Sometimes it pours and the sun shines at the same time.

Nobody bothers me. By now I am part of the restaurant's family, like Zulu, the black Lab who splashes after

Frisbees, and the stray cats who silently wander up to politely wait for scraps. Louie's four-legged wards eat better than any human. It is a comfort to watch the world treat its creatures kindly. I cannot complain about my days.

It is the nights I dread.

When my thoughts creep back into dark crevices and spin their fearful webs I pitch myself into crowded Old Town streets, drawn to noisy bars like a moth to light. Walt and PJ have refined my nocturnal habits to an art. Walt returns to the rooming house first, at twilight because his silver jewelry business in Mallory Square grinds to a halt after dark. We open bottles of beer and wait for PJ. Then out we go, bar to bar, usually ending up at Sloppy Joe's. We are becoming inseparable. I hope the two of them will always be inseparable. Their love no longer seems out of the ordinary to me. Nothing does, except the death I see.

Men emaciated and wan, their eyes windows through which I see tormented souls. AIDS is a holocaust consuming the offerings of this small island. Odd I should feel at home with the exiled and the dying. I may be survived by all of them. When I lie awake at night listening to the whirring of the window fan I'm seized by images of how it will happen.

Every time I hear a telephone ring, I remember. Every time I hear someone walking behind me, I turn around. At night I look in my closet, behind the curtain and under my bed, then prop a chair in front of the door.

Dear God, I don't want to go home.

Beryl

September 30
KEY WEST

Dear M,

Yesterday at Louie's, Brent came out to the porch and said the phone was for me. My heart raced as I went inside and was answered by long distance static and the line going dead.

The way that made me feel! I've been telling myself I'm too paranoid. He would have said something, and delighted in my fear. It's impossible he knows where I am, impossible he could have tracked me here. One of the waiters is named Stu. He recently broke off with a friend up north, then moved here. Maybe his friend called and the connection was bad. It sounded like he asked for "Straw" instead of "Stu," and then when I answered he hung up.

I wish I had never told anyone my nickname. I am Beryl. I am Straw. I am frightened.

The book isn't finished. But I'm almost out of money, and the weather has turned. This morning it's dark and there's a fierce wind. I've stayed in my room because if I tried to work at Louie's the pages would blow out to sea. Streetlights have blinked on. Palm trees are struggling against the wind, fronds like inside-out umbrellas. The world moans outside my window like something wounded, and when the rain hits the glass it sounds as if a dark army has marched in and Key West is under siege.

I must leave soon. I will miss the island. I will miss PJ and Walt. They have made me feel cared for and safe. I don't know what I'll do when I get back to Richmond. Perhaps I should move right away, but I don't know where I will go.

Beryl

1

Returning the Key West letters to their manila folder, I got out a packet of surgical gloves, tucked it inside my black medical bag, and took the elevator down one floor to the morgue.

The tile hallway was damp from being mopped, the autopsy suite locked and closed for business. Diagonally across from the elevator was the stainless-steel refrigerator, and opening its massive door, I was greeted by the familiar blast of cold, foul air. I located the gurney inside without bothering to check toe tags, recognizing the slender foot protruding from a white sheet. I knew every inch of Beryl Madison.

Smoky-blue eyes stared dully from slitted lids, her face slack and marred with pale open cuts, most of them on the left side. Her neck was laid wide open to her spine, the strap muscles severed. Closely spaced over her left chest and breast were nine stab wounds spread open likelarge red buttonholes and almost perfectly vertical. They had been inflicted in rapid succession, one right after the other, the force so violent there were hilt marks in her skin. Cuts to her forearms and hands ranged from a quarter of an inch to four and a half inches in length. Counting two on her back, and excluding her stab wounds and cut throat, there were twenty-seven cutting injuries, all of them inflicted while she was attempting to ward off the slashing of a wide, sharp blade.

I would not need photographs or body diagrams. When I closed my eyes I could see Beryl Madison's face. I could see in sickening detail the violence inflicted upon her body. Her left lung was punctured four times. Her carotid arteries were almost transected. Her aortic arch, pulmonary artery, heart, and pericardial sac were penetrated. She was, for all practical purposes, dead by the time the madman almost decapitated her.

I was trying to make sense of it. Someone had threatened to murder her. She fled to Key West. She was terrified beyond reason. She did not want to die. The night she returned to Richmond it happened.

Why did you let him into your house? Why in God's name did you?

Rearranging the sheet, I returned the gurney to the others bearing bodies against the refrigerator's back wall. By this time tomorrow her body would be cremated, her ashes en route to California. Beryl Madison would have turned thirty-four next month. She had no living relatives, no one in this world, it seemed, except a half sister in Fresno. The heavy door sucked shut.

The tarmac of the parking lot behind the Office of the Chief Medical Examiner was warm and reassuring beneath my feet, and I could smell the creosote of nearby railroad trestles baking in the unseasonably warm sun. It was Halloween.

The bay door was open wide, one of my morgue assistants hosing off the concrete. He playfully arched water, slapping it close enough for me to feel mist around my ankles.

"Hey, Dr. Scarpetta, you keeping banker's hours now?" he called out.

It was a little past four-thirty. I rarely left the office before six.

"Need a lift somewhere?" he added.

"I've got a ride. Thanks," I answered.

I was born in Miami. I was no stranger to the part of the world where Beryl had hidden during the summer. When I closed my eyes I saw the colors of Key West. I saw bright greens and blues and sunsets so gaudy only God can get away with them. Beryl Madison should never have come home.

A brand-new LTD Crown Victoria, shining like black glass, slowly pulled into the lot. Expecting the familiar beat-up Plymouth, I was startled when the new Ford's window hummed open. "You waiting for the bus or what?" Mirrored shades reflected my surprised face. Lieutenant Pete Marino was trying to look blasé as electronic locks opened with a firm click.

"I'm impressed," I said, settling into the plush interior.

"Went with my promotion." He revved the engine. "Not bad, huh?"

After years of broken-down dray horses, Marino had finally gotten himself a stallion.

I noticed the hole in the dash as I got out my cigarettes.

"You been plugging in your bubble light or just your electric razor?"

"Oh, hell," he complained. "Some drone swiped my lighter. At the car wash. I mean, I'd only had the car a day, you believe it? I take her in, right? Was too busy bitching after the fact, the brushes broke off the antenna, was giving the drones holy hell about that . . ."

Sometimes Marino reminded me of my mother.

". . . wasn't until later I noticed the damn lighter gone." He paused, digging in his pocket as I rummaged through my purse for matches.

"Yo, Chief, thought you was gonna quit smoking," he said rather sarcastically, dropping a Bic lighter in my lap.

"I am," I muttered. "Tomorrow."

The night Beryl Madison was murdered I was out enduring an overblown opera followed by drinks in an overrated English pub with a retired judge who became something less than honorable as the evening progressed. I wasn't wearing my pager. Unable to reach me, the police had summoned Fielding, my deputy chief, to the scene. This would be the first time I had been inside the slain author's house.

Windsor Farms was not the sort of neighborhood where one would expect anything so hideous to happen. Homes were large and set back from the street on impeccably landscaped lots. Most had burglar alarm systems, and all featured central air, eliminating the need for open windows. Money can't buy eternity, but it can buy a certain degree of security. I had never had a homicide case from the Farms.

"Obviously she had money from somewhere," I observed as Marino halted at a stop sign.

A snowy-haired woman walking her snowy Maltese squinted at us as the dog sniffed a tuft of grass, which was followed by the inevitable.

"What a worthless fuzz ball," he said, staring disdainfully at the woman and the dog moving on. "Hate mutts like that. Yap their damn heads off and piss all over the place. Gonna have a dog, ought to be something with teeth."

"Some people simply want company," I said.

"Yeah." He paused, then picked up on my earlier statement. "Beryl Madison had money, most of it tied up in her crib. Apparently whatever savings she had, she blew the dough down there in Queer West. We're still sorting through her paperwork."

"Had any of it been gone through?"

"Don't look like it," he replied. "Found out she didn't do half bad as a writer—bucks-wise. Appears she used several pen names. Adair Wilds, Emily Stratton, Edith Montague." The mirrored shades turned my way again.

None of the names were familiar except Stratton. I said, "Her middle name is Stratton."

"Maybe accounting for her nickname, Straw."

"That and her blond hair," I remarked.

Beryl's hair was honey blond streaked gold by the sun. She was petite, with even, refined features. She may have been striking in life. It was hard to say. The only photograph from life I had seen was the one on her driver's license.

"When I talked to her half sister," Marino was explaining, "I found out Beryl was called Straw by the people she was close to. Whoever she was writing down there in the Keys, this person was aware of her nickname. That's the impression I get." He adjusted the visor. "Can't figure why she Xeroxed those letters. Been chewing on that. I mean, how many people do you know who make photocopies of personal letters they write?"

"You've indicated she was an inveterate record keeper," I reminded him.

"Right. That's bugging me, too. Supposedly the squirrel's been threatening her for months. What'd he do? What'd he say? Don't know, because she didn't tape his calls or write nothing down. The lady makes photocopies of personal letters but don't keep a record when someone's threatening to whack her. Tell me if that makes sense."

"Not everybody thinks the way we do."

"Well, some people don't *think* because they're in the middle of something they don't want nobody to know about," he argued.

Pulling into a drive, he parked in front of the garage door. The grass was badly overgrown and spangled with tall dandelions swaying in the breeze, and there was a FOR SALE sign planted near the mailbox. Still tacked across the gray front door was a ribbon of yellow crime-scene tape.

"Her ride's inside the garage," Marino said as we got out. "A nice black Honda Accord EX. Some details about it you might find interesting."

We stood on the drive and looked around. The slanted rays of the sun were warm on the back of my shoulders and neck. The air was cool, the pervasive hum of autumn insects the only sound. I took a slow, deep breath. I was suddenly very tired.

Her house was International style, modern and starkly simplistic with a horizonal frontage of large windows supported by ground-floor piers, bringing to mind a ship with an open lower deck. Built of fieldstone and gray-stained wood, it was the sort of house a wealthy young couple might build—big rooms, high ceilings, a lot of expensive and wasted space. Windham Drive dead-ended at her lot, which explained why no one had heard or seen anything until it was too late. The house was cloistered by oaks and pines on two sides, drawing a curtain of foliage between Beryl and her nearest neighbors. In back, the yard sharply dropped off into a ravine of underbrush and boulders, leveling out into an expanse of virgin timber stretching as far as I could see.

"Damn. Bet she had deer," Marino said as we wandered around back. "Something, huh? You look out your windows, think you got the world to yourself. Bet the view's something when it snows. Me, I'd love a crib like this. Build a nice fire in the winter, pour yourself a little bourbon, and just look out at the woods. Must be nice to be rich."

"Especially if you're alive to enjoy it."

"Ain't that the truth," he said.

Fall leaves crackled beneath our shoes as we rounded the west wing. The front door was level with the patio, and I noted the peephole. It stared at me like a tiny empty eye. Marino flicked a cigarette butt, sent it sailing into the grass, then dug in a pocket of his powder-blue trousers. His jacket was off, his big belly hanging over his belt, his short-sleeved white shirt open at the neck and wrinkled around his shoulder holster.

He produced a key attached to a yellow evidence tag, and as I watched him open the dead-bolt lock I was startled anew by the size of his hands. Tan and tough, they reminded me of baseball mitts. He would never have made a musician or a dentist. Somewhere in his early fifties, with thinning gray hair and a face as shopworn as his suits, he was still formidable enough to give most people pause. Big cops like him rarely get in fights. The street punks take one look and sit on their bravado.

We stood in a rectangle of sunlight inside the foyer and worked on pairs of gloves. The house smelled stale and dusty, the way houses smell when they have been shut up for a while. Though the Richmond police department's Identification Unit, or ID, had thoroughly processed the scene, nothing had been moved. Marino had assured me the house would look exactly as it had when Beryl's body was found two nights earlier. He shut the door and flipped on a light.

"As you can see," his voice echoed, "she had to have let the guy in. No sign of forcible entry, and the joint's got a triple A burglar alarm." He directed my attention to the panel of buttons by the door, adding, "Deactivated at the moment. But it was in working order when we got here, screaming bloody murder, which is why we found her so fast to begin with."

He went on to remind me the homicide was originally called in as an audible alarm. At shortly after eleven P.M., one of Beryl's neighbor's dialed 911 after the alarm had been going for nearly thirty minutes. A patrol unit responded and the officer found the front door ajar. Minutes later he was on his radio requesting backups.

The living room was in shambles, the glass coffee table on its side. Magazines, a crystal ashtray, several art deco bowls and a flower vase were strewn over the dhurrie rug.

A pale blue leather wingchair was overturned, a cushion from the matching sectional sofa nearby. On the white-washed wall left of a door leading into a hallway were dark spatters of dried blood.

"Does her alarm have a time delay?" I asked.

"Oh, yeah. You open the door and the alarm hums about fifteen seconds, long enough for you to punch in your code before it goes off."

"Then she must have opened the door, deactivated the alarm, let the person in, and then reset the alarm while he was still here. Otherwise, it would never have gone off later, when he left. Interesting."

"Yeah," Marino replied, "interesting as shit."

We were inside the living room, standing near the overturned coffee table. It was sooty with dusting powder. The magazines on the floor were news and literary publications, all of them several months old.

"Did you find any recent newspapers or magazines?" I asked. "If she bought a paper locally, it could be important. Anywhere she went after getting off the plane is worth checking."

I saw his jaw muscles flex. Marino hated it when he assumed I was telling him how to do his job.

He said, "There were a couple of things upstairs in her bedroom where her briefcase and bags was. A Miami *Herald* and something called the *Keynoter*, has mostly real estate listings for the Keys. Maybe she was thinking of moving down there? Both papers came out Monday. She must've bought them, maybe picked them up in the airport on her way back to Richmond."

"I'd be interested in what her realtor has to say . . ."

"Nothing, that's what he has to say," he interrupted.

"Has no idea where Beryl was and only showed her house once while she was gone. Some young couple. Decided the price was too high. Beryl was asking three hundred Gs for the joint." He looked around, his face impervious. "Guess someone could get a deal now."

"Beryl took a taxi home from the airport the night she got in." I doggedly pursued the details.

He got out a cigarette and pointed with it. "Found the receipt in the foyer there, on that little table by the door. Already checked out the driver, a guy named Woodrow Hunnel. Dumb as a bag of hammers. Said he was waiting in the line of cabs at the airport. She flagged him down. This was close to eight, it was raining cats and dogs. He let her out here at the house maybe forty minutes later, said he carried her two suitcases to the door, then split. The fare was twenty-six bucks, including the tip. He was back at the airport about half an hour later picking up another fare."

"You're sure, or is this what he told you?"

"Sure as I'm damn standing here." He tapped the cigarette on his knuckle and began fingering the filtered tip with his thumb. "We checked out the story. Hunnel was shooting straight with us. He didn't touch the lady. There wasn't time."

I followed his eyes to the dark spatters near the doorway. The killer's clothing would have been bloody. It wasn't likely a cabdriver with bloody clothes was going to be picking up fares.

"She hadn't been home long," I said. "Got in around nine and a neighbor calls in her alarm at eleven. It had been going for a half hour, meaning the killer was gone by around ten-thirty."

"Yeah," he answered. "That's the hardest part to figure. Based on those letters, she was scared shitless. So she sneaks back to the city, locks herself inside her house, even has her three-eighty on the kitchen counter—show you that when we get there. Then, boom! The doorbell rings or what? Next thing you know, she's let the squirrel in and reset the burglar alarm behind him. Had to be somebody she knew."

"I wouldn't rule out a stranger," I said. "If the person is very smooth, she may have trusted him, let him in for some other reason."

"At that hour?" His eyes flicked me as they went around the room. "What? He's selling magazine subscriptions, Good Humor bars at ten o'clock at night?"

I didn't reply. I didn't know.

We stopped at the open doorway leading into a hallway. "This is the first blood," Marino said, looking at the dried spatters on the wall. "She got cut right here, the first cut. I figure she's running like hell and he's slashing."

I envisioned the cuts on Beryl's face, arms, and hands.

"My guess," he went on, "is he cut her left arm or back or face at this point. The blood on the wall here's cast off from blood slinging off the blade. He'd already cut her at least once, the blade was bloody, and when he swung again drops flew off and hit the wall."

The stains were elliptical, about six millimeters in diameter, and became increasingly elongated the farther they arched left of the doorframe. The spread of drops spanned at least ten feet. The assailant had been swinging with the vigor of a hard-hitting squash player. I felt the emotion of the crime. It wasn't anger. It was worse than that. *Why did she let him in?*

"Based on the location of this spatter, I'm thinking the drone was right about here," Marino said, positioning himself several yards back from the doorway and slightly to the left of it. "He swings, cuts her again, and as the blade follows through, blood flies off and hits the wall. The pattern, as you can see, starts here." He gestured toward the highest drops, which were almost level with the top of his head. "Then sweeps down, stopping several inches from the floor." He paused, his eyes challenging me. "You examined her. What do you think? He's right-handed or left-handed?"

The cops always wanted to know that. No matter how often I told them it was anybody's guess, they still asked.

"It's not possible to tell from this blood spatter," I said, the inside of my mouth dry and tasting like dust. "It depends entirely on where he was standing in relation to her. As for the stab injuries to her chest, they're slightly angled from left to right. That might make him left-handed. But again, it depends on where he was in relation to her."

"I just think it's interesting almost all her defense injuries are located on the left side of her body. You know, she's running. He's coming at her from the left instead of the right. Makes me suspicious he's left-handed."

"It all depends on the victim and assailant's positions in relation to each other," I repeated impatiently.

"Yo," he muttered shortly. "Everything depends on something."

Through the doorway was a hardwood floor. A runway had been chalked off to enclose drips of blood leading to a stairway some ten feet to our left. Beryl had fled this way and up the stairs. Her shock and terror were greater than her pain. On the left wall at almost every step was a bloody smear made by her cut fingers reaching out for balance and dragging across the paneling.

The black spots were on the floor, on the walls, on the ceiling. Beryl had run to the end of the upstairs hall, where she was momentarily cornered. In this area there was a great deal of blood. The chase resumed after she apparently fled from the end of the hall into her bedroom, where she may have eluded him by climbing over the queen-size bed as he came around it. At this point, either she threw her briefcase at him or, more likely, it was on top of the bed and was knocked off. The police found it on the rug, open and upside down like a tent, papers scattered nearby, including the photocopies of the letters she had written from Key West.

"What other papers did you find in here?" I asked.

"Receipts, a couple tourist guides, including a brochure with a street map," Marino answered. "I'll make copies for you if you want."

"Please," I said.

"Also found a stack of typed pages on her dresser there." He pointed. "Probably what she was writing in the Keys. A lot of notes scribbled in the margins in pencil. No prints worth nothing, a few smudges and a few partials that are hers."

Her bed was stripped to the bare mattress, its blood-stained quilted spread and sheets having been sent to the lab. She had been slowing down, losing motor control, getting weak. She had stumbled back out into the hall, where she'd fallen over an Oriental prayer rug I remembered from the scene photographs. There were bloody drag marks and handprints on the floor. Beryl had crawled into the guest bedroom beyond the bath, and it was here, finally, that she died.

"Me," Marino was saying, "I think it wasn't any fun unless he chased her. He could've grabbed her, killed her down there in the living room, but that would've ruined the sport. He was probably smiling the whole time, her bleeding and screaming and begging. When she finally makes it in here, she collapses. The gig's up. No fun anymore. He ends it."

The room was wintry, decorated in yellow as pale as January sunshine. The hardwood floor was black near the twin bed, and there were black streaks and splashes on the whitewashed wall. In the scene photographs Beryl was on her back, her legs spread, her arms up around her head, her face turned toward the curtained window. She was nude. When I had first studied the photographs I could not tell what she looked like or even the color of her hair. All I saw was red. The police had found a pair of bloody khaki slacks near her body. Her blouse and undergarments were missing.

"The cabdriver you mentioned—Hunnel or whatever his name was—did he remember what Beryl was wearing when he picked her up at the airport?" I asked.

"It was dark," Marino replied. "He wasn't sure but thought she was wearing pants and a jacket. We know she was wearing pants when she was attacked, the khaki ones we found in here. There was a matching jacket on a chair inside her bedroom. I don't think she changed clothes when she got home, just tossed her jacket on the chair. Whatever else she was wearing—a blouse, her underclothes—the killer took them."

"A souvenir," I thought aloud.

Marino was staring at the dark-stained floor where her body had been found.

He said, "The way I'm seeing it, he has her down in here, takes her clothes off, rapes her or tries to. Then he stabs her and nearly cuts her head off. A damn shame about her PERK," he added, referring to her Physical Evidence Recovery Kit, swabs from which were negative for sperm. "Guess we can kiss DNA good-bye."

"Unless some of the blood we're analyzing is his," I replied. "Otherwise, yes. Forget DNA."

"And no hairs," he said.

"None except a few consistent with hers."

The house was so quiet our voices were unnervingly loud. Everywhere I looked I saw the ugly stains. I saw the images in my mind: the stab wounds, the hilt marks, the savage wound in her neck gaping like a yawning red mouth. I went out into the hall. The dust was irritating my lungs. It was hard to breathe.

I said, "Show me where you found her gun."

When the police had arrived at the scene that night, they'd found Beryl's .380 automatic on the kitchen counter near the microwave oven. The gun was loaded, the safety on. The only partial prints the lab could identify were her own.

"She kept the box of cartridges inside a table by her bed," Marino said. "Probably kept the gun there, too. I figure she carried her bags upstairs, unpacked and dumped most of her clothes in the bathroom hamper, and put her suitcases back in the bedroom closet. At some point during all this, she got out her piece. A sure sign she was antsy as hell. What you wanta bet she checked out every room with it before she started winding down?"

"I know I would have," I commented.

He looked around the kitchen. "So maybe she came in here for a snack."

"She may have thought about a snack, but she didn't eat one," I answered. "Her gastric contents were about fifty milliliters, or less than two ounces, of dark brown fluid. Whatever she ate last was fully digested by the time she died—or better put, by the time she was attacked. Digestion shuts down during acute stress or fear. If she'd just eaten a snack when the killer got to her, the food wouldn't have cleared her stomach."

"Not much to munch on anyway," he said as if this were an important point to make as he opened the refrigerator door.

Inside we found a shriveled lemon, two sticks of butter, a block of moldy Havarti cheese, condiments, and a bottle of tonic water. The freezer was a little more promising, but not much. There were a few packages of chicken breasts, Le Menus, and lean ground beef. Cooking, it appeared, was not a pleasure for Beryl but a utilitarian exercise. I knew what my own kitchen was like. This one was depressingly sterile. Motes of dust were suspended in the pale light seeping through slits of the gray designer blinds in the window over the sink. The drainboard and sink were empty and dry. The appliances were modern and looked unused.

"The other thought is she came in here for a drink," Marino speculated.

"Her STAT alcohol was negative," I said.

"Don't mean she didn't think about it."

He opened a cabinet above the sink. There wasn't an inch to spare on three shelves: Jack Daniel's, Chivas Regal, Tanqueray, liqueurs, and something else that caught my attention. In front of the Cognac on the top shelf was a bottle of Haitian Barbancourt Rhum, aged fifteen years and as expensive as unblended Scotch.

Lifting it out with a gloved hand, I set it on the counter. There was no strip stamp, and the seal around the gold cap was unbroken.

"I don't think she got this around here," I told Marino. "My guess is she got it in Miami, Key West."

"So you're saying she brought it back from Florida?"

"It's possible. Clearly, she was a connoisseur of good booze. Barbancourt's wonderful."

"Guess I should start calling you Doc-tor Connoisseur," he said.

The bottle of Barbancourt wasn't dusty, even though many of the bottles near it were.

"It might explain why she was in the kitchen," I went on. "Perhaps she came downstairs to put away the rum. She may have been contemplating a nightcap when someone arrived at her door."

"Yeah, but what it don't explain is why she left her piece in here on the counter when she answered the door. She was supposed to be spooked, right? Still makes me think she was expecting company, knew the squirrel. Hey, she's got all this fancy booze, right? She drinks the stuff alone? Don't make sense. Makes more sense to think she did a little entertaining from time to time, had some guy in. Hell, maybe it's this 'M' she was writing down there in the Keys. Maybe that's who she was expecting the night she was whacked."

"You're entertaining the possibility 'M' is the killer," I said.

"Wouldn't you be?"

He was getting combative, and his toying with the unlit cigarette was beginning to grate on my nerves.

"I would entertain every possibility," I replied. "For example, I would also entertain the possibility she *wasn't* expecting company. She was in the kitchen putting away her rum and possibly thinking of pouring herself a drink. She was nervous, had her automatic nearby on the counter. She was startled when the doorbell rang or someone started knocking—"

"Right," he cut me off. "She's startled, jumpy. So why does she leave her piece here in the kitchen when she goes to the damn door?"

"Did she practice?"

"Practice?" he said as our eyes met. "Practice *what*?"

"Shooting."

"Hell . . . I donno . . ."

"If she didn't, it wasn't a natural reflex for her to arm herself but a conscious deliberation. Women carry Mace in their pocketbooks. They're assaulted and the Mace never enters their minds until after the fact because defending themselves isn't a reflex."

"I don't know . . ."

I *did* know. I had a Ruger .38 revolver loaded with Silvertips, one of the most destructive cartridges money could buy. The only reason it would occur to me to arm myself with the handgun was I practiced, took it down to the range inside my building several times a month. When I was home alone, I was more comfortable with the handgun than without it.

There was something else. I thought of the living room, of the fireplace tools upright in their brass stand on the hearth. Beryl had struggled with her assailant in that room and it never occurred to her to arm herself with the poker or the shovel. Defending herself was not a reflex. Her only reflex was to run, whether it was up the stairs or to Key West.

I explained, "She may have been a stranger to the gun, Marino. The doorbell rings. She's unnerved, confused. She goes into the living room and looks through the peephole. Whoever it is, she trusts the person enough to open the door. The gun is forgotten."

"Or else she was expecting her visitor," he said again.

"That is entirely possible. Providing somebody knew she was back in town."

"So maybe *he* knew," he said.

"And maybe he's 'M.' " I told him what he wanted to hear as I replaced the bottle of rum on the shelf.

"Bingo. Making more sense now, isn't it?"

I shut the cabinet door. "She was threatened, terrorized for months, Marino. I find it hard to believe it was a close friend and Beryl wasn't the least bit suspicious."

He looked annoyed as he glanced at his watch and dug another key out of a pocket. It made no sense at all that Beryl would have opened the door to a stranger. But it made even less sense that someone she trusted could have done this to her. *Why did she let him in?* The question wouldn't stop nagging at me.

A covered breezeway joined the house to the garage. The sun had dipped below the trees.

"I'll tell you right off," Marino said, the lock clicking open, "I only went in here right before I called you. Could've busted down the door the night of her murder but didn't see no point." He shrugged, lifting those massive shoulders of his as if to make sure I understood he really could tackle a door or a tree or a Dumpster if he were so inclined. "She hadn't been in here since she left for Florida. Took us a while to find the friggin' key."

It was the only paneled garage I had ever seen, the floor a gorgeous dragon skin of expensive red Italian tile.

"Was this *really* designed to be a garage?" I asked.

"It's got a garage door, don't it?" He was pulling several more keys out of a pocket. "Some place to keep your ride out of the rain, huh?"

The garage was airless and smelled dusty, but it was spotless. Other than a rake and a broom leaning against a corner, there was no sign of the usual tools, lawnmowers, and other impedimenta one would expect to find. The garage looked more like a car dealership showroom, the black Honda parked in the center of the tile floor. The car was so clean and shiny it could have passed for new and never driven.

Marino unlocked the driver's door and opened it.

"Here. Be my guest," he said.

Momentarily, I was settled back in the soft ivory leather seat, staring through the windshield at the paneled wall.

Stepping back from the car, he added, "Just sit there, okay? Get the feel of it, look around the interior, tell me what comes to mind."

"You want me to start it?"

He handed me the key.

"Then please open the garage door so we don't asphyxiate ourselves," I added.

Frowning as he glanced around, he found the right button and cracked the door.

The car turned over the first time, the engine dropping several octaves and purring throatily. The radio and air conditioning were on. The gas tank was a quarter full, the odometer registering less than seven thousand miles, the sunroof partially open. On the dash was a dry cleaning slip dated July eleventh, a Thursday, when Beryl took in a skirt and a suit jacket, garments she obviously never picked up. On the passenger's seat was a grocery receipt dated July twelth at ten-forty in the morning, when she bought one head of lettuce, tomatoes, cucumbers, ground beef, cheese, orange juice, and a roll of mints, the total nine dollars and thirteen cents out of a ten she gave the check-out clerk.

Next to the receipt was a slender white bank envelope that was empty. Beside it a pebbly tan Ray Ban sunglasses case—also empty.

In the backseat was a Wimbledon tennis racket, and a rumpled white towel I reached over the seat to get. Stamped in small blue letters on a terrycloth border was WESTWOOD RACQUET CLUB, the same name printed on a red vinyl tote bag I had noted upstairs in Beryl's closet.

Marino had saved his theatrics for last. I knew he had looked over all of these items and wanted me to see them *in situ*. They weren't evidence. The killer had never gone inside the garage. Marino was baiting me. He had been baiting me since we had first stepped inside the house. It was a habit of his that irritated the hell out of me.

Turning off the engine, I got out of the car, the door shutting with a muffled solid thud.

He looked speculatively at me.

"A couple of questions," I said.

"Shoot."

"Westwood is an exclusive club. Was she a member?"

A nod.

"You checked out when she last reserved a court?"

"Friday, July twelth, at nine in the morning. She had a lesson with the pro. Took a lesson once a week, that was about the extent of her playing."

"As I recall, she flew out of Richmond early Saturday morning, July thirteenth, arriving in Miami shortly after noon."

Another nod.

"So she took her lesson, then went straight to the grocery store. After that, she may have gone to the bank. Whatever the case, at some point after she did her shopping, she suddenly decided to leave town. If she'd known she was leaving town the next day, she wouldn't have bothered going to the grocery store. She didn't have time to eat everything she bought, and she didn't leave the food in the refrigerator. Apparently she threw away everything except the ground beef, the cheese and possibly the mints."

"Sounds reasonable," he said unemphatically.

"She left her glasses case and other items on the seat," I continued. "Plus, the radio and air conditioning were left on, the sunroof partially open. Looks like she drove into the garage, cut the engine, and hurried into the house with her sunglasses on. Makes me wonder if something happened while she was out in the car driving home from tennis and her errands . . ."

"Oh yeah. I'm pretty damn sure it did. Walk around, take a look at the other side—specifically at the passenger's door."

I did.

What I saw scattered my thoughts like marbles. Gouged into the glossy black paint right below the door handle was the name BERYL enclosed in a heart.

"Kind of gives you the creeps, don't it?" he said.

"If he did this while her car was parked at the club or the grocery store," I reasoned, "it seems someone would have seen him."

"Yo. So maybe he did it earlier." He paused, casually perusing the graffiti. "When's the last time you looked at *your* passenger's door?"

It could have been days. It could have been a week.

"She went grocery shopping." He finally lit the damn cigarette. "Didn't buy much." He took a deep, hungry drag. "And it probably all fit inside one bag, right? When my wife's got just one or two bags, she always sticks them up front, on the floor mat, maybe on the seat. So maybe Beryl went around to the passenger's side to put the groceries in the car. That's when she noticed what was scratched into the paint. Maybe she knew it had to have been done that day. Maybe she didn't. Don't matter. Freaked her right out, pushed her over the edge. She makes tracks home or maybe to the bank for cash. Books the next flight out of Richmond and runs to Florida."

I followed him out of the garage and back to his car. Night was falling fast, a chill in the air. He cranked the engine while I stared mutely out the side window at Beryl's house. Its sharp angles were deteriorating in the shadows, the windows dark. Suddenly the porch and living room lights blinked on.

"Geez," Marino muttered. "Trick or treat."

"A timer," I said.

"No kidding."

2

There was a full moon over Richmond as I followed the long road home. Only the most tenacious trick-or-treaters were still making the rounds, their ghastly masks and menacing child-size silhouettes lit up by my headlights. I wondered how many times my doorbell had gone unanswered. My house was a favorite because I was excessively generous with candy, not having children of my own to indulge. I would have four unopened bags of chocolate bars to dole out to my staff in the morning.

The phone started ringing as I was climbing the stairs. Just before my answering machine intervened, I snatched up the receiver. The voice was unfamiliar at first, then recognition grasped my heart.

"Kay? It's Mark. Thank God you're home . . ."

Mark James sounded as if he were talking from the bottom of an oil drum, and I could hear cars passing in the background.

"Where are you?" I managed to ask, and I knew I sounded unnerved.

"On Ninety-five, about fifty miles north of Richmond."

I sat down on the edge of the bed.

"At a phone booth," he went on to explain. "I need directions to your house." After another gust of traffic, he added, "I want to see you, Kay. I've been in D.C. all week, been trying to get you since late afternoon, finally took a chance and rented a car. Is it all right?"

I didn't know what to say.

"Thought we could have a drink, catch up," said this man who had once broken my heart. "I've got reservations at the Radisson downtown. Tomorrow morning, early, there's a flight out of Richmond back to Chicago. I just thought . . . Actually, there's something I want to discuss with you."

I couldn't imagine what Mark and I could have to discuss.

"Is it all right?" he asked again.

No, it wasn't all right! What I said was "Of course, Mark. It will be wonderful to see you."

After giving him directions, I went into the bathroom to freshen up, pausing long enough to take inventory. More than fifteen years had come and gone since our days together in law school. My hair was more ash than blond, and it had been long when Mark and I had last seen each other. My eyes were hazier, not as blue as they used to be. The unbiased mirror went on to remind me rather coldly that I would never see thirty-nine again and there was such a thing as face-lifts. In my memory Mark had remained barely twenty-four, when he became an object of passion and dependency that ultimately led to abject despair. After it was over, I did nothing but work.

He still drove fast and liked fine automobiles. Less than forty-five minutes later, I opened the front door and watched him get out of his rental Sterling. He was still the Mark I remembered, the same trim body and long-legged confident walk. Briskly mounting the steps, he smiled a little. After a quick hug, we stood awkwardly in the foyer for a moment and couldn't think of a significant thing to say.

"Still drinking Scotch?" I finally asked.

"That hasn't changed," he said, following me to the kitchen.

Retrieving the Glenfiddich from the bar, I automatically fixed his drink exactly as I had so long ago: two jiggers, ice, and a splash of seltzer water. His eyes followed me as I moved about the kitchen and set our drinks on the table. Taking a sip, he stared into his glass and began slowly swirling ice the way he used to when he was tense. I took a good, long look at him, at his refined features, high cheekbones, and clear gray eyes. His dark hair had begun to turn a little at the temples.

I shifted my attention to the ice slowly spinning inside his glass. "You're with a firm in Chicago, I assume?"

Leaning back in his chair, he looked up and said, "Doing strictly appeals, trial work only now and then. I run into Diesner occasionally. That's how I found out you're here in Richmond."

Diesner was the chief medical examiner in Chicago. I saw him at meetings and we were on several committees together. He had never mentioned he was acquainted with Mark James, and how he even knew I was once acquainted with Mark was a mystery.

"I made the mistake of telling him I'd known you in law school, think he brings you up from time to time to needle me," Mark explained, reading my thoughts.

That I could believe. Diesner was as gruff as a billy goat, and he was none too fond of defense attorneys. Some of his battles and theatrics in court had become the stuff of legends.

Mark was saying, "Like most forensic pathologists, he's pro prosecution. I represent a convicted murderer and I'm the bad guy. Diesner will make a point of looking for me and as a by-the-way telling me about the latest journal article you published or some gruesome case you worked. Dr. Scarpetta. The famous Chief Scarpetta." He laughed, but his eyes didn't.

"I don't think it's fair to say we're pro prosecution," I answered. "It seems that way because if the evidence is pro defendant, the case never sees a courtroom."

"Kay, I know how it works," he said in that give-it-a-rest tone of voice I remembered so well. "I know what you see. And if I were you, I'd want all the bastards to fry, too."

"Yes. You know what I see, Mark," I started to say. It was the same old argument. I couldn't believe it. He had been here less than fifteen minutes and we were picking up right where we had left off. Some of our worst fights used to be over this very subject. I was already an M.D. and enrolled in law school at Georgetown when Mark and I met. I had seen the darker side, the cruelty, the random tragedies. I had placed my gloved hands on the bloody spoils of suffering and death. Mark was the splendid Ivy Leaguer whose idea of a felony was for someone to nick the paint on his Jaguar. He was going to be a lawyer because his father and grandfather were lawyers. I was Catholic, Mark was Protestant. I was Italian, he was as Anglo as Prince Charles. I was brought up poor, he was brought up in one of the wealthiest residential districts of Boston. I had once thought ours would be a marriage made in heaven.

"You haven't changed, Kay," he said. "Except maybe you radiate a certain resolve, a hardness. I bet you're a force to be reckoned with in court."

"I wouldn't like to think I'm hard."

"I don't mean it as a criticism. I'm saying you look terrific." He glanced around the kitchen. "And successful. You happy?"

"I like Virginia," I answered, looking away from him. "My only complaint is the winters, but I suppose you have a bigger complaint in that department. How do you stand Chicago six months out of the year?"

"Never gotten used to it, you want to know the truth. You'd hate it. A Miami hothouse flower like you wouldn't last a month." He sipped his drink. "You're not married."

"I was."

"Hmmmm." He frowned as he thought. "Tony somebody . . . I recall you started seeing Tony . . . Benedetti, right? The end of our third year."

Actually, I was surprised Mark would have noticed, much less remembered. "We're divorced, have been for a long time," I said.

"I'm sorry," he said softly.

I reached for my drink.

"Seeing anybody nice?" he asked.

"No one at the moment, nice or otherwise."

Mark didn't laugh as much as he used to. He volunteered matter-of-factly, "I almost got married a couple of years ago but it didn't work out. Or maybe I should be honest enough to say that at the last minute I panicked."

It was hard for me to believe he had never been married. He must have read my mind again.

"This was after Janet died." He hesitated. "I *was* married."

"Janet?"

He was swirling the ice in his glass again. "Met her in Pittsburgh, after Georgetown. She was a tax lawyer in the firm."

I was watching him closely, perplexed by what I saw. Mark had changed. The intensity that had once drawn me to him was different. I couldn't put my finger on it, but it was darker.

"A car accident," he was explaining. "A Saturday night. She went out for popcorn. We were going to stay up, watch a late movie. A drunk driver crossed over into her lane. Didn't even have his headlights on."

"God, Mark. I'm sorry," I said. "How awful."

"That was eight years ago."

"No children?" I asked quietly.

He shook his head.

We fell silent.

"My firm's opening an office in D.C.," he said as our eyes met.

I did not respond.

"It's possible I may be relocated, move to D.C. We've been expanding like crazy, got a hundred-some lawyers and offices in New York, Atlanta, Houston."

"When would you be moving?" I asked very calmly.

"It could be by the first of the year, actually."

"You're definitely going to do it?"

"I'm sick to death of Chicago, Kay, need a change. I wanted to let you know—that's why I'm here, at least the major reason. I didn't want to move to D.C. and have us run into each other at some point. I'll be living in northern Virginia. You have an office in northern Virginia. Odds are we would run into each other in a restaurant, at the theater one of these days. I didn't want that."

I imagined sitting inside the Kennedy Center and spotting Mark three rows ahead whispering into the ear of his beautiful young date. I was reminded of the old pain, a pain once so intense it was physical. He'd had no competition. He had been my entire emotional focus. At first a part of me had sensed it wasn't mutual. Later, I was sure of it.

"This was my *major* reason," he repeated, now the lawyer making his opening statement. "But there's something else that really has nothing to do with us personally."

I remained silent.

"A woman was murdered here in Richmond a couple of nights ago. Beryl Madison . . ."

The look of astonishment on my face briefly stopped him.

"Berger, the managing partner, told me about it when he called me at my hotel in D.C. I want to talk to you about it—"

"How does it concern you?" I asked. "Did you *know* her?"

"Remotely. I met her once, in New York last winter. Our office there dabbles in entertainment law. Beryl was having publishing problems, a contract dispute, and she retained Orndorff & Berger to set things straight. I happened to be in New York on the same day she was conferring with Sparacino, the lawyer who took her case. Sparacino ended up inviting me to join the two of them for lunch at the Algonquin."

"If there's any possibility this *dispute* you mentioned could be connected with her murder, you need to be talking to the police, not to me," I said, getting angry.

"Kay," he replied. "My firm doesn't even know I'm talking to you, okay? When Berger called yesterday, it was about something else, all right? He happened to mention Beryl Madison's murder in the course of the conversation, said for me to check the area papers, see what I could find out."

"Right. Translated into see what you could find out from your ex—" I felt a flush creeping up my neck. Ex-*what*?

"It isn't like that." He glanced away. "I was thinking about you, thinking of calling you up before Berger called, before I even knew about Beryl. For two damn nights I actually had my hand on the phone, had already gotten your number from Information. But I couldn't bring myself to do it. And maybe I never would have had Berger not told me what happened. Maybe Beryl gave me the excuse. I'll concede that much. But it's not the way you think . . ."

I didn't listen. It dismayed me that I wanted to believe him so much. "If your firm has an interest in her murder, tell me what it is, exactly."

He thought for a moment. "I'm not sure if we have an interest in her murder legitimately. Maybe it's personal, a sense of horror. A shock for those of us who had any exposure to her while she was alive. I will also tell you that she was in the midst of a rather bitter dispute, was getting royally screwed because of a contract she signed eight years ago. It's very complicated. Has to do with Cary Harper."

"The novelist?" I said, baffled. "*That* Cary Harper?"

"As you probably know," Mark said, "he doesn't live far from here, in some eighteenth-century plantation called Cutler Grove. It's on the James River, in Williamsburg."

I was trying to remember what I had read about Harper, who produced one novel some twenty years ago that won a Pulitzer Prize. A legendary recluse, he lived with a sister. Or was it an aunt? There had been much speculation about Harper's private life. The more he refused interviews and eluded reporters, the more the speculation grew.

I lit a cigarette.

"I was hoping you'd quit," he said.

"It would take the removal of my frontal lobe."

"Here's what little I know. Beryl had some sort of relationship with Harper when she was in her teens, early twenties. For a time, she actually lived in the house with him and his sister. Beryl was the aspiring writer, the talented daughter Harper never had. His protégée. It was through his connections she got her first novel published when she was only twenty-two, some sort of quasi-literary romance she published under the name Stratton. Harper even conceded to giving a comment for the book jacket, some quote about this exciting new writer he'd discovered. It raised a lot of eyebrows. Her novel was more a commercial book than literature, and no one had heard a word from Harper in years."

"What does this have to do with her contract dispute?"

Mark answered wryly, "Harper may be a sucker for a hero-worshiping young lady, but he's a cagey bastard. Before he got her published, he forced her to sign a contract prohibiting her from ever writing a word about him or anything relating to him as long as he and his sister are alive. Harper's only in his mid-fifties, his sister a few years older. Basically, the contract trussed Beryl for life, preventing her from writing her memoirs because how could she do that and leave out Harper?"

"Maybe she could," I replied, "but minus Harper, the book wouldn't sell."

"Exactly."

"Why did she resort to pen names? Was this part of her agreement with Harper?"

"I think so. My guess is he wanted Beryl to remain his secret. He granted her literary success but wanted her locked away from the world. The name Beryl Madison's not exactly well known, even though her novels have been financially successful."

"Am I to assume she was on the verge of violating this contract, and that's why she sought out Orndorff & Berger?"

He sipped his drink. "Let me remind you that she wasn't my client. So I don't know all of the details. But my impression is that she was burned out, wanted to write something of significance. And this is the part that you probably already know about. Apparently she was having problems, somebody was threatening her, harassing her . . ."

"When?"

"Last winter, about the time I met her at lunch. I guess it was late February."

"Go on," I said, intrigued.

"She had no idea who was threatening her. Whether this began before she decided to write what she was currently working on or afterward, I can't say with certainty."

"How was she going to get away with violating her contract?"

"I'm not sure she would have, not entirely," Mark replied. "But the direction Sparacino was going was to inform Harper he had a choice. He could cooperate, and the finished product would be fairly harmless—in other words, Harper would have limited powers of censorship. Or else he could be a son of a bitch and Sparacino would give the newspapers, 'Sixty Minutes,' a crack at it. Harper was in a bind. Sure, he could sue Beryl, but she didn't have that much cash, a drop in the bucket compared to what he's worth. A suit would only make everybody run out to buy Beryl's book. Harper really couldn't win."

"Couldn't he have gotten an injunction to stop the publication?" I asked.

"More publicity. And to halt the presses would have run him into the millions."

"Now she's dead." I watched my cigarette smoldering in the ashtray. "The book isn't finished, I presume. Harper doesn't have any worries. Is this what you're getting at, Mark? That Harper may be involved in her murder?"

"I'm just giving you the background," he said.

Those clear eyes were looking into mine. Sometimes they could be so incredibly unreachable, I remembered uncomfortably.

"What do you think?" he was asking.

I did not say what I really thought, which was that it struck me as very strange that Mark was telling me all this. It did not matter that Beryl was not his client. He was familiar with the canons of legal ethics, which make it quite clear that the knowledge of one member of a firm is imputed to all its members. He was just a shade away from impropriety, and this was as out of character for the scrupulous Mark James I remembered as if he had shown up at my house sporting a tattoo.

"I think you'd better have a talk with Marino, the head of the investigation," I replied. "Or else I'd better tell him what you just told me. In either event, he'll be looking up your firm, asking questions."

"Fine. I don't have a problem with that."

We fell silent for a moment.

"What was she like?" I asked, clearing my throat.

"As I said, I met her only once. But she was memorable. Dynamic, witty, attractive, dressed in white. A fabulous winter-white suit. I'd also describe her as rather distant. She kept a lot of secrets. There was a depth to her no one was ever going to reach. And she drank a lot, at least she did that day at lunch—had three cocktails, which struck me as rather excessive considering it was the middle of the day. It may not have been in character, though. She was nervous, upset, tense. Her reason for coming to Orndorff & Berger wasn't a happy one. I'm sure all this business about Harper had to be upsetting her."

"What did she drink?"

"Pardon?"

"The three cocktails. What were they?" I asked.

He frowned, staring off across the kitchen. "Hell, I don't know, Kay. What difference does it make?"

"I'm not sure it makes a difference," I said, recalling her liquor cabinet. "Did she talk about the threats she'd been getting? In your presence, I mean?"

"Yes. And Sparacino's mentioned them. All I know is she started receiving phone calls that were very specific in nature. Always the same voice, wasn't somebody she knew, or at least this is what she said. There were other strange events. I can't remember the details—it was a long time ago."

"Was she keeping a record of these events?" I asked.

"I don't know."

"And she had no idea who was doing this or why?"

"That's the impression she gave." He scooted back his chair. It was getting close to midnight.

As I led him to the front door, something suddenly occurred to me. "Sparacino," I said. "What's his first name?"

"Robert," he replied.

"He doesn't go by the initial M, does he?"

"No," he said, looking curiously at me.

There was a tense pause.

"Drive carefully."

"Good night, Kay," he said, hesitating.

Maybe it was my imagination, but for an instant I thought he was going to kiss me. Then he walked briskly down the steps, and I was back inside my house when I heard him drive off.

* * *

The following morning was typically frantic. Fielding informed us in staff meeting that we had five autopsies, including a "floater," or decomposed body from the river, a prospect that never failed to make everybody groan. Richmond had sent in its two latest shootings, one of which I managed to post before dashing off to the John Marshall Court House to testify in another homicidal shooting, and afterwards to the Medical College to have lunch with one of my student advisees. All the while, I was working hard at pushing Mark's visit completely from my mind. The more I tried not to think about him, the more I thought about him. He was cautious. He was stubborn. It was out of character for him to contact me after more than a decade of silence.

It wasn't until early afternoon that I gave in and called Marino.

"Was just about to ring you up," he launched in before I had barely said two words. "On my way out. Can you meet at Benton's office in an hour, hour and a half?"

"What's this about?" I hadn't even told him why I was calling.

"Got my hands on Beryl's reports. Thought you'd wanna be there."

He hung up as he always did, without saying good-bye.

At the appointed time, I drove along East Grace Street and parked in the first metered space I could find within a reasonable walk of my destination. The modern ten-story office building was a lighthouse watching over a depressing shore of junk shops parading as antique stores and small ethnic restaurants whose "specials" weren't. Street people drifted along cracked sidewalks.

Identifying myself at the guard station inside the lobby, I took the elevator to the fifth floor. At the end of the hall was an unmarked wooden door. The location of Richmond's FBI field office was one of the city's best-kept secrets, its presence as unannounced and unobtrusive as its plainclothes agents. A young man sitting behind a counter that stretched halfway across the back wall glanced at me as he talked on the phone. Placing his hand over the mouthpiece, he raised his eyebrows in a "May I help you?" expression. I explained my reason for being here, and he invited me to take a seat.

The lobby was small and decidedly male, with furniture upholstered in sturdy dark-blue leather, the coffee table stacked with various sports magazines. On paneled walls were a rogue's gallery of past directors of the FBI, service awards, and a brass plaque engraved with the names of agents who had died in action. The outer door opened occasionally, and tall, fit men in somber suits and sunglasses passed through without a glance in my direction.

Benton Wesley could be as Prussian as the rest of them, but over the years he had won my respect. Beneath his Bureau boilerplate was a human being worth knowing. He was brisk and energetic, even when he was sitting, and he was typically dapper in his dark suit trousers and starched white shirt. His necktie was fashionably narrow and perfectly knotted, the black holster on his belt lonely for its ten-millimeter, which he almost never wore indoors. I hadn't seen Wesley in a while and he hadn't changed. He was fit and handsome in a hard way, with premature silver-gray hair that never failed to surprise me.

"Sorry to keep you waiting, Kay," he said, smiling.

His handshake was reassuringly firm and absent of any

hint of macho. The grip of some cops and lawyers I know are a thirty-pound squeeze on a three-pound trigger that damn near breaks my fingers.

"Marino's here," Wesley added. "I needed to go over a few more things with him before we brought you in."

He held the door and I followed him down an empty hallway. Steering me inside his small office, he left to get coffee.

"The computer finally came up last night," Marino said. He was leaning back comfortably in his chair and examining a .357 revolver that looked brand new.

"Computer? What computer?" Had I forgotten my cigarettes? No. On the bottom of my purse again.

"At HQ. Goes down all the friggin' time. Anyway, I finally got hard copies of those offense reports. Interesting. Least I think so."

"Beryl's?" I asked.

"You got it." He set the handgun on Wesley's desk, adding, "Nice piece. The lucky bastard won it as a door prize at the police chiefs' convention in Tampa last week. Me, I can't even win two bucks in the lottery."

My attention drifted. Wesley's desk was cluttered with telephone messages, reports, videotapes, and thick manila envelopes containing details and photographs, I assumed, of various crimes police jurisdictions had brought to his attention. Behind panes of glass in the bookcase against one wall were macabre weapons—a sword, brass knuckles, a zip gun, an African spear—trophies from the hunt, gifts from grateful protégés. An outdated photograph showed William Webster shaking hands with Wesley before a backdrop of a Marine Corp helicopter at Quantico. There wasn't the faintest hint Wesley had a wife and three kids. FBI agents, like most cops, jealously guard their personal lives from the world, especially if they have gotten close enough to evil to feel its horror. Wesley was a suspect profiler. He knew what it was to review photographs of unthinkable slaughter and then visit penitentiaries and stare the Charles Mansons, the Ted Bundys, straight in the eye.

Wesley was back with two Styrofoam cups of coffee, one for Marino, one for me. Wesley always remembered I drink my coffee black and need an ashtray within easy reach.

Marino collected a thin stack of photocopied police reports from his lap and began to go through them.

"For starters," he said, "there's only three of 'em. Three reports we got a record of. The first one's dated March eleventh, nine-thirty on a Monday morning. Beryl Madison dialed 911 the night before and requested that an officer come to her house to take a complaint. The call, unsurprisingly, was given a low priority because the street was hopping. A uniform man didn't swing by until the next morning, uh, Jim Reed, been with the department about five years." He glanced up at me.

I shook my head. I didn't know Reed.

Marino began skimming the report. "Reed reported the complainant, Beryl Madison, was very agitated and stating she'd received a phone call of a threatening nature at eight-fifteen the night before—Sunday night. During this phone call, a voice she identified as male, and possibly wnite, said the following: 'Bet you've been missing me, Beryl. But I'm always watching over you even though you can't see me. I see you. You can run but you can't hide.' The complainant went on to report that this caller stated he'd observed Miss Madison buying a newspaper in front of a Seven-Eleven earlier that morning. The subject described what she'd been wearing, 'a red warm-up suit and no bra.' She confirmed she did drive to the Seven-Eleven on Rosemount Avenue at approximately ten o'clock Sunday morning, and that she was dressed in the described fashion. She parked in front of the Seven-Eleven and bought a *Washington Post* from a vending machine and didn't go inside the store or notice anybody in the area. She was upset the caller knew these details and stated he must be following her. When asked if she was aware of anybody following her at any time, she stated she was not."

Marino turned to the second page, the confidential section of the report, and resumed: "Reed reports here Miss Madison was reluctant to divulge specific details pertaining to the actual threat communicated by the caller. When questioned at length, she finally stated the caller became 'obscene' and said when he imagined what she looked like with her clothes off it made him want to 'kill' her. At this point, Miss Madison hung up the phone, she said."

Marino placed the photocopy on the edge of Wesley's desk.

"What advice did Officer Reed give her?" I asked.

"The usual," Marino said. "Advised her to start keeping a log. When she got a call, to write down the date, time and what occurred. He also advised her to keep her doors locked, her windows shut and locked, maybe to think about getting an alarm system installed. And if she noted any strange vehicles, to write down the plate numbers, call the police."

I remembered what Mark had told me about his lunch with Beryl last February. "Did she say that this threat, the one she reported on March eleventh, was the first one she'd gotten?"

It was Wesley who replied as he reached for the report, "Apparently not." He flipped a page. "Reed mentions she claimed to have been receiving harassing calls since the first of the year, but didn't notify the police until this occasion. It seems the previous calls were infrequent and not as specific as the one she received Sunday night, the night of March tenth."

"She was certain the previous calls were made by the same man?" I asked Marino.

"She told Reed the voice sounded the same," he replied. "A white male she described as soft-spoken and articulate. It wasn't the voice of anyone she knew—or at least this was what she claimed."

Marino resumed, the second report in hand: "Beryl called Officer Reed's pager number on a Tuesday evening at seven-eighteen. She said she needed to see him, and he arrived at her house less than an hour later, at shortly after eight. Again, according to his report, she was very upset, stating she'd got another threatening call right before she'd dialed Reed's pager number. It was the same voice, the same subject who'd called in the past, she said. In this instance his message was similar to the March tenth call."

Marino began reading the report word for word. " 'I know you've been missing me, Beryl. I'll be coming for you soon. I know where you live, know everything about you. You can run but you can't hide.' He went on to state he knew she drove a new car, a black Honda, and he'd broken off the antenna the night before while it was parked in her driveway. The complainant confirmed that her car had been parked in her driveway the night before, and when she went out this same Tuesday morning she did notice the antenna was broken. It was still attached to the car, but bent back at an extreme angle and too damaged to be operative. This officer did go out to look at the vehicle and found the antenna to be in the condition the complainant described."

"What action did Officer Reed take?" I asked.

Marino flipped to the second page and said, "Advised her to begin parking her car inside the garage. She stated she never used the garage, was planning to turn it into an office. He then suggested she ask her neighbors to begin watching out for strange vehicles in the area or anybody on her property at any time. He notes in this report she inquired as to whether she should get a handgun."

"That's all?" I asked. "What about the log Reed told her to keep. Any mention of that?"

"No. He also made the following note in the confidential part of the report: 'Complainant's response to the damaged antenna seemed excessive. She became extremely upset and at one point was abusive to this officer.' " Marino looked up. "Translated, Reed's implying he didn't believe her. Maybe she broke the antenna herself, was making up the shit about the threatening calls."

"Oh, Lord," I muttered in disgust.

"Hey. You got any idea how many frootloops call in this kind of crap on a regular basis? Ladies call all the time, got cuts on 'em, scratches, screaming rape. Some of 'em make it up. They got some screw loose that makes 'em need the attention. . . ."

I knew all about fictitious illnesses and injuries, about Munchausens and maladjustments and manias that will cause people to wish and even induce terrible sickness and violence upon themselves. I didn't need a lecture from Marino.

"Go on," I said. "What happened next?"

He placed the second report on Wesley's desk and began reading the third one. "Beryl called Reed again, this time on July sixth, a Saturday morning at eleven-fifteen. He responded to her house that afternoon at four o'clock and found the complainant hostile and upset . . ."

"I guess so," I said shortly. "She'd been waiting five damn hours for him."

"On this occasion"—Marino ignored me and read word for word—"Miss Madison stated the same subject called her at eleven A.M. and communicated the following message: 'Still missing me? Soon, Beryl, soon. I came by last night for you. You weren't home. Do you bleach your hair? I hope not.' At this point, Miss Madison, who is blond, said she tried to talk to him. She pleaded with him to leave her alone, asked him who he was and why he was doing this to her. She said he didn't respond and hung up. She did confirm she was out the night before when the caller claimed to have come by. When this officer asked her where she was, she became evasive and would state only that she was out of town."

"And what did Officer Reed do this time to help the lady in distress?" I asked.

Marino looked blandly at me. "He advised her to get a dog, and she stated she was allergic to dogs."

Wesley opened a file folder. "Kay, you're looking at this in retrospect, in light of a terrible crime already committed. But Reed was coming at it from the other end.

Look at it through his eyes. Here's this young woman who lives alone. She's getting hysterical. Reed does the best he can for her—even gives her his pager number. He responds quickly, at least at first. But she's evasive when asked pointed questions. She's got no evidence. Any officer would have been skeptical."

"If it had been me," Marino concurred, "I know what I would have thought. I would have been suspicious the lady was lonely, wanted the attention, wanted to feel like someone gave a rat's ass about her. Or maybe she'd been burned by some guy and was setting the stage to pay him back."

"Right," I said before I could stop myself. "And if it had been her husband or boyfriend threatening to kill her, you'd think the same thing. And Beryl would still turn up dead."

"Maybe," Marino said testily. "But if it was her husband—saying she had one—at least I would have a damn suspect and could get a damn warrant and the judge could slap the drone with a restraining order."

"Restraining orders aren't worth the paper they're written on," I retorted, my anger nudging me closer to the limits of self-control. Not a year went by that I didn't autopsy half a dozen brutalized women whose husbands or boyfriends had been slapped with restraining orders.

After a long silence, I asked Wesley, "Didn't Reed at any point suggest placing a trap on her line?"

"Wouldn't have done any good," he answered. "Pin taps or traps aren't easy to get. The phone company needs a long list of calls, hard evidence the harassment is occurring."

"She didn't have hard evidence?"

Wesley slowly shook his head. "It would take more calls than she was getting, Kay. A lot of them. A pattern of when they were occurring. A solid record of them. Without all that, you can forget a trap."

"By all appearances," Marino added, "Beryl was getting only one or two calls a month. And she wasn't keeping the damn log Reed told her to keep. Or if she was, we haven't found it. Apparently she didn't tape any of the calls either."

"Good God," I muttered. "Someone threatens your life and it takes a damn act of Congress to get anyone to take it seriously."

Wesley didn't reply.

Marino snorted. "It's like in your place, Doc. No such thing as preventive medicine. We're nothing but a damn cleanup crew. Can't do a damn thing until after the fact, when there's hard evidence. Like a dead body."

"Beryl's behavior ought to have been evidence enough," I answered. "Look over these reports. Everything Officer Reed suggested, she did. He told her to get an alarm system and she did. He told her to start parking her car in the garage and she did, even though she was planning to turn the garage into an office. She asked him about a handgun, then went out and bought one. And whenever she called Reed it was *directly after* the killer had called and threatened her. In other words, she didn't wait and call the police hours, days later."

Wesley began spreading out the photocopies of Beryl's letters from Key West, the scene sketches and report, and a series of Polaroid photographs of her yard, the inside of her house, and finally of her body in the bedroom upstairs. He perused the items in silence, his face hard. He was sending the clear signal it was time to move on, we had argued and complained enough. What the police did or didn't do wasn't important. Finding the killer was.

"What's bothering me," Wesley began, "is there's an inconsistency in the MO. The history of threats she was receiving are in keeping with a psychopathic mentality. Someone who stalked and threatened Beryl for months, someone who seemed to know her only from a distance. Unquestionably, he derived most of his pleasure from fantasy, the antecedent phase. He drew it out. He may have finally struck when he did because she'd frustrated him by leaving town. Maybe he feared she was going to move altogether, and he murdered her the moment she got back."

"She finally pissed him off big time," Marino interjected.

Wesley continued looking at the photographs. "I'm seeing a lot of rage, and this is where the inconsistency comes in. His rage seems personally directed at her. The mutilation of her face, specifically." He tapped a photograph with an index finger. "The face is the person. In the typical homicide committed by a sexual sadist, the victim's face isn't touched. She's depersonalized, a symbol. In a sense, she has no face to the killer because she's a nobody to him. Areas of the body he mutilates, if he's into mutilation, are the breasts, the genitalia . . ." He paused, his eyes perplexed. "There are personal elements in Beryl's murder. The cutting of her face, the overkill, fit with the killer's being someone she knew, perhaps even well. Someone who had a private, intense obsession with her. But watching her from a distance, stalking her, don't fit with that at all. These are acts more in keeping with a stranger killer."

Marino was toying with Wesley's .357 door prize again. Idly spinning the cylinder, he said, "Want my opinion? I think the squirrel's got a God complex. You know, as long as you play by his rules he don't whack you. Beryl broke the rules by leaving town and sticking a FOR SALE sign in her yard. No fun anymore. You break the rules, you get punished."

"How are you profiling him?" I asked Wesley.

"White, mid-twenties to mid-thirties. Bright, from a broken home in which he was deprived of a father figure. He may also have been abused as a child, physically, psychologically, or both. He's a loner. This doesn't mean he lives alone, however. He could be married because he's skilled at maintaining a public persona. He leads a double life. There is the one man the world sees, then this darker side. He's obsessive-compulsive, and he's a voyeur."

"Yo," Marino muttered sardonically. "Sounds like half the drones I work with."

Wesley shrugged. "Maybe I'm shooting blanks, Pete. I haven't sorted through it yet. He could be some loser still living at home with his mother, could have priors, been in and out of institutions, prisons. Hell, he could work downtown in a big securities firm and have no criminal or psychiatric history at all. It seems he usually called Beryl at night. The one call we know about that he made during the day was on a Saturday. She worked out of her home, was there most of the time. He called when it was convenient for him versus when he was likely to find her in. I'm leaning toward thinking he has a regular nine to five job and is off on the weekends."

"Unless he was calling her while he was at work," Marino said.

"There's always that possibility," Wesley conceded.

"What about his age?" I asked. "You don't think it's possible he might be older than you just proposed?"

"It would be unusual," Wesley said. "But anything's possible."

Sipping my coffee, which was cool by now, I got around to telling them what Mark had told me about Beryl's contract conflicts and her enigmatic relationship with Cary Harper. When I was finished, Wesley and Marino were staring curiously at me. For one thing, this Chicago lawyer's impromptu visit late at night did sound a little odd. For another, I had thrown them a curve. The thought probably had not occurred to Marino or Wesley and, before last night, certainly not to me, that there actually might be a motive in Beryl's slaying. The most common motive in sexual homicides is no motive at all. The perpetrators do it because they enjoy it and because the opportunity is there.

"A buddy of mine's a cop in Williamsburg," Marino commented. "Tells me Harper's a real squirrel, a hermit. Drives around in an old Rolls-Royce and never talks to nobody. Lives in this big mansion on the river, never has nobody in, nothing. And the guy's *old*, Doc."

"Not so old," I disagreed. "In his mid-fifties. But yes, he's reclusive. I think he lives with his sister."

"It's a long shot," Wesley said, and he looked very tense. "But see how far you can run with it, Pete. If nothing else, maybe Harper would have a few guesses about this 'M' Beryl was writing. Obviously, it was someone she knew well, a friend, a lover. Someone out there has got to know who it is. We find that out, we're getting somewhere."

Marino didn't like it. "I know what I've heard," he said.

"Harper ain't going to talk with me and I don't got probable cause to force him into it. I also don't think he's the guy who whacked Beryl even if he did have motive, maybe. Seems to me he would have done it and been done with it. Why draw it out for nine, ten months? And she'd recognize his voice if it was him calling."

"Harper could have hired somebody," Wesley said.

"Right. And we would have found her a week later with a nice clean gunshot wound in the back of her head," Marino answered. "Most hit men don't stalk their victims, call 'em up, use a blade, rape 'em."

"Most of them don't," Wesley agreed. "But we can't be sure rape occurred, either. There was no seminal fluid." He glanced at me, and I nodded a confirmation. "The guy may be dysfunctional. Then again, the crime could be staged, her body positioned to looked like a sexual assault when it really wasn't. It all depends on who was hired, if this is the case, and what the plan was. For example, if Beryl turned up shot while she was in the middle of a dispute with Harper, the cops put him first on the list. But if her murder looks like the work of a sexual sadist, a psychopath, Harper doesn't enter anybody's mind."

Marino was staring off at the bookcase, his meaty face flushed. Slowly turning uneasy eyes on me, he said, "What else you know about this book she was writing?"

"Only what I've said, that it was autobiographical and possibly threatening to Harper's reputation," I replied.

"That's what she was working on down there in Key West?"

"I would assume so. I can't be certain," I said.

He hesitated. "Well, I hate to tell you, but we didn't find nothing like that inside her house."

Even Wesley looked surprised. "The manuscript in her bedroom?"

"Oh, yeah." Marino reached for his cigarettes. "I've glanced at it. Another novel with all this Civil War/romance shit in it. Sure don't sound like this other thing the doc's describing."

"Does it have a title or a date on it?" I asked.

"Nope. Don't even look like it's all there, for that matter. About this thick." Marino measured off about an inch with his fingers. "Got a lot of notes written in the margins, about ten more pages written in longhand."

"We'd better take a second look through all of her papers, her computer disks, make sure this autobiographical manuscript isn't there," Wesley said. "We also need to find out who her literary agent or editor is. Maybe she mailed the manuscript to someone before she left Key West. What we'd better make sure of is that she didn't return to Richmond with the thing. If she did and now it's gone, that's significant, to say the least."

Glancing at his watch, Wesley pushed back his chair as he announced apologetically, "I've got another appointment in five minutes." He escorted us out to the lobby.

I couldn't get rid of Marino. He insisted on walking me to my car.

"You got to keep your eyes open." He was at it again, giving me one of the "street smart" lectures he had given me numerous times in the past. "A lot of women, they never think about that. I see 'em all the time walking along and not having the foggiest idea who's looking at 'em, maybe following 'em. And when you get to your car, have your damn keys out and look *under* it, okay? Be surprised how many women don't think about that either. If you're driving along and realize someone's following you, what do you do?"

I ignored him.

"You head to the nearest fire station, okay? Why? Because there's always somebody there. Even at two in the morning on Christmas. That's the first place you head."

Waiting for a break in traffic, I began digging for my keys. Glancing across the street, I noticed an ominous white rectangle under the wiper blade of my state car. Hadn't I put in enough change? Damn.

"They're all over the place," Marino went on. "Just start looking for 'em on your way home or when you're running around doing your shopping."

I shot him one of my looks, then hurried across the street.

"Hey," he said when we got to my car, "don't get hot at me, all right? Maybe you should feel lucky I hover over you like a guardian angel."

The meter had run out fifteen minutes ago. Snatching the ticket off the windshield, I folded it and stuffed it in his shirt pocket.

"When you *hover* back to headquarters," I said, "take care of this, please."

He was scowling at me as I drove off.

3

Ten blocks away I pulled into another metered space and dropped in my last two quarters. I kept a red MEDICAL EXAMINER plate in plain view on the dash of my state car. Traffic cops never seemed to look. Several months ago, one of them had the nerve to write me up while I was downtown working a homicide scene the police had called me to in the middle of the day.

Hurrying up cement steps, I pushed through a glass door and went inside the main branch of the public library, where people moved about noiselessly and wooden tables were stacked with books. The hushed ambiance inspired the same reverence in me as it had when I was a child. Locating a row of microfiche machines halfway across the room, I began pulling up an index of books written under Beryl Madison's various pen names and jotting down the titles. The most recent work, a historical novel set during the Civil War and published under the pen name Edith Montague, had come out a year and a half ago. Probably irrelevant, and Mark was right, I thought. Over the past ten years, Beryl had published six novels. I had never heard of a single one of them.

Next I began a search of periodicals. Nothing. Beryl wrote books. Apparently she had not published anything, nor had there been any interviews of her, in magazines. Newspaper clips should be more promising. There were a few book reviews published in the Richmond *Times* over the past few years. But they were useless because they referred to the author by pen name. Beryl's killer knew her by her real name.

Screen after screen of hazy white type went by. "Maberly," "Macon," and finally "Madison." There was one very short piece about Beryl published in the *Times* last November:

AUTHOR TO LECTURE

> Novelist Beryl Stratton Madison will lecture to the Daughters of the American Revolution this Wednesday at the Jefferson Hotel at Main and Adams streets. Ms. Madison, protégée of Pulitzer Prize-winner Cary Harper, is most known for historical fiction set during the American Revolution and the Civil War. She will speak on "The Viability of Legend as a Vehicle for Fact."

Jotting down the pertinent information, I lingered long enough to locate several of Beryl's books and check them out. Back at the office, I busied myself with paperwork, my attention continually tugged toward the phone. *It's none of your business.* I was well aware of the boundary separating my jurisdiction from that of the police.

The elevator across the hall opened and custodians began talking in loud voices as they went to the janitorial closet several doors down. They always arrived at around six-thirty. Mrs. J. R. McTigue, listed in the paper as being in charge of reservations, wasn't going to answer anyway. The number I had copied was probably the DAR's business office, which would have closed at five.

The phone was picked up on the second ring.

After a pause, I asked, "Is this Mrs. J. R. McTigue?"

"Why, yes. I'm Mrs. McTigue."

It was too late. There was no point in being anything other than direct. "Mrs. McTigue, this is Dr. Scarpetta . . ."

"Dr. *who*?"

"Scarpetta," I repeated. "I'm the medical examiner investigating the death of Beryl Madison . . ."

"Oh, my! Yes, I read about that. Oh, my, oh, my. She was such a lovely young woman. I just couldn't believe it when I heard—"

"I understand she spoke at the November DAR meeting," I said.

"We were so thrilled when she agreed to come. You know, she didn't do much of that sort of thing."

Mrs. McTigue sounded quite elderly, and already I had the sinking feeling this had been the wrong move. Then she surprised me.

"You see, Beryl did it as a favor. That's the only reason it happened. My late husband was a friend of Cary Harper, the writer. I'm sure you've heard of him. Joe set it up, really. He knew it would mean so much to me. I've always loved Beryl's books."

"Where do you live, Mrs. McTigue?"

"The Gardens."

Chamberlayne Gardens was a retirement home not far

from downtown. It was just one more grim landmark in my professional life. Over the past few years, I'd had several cases from the Gardens and virtually every other retirement community or nursing home in the city.

"I'm wondering if I could stop by for a few minutes on my way home," I said. "Would that be possible?"

"I think so. Why, yes. I suppose that would be fine. You're Dr. *who*?"

I repeated my name slowly.

"I'm in apartment three-seventy-eight. When you come into the lobby, take the elevator up to the third floor."

I already knew a lot about Mrs. McTigue because of where she lived. Chamberlayne Gardens catered to the elderly who did not have to rely on Social Security to survive. Deposits for its apartments were substantial, the monthly fee steeper than most people's mortgages. But the Gardens, like others of its kind, was a gilded cage. No matter how lovely it was, no one really wanted to be there.

On the western fringes of downtown, it was a modern brick high rise that looked like a depressing blend of a hotel and a hospital. Parking in a visitor slot, I headed toward a lighted portico that promised to be the main entrance. The lobby gleamed with Williamsburg reproductions, many of the pieces bearing arrangements of silk flowers in heavy cut-crystal vases. On top of the wall-to-wall red carpet were machine-made Oriental rugs, and overhead was a brass chandelier. An old man was perched on a couch, cane in hand, eyes vacant beneath the brim of a tweedy English cap. A decrepit woman was trekking across the rug with a walker.

A young man looked bored behind a potted plant on the front desk and paid me no mind as I headed to the elevator. The doors eventually opened and took forever to close, as is common in places where people need plenty of time to ambulate. Riding up three floors alone, I stared abstractedly at the bulletins taped to the paneled interior, reminders of field trips to area museums and plantations, of bridge clubs, arts and crafts, and a deadline for knitted items needed by the Jewish Community Center. Many of the announcements were outdated. Retirement homes, with their cemetery names like Sunnyland or Sheltering Pines or Chamberlayne Gardens, always made me feel slightly queasy. I didn't know what I would do when my mother could no longer live alone. Last time I called her she was talking about getting a hip replacement.

Mrs. McTigue's apartment was halfway down on the left, and my knock was promptly answered by a wizened woman with scanty hair tightly curled and yellowed like old paper. Her face was dabbed with rouge, and she was bundled in an oversize white cardigan sweater. I smelled floral-scented toilet water and the aroma of baking cheese.

"I'm Kay Scarpetta," I said.

"Oh, it's so nice of you to come," she said, lightly patting my offered hand. "Will you have tea or something a little stronger? Whatever you like, I have it. I'm drinking port."

All this as she led me into the small living room and showed me to a wing chair. Switching off the television, she turned on another lamp. The living room was as overwhelming as the set of the opera *Aïda*. On every available space of the faded Persian rug were heavy pieces of mahogany furniture: chairs, drum tables, a curio table, crowded bookcases, corner cupboards jammed with bone china and stemware. Closely spaced on the walls were dark paintings, bell pulls, and several brass rubbings.

She returned with a small silver tray bearing a Waterford decanter of port, two matching pieces of stemware, and a small plate arranged with homemade cheese biscuits. Filling our glasses, she offered me the plate and lacy linen napkins that looked old and freshly ironed. It was a ritual that took quite a long time. Then she seated herself on a worn end of a sofa where I suspected she sat most hours of the day while she was reading or watching television. She was pleased to have company even if the reason for it was somewhat less than sociable. I wondered who, if anyone, ever came to see her.

"As I mentioned earlier, I'm the medical examiner working Beryl Madison's case," I said. "At this point there is very little those of us investigating her death know about her or the people who might have known her."

Mrs. McTigue sipped her port, her face blank. I was so accustomed to going straight to the point with the police and attorneys I sometimes forgot the rest of the world needs lubrication. The biscuit was buttery and really very good. I told her so.

"Why, thank you." She smiled. "Please help yourself. There's plenty more."

"Mrs. McTigue," I tried again, "were you acquainted with Beryl Madison before you invited her to speak to your group last fall?"

"Oh, yes," she replied. "At least I was indirectly, because I've been quite a fan of hers for years. Her books, you see. Historical novels are my favorite."

"How did you know she wrote them?" I asked. "Her books were written under pen names. There is no mention of her real name on the jacket or in an author's note." I had glanced through several of Beryl's books on my way out of the library.

"Very true. I suppose I'm one of the few people who knew her identity—because of Joe."

"Your husband?"

"He and Mr. Harper were friends," she answered. "Well, as much as anyone is really Mr. Harper's friend. They were connected through Joe's business. That's how it started."

"What was your husband's business?" I asked, deciding that my hostess was much less confused than I had previously assumed.

"Construction. When Mr. Harper bought Cutler Grove, the house was badly in need of restoration. Joe spent the better part of two years out there overseeing the work."

I should have made the connection right away. McTigue Contractors and McTigue Lumber Company were the biggest construction companies in Richmond, with offices throughout the commonwealth.

"This was well over fifteen years ago," Mrs. McTigue went on. "And it was during the time Joe was working at the Grove that he first met Beryl. She came to the site several times with Mr. Harper, and soon moved into the house. She was very young." She paused. "I remember Joe telling me back then that Mr. Harper had adopted a beautiful young girl who was a very talented writer. I think she was an orphan. Something sad like that. This was all kept very quiet, of course." She carefully set down her glass and slowly made her way across the room to the secretary. Sliding open a drawer, she pulled out a legal-size creamy envelope.

"Here," she said. Her hands trembled as she presented it to me. "It's the only picture of them I have."

Inside the envelope was a blank sheet of heavy rag stationery, an old, slightly overexposed black-and-white photograph protected within its folds. On either side of a delicately pretty blond teen-age girl were two men, imposing and tan and dressed for outdoors. The three figures stood close to each other, squinting in the glare of a brilliant sun.

"That's Joe," Mrs. McTigue said, pointing to the man standing to the left of a girl I was certain was the young Beryl Madison. The sleeves of his khaki shirt were rolled up to the elbows of his muscular arms, his eyes shielded by the brim of an International Harvester cap. To Beryl's right was a big white-haired man who Mrs. McTigue went on to explain was Cary Harper.

"It was taken by the river," she said. "Back then when Joe was working on the house. Mr. Harper had white hair even then. I 'spect you've heard the stories. Supposely his hair turned white while he was writing *The Jagged Corner*, when he was barely in his thirties."

"This was taken at Cutler Grove?"

"Yes, at Cutler Grove," she answered.

I was haunted by Beryl's face. It was a face too wise and knowing for one so young, a wistful face of longing and sadness that I associate with children who have been mistreated and abandoned.

"Beryl was just a child then," Mrs. McTigue said.

"I suppose she would have been sixteen, maybe seventeen?"

"Well, yes. That sounds about right," she replied, watching me fold the sheet of paper around the photograph and tuck both back inside the envelope. "I didn't find this until after Joe passed on. I 'spect one of the members of his crew must have taken it."

She returned the envelope to its drawer, and when she had reseated herself, she added, "I think one of the reasons Joe got on so well with Mr. Harper is Joe was a one-way street when it came to other people's business. There was quite a lot I'm sure he never even told me." Smiling wanly, she stared off at the wall.

"Apparently, Mr. Harper told your husband about Beryl's books when they began to get published," I commented.

She shifted her attention back to me and looked surprised. "You know, I'm not sure Joe ever told me how he knew that, Dr. Scarpetta—such a lovely name. Spanish?"

"Italian."

"Oh! I'll bet you're quite a cook, then."

"It's something I enjoy," I said, sipping my port. "So apparently Mr. Harper told your husband about Beryl's books."

"Oh, my." She frowned. "How curious you should bring that up. It's something I never considered. But Mr. Harper must have told him at some point. Why, yes, I can't think of how else Joe would have known. But he did. When *Flag of Honor* first came out, he gave me a copy of it for Christmas."

She got up again. Searching several bookshelves, she pulled out a thick volume and carried it over to me. "It's autographed," she added proudly.

I opened it and looked at the generous signature of

"Emily Stratton," which had been penned in December ten years before.

"Her first book," I said.

"Possibly one of the few she ever signed." Mrs. McTigue beamed. "I believe Joe got it through Mr. Harper. Of course, there's no other way he could have gotten it."

"Do you have any other signed editions?"

"Not of hers. Now, I have all of her books, have read every one of them, most of them two or three times." She hesitated, her eyes widening. "Did it happen the way the papers depicted?"

"Yes." I wasn't telling the whole truth. Beryl's death was much more brutal than anything reported by the news.

She reached for another cheese biscuit, and for an instant seemed on the verge of tears.

"Tell me about last November," I said. "It was almost a year ago when she came to speak to your group, Mrs. McTigue. This was for the Daughters of the American Revolution?"

"It was our annual author's luncheon. The highlight of the year, when we have in a special speaker, an author —usually someone quite well known. It was my turn to head the committee, to work out the arrangements, find the speaker. I knew from the start I wanted Beryl, but immediately ran into obstacles. I had no idea how to locate her. She didn't have a listed telephone number and I had no idea where she lived, had no earthly idea she lived right here in Richmond! Finally, I asked Joe to help me out." She hesitated, laughing uncomfortably. "You know, I 'spect I wanted to see if I could take care of the matter on my own. And Joe was so busy. Well, he called

Mr. Harper one night, and the very next morning my telephone rang. I'll never forget my surprise. Why, I was almost speechless when she identified herself."

Her telephone. It hadn't occurred to me that Beryl's number was unlisted. There was no mention of this detail in the reports Officer Reed had taken. Did Marino know?

"She accepted the invitation, much to my delight, then asked the usual questions," Mrs. McTigue said. "What size group we expected. I told her between two and three hundred. The time, how long she should talk, that sort of thing. She was most gracious, charming. Not chatty, though. And it was unusual. She didn't care to bring books. Authors always want to bring books, don't you know. They sell them afterward, autograph them. Beryl said that wasn't her practice, and she refused the honorarium as well. It was quite out of the ordinary. She was very sweet and modest, I thought."

"Was your group all women?" I asked.

She tried to remember. "I think a few members did bring their husbands, but most of those who attended were women. Almost always are."

I expected as much. It was improbable Beryl's killer had been among her admirers that November day.

"Did she accept invitations like yours very often?" I asked.

"Oh, no," Mrs. McTigue was quick to say. "I know she didn't, at least not around here. I would have heard about something like that and been the first to sign up. She struck me as a very private young woman, someone who wrote for the joy of it and didn't really care for the attention. Explaining why she used pen names. Writers who mask their identities the way she did rarely venture out in public. And I'm sure she wouldn't have made the exception in my case had it not been for Joe's connections with Mr. Harper."

"Sounds like he would do most anything for Mr. Harper," I commented.

"Why, yes. I 'spect that's so."

"Have you ever met him?"

"Yes."

"What was your impression of him?"

"I 'spect he may have been shy," she said. "But I sometimes thought he was an unhappy man and perhaps considered himself a bit better than everybody else. I will say he cut an impressive figure." She was staring off again, and the light had gone out of her eyes. "Certainly my husband was devoted to him."

"When was the last time you saw Mr. Harper?" I asked.

"Joe passed away last spring."

"You haven't seen Mr. Harper since your husband died?"

She shook her head and left me for a private bitter place I knew nothing of. I wondered what had really transpired between Cary Harper and Mr. McTigue. Bad business deals? An influence on Mr. McTigue that eventually made him less than the man his wife had loved? Perhaps it was simply that Harper was egotistical and rude.

"He has a sister, I understand. Cary Harper lives with his sister?" I said.

Mrs. McTigue baffled me by pressing her lips together, her eyes tearing up.

Setting my glass on an end table, I reached for my pocketbook.

She followed me to the door.

I persisted, carefully. "Did Beryl ever write to you or perhaps to your husband?"

She shook her head.

"Are you aware of any other friends she had? Did your husband ever mention anyone?"

Again, she shook her head.

"What about anyone she may have referred to as 'M,' the initial M?"

Mrs. McTigue stared sadly into the empty hallway, her hand on the door. When she looked at me, her eyes were weepy and unfocused. "There's a 'P' and an 'A' in two of her novels. Union spies, I believe. Oh, my. I don't think I turned the oven off." She blinked several times as if staring into sunlight. "You'll come see me again, I hope?"

"That would be very nice." Kindly touching her arm, I thanked her and left.

I called my mother as soon as I got home and for once was relieved to receive the usual lectures and reminders, to hear that strong voice loving me in its no-nonsense way.

"It's been in the eighties all week and I saw on the news it's been dropping as low as forty in Richmond," she said. "That's almost freezing. It hasn't snowed yet?"

"No, Mother. It hasn't snowed. How's your hip?"

"As well as can be expected. I'm crocheting a lap robe, thought you could cover your legs with it while you work in your office. Lucy's been asking about you."

I hadn't talked to my niece in weeks.

"She's working on some science project at school right now," my mother went on. "A talking robot, of all things. Brought it over the other night and scared poor Sinbad under the bed. . . ."

Sinbad was a sinful, bad, mean, nasty cat, a gray- and black-striped stray who had tenaciously begun following Mother while she was shopping in Miami Beach one morning. Whenever I came to visit, Sinbad's hospitality extended to his perching on top of the refrigerator like a vulture and giving me the fish-eye.

"You'll never guess who I saw the other day," I began a little too breezily. The need to tell someone was overwhelming. My mother knew my past, or at least most of it. "Do you remember Mark James?"

Silence.

"He was in Washington and stopped by."

"Of course I remember him."

"He stopped by to discuss a case. You remember, he's a lawyer. Uh, in Chicago." I was rapidly retreating. "He was on business in D.C." The more I said, the more her disapproving silence closed in on me.

"*Huh.* What I remember is he nearly killed you, Katie."

When she called me "Katie" I was ten years old again.

4

An obvious advantage of having the forensic science labs inside my building was I didn't have to wait for paper reports. Like me, the scientists often knew a lot before they began writing anything down. I had submitted Beryl Madison's trace evidence exactly one week ago. It would probably be several more weeks before the report was on my desk, but Joni Hamm would already have her opinions and private interpretations. Having finished the morning's cases and in a mood to speculate, I keyed myself up to the fourth floor, a cup of coffee in hand.

Joni's "office" was little more than an alcove sandwiched between the trace and drug analysis labs at the end of the hall. When I walked in she was sitting at a black countertop peering into the ocular lens of a stereoscopic microscope, a spiral notebook at her elbow filled with neatly written notes.

"A bad time?" I inquired.

"No worse than any other time," she said, glancing around distractedly.

I pulled up a chair.

Joni was a petite young woman with short black hair and wide, dark eyes. A Ph.D. candidate taking classes at night and the mother of two young children, she always looked tired and a bit harried. But then, most of the lab workers did, and in fact the same was often said of me.

"Checking in on Beryl Madison," I said. "What have you found?"

"More than you bargained for, I have a feeling." She turned back through pages in the notebook. "Beryl Madison's trace is a nightmare."

I wasn't surprised. I had turned in a multitude of envelopes and evidence buttons. Beryl's body was so bloody it had picked up debris like flypaper. Fibers, in particular, were difficult to examine because they had to be cleaned before Joni could put them under the scope. This required placing each individual fiber inside a container of soapy solution, which in turn was placed inside an ultrasound bath. After blood and dirt were gently agitated free, the solution was strained through sterile filter paper and each fiber was mounted on a glass slide.

Joni was scanning her notes. "If I didn't know better," she went on, "I'd suspect Beryl Madison was murdered somewhere other than her house."

"Not possible," I answered. "She was murdered upstairs, and she hadn't been dead long when the police got there."

"I understand that. We'll start with fibers indigenous to her house. There were three collected from the bloody areas of her knees and palms. They're wool. Two of them dark red, one gold."

"Consistent with the Oriental prayer rug in the upstairs hallway?" I recalled from the scene photographs.

"Yes," she said. "A very good match with the exemplars brought in by the police. If Beryl Madison were on her hands and knees and on the rug, it would explain the fibers you collected and their location. That's the easy part."

Joni reached for a stack of stiff cardboard slide folders, sorting through them until she found what she was looking for. Opening the flaps, she perused rows of glass slides as she talked. "In addition to those fibers, there were a number of white cotton fibers. They're useless, could have come from anywhere and possibly were transferred from the white sheet covering her body. I also looked at ten other fibers collected from her hair, the bloody areas of her neck and chest, and her fingernail scrapings. Synthetics." She glanced up at me. "And they aren't consistent with any of the exemplars the police sent in."

"They don't match up with her clothing or bed covers?" I asked.

Joni shook her head and said, "Not at all. They appear foreign to the scene, and because they were adhering to blood or were under her nails, the likelihood is strong they're the result of a passive transfer from the assailant to her."

This was an unexpected reward. When Deputy Chief Fielding finally got hold of me the night of Beryl's murder, I had instructed him to wait for me at the morgue. I got there shortly before one A.M. and we spent the next several hours examining Beryl's body under the laser and collecting every particle and fiber that lit up. I had just assumed most of what we found would prove worthless debris from Beryl's own clothing or house. The idea of finding ten fibers deposited by the assailant was astonishing. In most cases I was lucky to find one unknown fiber and considered myself blessed to find two or three. I frequently had cases where I didn't find any. Fibers are hard to see, even with a lens, and the slightest disturbance of the body or the faintest stirring of air can dislodge them long before the medical examiner arrives at the scene or the body is transported to the morgue.

"What sort of synthetics?" I asked.

"Olefin, acrylic, nylon, polyethylene, and Dynel, with the majority of them being nylon," Joni replied. "The colors vary: red, blue, green, gold, orange. Microscopically they're inconsistent with each other as well."

She began placing one slide after another on the stereoscope's stage and peering through the lens.

She explained, "Logitudinally, some are striated, some aren't. Most of them contain titanium dioxide in a variety of densities, meaning some are a semidull luster, others dull, a few bright. The diameters are all rather coarse, suggestive of carpet-type fibers, but on cross section the shapes vary."

"*Ten* different origins?" I asked.

"That's the way it looks at this point," she said. "Definitely atypical. If these fibers were transferred by the assailant, he was carrying an unusual variety of fibers on his person. Obviously, the coarser ones aren't from his clothing because they're carpet-type fibers. And they're not from any of the carpets inside her house. For him to have such a variety is peculiar for another reason. You pick up fibers all day long, but they don't stay with you. You sit somewhere and pick up fibers, and a little later they're brushed off when you sit somewhere else. Or the air dislodges them."

It got more perplexing. Joni turned another page in her notebook and said, "I've also put the vacuumings under the scope, Dr. Scarpetta. The debris Marino vacuumed off the prayer rug, in particular, is a real hodgepodge." She skimmed a list. "Tobacco ash, pinkish paper particles consistent with the stamp on cigarette packs, glass beads, a couple bits of broken glass consistent with beer bottle and headlight glass. As usual, there are pieces and parts of bugs, vegetable debris, also one spherical metal ball. And a lot of salt."

"As in table salt?"

"That's right," she said.

"All this was on her prayer rug?" I asked.

"Also from the area of the floor where her body was found," she replied. "And a lot of the same debris was on her body, in her nail scrapings, and in her hair."

Beryl didn't smoke. There was no reason for tobacco ash or particles from a cigarette pack stamp to be found inside her house. Salt is associated with food, and it didn't make sense for salt to be upstairs or on her body.

"Marino brought in six different vacuumings, all of them from carpets and areas of the floor where blood was found," Joni said. "In addition, I've looked at the control sample vacuumings taken from areas of her house or carpets where there was no blood or evidence of a struggle —areas where the police think the killer didn't go. The vacuumings are significantly different. The debris I just listed was found only in those areas where the killer was thought to have been, suggesting that most of this material was transferred from him to the scene and her body. It may have been clinging to his shoes, his clothing, his hair. Everywhere he went, everything he brushed up against collected some of this debris."

"He must be a veritable Pig Pen," I said.

"This stuff is almost invisible to the naked eye," the ever-serious Joni reminded me. "He probably wouldn't have a clue he was carrying so much trace on his person."

I studied her handwritten lists. There were only two types of cases from my past experience that might account for such an abundance of debris. One was when a body was dumped in a landfill or some other dirty place such as a road shoulder or gravel parking lot, the other when it was transported from one scene to another in the dirty trunk or on the dirty floor of a car. Neither scenario applied to Beryl.

"Break it down for me by color," I said. "Which of these are likely to be carpet versus garment fibers?"

"The six nylon fibers are red, dark red, blue, green, greenish yellow, and dark green. The greens may actually be black," she added. "Black doesn't look black under the scope. All of these are coarse, consistent with carpet-type fibers, and I'm suspicious some of them may be from vehicle versus household carpeting."

"Why?"

"Because of the debris I found. For example, the glass beads are often associated with reflectorized paint, such as is used in street signs. The metal spheres I find quite often in car vacuumings. They're solder balls from the assembling of the vehicle's undercarriage. You don't see them, but they're there. Bits of broken glass—broken glass is all over the place, especially along road shoulders and in parking lots. You pick it up on the bottom of your shoes and track it into your car. Same goes for the cigarette debris. Finally, we're left with salt, and that makes me most suspicious the origin of Beryl's trace is vehicular. People go to McDonald's. They eat french fries inside their cars. Probably every car in this city has salt in it."

"Let's say you're right," I said. "Let's say these fibers are from car carpeting. That still doesn't explain why there would be possibly six different nylon carpet fibers. It's not likely this guy has six different types of carpet inside his vehicle."

"No, that's not likely," Joni said. "But the fibers could have been transferred to the inside of his car. Maybe he works in a profession that exposes him to carpets. Maybe he has an occupation that puts him in and out of different cars throughout the day."

"A car wash?" I asked, envisioning Beryl's car. It was spotless inside and out.

Joni thought about this, her young face intense. "Could very well be something like that. If he works in one of these car washes where attendants clean the interiors, the trunks, he'd be exposed to a variety of carpet fibers all day long. It's inevitable he's going to pick up some of them. Another possibility is he works as a car mechanic."

I reached for my coffee. "Okay. Let's get to the other four fibers. What can you tell me about them?"

She glanced over her paperwork. "One is acrylic, one olefin, one polyethylene, the other Dynel. Again, the first three are consistent with carpet-type fibers. The Dynel fiber is interesting because I don't see Dynel very often. It's generally associated with fake fur coats, furlike rugs, wigs. But this Dynel fiber is rather fine, more consistent with garment material."

"The only clothing fiber you found?"

"I'm inclined that way," she answered.

"Beryl was thought to have been wearing a tannish pants suit . . ."

"It's not Dynel," she said. "At least her slacks and jacket aren't. They're a cotton and polyester blend. It's possible her blouse was Dynel, no way to know since it hasn't turned up." She retrieved another slide from the file folder and mounted it on the stage. "As for the orange fiber I mentioned, the only acrylic one I found, it has a shape at cross section I've never seen before."

She drew a diagram to demonstrate, three circles joined in the center, bringing to mind a three-leaf clover without a stem. Fibers are manufactured by forcing a melted or dissolved polymer through the very fine holes of a spinneret. Cross-sectionally, the resulting filaments, or fibers, will be the same shape as the spinneret holes, just as a line of toothpaste will be the same cross-sectional shape as the opening in the tube it was squeezed through. I had never seen the clover-leaf shape before, either. Most acrylics are a peanut, dog bone, dumbbell, round, or mushroom shape at cross section.

"Here." Joni moved to one side, making room for me.

I peered through the ocular lens. The fiber looked like a blotchy twisted ribbon, its varying shades of bright orange lightly peppered with black particles of titanium dioxide.

"As you can see," she explained, "the color is also a little awkward. The orange. Uneven, and moderately dense with delustering particles to dull the fiber's shine.

All the same, the orange is garish, a real Halloween orange, which I find peculiar for clothing or carpet fibers. The diameter is moderately coarse."

"Which would make it consistent with carpeting," I ventured. "Despite the peculiar color."

"Possibly."

I began thinking about what materials I had come across that were bright orange. "What about traffic vests?" I asked. "They're bright orange, and a fiber from that would fit with the vehicle-type debris you've identified."

"Unlikely," she replied. "Most traffic vests I've seen are nylon versus acrylic, usually a very coarse mesh that isn't likely to shed. In addition, windbreakers and jackets you might associate with road crews or traffic cops are smooth, also unlikely to shed, and they're usually nylon." She paused, adding thoughtfully, "It also seems to me you aren't likely to find much, if any, delustering particles—you wouldn't want a traffic vest to appear dull."

I backed away from the stereoscope. "Whatever the case, this fiber is so distinctive I suspect it's patented. Someone out there should recognize it even if we don't have a known material for comparison."

"Good luck."

"I know. Proprietary blackouts," I said. "The textile industry is as secretive about their patents as people are about their assignations."

Joni stretched her arms and massaged the back of her neck. "It's always struck me as miraculous the Feds were able to get so much cooperation in the Wayne Williams case," she said, referring to the grisly twenty-two-month spree in Atlanta, in which it is believed that as many as thirty black children were murdered by the same serial killer. Fibrous debris recovered from twelve of the victims' bodies was linked to the residence and automobiles used by Williams.

"Maybe we should get Hanowell to take a look at these fibers, especially this orange one," I said.

Roy Hanowell was an FBI special agent in the Microscopic Analysis Unit in Quantico. He examined the fibers in the Williams case, and ever since had been inundated with other investigative agencies worldwide wanting him to look at everything from cashmere to cobwebs.

"Good luck," Joni said again, just as drolly.

"You'll call him?" I asked.

"I doubt he'll be inclined to look at something that's already been examined," she said, adding, "You know how the Feds are."

"We'll both call him," I decided.

When I returned to my office there were half a dozen pink telephone messages. One jumped out at me. Written on it was a number with a New York City exchange and the note: "Mark. Please return call ASAP." There was only one reason I could think of for his being in New York. He was seeing Sparacino, Beryl's attorney. Why was Orndorff & Berger so intensely interested in Beryl Madison's murder?

The telephone number apparently was Mark's direct line because he picked up on the first ring.

"When's the last time you were in New York?" he asked casually.

"I beg your pardon?"

"There's a flight leaving Richmond in exactly four hours. It's nonstop. Can you can be on it?"

"What is this about?" I asked quietly, my pulse quickening.

"I don't think it wise to discuss the details over the phone, Kay," he said.

"I don't think it wise for me to come to New York, Mark," I responded.

"Please. It's important. You know I wouldn't ask if it wasn't."

"It's not possible . . ."

"I just spent the morning with Sparacino," he interrupted as long-suppressed emotions wrestled with my resolve. "There's a couple of new developments having to do with Beryl Madison and your office."

"My office?" I no longer sounded unmoved. "What could you possibly be discussing that has to do with my office?"

"Please," he said again. "Please come."

I hesitated.

"I'll meet you at La Guardia." Mark's urgency cut off my attempts at retreat. "We'll find someplace quiet to talk. The reservation's already made. All you need to do is pick up your ticket at the check-in counter. I've booked a room for you, taken care of everything."

Oh God, I thought as I hung up, and then I was inside Rose's office.

"I have to go to New York this afternoon," I explained in a tone that invited no questions. "It has to do with Beryl Madison's case, and I'll be out of the office at least through tomorrow." I evaded her eyes. Though my secretary knew nothing about Mark, I feared that my motivation was as obvious as a billboard.

"Is there a number where you can be reached?" Rose asked.

"No."

Opening the calendar, she immediately began scanning for the appointments she would need to cancel as she informed me, "The *Times* called earlier, something about doing a features article, a profile of you."

"Forget it," I answered irritably. "They just want to corner me about Beryl Madison's case. It never fails. Whenever there's a particularly brutal case I refuse to discuss, suddenly every reporter in town wants to know where I went to college, if I have a dog or ambivalence about capital punishment, and what my favorite color, food, movie, and mode of death are."

"I'll decline," she muttered, reaching for the phone.

I left the office in time to make it home, throw a few things into a suit bag, and beat the rush-hour traffic. As Mark promised, my ticket was waiting for me at the airport. He had booked me in first class, and within the hour I was settled in a row all to myself. For the next hour I sipped Chivas on the rocks and tried to read as my thoughts shifted like the clouds in the darkening sky beyond my oval window.

I wanted to see Mark. I realized it wasn't professional necessity, but a weakness that I had believed I had completely overcome. I was alternately thrilled and disgusted with myself. I did not trust him, but I wanted to desperately. *He's not the Mark you once knew, and even if he was, remember what he did to you.* And no matter what my mind said, my emotions would not listen.

I went through twenty pages of a novel written by Beryl Madison as Adair Wilds and had no earthly idea what I had read. Historical romances are not my favorite, and this one, in truth, wouldn't win any prizes. Beryl wrote well, her prose sometimes breaking into song, but the story limped along on wooden feet. It was the sort of pulp that was written almost to formula, and I wondered if she might have succeeded at the literature she aspired to write had she lived.

The pilot's voice suddenly announced we would be landing in ten minutes. Below, the city was a dazzling circuit board with tiny lights moving along highways and tower lights winking red from the tops of skyscrapers.

Minutes later, I pulled my suit bag out of the storage compartment and passed through the boarding bridge into the madness of La Guardia. I turned, rather startled, at the pressure of a hand on my elbow. Mark was behind me, smiling.

"Thank God," I said with relief.

"What? You thought I was a purse snatcher?" he asked dryly.

"If you had been, you wouldn't be standing," I said.

"I don't doubt that." He began steering me through the terminal. "Your only bag?"

"Yes."

"Good."

Out front, we got a cab piloted by a bearded Sikh in a maroon turban whose name was Munjar, according to the ID clamped to his visor. He and Mark shouted at each other until Munjar appeared to understand our destination.

"You haven't eaten, I hope," Mark said to me.

"Nothing but smoked almonds . . ." I fell against his shoulder as we screeched from lane to lane.

"There's a good steak house not far from the hotel," Mark said loudly. "Figured we'd just eat there since I don't know a damn thing about getting around in this city."

Just getting to the hotel would do, I thought, as Munjar began an unsolicited monologue about how he had come to this country to get married, and had a December wedding planned even though he had no prospects for a wife at the moment. He went on to inform us that he had been driving a cab for only three weeks, and had learned how to drive in the Punjab, where he had started driving a tractor at the age of seven.

The traffic was bumper to bumper, with yellow cabs whirling dervishes in the dark. When we arrived in midtown we passed a steady flow of people in evening dress adding to the long line outside Carnegie Hall. The bright lights and people in furs and black ties stirred old memories. Mark and I used to love the theater, the symphony, the opera.

The cab stopped at the Omni Park Central, an impressive tower of lights near the theater district at the corner of Fifty-fifth and Seventh. Mark snatched up my bag and I followed him inside the elegant lobby, where he checked me in and had my bag sent up to my room. Minutes later we were walking through the sharp night air. I was grateful I had brought my overcoat. It felt cold enough to snow. In three blocks we were at Gallagher's, the nightmare of every cow and coronary artery and the fantasy of every red meat lover. The front window was a meat locker behind glass, an enormous display of every cut of meat imaginable. Inside was a shrine to celebrities, autographed photographs covering the walls.

The din was loud and the bartender mixed our drinks very strong. I lit a cigarette and took a quick survey. Tables were arranged close together, typical for New York restaurants. Two businessmen were engrossed in conversation to our left, the table to our right empty, the one beyond that occupied by a strikingly handsome young man working on the *New York Times* and a beer. I took a long look at Mark, trying to read his face. He was tight around the eyes and playing with his Scotch.

"Why am I really here, Mark?" I asked.

"Maybe I just wanted to take you out to dinner," he said.

"Seriously."

"I'm serious. You aren't enjoying yourself?"

"How can I enjoy myself when I'm waiting for a bomb to drop?" I said.

He unbuttoned his suit jacket. "We'll order first, then we'll talk."

He used to do this to me all the time. He would get me going only to make me wait. Maybe it was the lawyer in him. It used to drive me crazy. It still did.

"The prime rib comes highly recommended," he said as we looked over the menus. "That's what I'm going to have, and a spinach salad. Nothing fancy. But the steaks are supposed to be the best in town."

"You've never been here?" I asked.

"No. Sparacino has," he answered.

"He recommended this place? And the hotel, too, I presume?" I asked, my paranoia kicking in.

"Sure," he replied, interested in the wine list now. "It's

SOP. Clients fly to town and stay in the Omni because it's convenient to the firm."

"And your clients eat here, too?"

"Sparacino's been here before, usually after the theater. That's how he knows about it," Mark said.

"What else does Sparacino know about?" I asked. "Did you tell him you were meeting me?"

He met my eyes and said, "No."

"How is that possible if your firm is putting me up and if Sparacino recommended the hotel and the restaurant?"

"He recommended the hotel to *me*, Kay. I have to stay somewhere. I have to eat. Sparacino invited me to go out with a couple of other lawyers tonight. I declined, said I needed to look over some paperwork and would probably just find a steak somewhere. What did he recommend? And so on."

It was beginning to dawn on me and I wasn't sure if I felt embarrassed or unnerved. Probably it was both. Orndorff & Berger wasn't paying for this trip. Mark was. His firm knew nothing about it.

The waiter was back and Mark placed the order. I was fast losing my appetite.

"I flew in last night," he resumed. "Sparacino got hold of me in Chicago yesterday morning, said he needed to see me right away. As you may have guessed, it's about Beryl Madison." He looked uncomfortable.

"And?" I prodded him, my uneasiness increasing.

He took a deep breath and said, "Sparacino knows about my connection, uh, about you and me. Our past . . ."

My stare stopped him.

"Kay . . ."

"You bastard." I pushed back my chair and dropped my napkin on the table.

"Kay!"

Mark grabbed my arm, pulling me back into the seat. I angrily shook him off and sat rigidly in my chair, glaring at him. It was in a Georgetown restaurant many years ago that I had snatched off the heavy gold bracelet he had given me and dropped it into his clam chowder. It was a childish thing to do. It was one of the rare moments in my life when I had completely lost my composure and made a scene.

"Look," he said, lowering his voice, "I don't blame you for what you're thinking. But it isn't like that. I'm not taking advantage of our past. Just listen for a minute, please. It's very involved, has to do with things you know nothing about. I have your best interests in mind, I swear. I'm not supposed to be talking to you. If Sparacino, if Berger knew, my ass would be nailed to the nearest tree."

I didn't say anything. I was so upset I couldn't think.

He leaned forward. "Start with this thought. Berger's after Sparacino and, right now, Sparacino's after you."

"After *me*?" I blurted out. "I've never met the man. How could he be after me?"

"Again, it's all got to do with Beryl," he repeated. "The truth is, he's been her lawyer since the beginning of her career. He didn't join our firm until we opened the office here in New York. Before that, he was on his own. We needed an attorney who specialized in entertainment law. Sparacino's been in New York for thirty-some years. He had all the connections. He brought over his clients, brought us a lot of business up front. You remember my mentioning when I first met Beryl, the lunch at the Algonquin?"

I nodded, the fight in me fading.

"That was a setup, Kay. I wasn't there by accident. Berger sent me."

"Why?"

Glancing around the restaurant, he replied, "Because Berger's worried. The firm's just getting started in New York, and you've got to be aware how hard it is to break into this city, to build up a solid clientele, a good reputation. Last thing we need is an asshole like Sparacino driving the firm's name into the gutter."

He fell silent as the waiter appeared with the salads and ceremoniously uncorked a bottle of cabernet sauvignon. Mark took the obligatory first sip and glasses were filled.

"Berger knew when he hired Sparacino the guy's flamboyant, likes to play fast and loose," Mark resumed. "You think, well, it's just his style. Some lawyers are conservative, others like to make a lot of noise. Problem is, it wasn't until some months back that Berger and a few of us began to see just how far Sparacino was willing to go. You remember Christie Riggs?"

It took a moment for the name to click. "The actress who married the quarterback?"

Nodding, he said, "Sparacino masterminded that one from soup to nuts. Christie's a struggling model doing a few TV commercials here in the city. This was about two years ago, at the same time Leon Jones was making the covers of all the magazines. The two of them meet at a party and some photographer snaps a picture of them leaving together and getting inside Jones's Maserati. Next thing, Christie Riggs is sitting in the lobby of Orndorff & Berger. She's got an appointment with Sparacino."

"Are you telling me Sparacino was behind what happened?" I asked in disbelief.

Christie Riggs and Leon Jones had been married last year and divorced about six months later. Their tempestuous relationship and dirty divorce had entertained the world night after night on the news.

"Yes." Mark sipped his wine.

"Explain."

"Sparacino fixes on Christie," he said. "She's gorgeous, smart, ambitious. But the real thing she's got going for her at the moment is she's dating Jones. Sparacino gives her the game plan. She wants to be a household name. She wants to be rich. All she's got to do is draw Jones into her web and later start crying in front of cameras about their lives behind shut doors. She accuses him of slapping her around, says he's a drunk, a psychopath, fooling around with cocaine, smashing up the furniture. Next thing you know, she and Jones are splitting and she's signed a million-dollar book contract."

"Makes me have a little more sympathy for Jones," I muttered.

"The worse part is I think he really loved her and didn't have the smarts to know what he was up against. He started playing lousy ball, ended up in the Betty Ford Clinic. He's since dropped out of sight. One of America's greatest quarterbacks is washed up, ruined, and indirectly you can thank Sparacino for it. This kind of muckraking and slandering isn't our style. Orndorff & Berger is an old, distinguished firm, Kay. When Berger began to get a scent of what his entertainment lawyer was doing, Berger wasn't exactly happy."

"Why doesn't your firm just get rid of him?" I asked, picking at my salad.

"Because we can't prove anything, not at this point. Sparacino knows how to slide through without a snag. He's powerful, especially in New York. It's like grabbing hold of a snake. How the hell do you let go without getting bit? And the list goes on." Mark's eyes were angry. "When you start looking back through Sparacino's professional history and examine some of the cases he handled when he was a one-man show, it really makes you wonder."

"What cases, for example?" I almost hated to ask.

"A lot of suits. Some hatchet writer decides to do an unauthorized biography of Elvis, John Lennon, Sinatra, and when it comes pub time, the celebrity, his relatives sue the biographer and it makes the network talk shows, *People* magazine. The book comes out anyway, with the benefit of incredible free publicity. Everybody's fighting over it because it's got to be juicy to have caused such a stink. We're suspicious Sparacino's method is to represent the writer, then go behind the scenes and offer the 'victim' or 'victims' money under the table to raise hell. It's all staged, works like a charm."

"Makes you wonder what to believe." In fact, I wondered that most of the time.

The prime rib arrived. When the waiter was gone I asked, "How in the world did Beryl Madison ever get hooked up with him?"

"Through Cary Harper," Mark said. "That's the irony. Sparacino represented Harper for a number of years. When Beryl was coming along, Harper sent her to him. Sparacino has been shepherding her since the beginning, a combination agent, lawyer and godfather. I think Beryl was very vulnerable to older powerful men, and her career was pretty bland until she decided to do this autobiographical work. My guess is Sparacino originally suggested it. Whatever the case, Harper hasn't published anything since his Great American Novel. He's history, only valuable to someone like Sparacino if there's a possibility for exploitation."

I considered. "Is it possible Sparacino was playing his game with them? In other words, Beryl decides to break her silence—and break her contract with Harper—and Sparacino plays both sides. Goes behind the scenes and goads Harper into causing a problem."

He refilled our glasses and answered, "Yes, I think he was staging a dogfight and neither Beryl nor Harper was aware of it. As I've said, it's Sparacino's style."

We ate in silence for a moment. Gallagher's was living up to its reputation. You could cut the prime rib with a fork.

Mark finally said, "What's so awful, at least for me, Kay"—he looked up at me, his face hard—"that day we had lunch at the Algonquin, when Beryl mentioned she was being threatened, that someone was threatening to kill her . . ." He hesitated. "To tell you the truth, knowing what I did about Sparacino . . ."

"You didn't believe her." I finished the sentence for him.

"No," he confessed. "I didn't. Frankly, it struck me as another publicity stunt. I was suspicious Sparacino put her up to it, had her stage the whole thing to help sell her book. Not only does she have this battle with Harper, but now someone's threatening to kill her. I didn't give what she said much credence." He paused. "And I was wrong."

"Sparacino wouldn't go that far," I dared to suggest. "You're not implying . . ."

"I really think it's more likely he might have agitated Harper to the point he freaked, got so enraged maybe he came to see her and lost it. Or Harper hired someone else to do it."

"If that's the case," I said quietly, "he must have a lot to hide about what went on when Beryl lived with him."

"He might," Mark said, returning his attention to his meal. "Even if he doesn't, he knows Sparacino, knows how he operates. Truth or fiction, it doesn't matter. When Sparacino wants to raise a stink, he does, and nobody remembers the outcome, only the accusations."

"And now he's after me?" I asked dubiously. "I don't understand. How do I fit in?"

"Simple. Sparacino wants Beryl's manuscript, Kay. Now more than ever the book's a hot property because of what happened to the author." He looked up at me. "He believes the manuscript was turned in to your office as evidence. Now it's missing."

I reached for the sour cream and was very calm when I asked, "What makes you think it's missing?"

"Sparacino somehow managed to get his hands on the police report," Mark said. "You've seen it, I assume?"

"It was fairly routine," I answered.

He jogged my memory. "On the back sheet's an itemized list of evidence collected—including papers found on her bedroom floor and a manuscript from her dresser."

Oh, God, I thought. Marino *had* found a manuscript. It was simply that he had found the wrong one.

"He talked to the investigator this morning," Mark said. "A lieutenant named Marino. He told Sparacino the cops don't have it, said all evidence was turned into the labs in your building. He suggested Sparacino call the medical examiner—you, in other words."

"It's *pro forma*," I said. "The cops send everyone to me and I send everyone back to them."

"Try telling Sparacino that. He's claiming it was turned in to you, that it came in with Beryl's body. And now it's missing. He's holding your office responsible."

"That's ridiculous!"

"Is it?" Mark looked speculatively at me. I felt as if I were being cross-examined when he said, "Isn't it true some evidence comes in with the body and you personally receipt it to the labs or store it in your evidence room?"

Of course it was true.

"Are you part of the chain of evidence in Beryl's case?" he asked.

"Not in terms of what was found at the scene, such as in the instance of any personal papers," I said tensely. "Those were receipted to the labs by the cops, not by me. In fact, most of the items collected from her house would be in the P.D.'s property room."

Again he said, "Try telling Sparacino that."

"I never saw the manuscript," I said flatly. "My office doesn't have it, never had it. And as far as I know, it hasn't turned up, period."

"It hasn't turned up? You mean it wasn't in her house? The cops didn't find it?"

"No. The manuscript they found isn't the one you're talking about. It's an old one, possibly from a book published years ago, and it's incomplete, just a couple hundred pages at most. It was in her bedroom on the dresser. Marino took it in, had Fingerprints check in the event the killer might have touched it."

He leaned back in his chair.

"If you didn't find it," he asked quietly, "then where is it?"

"I have no idea," I answered. "I suppose it could be anywhere. Perhaps she mailed it to someone."

"She have a computer?"

"Yes."

"You check out her hard disk?"

"Her computer doesn't have a hard disk, just two floppy drives," I said. "Marino's checking the floppies. I don't know what's on them."

"Doesn't make sense," he went on. "Even if she did mail the manuscript to someone, it doesn't make sense she wouldn't have made a copy first, that there wasn't a copy somewhere inside her house."

"It doesn't make sense her godfather Sparacino wouldn't have a copy," I said pointedly. "I can't believe he hasn't seen the book. In fact, I can't believe he doesn't have a draft somewhere, maybe even the latest version."

"He says he doesn't, and I'm inclined to believe him for one good reason. From what I've gathered about Beryl, she was very private when it came to her writing, didn't let anybody—including Sparacino—see what she was doing until it was finished. She'd kept him posted on her progress through telephone conversations, letters. According to him, the last time he heard from her was about a month ago. She supposedly told him she was busy revising and should have the book ready to submit for publication by the first of the year."

"A month ago?" I asked warily. "She wrote to him?"

"Called him."

"From where?"

"Hell, I don't know. Richmond, I guess."

"Is that what he told you?"

Mark thought for a moment. "No, he didn't mention *where* she was calling from." He paused. "Why?"

"She'd been out of town for a while," I replied as if it didn't matter. "I'm just wondering if Sparacino knew where she was."

"The cops don't know where she was?"

"There's a lot the cops don't know," I said.

"That's not an answer."

"A better answer is we really shouldn't be discussing her case, Mark. I've already said too much, and I'm not sure why you're so interested."

"And you're not sure my motives are pure," he said. "You're not sure that I'm not trying to wine you and dine you because I want information."

"Yes, to be honest," I answered as our eyes met.

"I'm worried, Kay." I could tell by the tension in his face—a face that still had power over me—that he was. I could scarcely take my eyes off him.

"Sparacino's up to something," he said. "I don't want you squeezed." He drained the last of the wine into our glasses.

"What's he going to do, Mark?" I asked. "Call me and demand a manuscript I don't have? So what?"

"I have a feeling he knows you don't have it," he said. "Problem is, it doesn't matter. Yes, he wants it. And he'll get it eventually, has to unless it's lost. He's the executor of her estate."

"That's cozy," I said.

"I just know he's up to something." He seemed to be talking to himself.

"Another one of his publicity schemes?" I offered a bit too breezily.

He sipped his wine.

"I can't imagine what," I went on. "Not anything involving me."

"I can imagine it," he said seriously.

"Then please spell it out," I said.

He did. "Headline: 'Chief Medical Examiner Refuses to Release Controversial Manuscript.' "

I laughed. "That's ridiculous!"

He didn't smile. "Think about it. A controversial autobiography written by a reclusive woman who ends up brutally murdered. Then the manuscript disappears and the medical examiner is accused of stealing it. The damn thing's disappeared from the *morgue*. Christ. When the book finally comes out, it will be a runaway bestseller and Hollywood will be fighting over the movie rights."

"I'm not worried," I said unconvincingly. "It's all so farfetched, I can't imagine it."

"Sparacino's a whiz at making something out of nothing, Kay," he warned. "I just don't want you ending up like Leon Jones." He looked around for the waiter, his eyes freezing in the direction of the front door. Quickly looking down at his half-eaten prime rib, he mumbled, "Oh, shit."

It took every bit of my self-restraint not to turn around. I didn't look up or act the least bit aware until the big man was at our table.

"Well, hello, Mark. Thought I might find you here."

He was a soft-spoken man in his late fifties or early

sixties, with a fleshy face made hard by small eyes as blue as they were lacking in warmth. Flushed, he was breathing hard, as if the exertion of merely carrying his formidable weight strained every cell in his body.

"On a whim, I decided to wander by and offer you a drink, old boy." Unbuttoning his cashmere coat, he turned to me, offering his hand and a smile. "I don't believe we've met. Robert Sparacino."

"Kay Scarpetta," I said with surprising poise.

5

Somehow we had managed to drink liqueur with Sparacino for an hour. It was awful. He acted as if I were a stranger. But he knew who I was, and I was sure the encounter hadn't been accidental. In a city the size of New York, how could it have been accidental?

"You sure there's no way he knew I was coming?" I asked.

"I don't see how," Mark said.

I could feel the urgency in his fingertips as he steered me right on to Fifty-fifth Street. Carnegie Hall was empty, a few people strolling past on the sidewalk. It was getting close to one A.M., and my thoughts were floating in alcohol, nerves taut.

Sparacino had gotten more animated and obsequious with each Grand Marnier until he was finally slurring his words.

"He doesn't miss a trick. You think he's soused and

won't remember a thing in the morning. Hell, he's on red alert even when he's sound asleep."

"You're not making me feel any better," I said.

We headed straight for the elevator, where we rode up in self-conscious silence, watching the floor light blink from number to number. Our feet were quiet on the carpeted hallway. Hoping my bag was there, I was relieved to see it on the bed when I stepped inside my room.

"Are you nearby?" I asked.

"A couple doors down." His eyes were darting around. "You going to offer me a nightcap?"

"I didn't bring anything . . ."

"There's a bar fully stocked. Take my word for it," he said.

We needed another drink like a hole in the head.

"What's Sparacino going to do?" I asked.

The "bar" was a small refrigerator filled with beer, wine, and jigger-sized bottles.

"He sees us together," I added. "What's going to happen?"

"Depends on what I tell him," Mark said.

I handed him a plastic cup of Scotch. "Let me ask it this way. What are you planning to tell him, Mark?"

"A lie."

I sat down on the edge of the bed.

He pulled a chair close and began slowly swirling the amber liquor. Our knees were almost touching.

"I'll tell him I was trying to find out what I could from you," he said, "trying to help him out."

"That you were using me," I said, my thoughts breaking apart like a bad radio transmission. "That you were able to do that. Because of our past."

"Yes."

"And that's a lie?" I demanded.

He laughed, and I had forgotten how much I loved the sound of his laugh.

"I fail to see the humor," I protested. It was hot inside the room. I felt flushed from the Scotch. "If that's a lie, Mark, then what's the truth?"

"Kay," he said, still smiling, and his eyes wouldn't let me go. "I've already told you the truth." He was silent for a moment. Then he leaned over and touched my cheek, and I was frightened by how much I wanted him to kiss me.

He leaned back in his chair. "Why don't you stay, at least until tomorrow afternoon? Maybe we should both go talk to Sparacino in the morning."

"No," I said. "That's exactly what he'd like me to do."

"Whatever you say."

Hours later, after Mark left, I lay awake staring up into the darkness, aware of the cool emptiness of the other side of the bed. In the old days Mark never stayed the night, and the next morning I would go around the apartment collecting various articles of clothing, dirty glasses, dishes, and wine bottles, and emptying the ashtrays. Both of us smoked then. We would sit up until one, two, three A.M., talking, laughing, touching, drinking, smoking. We also argued. I hated the debates, which all too often turned into vicious exchanges, blow for blow, tit for tat, Code section this for philosophical that. I was always waiting to hear him say he was in love with me. He never did. In the morning I had the same empty feeling I'd had as a child when Christmas was over and I helped my mother gather up the discarded gift paper strewn under the tree.

I didn't know what I wanted. Maybe I never had. The emotional distance was never worth the togetherness, and yet I didn't learn. Nothing had changed. Had he reached for me, I would have forgotten to behave sensibly. Desire has no reason, and the need for intimacy had never stopped. I had not conjured up the images in years, his lips on mine, his hands, the urgency of our hunger. Now I was tormented by the memories.

I had forgotten to request a wake-up call and didn't bother with the clock by the bed. Setting my mental alarm for six, I woke up exactly on time. I sat straight up and felt as bad as I looked. A hot shower and careful grooming did not hide the dark puffy circles under my eyes or my wan complexion. The bathroom lighting was brutally honest. I called United Airlines and was tapping on Mark's door at seven.

"Hi," he said, looking disgustingly fresh and chipper. "You change your mind?"

"Yes," I said. The familiar scent of his cologne re-arranged my thoughts like bright shards of glass inside a kaleidoscope.

"I knew you would," he said.

"And how did you know that?" I asked.

"Never knew you to duck a fight," he said, watching me in the dresser mirror as he resumed knotting his tie.

Mark and I had agreed to meet at the Orndorff & Berger offices in the early afternoon. The firm's lobby was a heartless, deep space. Rising from black carpet was a massive black console beneath polished-brass track lighting, with a solid block of brass serving as a table between two black acrylic chairs nearby. Remarkably, there was no other furniture, no plants or paintings, nothing else but a few pieces of twisted sculpture desposited like shrapnel to break the vast emptiness of the room.

"May I help you?" The receptionist gave me a practiced smile from the depths of her station.

Before I could respond, a door indistinguishable from the dark walls silently opened and Mark was taking my suit bag and ushering me inside a long, wide hallway. We passed doorway after doorway opening onto spacious offices with plate-glass windows offering a gray vista of Manhattan. I didn't see a soul. I supposed everybody was at lunch.

"Who in God's name designed your lobby?" I whispered.

"The person we're going to see," Mark said.

Sparacino's office was twice the size of the others I had passed, his desk a beautiful block of ebony scattered with polished gemstone paperweights and surrounded by walls of books. No less intimidating than he had seemed last night, this lawyer to luminaries and the literati was dressed in what looked like an expensive John Gotti suit, the handkerchief in his breast pocket offering a contrasting touch of bloodred. He did not budge from his casual repose when we walked in and helped ourselves to chairs. For a chilly moment he did not even look at us.

"Understand you're on your way to lunch," he finally said as cool blue eyes lifted up and thick fingers shut a file folder. "I promise not to hold you up long, Dr. Scarpetta. Mark and I have been reviewing a few details pertaining to the case of my client, Beryl Madison. As her attorney and the executor of her estate, I have some fairly clear needs, and I'm confident you can assist me in complying with her wishes."

I said nothing, my search for an ashtray fruitless.

"Robert needs her papers," Mark said unemphatically. "Specifically the manuscript of the book she was writing, Kay. I was explaining to him before you got here that the medical examiner's office is not the custodian of these personal effects, at least not in this instance."

We had rehearsed this meeting over breakfast. Mark was supposed to "handle" Sparacino before I arrived. Already I was getting the feeling that I was the one being handled.

I looked straight at Sparacino and said, "The items receipted to my office are of an evidentiary nature and do not include any papers you might need."

"You're telling me you don't have the manuscript," he said.

"That's correct."

"You don't know where it is, either," he said.

"I have no idea."

"Well, now, I've got a few problems with what you're saying."

His face was expressionless as he opened the file folder and produced a photocopy I recognized as Beryl's police report.

"According to the police, a manuscript was recovered at the scene," he said. "Now I'm being told there isn't a manuscript. Can you help me make sense of that?"

"Pages of a manuscript were recovered," I answered. "But I don't think they're what you're interested in, Mr. Sparacino. They do not appear to be part of a current work and, more to the point, they were never receipted to me."

"How many pages?" he asked.

"I've not actually seen them," I said.

"Who has?"

"Lieutenant Marino. He's the one you really need to talk to," I said.

"I already have, and he tells me he hand delivered this manuscript to you."

I did not believe Marino had actually said such a thing. "A miscommunication," I replied. "I think Marino must have been referring to his receipting a partial manuscript to the forensic labs, pages of which may be an earlier work. The Bureau of Forensic Science is a separate division. It happens to be located in my building."

I glanced at Mark. His face was hard and he was perspiring.

Leather creaked as Sparacino shifted in the chair.

"I'm going to shoot straight with you, Dr. Scarpetta," he said. "I don't believe you."

"I have no control over what you believe or don't believe," I replied very calmly.

"I've been giving the matter a lot of thought," he said, just as calmly. "The fact is, the manuscript's a lot of worthless paper unless you realize its value to certain parties. I know of at least two people, not including publishers, who would pay a high price for the book she was working on when she died."

"All of this is of no concern to me," I answered. "My office does not have the manuscript you've mentioned. Furthermore, we never had it."

"Someone has it." He stared out the window. "I knew Beryl better than anyone did, knew her habits, Dr. Scarpetta. She'd been out of town for quite a while, had been home only a few hours before she was murdered. I find it impossible to think she didn't have her manuscript close by. In her office, in her briefcase, in a suitcase." The small blue eyes fixed back on me. "She doesn't have a lock box in a bank, no other place she might have kept it—not that she would have, anyway. She had it with her while she was out of town, was working on it. Obviously, when she came back to Richmond she would have had the manuscript with her."

"She'd been out of town for quite a while," I repeated. "You're sure of that?"

Mark wouldn't look at me.

Sparacino leaned back in his chair and laced his fingers over his big belly.

He said to me, "I knew Beryl wasn't home. I had been trying to call her for weeks. Then she called me about a month ago. She wouldn't tell me where she was but said she was, quote, safe, and proceeded to give me a progress report on her book, said she was hard at work on it. To make a long story short, I didn't pry. Beryl was running scared because of this psycho threatening her. It didn't really matter to me where she was, just that she was well and working hard at meeting her deadline. Might sound insensitive, but I had to be pragmatic."

"We don't know where Beryl was," Mark informed me. "Apparently, Marino wouldn't say."

His choice of pronouns bit into me. "We" as in he and Sparacino.

"If you're asking me to answer that question—"

"That's exactly what I'm asking," Sparacino cut in. "It's going to come out eventually that for the past few months she was staying in North Carolina, Washington,

Texas—hell, wherever it was. I need to know *now*. You're telling me your office doesn't have the manuscript. The police are telling me they don't have it. One sure way for me to get to the bottom of this is to find out where she was last, begin tracking the manuscript that way. Maybe someone drove her to the airport. Maybe she made friends wherever she was. Maybe someone has an inkling as to what happened to her book. For example, did she have it in hand when she boarded the plane?"

"You'll have to get that information from Lieutenant Marino," I replied. "I'm not at liberty to discuss the details of her case with you."

"I didn't expect you to be," Sparacino said. "Probably because you know she had it with her when she got on that plane to come home to Richmond. Probably because it came into your office with her body and now it's gone." He paused, his eyes cold on mine. "How much did Cary Harper or his sister or both pay you to turn it over to them?"

Mark was tuned out, his face without expression.

"How much? Ten, twenty, fifty thousand?"

"I believe this terminates our conversation, Mr. Sparacino," I said, reaching for my pocketbook.

"No. I don't believe it does, Dr. Scarpetta," Sparacino answered.

He casually shuffled through the file folder. Just as casually, he tossed several sheets of paper across the desk in my direction.

I felt the blood drain from my face as I picked up what I recognized as photocopies of articles the Richmond newspapers had published more than a year ago. The story on top was depressingly familiar:

MEDICAL EXAMINER ACCUSED OF
STEALING FROM BODY

When Timothy Smathers was shot to death last month in front of his residence, he was wearing a gold wristwatch, a gold ring, and had $83 cash in his pants pockets, according to his wife, who was witness to the homicide allegedly committed by a disgruntled former employee. Police and members of the rescue squad responding to Smathers' residence after the shooting claim that these valuables accompanied Smathers' body when it was sent in to the Medical Examiner's Office for an autopsy. . . .

There was more, and I didn't have to read on to know what the other clippings said. The Smathers case had precipitated some of the worst publicity my office had ever received.

I passed the photocopies to Mark's outstretched hand. Sparacino had me on a hook and I was determined not to squirm.

"As you'll note if you've read the stories," I said, "there was a full investigation of that situation, and my office was cleared of any wrongdoing."

"Yes, indeed," Sparacino said. "You personally receipted the valuables in question to the funeral home. It was after this that the items disappeared. The problem was proving it. Mrs. Smathers is still of the opinion the OCME stole her husband's jewelry and money. I've talked to her."

"Her office was cleared, Robert," Mark offered in a monotone as he looked over the articles. "Even so, it says here that Mrs. Smathers was issued a check for an amount commensurate with what the items were worth."

"That's correct," I said coldly.

"There's no price tag on sentimental value," Sparacino remarked. "You could have issued her a check for *ten times* the amount, and she's going to be unhappy."

That was definitely a joke. Mrs. Smathers, whom the police still suspected was behind her husband's murder, married a wealthy widower before the grass had even started growing on her husband's grave.

"And as the news stories point out," Sparacino was saying, "your office was unable to produce the evidence receipt that would verify you did indeed turn over Mr. Smathers's personal effects to the funeral home. Now, I know the details. The receipt was supposedly misplaced by your administrator, who has since gone to work elsewhere. It boiled down to your word against the funeral home's, and though the matter was never resolved, at least not to my satisfaction, by now nobody remembers or cares."

"What's your point?" Mark asked in the same flat tone.

Sparacino glanced at Mark, then returned his attention to me. "The Smathers situation, unfortunately, isn't the end of this sort of accusation. Last July your office received the body of an elderly man named Henry Jackson, who died of natural causes. His body came into your office with fifty-two dollars cash in a pocket. Again, it seems, the money disappeared and you were forced to issue a check to the dead man's son. The son complained to a local television news station. I've got a videotape of what went out over the air if you'd like to see it."

"Jackson came in with fifty-two dollars cash in his pockets," I responded, about to lose my temper. "He was badly decomposed, the money so putrid not even the most desperate thief would have touched it. I don't know what happened to it, but it seems likely the money inadvertently got incinerated along with Jackson's equally putrid and maggot-infested clothing."

"Jesus," Mark muttered under his breath.

"Your office has got a problem, Dr. Scarpetta." Sparacino smiled.

"Every office has its problems," I snapped, getting up. "You want Beryl Madison's property, deal with the police."

"I'm sorry," Mark said when we were riding down on the elevator. "I had no idea the bastard was going to hit you with this shit. You could have told me, Kay . . ."

"Told you?" I stared incredulously at him. "Told you *what?*"

"About the items missing, the bad publicity. It's just the sort of stink Sparacino thrives on. I didn't know and I walked both of us into an ambush. Damn!"

"I didn't tell you," I said, my voice rising, "because it isn't relevant to Beryl's case. The situations he mentioned were tempests in a teapot, the sort of housekeeping snafus that inevitably occur when bodies land on the doorstep in every possible condition and where funeral homes and cops are in and out all day long to pick up personal effects—"

"Please don't get angry with me."

"I'm not angry with you!"

"Look, I've warned you about Sparacino. I'm trying to protect you from him."

"Maybe I'm not sure what you're trying to do, Mark."

We continued to talk in heated voices as he cast about for a cab. The street was almost at a standstill. Horns were blaring, engines rumbling, and my nerves were to the point of snapping. A cab finally appeared and Mark opened the back door, placing my suit bag on the floor. When he handed the driver a couple of bills after I got in, I realized what was happening. Mark wasn't joining me. He was sending me back to the airport alone and without lunch. Before I could roll down the window to talk to him, the cab jerked back out into traffic.

I rode in silence to La Guardia and still had three hours to spare before my flight departed. I was angry, hurt, and bewildered. I couldn't stand parting like this. Finding an empty chair inside a bar, I ordered a drink and lit a cigarette. I watched blue smoke curl up and dissipate in the hazy air. Minutes later I was feeding a quarter into a pay phone.

"Orndorff & Berger," the businesslike female voice announced.

I envisioned the black console as I said, "Mark James, please."

After a pause, the woman replied, "I'm sorry, you must have the wrong number."

"He's with your Chicago office. He's visiting. In fact, I met him at your office earlier today," I said.

"Can you hold?"

I was treated to a Muzak rendition of Jerry Rafferty's "Baker Street" for what must have been two minutes.

"I'm sorry," the receptionist informed me when she returned, "there's no one here by that name, ma'am."

"He and I met in your lobby less than two hours ago," I exclaimed impatiently.

"I checked, ma'am. I'm sorry, but perhaps you have us confused with another firm."

Cursing under my breath, I slammed down the receiver.

Dialing directory assistance, I got the number for Orndorff & Berger's Chicago office and stabbed in my credit card number. I would leave a message for Mark telling him to call me as soon as possible.

My blood ran cold when the Chicago receptionist announced, "I'm sorry, ma'am. There is no Mark James at this firm."

6

Mark wasn't listed in the Chicago directory. There were five Mark Jameses and three M Jameses, and after I got home I tried each number and either got a woman or some unfamiliar man on the line. I was so bewildered I couldn't sleep.

It didn't occur to me until the next morning to call Diesner, the chief medical examiner in Chicago whom Mark had claimed to run into.

Deciding being direct was my best recourse, I said to Diesner after the usual pleasantries, "I'm trying to track down Mark James, a Chicago lawyer I believe you might know."

"James . . ." Diesner repeated thoughtfully. "Afraid the name's not familiar, Kay. You say he's a lawyer here in Chicago?"

"Yes." My heart sank. "With Orndorff & Berger."

"Now, I know Orndorff & Berger. A very well respected firm. But I can't recall, uh, a Mark James . . ." I heard a drawer opening and pages flipping. After a long moment, Diesner was saying, "Nope. Don't see him listed in the Yellow Pages either."

After I hung up, I poured myself another cup of black coffee and stared out the kitchen window at the empty bird feeder. The gray morning threatened rain. I had a desk downtown requiring a bulldozer. It was Saturday. Monday was a state holiday. The office would be deserted, my staff already enjoying the three-day weekend. I should go in and take advantage of the peace and quiet. But I didn't care. I couldn't think of anything but Mark. It was as if he didn't exist, as if the man was imaginary, a dream. The more I tried to sort through it, the more tangled my thoughts became. What the hell was going on?

To the point of desperation, I tried to get Robert Sparacino's home number from Directory Assistance and was secretly relieved to find it was unlisted. It would be suicidal for me to call him. Mark had lied to me. He told me he worked for Orndorff & Berger, told me he lived in Chicago and knew Diesner. None of it was true! I kept hoping the phone would ring, hoping Mark would call. I straightened up the house, did the laundry and ironing, put on a pot of tomato sauce, made meatballs, and went through the mail.

The phone didn't ring until five P.M.

"Yo, Doc? Marino here," the familiar voice greeted me. "Don't mean to be bothering you on the weekend, but been trying to find you for two damn days. Wanted to make sure you was all right."

Marino was playing guardian angel again.

"Got a videotape I want you to see," he said. "Thought if you was going to be in, I'd just drop it by your house. You got a VCR?"

He knew I did. He had "dropped by" videotapes before. "What sort of videotape?" I asked.

"This drone I spent the entire morning with. Interviewing him about Beryl Madison." He paused. I could tell he was pleased with himself.

The longer I knew Marino, the more he had begun subjecting me to show-and-tell. In part I attributed this phenomenon to his saving my life, a horrific event that had served to bond us into an unlikely pair.

"You on duty?" I asked.

"Hell, I'm always on duty," he grumbled.

"Seriously."

"Not officially, okay? Knocked off at four, but the wife's off in Jersey visiting her mother and I got more loose ends to tie up than a damn rug maker."

His wife was gone. His kids were grown. It was a gray, raw Saturday. Marino didn't want to go home to an empty house. I wasn't exactly feeling contented and cheery inside my empty house, either. I stared at the pot of sauce simmering on the stove.

"I'm not going anywhere," I said. "Drop by with your videotape and we'll watch it together. You like spaghetti?"

He hesitated. "Well . . ."

"With meatballs. And I'm getting ready to make the pasta now. You'll eat with me?"

"Yeah," he said. "I guess I can do that."

When Beryl Madison wanted a clean car, it was her habit to visit Masterwash on Southside.

Marino had found this out by hitting every high-class car wash in the city. There weren't that many, a dozen at most that offered to roll your driverless car automatically through an assembly line of "hula skirts" gyrating over sudsy paint as spray jets fired needle streams of water. Following a quick hot-air drying, the car was manned by a human being and driven to a bay where attendants vacuumed, waxed, buffed, dressed the bumpers, and all the rest of it. A Masterwash "Super Deluxe," Marino informed me, was fifteen dollars.

"I was lucky as hell," Marino said as he guided spaghetti onto his fork with a soup spoon. "How do you track down something like that, huh? The drones wipe off, what, seventy, a hundred rides a day? And you think they're gonna notice a black Honda? Hell, no."

He was the happy hunter. He had bagged the big one. I knew when I had given him the preliminary fiber report last week he would start hitting every car wash and body shop in the city. One thing about Marino, if there was one bush in the desert, he had to look behind it.

"Hit pay dirt yesterday," he went on. "Buzzed by Masterwash. Was close to last on my list because of its location. Me, I figured Beryl would take her Honda to some West Endy joint. But she didn't, took it Southside, and the only reason I can figure for that is the place has a body and detail shop. Turns out she took her car in shortly after she bought it last December and had one of those hundred-buck jobs done to seal the undercoating and paint. Next thing, she's opened an account there, made herself a member so she could get two bucks knocked off each wash and the perk of the week thrown in free."

"That's how you found out about it?" I asked. "Because of this membership deal?"

"Oh, yeah," he said. "They don't have a computer. Had

to look through all their damn receipts. But I found a copy of when she paid for her membership, and based on the condition of her car when we found it in her garage, I was guessing she had it washed not long before she ran off to Key West. Been rooting through her paperwork, too, looking at her charge-card bills. Only one listing for Masterwash, and that's the hundred-buck job I told you about. Apparently she paid cash when she had her ride cleaned after that."

"The car wash attendants," I said. "What do they wear?"

"Nothing orange that might fit with that oddball fiber you found. Most of 'em wear jeans, running shoes—all of 'em have on these blue shirts with 'Masterwash' embroidered in white on the pocket. I looked over everything while I was there. Nothing hit me. Only other fabric-type shit I saw was the barrels of white towels they use to wipe down the cars."

"Doesn't sound very promising," I remarked, pushing away my plate. At least Marino had an appetite. My stomach was still knotted from New York, and I was debating whether to tell him what had happened.

"Maybe not," he said. "But one guy I talked to made my antenna go up."

I waited.

"Name's Al Hunt, twenty-eight, white. Zeroed in on him right away. Saw him standing out there supervising the busy beavers. Something clicked. He looked out of place. Clean-cut, smart, like he ought have been wearing a three-piece suit and carrying a briefcase. I start asking myself, 'What's a guy like him doing in a dead end like this?' " He paused to sop his plate with garlic bread. "So

I wander his way and start shooting the breeze. I ask him about Beryl, show him her picture from her driver's license. Ask if maybe he remembers seeing her there, and boom! He starts getting antsy."

I couldn't help but think I would start getting antsy, too, if Marino "wandered" my way. He probably ran over the poor man like a Mack truck.

"Then what?" I asked.

"Then we go inside, get coffee, and get down to serious business," Marino replied. "This Al Hunt's a first-class squirrel. To start with, the guy's been to graduate school. Gets a master's degree in psychology, then goes to work as a *male nurse* at Metropolitan for a couple years, if you can friggin' believe that. And when I ask him why he left the hospital for Masterwash, I find out his old man owns the damn place. Old man Hunt's got his fingers in pies all over the city. Masterwash is just one of his investments. He also owns a number of parking lots and is a slumlord for half of Northside. I'm supposed to automatically assume young Al's being groomed to move into his daddy's shoes, right?"

I was getting interested.

"Thing is, though, Al ain't wearing a suit even if he looks like he should be, right? Translated, Al's a loser. The old man don't trust him in pinstripes and sitting behind a desk. I mean, the guy's standing out there in the lot telling drones how to wax cars and dress the bumpers. Tells me right away something's off up here." He pointed a greasy finger at his head.

"Maybe you should ask his father that," I said.

"Right. He's going to tell me his great white hope's a dumb ass."

"How do you plan to follow up?"

"Already did," he answered. "Witness the videotape I brought, Doc. Spent the entire morning with Al Hunt down at HQ. This guy will talk the wood off a door, and he's overly curious about what happened to Beryl, said he read about it in the papers—"

"How did he know who Beryl was?" I interrupted. "The papers and television stations didn't have any photographs of her. Did he recognize her name?"

"Said he didn't, had no idea it was the blond lady he'd seen at the car wash until I showed him the picture on her driver's license. Then he put on the big act of being shocked, real tore up about it. He was hanging on my every word, wanted to talk about her, was real intense for someone who supposedly didn't know her from Adam's house cat." He placed his rumpled napkin on the table. "Best thing's for you to hear it yourself."

I put on a pot of coffee, gathered the dirty dishes, and we went into the living room and started the tape. The setting was familiar. I had seen it numerous times before. The police department's interrogation room was a small, paneled cubicle with nothing but a bare table in the middle of the carpeted floor. Near the door was a light switch, and only an expert or the initiated would notice the top screw was missing. On the other side of the tiny black hole was a video room equipped with a special wide-angle camera.

At a glance, Al Hunt didn't look frightening. He was fair, with receding light blond hair and a pasty complexion. He wouldn't have been unattractive were it not for a weak chin that caused his face to disappear into his neck. He was wearing a maroon leather jacket and jeans;

his tapered fingers nervously fidgeting with a can of 7-Up as he watched Marino, who was sitting directly across from him.

"What was it about Beryl Madison, exactly?" Marino asked. "What made you notice her? You get a lot of cars in your car wash every day. Do you remember all your clients?"

"I remember more of them than you might think," Hunt replied. "Regular customers in particular. Maybe I don't remember their names, but I remember their faces because most people generally stand out in the lot while the attendants are wiping down their cars. Many of the customers supervise, if you know what I mean. They keep an eye on their cars, make sure nothing is forgotten. Some of them will pick up one of the cloths and help out, especially if they're in a hurry—if they're the kind of people who can't stand still, have to be doing something."

"Was Beryl that kind of person? Did she supervise?"

"No, sir. We have a couple of benches out there. It was her habit to sit outside on a bench. Sometimes she read the paper, a book. She really didn't pay any attention to the attendants and wasn't what I would call friendly. Maybe that's why I noticed her."

"What do you mean?" Marino asked.

"I mean she sent out these signals. I picked up on them."

"Signals?"

"People send out all kinds of signals," Hunt explained. "I'm attuned to them, pick them up. I can tell a lot about a person by the signals he or she sends out."

"Am I sending out signals, Al?"

"Yes, sir. Everybody sends them."

"What signals am I sending?"

Hunt's face was very serious as he answered, "Pale red."

"Huh?" Marino looked baffled.

"I pick up signals as colors. Maybe you think that's strange, but it's not unique. There are some of us who sense colors radiating from others. These are the signals I'm referring to. The signals I pick up from you are a pale red. Somewhat warm but also somewhat angry. Like a warning signal. It draws you in but suggests a danger of some sort—"

Marino stopped the tape and smiled snidely at me.

"Is the guy a squirrel or what?" he asked.

"Actually, I think he's rather astute," I said. "You *are* sort of warm, angry, and dangerous."

"Shit, Doc. The guy's goofy. To hear him talk, the whole friggin' population's a walking rainbow."

"There's some psychological validity to what he's saying," I replied matter-of-factly. "Various emotions are associated with colors. It's a legitimate basis for color schemes chosen for public places, hotel rooms, institutions. Blue, for example, is associated with depression. You won't find many psychiatric hospital rooms decorated in blue. Red is angry, violent, passionate. Black is morbid, ominous, and so on. As I recall, you told me Hunt has a master's degree in psychology."

Marino looked annoyed and restarted the tape.

"—I assume this may have to do with the role you're playing. You're a detective," Hunt was saying. "You need my cooperation at the moment, but you also don't trust me and could be dangerous to me if I have something to hide. That's the warning part of the pale red I sense. The warm part is your outgoing personality. You want people to feel close to you. Maybe you want to be close to people. You act tough, but you want people to like you . . ."

"All right," Marino interrupted."What about Beryl Madison? You pick up colors from her, too?"

"Oh, yes. That struck me right away about her. She was different, really different."

"How so?" Marino's chair creaked loudly as he leaned back and crossed his arms.

"Very aloof," Hunt replied. "I picked up arctic colors from her. Cool blue, pale yellow like weak sunlight, and white so cold it was hot like dry ice, as if she would burn you if you ever touched her. It's the white part that was different. I pick up the pastel shades from a lot of women. Feminine shades that fit with the colors they wear. Pink, yellow, light blues and greens. The ladies passive, cool, fragile. Sometimes I'll see a woman who sends out dark, strong colors like navy or burgundy or red. She's a stronger type. Usually aggressive, may be a lawyer or doctor or businesswoman, and often wears suits in the colors I just described. They're the type who stand out by their cars, their hands on their hips as they supervise everything the attendants are doing. And they don't hesitate to point out streaks on the windshield or any spots of dirt."

"Do you like that type of woman?" Marino asked.

He hesitated. "No, sir. To be honest."

Marino laughed, leaned forward and said to him, "Hey. Me, I don't like those types either. Like the pastel babes better."

I gave the real Marino one of my looks.

He ignored me as on-screen he said to Hunt, "Tell me some more about Beryl, about what you picked up."

Hunt frowned, thinking hard. "The pastel shades she sent out weren't all that unusual except I didn't interpret them as fragile, exactly. Not passive, either. The shades were cooler, arctic, as I've said, versus flower shades. As if she were telling the world to keep away from her, to give her a lot of space."

"Like maybe she was frigid?"

Hunt fidgeted with his 7-Up can again. "No, sir, I don't think I can say that. In fact, I don't think I was picking up that. Distance is what came to mind. A vast distance one would have to travel to get to her. But if you did, if she ever let you get close, she would burn you with her intensity. That's where the white-hot signals came in, the thing that made her stand out to me. She was intense, very intense. I had the feeling she was very intelligent, very complicated. Even when she was off sitting alone on her bench and not paying anybody any attention, her mind was working. She was picking up on everything around her. She was distant and white-hot like a star."

"Did you notice she was single?"

"She wasn't wearing a wedding ring," Hunt replied without pause. "I assumed she was single. I didn't notice anything about her car to tell me otherwise."

"I don't get it." Marino looked confused. "How could you tell from her car?"

"I think it was the second time she brought it in. I was watching one of the guys clean out the interior and there wasn't anything masculine inside. Her umbrella, for example—it was on the floor in back and was one of these slender blue umbrellas women usually carry, versus the black ones with big wooden handles men carry. Her dry cleaning was also in the back and it looked like women's clothing in the bags, no men's garments. Most married ladies pick up their husband's clothing when they pick up their own. Also, the trunk. No tools, jumper cables. Nothing masculine. It's interesting, but when you see cars all day long, you start to notice these details and make assumptions about the drivers without really thinking about it."

"Sounds like you did think about it in her case," Marino said. "Did it ever cross your mind to ask her out, Al? You sure you didn't know her name, didn't notice it on her dry cleaning slip, maybe on a piece of mail she left inside her car?"

Hunt shook his head. "I didn't know her name. Maybe I didn't want to know it."

"Why not?"

"I don't know . . ." He became uneasy, confused.

"Come on, Al. You can tell me. Hey, maybe I would have wanted to ask her out, you know? She's a good-looking lady, interesting. Hey, I would have thought about it, probably would have gotten her name on the sly, maybe even tried to ring her up."

"Well, I didn't." Hunt stared down at his hands. "I didn't try any of that."

"Why not?"

Silence.

Marino said, "Maybe because you had a woman like her once and she burned you?"

Silence.

"Hey, it happens to all of us, Al."

"In college," Hunt replied almost inaudibly. "I went out with a girl. For two years. She ended up with some guy in med school. Women like that . . . they look for certain types. You know, when they start thinking about settling down."

"They look for the big shots." Marino's voice was getting sharp around the edges. "The lawyers, doctors, bankers. They don't look for guys working in car washes."

Hunt's head jerked up. "I wasn't working in a car wash then."

"Don't matter, Al. The blue-chip babes like Beryl Madison ain't likely to give you the time of day, right? Bet Beryl didn't even know you were alive, right? Bet she wouldn't have recognized you if you'd run into her damn car on a street somewhere . . ."

"Don't say things like that—"

"True or false?"

Hunt stared at his clenched fists.

"So maybe you had a thing for Beryl, huh?" Marino continued relentlessly. "Maybe you was thinking about this white-hot lady all the time, fantasizing, wondering what it would be like to get with her, date her, have sex with her. Maybe you just didn't have the guts to talk to her directly because you figured she'd consider you a low-life, beneath her—"

"Stop it! You're picking on me! Stop it! Stop it!" Hunt cried shrilly. "Leave me alone!"

Marino stared unemotionally across the table at him.

"Sound just like your old man, don't I, Al?" Marino lit up a cigarette and waved it as he talked. "Old Man Hunt who thinks his only kid's a fuckin' fairy because you're not a mean-ass-son-of-a-bitch slumlord who don't give a shit about anybody's welfare or feelings." He exhaled a stream of smoke, then spoke gently. "I know about the Almighty Old Man Hunt. Also know he told all his buddies you was a pansy, was ashamed to have his blood in your veins when you went to work as a male nurse. Fact is, you came over to his damn car wash because he said if you didn't, you'd be disinherited."

"You know that? How did you know that?" Hunt stammered.

"I know a lot of things. Also know, as a matter of fact, the people at Metropolitan said you was topflight, had a real gentle way with patients. They was sorry as hell to see you leave. Think the word they used to describe you was 'sensitive,' maybe too sensitive for your own good, huh, Al? Explaining why you don't date, don't have no ladies. You're scared. Beryl scared the shit out of you, didn't she?"

Hunt took a deep breath.

"That why you didn't want to know her name? Then you wouldn't be tempted to call her, try anything?"

"I just noticed her," Hunt responded nervously.

"Really, there wasn't anything more to it than that. I didn't think about her in the manner you've suggested. I was just, uh, just very aware of her. But I didn't cultivate it. I never even talked to her until the last time she came in—"

Marino hit the Stop button again. He said, "This is the important part . . ." He paused and looked closely at me. "Hey, you all right?"

"Was it really necessary to be so brutal?" I answered emotionally.

"You ain't been around me much if you think that was brutal," Marino said.

"Sorry. I forgot I was sitting in my living room with Attila the Hun."

"It's all acting," he said, hurt.

"Remind me to nominate you for an Academy Award."

"Come off it, Doc."

"You absolutely demoralized him," I said.

"It's a tool, okay? You know, a way to shake things loose, make people say things maybe they wouldn't have thought of otherwise." He turned back toward the set and added, as he hit the Play button, "The entire interview was worth what he tells me next."

"When was this?" Marino asked Hunt. "The last time she came in was when?"

"I'm not sure of the exact date," Hunt answered. "A couple months ago, but I do remember it was a Friday, uh, late morning. The reason I remember is I was supposed to have lunch with my father that day. I always have lunch with him on Friday so we can discuss the business." He reached for his 7-Up. "I always dress a little better on Friday. I was wearing a tie that day."

"So Beryl comes in late morning on this Friday to have her car washed," Marino prompted him. "And on this occasion you talked to her?"

"She actually talked to me first," Hunt replied as if this was important. "Her car was coming out of the bay when she walked up to me, told me she spilled something on the carpet inside the trunk and wanted to know if we could get it out. She took me to her car, opened the trunk, and I saw the carpet was soaked. Apparently, she had groceries in the trunk and a half-gallon bottle of orange juice broke. I guess that's why she decided to drive her car in to be washed right away."

"Was the groceries still in the trunk when she brought her car in?"

"No," Hunt replied.

"Do you remember what she was wearing that day?"

Hunt hesitated. "Tennis clothes, sunglasses. Uh, it looked like she'd just played. I remember because I'd never seen her come in like that. In the past she was always in street clothes. I also remember her tennis racket and a few other things were in the trunk because she took these things out when we started shampooing. I remember she wiped them off and placed them in the backseat."

Marino pulled a datebook out of his breast pocket. Opening it and flipping back several pages, he said, "Is it possible this was the second week of July? Friday the twelth?"

"It could have been."

"Do you remember anything else? Did she say anything else?"

"She was almost friendly," Hunt answered. "I remember that well. I assume it was because I was helping her out, making sure we took care of her trunk when I really didn't have to. I could have told her she'd have to take her car to the detail shop and pay thirty dollars for a shampoo. But I wanted to help her. And I was hanging around while the guys worked when I happened to notice the passenger's side of her car. The door was messed up. It was weird. It looked as if someone had taken his key and gouged a heart and some letters on the door right below the handle. When I asked her how it happened, she went around to the door and inspected the damage. She just stood there staring. I swear, she turned white as a sheet. Apparently she hadn't noticed the damage until I pointed it out. I tried to calm her down, told her I didn't blame her for being upset. The Honda's brand new, not a scratch on it, about a twenty-thousand-dollar car. Then some jerk does something like that. Probably some kid with nothing better to do."

"What else did she say, Al?" Marino asked. "Did she have any explanation for the damage?"

"No, sir. She didn't say much of anything. It's like she got scared, was looking around, really upset. Then she asked me where the nearest phone was and I told her there was a pay phone inside. By the time she came back out, the car was finished and she left—"

Marino stopped the tape and popped it out of the VCR. Remembering coffee, I went into the kitchen and fixed two cups.

"Looks like that answers one of our questions," I said when I returned.

"Oh, yeah," Marino said, reaching for the cream and sugar. "The way I'm picturing it, Beryl probably used the pay phone to call her bank or maybe the airlines to make a reservation. Finding that little Valentine scratched in her door was the last straw. She freaked. From the car wash she heads straight to her bank. I've checked out where she had her account. On July twelfth at twelve-fifty P.M., she withdrew almost ten thousand dollars cash, cleaning out her account. Was a top-drawer customer. Didn't get an argument."

"Did she get traveler's checks?"

"No, if you can believe it," he said. "Tells me she was more scared of someone finding her than she was of being robbed. She pays cash for everything down there in the Keys. No one has to know her name if she's not using credit cards or traveler's checks."

"She must have been terrified," I said quietly. "I can't imagine carrying that much cash. I'd have to be crazy or frightened to the point of utter desperation."

He lit a cigarette. I did the same.

Shaking out the match, I asked, "Do you think it's possible the heart was scratched on her car while it was being washed?"

"I asked Hunt the same question to see how he reacted," Marino replied. "He swore it couldn't have been done at the car wash, said someone would have seen it, seen the person doing it. I'm not so sure. Hell, you leave fifty cents in your change box at those joints and it's gone when you get your ride back. People steal like bandits. Change, umbrellas, checkbooks, you name it, and no one saw a thing when you ask. Hunt could have done it, for all I know."

"He is a little unusual," I conceded. "I find it peculiar he was so vividly aware of Beryl. She was one of a very large number of people through that place every day. She was coming in what? Once a month, maybe less?"

He nodded. "But she stood out like a neon sign to him. Could be perfectly innocent. Then again, maybe not."

I recalled what Mark had said about Beryl's being "memorable."

Marino and I sipped our coffees in silence, darkness settling over my thoughts again. Mark. There had to be some mistake, some logical explanation for why he wasn't listed with Orndorff & Berger. Perhaps his name had been left out of the directory or the firm had recently become computerized and he was improperly coded, and his name didn't come up when the receptionist keyed it into her computer. Maybe both receptionists were new and didn't know many of the lawyers. But why wasn't he listed in Chicago at all?

"You look like something's eating you," Marino finally said. "Been looking like that ever since I got here."

"I'm just tired," I answered.

"Bullshit." He sipped his coffee.

I almost choked on mine when he said, "Rose told me you skipped town. You have a productive little chat with Sparacino in New York?"

"When did Rose tell you that?"

"Don't matter. And don't go getting hot at your secretary," he said. "She just said you had to go out of town. Didn't say where, who, or what for. The rest of it I found out on my own."

"How?"

"You just told me, that's how," he said. "Didn't deny it, did you? So what did you and Sparacino talk about?"

"He said he talked to you. Maybe you should tell me about that conversation first," I answered.

"Nothing to it." Marino retrieved his cigarette from the ashtray. "He calls me the other night at home. Don't ask me how the hell he got my name and number. He wants Beryl's papers and I'm not about to hand them over. Maybe I would have been more inclined to be more cooperative, but the guy's an asshole. Started giving orders, acting like King Tut. Said he's the executor of her estate, started threatening."

"And you did the honorable thing by sending the shark to my office," I said.

Marino looked blankly at me. "No. I didn't even mention you."

"You're sure?"

"Sure I'm sure. The conversation lasted maybe three minutes. That was it. Your name didn't come up."

"What about the manuscript you listed in the police report? Did Sparacino ask about it?"

"He did," Marino said. "I didn't give him any details,

told him all her papers was being processed as evidence, gave him the usual about not being at liberty to discuss her case."

"You didn't tell him the manuscript you found was receipted to my office?" I asked.

"Hell, no." He looked strangely at me. "Why would I tell him that? It isn't true. I had Vander check the thing for prints, stood there while he did it. Then I took it back out of the building with me. It's in the property room with all her other shit even as we speak." He paused. "Why? What did Sparacino tell you?"

I got up to refill our coffee cups. When I returned, I told Marino everything. When I was finished, he was staring at me in disbelief, and there was something else in his eyes that thoroughly unnerved me. I think it was the first time I had ever seen Marino scared.

"What are you going to do if he calls?" he asked.

"If Mark does?"

"No. If the Seven Dwarfs does," Marino said sarcastically.

"Ask him to explain. Ask him how he can work for Orndorff & Berger, ask him how he can live in Chicago when there's no record of it." My frustration was mounting. "I don't know, but I'll try to find out what the hell is really going on."

Marino looked away, his jaw muscles flexing.

"You're wondering if Mark's involved . . . tied in with Sparacino, involved in illegal activities, crime," I said, barely able to put into words this chilling suspicion.

He angrily lit another cigarette. "What else am I supposed to think? You haven't seen your ex-Romeo for more than fifteen years, haven't even talked to him, heard a word about his whereabouts. It's like he fell off the edge of the earth. Then he's suddenly on your doorstep. How do you know what he's really been doing all this time? You don't. You only know what he tells you—"

We both started at the clangor of the telephone. I instinctively glanced at my watch as I went to the kitchen. It was not quite ten, and my heart was tight with fear as I picked up the receiver.

"Kay?"

"Mark?" I swallowed hard. "Where are you?"

"Home. Flew back to Chicago, just got in . . ."

"I tried to get you in New York and Chicago, at the office . . ." I stammered. "Called while I was at the airport."

There was a pregnant pause.

"Listen, I don't have much time. I just wanted to call to tell you I'm sorry about how it went and to make sure you're all right. I'll be in touch."

"Where are you?" I asked again. "Mark? Mark!"

I was answered by a dial tone.

7

The next day, Sunday, I slept through the alarm. I slept through Mass. I slept through lunch and felt sluggish and unsettled when I finally climbed out of bed. I could not remember my dreams, but I knew they had been unpleasant.

My telephone rang at a little past seven P.M. as I was chopping onions and peppers for an omelet I wasn't destined to eat. Minutes later I was speeding along a dark stretch of 64 East, a slip of paper on the dash scribbled with directions to Cutler Grove. My mind was like a computer program caught in a loop, thoughts going round and round, processing the same information. Cary Harper had been murdered. An hour ago he drove home from a Williamsburg tavern and was attacked as he got out of his car. It happened very fast. The crime was very brutal. Like Beryl Madison, he'd had his throat cut.

It was dark out, pockets of fog reflecting the low beams

of my headlights back into my eyes. Visibility was reduced to almost zero, and the highway I had traveled countless times in the past suddenly seemed strange. I wasn't sure where I was. I was tensely lighting a cigarette when I realized headlights were gaining on me. A dark car I could not make out rushed alarmingly close, then gradually dropped back. The car maintained the same distance from me mile after mile whether I sped up or slowed down. When I finally found the exit I was looking for, I turned off, as did the car behind me.

The unpaved road I turned onto next wasn't marked. The headlights remained fixed to my bumper. My .38 was at home. I had nothing but a small canister of chemical Mace in my medical bag. I was so relieved I said, "Thank you, Lord," out loud when the great house appeared around a bend, its semicircular drive pulsing with emergency lights and lined with cars. I parked, and the car still tailing me rocked to a halt at my rear. I stared in amazement as Marino climbed out and flipped his coat collar up around his ears.

"*Good God,*" I exclaimed irritably. "I can't believe it."

"Ditto," he grumbled, his long strides bringing him to my side. "I can't believe it, either." He scowled into the bright circle of lights set up around an old white Rolls-Royce parked near the mansion's back entrance. "Shit. That's all I got to say. Shit!"

Cops were all over the place. Their faces seemed unnaturally pale in the flood of artificial light. Engines rumbled loudly and the static of fragmented sentences from radios drifted on the damp frigid air. Crime-scene tape tied to the back-step railings sealed off the area in an ominous yellow rectangle.

A plainclothes officer wearing an old brown leather

jacket headed our way. "Dr. Scarpetta?" he said. "I'm Detective Poteat."

I was opening my medical bag to get out a packet of surgical gloves and a flashlight.

"No one's disturbed the body," Poteat informed me. "I done exactly what Doc Watts said to do."

Dr. Watts was a general practitioner, one of my five hundred appointed MEs statewide, and one of my top ten pains in the ass. After the police called him earlier this evening, he immediately called me. It was SOP to notify the chief medical examiner whenever there was a suspicious or unexpected death of a well-known personage. It was also SOP for Watts to avoid any case he could, to pass it along or pass it by because he couldn't be bothered with the inconvenience or the paperwork. He was notoriously bad about not responding to scenes, and I saw neither hide nor hair of him at this one.

"Got here about the same time the squad did," Poteat was explaining. "Made sure the guys didn't do nothing more'n necessary. Didn't turn him over or remove his clothes or nothing. He was DOA."

"Thank you," I said abstractedly.

"Looks like he was beaten about the head, cut. Maybe shot. Bird shot all over the place. You'll see in a minute. We ain't found a weapon. Appears he pulled in around quarter of seven, parked where his car is now. Best we can figure, he was attacked as he got out."

He looked over at the white Rolls-Royce. The area around it was thick with shadows cast by boxwoods older and taller than he was.

"Was the driver's door open when you got here?" I asked.

"No, ma'am," Poteat answered. "The car keys is on

the ground, like he had 'em in his hand when he went down. Like I said, we ain't touched nothing, was waiting till you got here or till the weather forced us to proceed. Gonna rain." He squinted up at the layer of dense clouds. "Could be snow. No sign of any disturbance inside the car, no sign of a struggle at all. We're figuring the assailant was waiting for him, hiding in the bushes prob'ly. All I can tell you is it happened mighty fast, Doc. His sister in there didn't hear a gun go off, nothing, she says."

I left him to talk to Marino as I ducked under the tape and approached the Rolls-Royce, my eyes instinctively probing everywhere I stepped. The car was parallel parked less than ten feet from the back steps, the driver's door toward the house. Rounding the hood with its distinctive ornament, I stopped and got out my camera.

Cary Harper was on his back, his head just inches from the car's front tire. The white fender was speckled and streaked with blood, his beige fisherman's knit sweater almost solid red. Not far from his hips was a ring of keys. In the glare of floodlights all I saw was glistening sticky red. His white hair was matted with blood, his face and scalp laid open by lacerations caused when he was struck with severe force by a blunt instrument that had split the skin. His throat was cut from ear to ear, almost severing his head from his neck, and everywhere I directed the flashlight bird shot glinted like tiny beads of pewter. There were hundreds of them on his body and around it, even a few scattered over the hood of the car. The bird shot had not been fired from any sort of gun.

I moved around taking photographs, then squatted and got out the long chemical thermometer, which I slid carefully under his sweater and wedged in the fold of his left arm. The temperature of the body was 92.4 degrees, the temperature of the air 31. The body was cooling at the rapid rate of approximately three degrees per hour because it was below freezing out and Harper wasn't heavyset or heavily dressed. Rigor had already started in the small muscles. I estimated he had been dead less than two hours.

Next I began looking for any trace evidence that might not survive the trip to the morgue. Fibers, hairs or any other debris adhering to blood could wait. I was worried about anything loose, slowly scanning his body and the area directly around it, when the narrow beam licked over something not far from his neck. I leaned closer without touching, puzzling over a small greenish lump of what looked remarkably like Play-Doh. Embedded in it were several more pellets. I was carefully sealing this inside a plastic envelope when the back door opened and I found myself staring directly up into the terrified eyes of a woman standing inside the foyer beside a police officer holding a metal clipboard.

Approaching footsteps belonged to Marino and Poteat. They ducked under the tape and were joined by the officer with the clipboard. The back door quietly shut.

"Will there be someone to stay with her?" I asked.

"Oh, yeah," the officer with the clipboard responded, his breath smoking out. "Miss Harper's got a friend coming, says she'll be okay. We'll have a couple units staked out nearby to make sure the guy doesn't come back for an encore."

"What we looking for?" Poteat asked me.

He slipped his hands in the pockets of his jacket and hunched his shoulders against the cold. Snowflakes as big as quarters were beginning to spiral down.

"More than one weapon," I replied. "The injuries to his head and face are blunt-force trauma." I pointed a bloody gloved finger. "Obviously, the injury to his neck was inflicted by a sharp instrument. As for the bird shot, the pellets aren't deformed, and it doesn't appear that any of them penetrated his body."

Marino looked positively baffled as he stared at the pellets scattered everywhere.

"That was my impression," Poteat said, nodding. "Don't appear the shot was fired, but I couldn't be sure. Then we're prob'ly not looking for a shotgun. A knife and maybe something like a tire tool?"

"Possibly but not necessarily," I answered. "All I can tell you with certainty right now is his neck was cut with something sharp, and he was beaten with something blunt and linear."

"That could be a lot of things, Doc," Poteat remarked, frowning.

"Yes, it could be a lot of things," I agreed.

Though I had my suspicions about the bird shot, I refrained from speculating, having learned the hard way from past experiences. Generalities often got interpreted literally, and at one crime scene the cops walked right past a bloody upholstery needle in the victim's living room because I had said that the weapon was "consistent with" an ice pick.

"The squad can move him," I announced, peeling off my gloves.

Harper was wrapped in a clean white sheet and zipped inside a body pouch. I stood next to Marino and watched the ambulance slowly head back down the dark, deserted drive. There were no lights or sirens—no need to rush when transporting the dead. The snow was coming down harder and it was sticking.

"You leaving?" Marino asked me.

"What are you going to do, follow me again?" I wasn't smiling.

He stared off at the old Rolls-Royce in the circle of milky light at the edge of the drive. Snowflakes melted as they hit the area of gravel stained with Harper's blood.

"I wasn't following you," Marino said seriously. "Got the radio message when I was almost back to Richmond—"

"Almost back to Richmond?" I interrupted. "Almost back from *where*?"

"From here," he said, fishing in a pocket for his keys. "Found out Harper was a regular at Culpeper's Tavern. I decide to buttonhole him. Was with him maybe a half hour before he basically tells me to screw myself. Then he splits. So I head out, am maybe fifteen miles from Richmond when Poteat gets a dispatcher to raise me and tell me what's gone down. I'm hauling ass back in this direction when I recognize your ride, stay with you to make sure you don't get lost."

"You're telling me you actually talked to Harper at the tavern tonight?" I asked in amazement.

"Oh, yeah," he said. "Then he leaves me and gets whacked about five minutes later." Agitated and restless, he started moving toward his car. "Gonna meet with Poteat, see what all I can find out. And I'll be by in the morning to look in on the post if you've got no objections."

I watched him walk off, shaking snow out of his hair. He was gone by the time I turned the key in the Plymouth's ignition. The wipers pushed back a thin layer of snow, then stopped cold in the middle of the windshield. The engine of my state car made one last sick attempt before it became the second DOA of the night.

The Harper library was a warm, vibrant room of red Persian rugs and antiques crafted from the finest woods. I was fairly certain the sofa was a Chippendale, and I had never touched, much less sat on, a genuine Chippendale anything before. The high ceiling was ornamented in rococo molding, the walls lined with books, most of them leatherbound. Directly across from me was a marble fireplace recently stoked with split logs.

Leaning forward, I stretched my hands toward the flames and resumed studying the oil portrait over the mantel. The subject was a lovely young girl in white seated on a small bench, her hair long and very blond, her hands loosely curled around a silver hairbrush in her lap. She shimmered darkly in the rising heat, her eyes heavy lidded, her moist lips parted, the deeply scooped neckline of her dress exposing a porcelain-white, undeveloped bosom. I was wondering why this peculiar portrait was so prominently displayed when Cary Harper's sister came in and shut the door as quietly as she had opened it.

"I thought this might warm you," she said, handing me a glass of wine.

Setting the tray on the coffee table, she seated herself on the red velvet cushion of a baroque side chair, tucking her feet to one side the way proper ladies are taught to sit by their proper female elders.

"Thank you," I said, and again I apologized.

The battery in my state car was no longer in this world, and jumper cables were not going to bring it back. The police had radioed for a wrecker, and had promised to give me a lift back to Richmond as soon as they finished processing the scene. There was no choice. I wasn't going to stand outside in the snow or sit for an hour inside a squad car. So I had knocked on Miss Harper's back door.

She sipped her wine and stared vacantly into the fire. Like the expensive objects surrounding her, she was beautifully crafted, one of the most elegant women I thought I had ever seen. Silver-white hair softly framed her patrician face. Her cheekbones were high, her features refined, her figure lithe but shapely in a beige cowl-necked sweater and corduroy skirt. When I looked at Sterling Harper, the word "spinster" definitely did not enter my mind.

She was silent. Snow coldly kissed the windows and the wind moaned around the eaves. I could not imagine living alone in this house.

"Do you have any other family?" I asked.

"None living," she said.

"I'm sorry, Miss Harper . . ."

"Really. You must stop saying that, Dr. Scarpetta."

A large cut-emerald ring flashed in the firelight as she lifted her glass again. Her eyes focused on me. I remembered the terror in those eyes when she opened the door while I was examining her brother. She was remarkably steady now.

"Cary knew better," she suddenly commented. "I suppose what surprises me most is the *way* it happened. I wouldn't have expected someone to be so bold as to wait for him at the house."

"And you didn't hear anything?" I asked.

"I heard him drive up. I heard nothing after that. When he didn't come inside the house, I opened the door to check. I immediately called 911."

"Did he frequent any other places besides Culpeper's?" I asked.

"No. No other place. He went to Culpeper's every night," she said, her eyes drifting away from me. "I warned him about going to that place, about the dangers in this day and age. He always carried cash, you see, and Cary was quite skilled at offending people. He never stayed at the tavern long. An hour, at the most two hours. He used to tell me it was for inspiration, to mingle with the common man. Cary had nothing else to say after *The Jagged Corner.*"

I had read the novel at Cornell and remembered only impressions: a gothic South of violence, incest, and racism as seen through the eyes of a young writer growing up on a Virginia farm. I remembered it had depressed me.

"My brother was one of these unfortunate talents who had but one book in him," Miss Harper added.

"There have been other very fine writers like that," I said.

"He lived only what he was forced to live when he was young," she went on in the same unnerving monotone. "After that he became the hollow man, the life of quiet desperation. His writing was a series of false starts that he would eventually toss into the fire, scowling as he watched the pages burn. Then he would roam about the house like a angry bull until he was ready to try again. That is the way it has been for more years than I care to recall."

"You seem awfully hard on your brother," I remarked quietly.

"I'm awfully hard on myself, Dr. Scarpetta," she said as our eyes met. "Cary and I are cut from the same cloth. The difference between the two of us is I don't feel compelled to be analytical about what can't be altered. He was constantly excavating his nature, his past, the forces that shaped him. It won him a Pulitzer Prize. As for me, I have chosen not to fight what has always been so clear."

"Which is?"

"The Harper family is at the end of its line, overbred and barren. There will be no one after us," she said.

The wine was an inexpensive domestic burgundy, dry with a faint metallic bite. How much longer until the police finished? I thought I'd heard the rumble of a truck a while ago, the wrecker coming to tow away my car.

"I accepted it as my lot in life to take care of my brother, to ease the family into extinction," Miss Harper said. "I will miss Cary only because he was my brother. I'm not going to sit here and lie about how wonderful he was." She sipped her wine again. "I'm sure I must sound cold to you."

Cold wasn't the word for it. "I appreciate your honesty," I said.

"Cary had imagination and volatile emotions. I have little of either, and were this not the case I couldn't have managed. Certainly, I wouldn't have lived here."

"Living in this house would be isolating." I supposed this was what Miss Harper meant.

"It isn't the isolation I mind," she said.

"What is it you mind, then, Miss Harper?" I queried, reaching for my cigarettes.

"Would you like another glass of wine?" she asked, one side of her face obscured by the shadow of the fire.

"No, thank you."

"I wish we'd never moved here. Nothing good happens in this house," she said.

"What will you do, Miss Harper?" The emptiness of her eyes chilled me. "Will you stay here?"

"I have no place else to go, Dr. Scarpetta."

"I would think selling Cutler Grove wouldn't be hard," I answered, my attention wandering back to the portrait over the mantel. The young girl in white smiled eerily in the firelight at secrets she would never tell.

"It is hard to leave your iron lung, Dr. Scarpetta."

"I beg your pardon?"

"I'm too old for change," she explained. "I'm too old to pursue good health and new relationships. The past breathes for me. It is my life. You are young, Dr. Scarpetta. Someday you will see what it is like to look back. You will find it inescapable. You will find your personal history drawing you back into familiar rooms where, ironically, events occurred that set into motion your eventual estrangement from life. You will find the hard furniture of heartbreak more comfortable and the people who failed you friendlier with time. You will find yourself running back into the arms of the pain you once ran away from. It is easier. That's all I can say. It is easier."

"Do you have any idea who did this to your brother?" I asked her directly, desperate to change the subject.

She said nothing as she stared wide-eyed into the fire.

"What about Beryl?" I persisted.

"I know she was being harassed months before it happened."

"Months before her death?" I asked.

"Beryl and I were very close."

"You knew she was being harassed?"

"Yes. The threats she was getting," she said.

"She *told you* she was being threatened, Miss Harper?"

"Of course," she said.

Marino had been through Beryl's phone bills. He hadn't found any long-distance calls made to Williamsburg. Nor had he turned up any letters written to her by Miss Harper or her brother.

"Then you maintained close contact with her over the years?" I said.

"Very close contact," she replied. "At least, as much as that was possible. Because of this book she was writing and the clear violation of her agreement with my brother. Well, it all got very ugly. Cary was enraged."

"How did he know what she was doing? Did she tell him what she was writing?"

"Her lawyer did," she said.

"Sparacino?"

"I don't know the details of what he told Cary," she said, her face hard. "But my brother was informed of Beryl's book. He knew enough to be extremely out of sorts. The lawyer agitated the matter behind the scenes. Going from Beryl to Cary, back and forth, acting as if he were an ally with one or the other, depending on whom he was talking to."

"Do you know the status of her book now?" I asked carefully. "Does Sparacino have it? Is it in the process of being published?"

"Several days ago he called Cary. I overheard snatches of their conversation, enough to ascertain the manuscript has disappeared. Your office was mentioned. I heard Cary say something about the medical examiner. You, I suppose. And at this point he was getting angry. I concluded

Mr. Sparacino was trying to determine whether it was possible my brother might have the manuscript."

"Is that possible?" I wanted to know.

"Beryl would never have turned it over to Cary," she answered with emotion. "It would make no sense for her to have relinquished her work to him. He was adamantly opposed to what she was doing."

We were silent for a moment.

Then I asked, "Miss Harper, what was your brother so afraid of?"

"Life."

I waited, watching her closely. She was staring into the fire again.

"The more he feared it, the more he retreated from it," she said in a strange voice. "Reclusiveness does peculiar things to one's mind. Turns it inside out, puts a spin on thoughts and ideas until they begin to bounce off center and at crazy angles. I think Beryl was the only person my brother ever loved. He clung to her. He had an overwhelming need to possess her, to keep her wedded to him. When he thought she was betraying him, that he no longer had power over her, his madness became more extreme. I'm sure he began to imagine all sorts of nonsense she might divulge about him. About our situation here."

When she reached for her wine again, her hand trembled. She was talking about her brother as if he had been dead for years. There was an edge to her voice when she spoke of him, the well of love for her brother lined with hard bricks of rage and pain.

"Cary and I had no one left when Beryl came along," she continued. "Our parents were dead. We had no one but each other. Cary was difficult. A devil who wrote like an angel. He needed taking care of. I was willing to facilitate his desire to leave his mark on the world."

"Such sacrifices are often accompanied by resentment," I ventured.

Silence. The light from the fire flickered on her exquisitely chiseled face.

"How did you find Beryl?" I asked.

"She found us. She was living in Fresno at the time with her father and stepmother. She was writing, was obsessed with writing." Miss Harper continued staring into the fire as she talked. "One day Cary got a letter from her through his publisher. Accompanying it was a short story written in longhand. I still remember it well. She showed promise, a germinal imagination that simply needed shepherding. Thus the correspondence began, and months later Cary invited her to visit us, sent her a ticket. Not long after that, he bought this house and began to restore it. He did it for her. A lovely young girl had brought magic into his world."

"And you?" I asked.

She did not reply at first.

Wood shifted in the fireplace and sparks popped.

"Life was not without its complications after she moved in with us, Dr. Scarpetta," she said. "I watched what went on between them."

"Between your brother and Beryl."

"I did not want to imprison her the way he did," she said. "In Cary's relentless attempts to hold on to Beryl and have her all to himself, he lost her."

"You loved Beryl very much," I said.

"It is impossible to explain," she said, her voice catching. "It was very difficult to manage."

I continued to probe. "Your brother didn't want you to have contact with her."

"Especially during the past few months, because of her book. Cary denounced and disowned her. Her name was not mentioned in this house. He forbade me to have any sort of contact with her."

"But you did," I answered.

"In a very limited way," she said with difficulty.

"That must have been very painful for you. To be cut off from someone so dear to you."

She looked away from me, interested in the fire again.

"Miss Harper, when did you find out about Beryl's death?"

She did not reply.

"Did someone call you?"

"I heard about it on the radio the next morning," she muttered.

Dear God, I thought. How awful.

She said nothing more. Her wounds were beyond my reach, and as much as I wanted to offer a word of comfort, there was nothing I could say. So we sat in silence for what seemed a very long time. When I finally stole a glance at my watch, I saw it was almost midnight.

The house was very quiet—too quiet, I realized with a start.

After the warmth of the library, the entrance hall was as chilly as a cathedral. I opened the back door and gasped in surprise. Beneath the milky swirl of snow the drive was a solid white blanket, with barely perceptible tire tracks left when the damn cops had driven off without me. My state car had been towed long ago, and they had forgotten I was still inside the house. Damn! Damn! Damn!

When I returned to the library, Miss Harper was placing another log on the fire.

"It appears my ride went off without me," I said, and I know I sounded upset. "I'll need to use a phone."

"I'm afraid that won't be possible," she answered unemphatically. "The phones went out not long after the policeman left. It seems to happen quite often when the weather's bad."

I watched her stab the burning logs. I watched ribbons of smoke curl out from under them as sparks swarmed up the chimney.

I had forgotten.

It hadn't occurred to me until now.

"Your friend . . ." I said.

She jabbed the log again.

"The police said a friend was on her way, would be staying with you tonight . . ."

Miss Harper slowly straightened up and turned around, her face flushed from the heat.

"Yes, Dr. Scarpetta," she said. "It was so kind of you to come."

8

Miss Harper returned with more wine as the tall case clock on the landing outside the library chimed twelve times.

"The clock," she seemed compelled to explain. "It's ten minutes slow. Always has been."

The mansion's phones really were out. I had checked. The walk to town was several miles through what was now at least four inches of snow. I wasn't going anywhere.

Her brother was dead. Beryl was dead. Miss Harper was the only one left. I hoped it was a coincidence. I lit a cigarette and took a swallow of wine.

Miss Harper didn't have the physical strength to have killed her brother and Beryl. What if the killer were after Miss Harper, too? What if he came back?

My .38 was at home.

The police would be staking out the area.

In what? Snowmobiles?

I realized Miss Harper was saying something else to me.

"I'm sorry," I said, forcing a smile.

"You look cold," she repeated.

Her face was placid as she seated herself on the baroque side chair and stared into the fire. The high flames sounded like a wind-whipped flag, and infrequent gusts of wind sent ashes blowing out on the hearth. But she appeared reassured by my company. Were I in her shoes, I wouldn't have wanted to be alone, either.

"I'm fine," I lied. I *was* cold.

"I'll be glad to get you a sweater."

"Please don't trouble yourself. I'm comfortable—really."

"It's quite impossible to heat this house," she went on. "The high ceilings. And it isn't insulated. You grow accustomed to it."

I thought of my gas-heated modern house in Richmond. I thought of my queen-size bed with its firm mattress and electric blanket. I thought of the carton of cigarettes in the cupboard near the refrigerator and of the good Scotch in my bar. I thought of the drafty, dusty dark upstairs of the Cutler Grove mansion.

"I'll be fine down here. On the sofa," I said.

"Nonsense. The fire will go out soon enough." She was fidgeting with a button on her sweater, her eyes not leaving the fire.

"Miss Harper," I tried one last time. "Do you have any idea who might have done this? To Beryl, to your brother. Or why?"

"You think it's the same man." She presented this as a statement of fact, not a question.

"I have to consider it."

"I wish I could tell you something that would help," she answered. "But perhaps it doesn't matter. Whoever it is, what's done is done."

"Don't you want him punished?"

"There has been enough punishment. It won't undo what has been done," she said.

"Wouldn't Beryl want him caught?"

She turned to me, her eyes wide. "I wish you had known her."

"I think I did. I do know her in a way," I said gently.

"I can't explain . . ."

"You don't need to, Miss Harper."

"It could have been so nice . . ."

I saw her grief for an instant, her face contorted, then controlled again. She didn't need to finish the thought. It could have been so nice now that there was no one to keep Beryl and Miss Harper apart. Companions. Friends. Life is so empty when you are alone, when there is no one to love.

"I'm sorry," I said with feeling. "I'm so terribly sorry, Miss Harper."

"It is the middle of November," she replied, looking away from me again. "Unusually early for snow. The thaw will come quickly, Dr. Scarpetta. You will be able to get out by late morning. Those who forgot you will remember by then. It really was so good of you to come."

She seemed to have known that I would be here. I had the uncanny impression she had somehow planned it. Of course, that wasn't possible.

"One thing I will ask you to do," she said.

"What is that, Miss Harper?"

"Come back in the spring. Come back when it is April," she said to the flames.

"I would like that," I answered.

"The forget-me-nots will be in bloom. The bowling green will be pale blue with them. It is so lovely, my favorite time of year. Beryl and I used to pick them. Have you ever studied them up close? Or are you like most people who take them for granted, never give them a thought because they are so small? They are so beautiful if you hold them close. *So beautiful*, as if made of porcelain and painted by the perfect hand of God. We would wear them in our hair and put them in bowls of water in the house, Beryl and I. You must promise to come back in April. You will promise me that, won't you?" She turned to me, and the emotion in her eyes pained me.

"Yes, yes. Of course I will," I replied, and I meant it.

"Is there anything special you eat for breakfast?" she asked as she got up.

"Whatever you fix for yourself will be fine."

"There's plenty in the refrigerator," she remarked oddly. "Bring your wine and I'll show you to your room."

Her hand trailed the banister as she led her guest up the magnificent carved stairway to the second floor. There were no overhead lights, just lamps to light our way, and the musty air was as cold as a cellar.

"I'm on the other side of the hallway, three doors down, if you need anything," she told me, and she showed me inside a small bedroom.

The furnishings were mahogany with satinwood inlays, and on pale-blue-papered walls were several oil paintings of loosely arranged flowers and a vista of the river. The canopied bed was turned down and piled high with comforters, and an open doorway led into the tiled bath. The air was stale and smelled of dust, as if windows were never opened and nothing but memories ever stirred in here. I was sure that no one had slept in this room in many, many years.

"In the top dresser drawer is a flannel gown. There are clean towels and other necessities in the bath," Miss Harper said. "Now then, if you're all set?"

"Yes. Thank you." I smiled at her. "Good night."

I shut the door and closed its feeble latch. The gown was the only garment inside the dresser, and tucked under it was a sachet that long ago had lost its scent. Every other drawer was empty. Inside the bath was a toothbrush still wrapped in cellophane, a tiny tube of toothpaste, a bar of lavender soap never used, and plenty of towels, as Miss Harper had promised. The sink was as dry as chalk, and when I turned the gold handles the water was liquid rust. It took forever to get clear and warm enough for me to dare to wash my face.

The gown, old but clean, was the washed-out blue of forget-me-nots, I thought. Getting in bed, I pulled the musty-smelling comforters up to my chin before switching off the lamp. The pillow was plump, and I could feel the prickly twill of feathers as I pushed and shoved it into a more comfortable shape. Wide awake, my nose cold, I sat up in the darkness of a room I was certain had once been Beryl's, and I finished my wine. The house was so still I imagined I could hear the all-absorbing quiet of the snow falling beyond the window.

I wasn't aware of dozing off, but when my eyelids flew open my heart was thudding violently, and I was afraid to move. I couldn't remember the nightmare. At first I wasn't sure where I was and if the noise I heard was real. The faucet in the bathroom was leaking, drops of water slowly clinking into the sink. Floorboards beyond my latched bedroom door creaked again, quietly.

My mind raced through an obstacle course of possibilities. The dropping temperature was causing wood to creak. Mice. Someone was slowly making his way down the hall. I strained to hear, holding my breath as slippered feet whispered past my shut door. Miss Harper, I concluded. It sounded as if she was going downstairs. I tossed and turned for what seemed like an hour. Eventually, I switched on the lamp and got out of bed. It was half past three, and there wasn't a hope I could go back to sleep. Shivering beneath my borrowed gown, I put on my overcoat, unlatched the door, and followed the pitch-black hallway until I recognized the shadowy shape of the curved banister at the top of the stairs.

The chilly entrance hall was dimly illuminated by moonlight seeping through small windows on either side of the front door. The snow had stopped and stars were out, tree branches and shrubbery formless beneath white frosting. I crept into the library, lured by the promise of heat from its crackling fire.

Miss Harper was sitting on the sofa, an afghan pulled around her. She was staring into the flames, her cheeks wet with tears she did not bother to brush away. Clearing my throat, I tentatively called her name, not wanting to startle her.

She did not move.

"Miss Harper?" I said again, louder. "I heard you come down . . ."

She was leaning against the serpentine-curved back of

the sofa, her eyes unblinking as they stared dully into the fire. Her head fell limply to one side when I quickly sat next to her and pressed my fingers against her neck. She was very warm but pulseless. Pulling her down to the rug, I went from her mouth to her sternum, desperately trying to breathe life into her lungs and force her heart to beat. I don't know how long this went on. When I finally gave up, my lips were numb, the muscles in my back and arms quivering. I was trembling all over.

The telephones were still out. I could not call anyone. There was nothing I could do. I stood before the library window, parted the curtains and looked out through tears at the incredible whiteness lit up by the moon. Beyond, the river was black and I could not see across it. Somehow I managed to get her body back on the sofa and I gently covered it with the afghan while the fire burned down and the girl in the portrait receded into the shadows. Sterling Harper's death had caught me unawares and left me stunned. I sat on the rug in front of the sofa and watched the fire die. I could not keep that alive, either. In fact, I didn't even try.

I did not cry when my father died. He had been sick so many years I became expert at cauterizing my emotions. He was in bed most of my childhood. When he finally died one evening at home, my mother's terrible grief drove me to a higher ground of detachment, and it was from this seemingly safer vantage point that I honed to perfection the art of surveying the wreckage of my family.

With what seemed unflappable reserve, I watched the anarchy that broke out between my mother and my younger sister, Dorothy, who had been consummately narcissistic and irresponsible since the day she was born.

I silently removed myself from the screaming matches and arguments while inwardly I ran for my life. AWOL from the wars within my house, I spent increasing lengths of time engaging the tutelage of the Gray Nuns after class or ensconcing myself in the library, where I began to realize the precocity of my mind and the rewards it would bring to me. I excelled in science and was intrigued by human biology. I was poring over *Gray's Anatomy* by the time I was fifteen, and it became the sine qua non of my self-education, the vessel of my epiphany. I was going to leave Miami for college. In an era when women were teachers, secretaries, and housewives, I was going to be a physician.

In high school I made all A's and played tennis and read during the holidays and summers while my family struggled on like wounded Confederate veterans in a world long since won by the North. I had little interest in dating and had few friends. Graduating at the top of my class, I went off to Cornell on a full scholarship; then it was Johns Hopkins for medical school, law school at Georgetown after that, then back to Hopkins for my pathology residency. I was only vaguely aware of what I was doing. The career I had embarked upon would forever return me to the scene of the terrible crime of my father's death. I would take death apart and put it back together again a thousand times. I would master its codes and take it to court. I would understand the nuts and bolts of it. But none of it brought my father back to life, and the child inside me never stopped grieving.

Embers shifted on the hearth, and I dozed in fits and starts.

Hours later the details of my prison began to materialize in the chilled blue of dawn. Pain shot through my back and legs as I stiffly got to my feet and went to the window. The sun was a pale egg over the slate-gray river, tree trunks black against the white snow. The fire was cold, and two questions were tapping at the back of my feverish brain. Would Miss Harper have died had I not been here? How convenient for her to die while I was inside her house. Why did she come down to the library? I imagined her making her way down the stairs, stoking the fire and settling on the sofa. While she stared into the flames, her heart simply stopped. Or was it the portrait she had been looking at in the end?

I switched on every lamp. Pulling a chair close to the hearth, I climbed up and lifted the unwieldy painting free of its hooks. The portrait did not seem so unsettling up close, the total effect disintegrating into subtle shades of color and delicate brush strokes in heavy oil paint. Dust floated free of the canvas as I climbed down and laid the painting on the floor. There was no signature or date, nor was the portrait nearly as old as I had assumed. The colors had been deliberately muted to look old, and there wasn't the slightest bit of cracking evident in the paint.

Turning it over, I examined the brown paper backing. Centered on it was a gold seal embossed with the name of a Williamsburg picture-framing shop. I made note of it and climbed back up on the chair, returning the painting to its hooks. Then I squatted before the fireplace and delicately probed the debris with a pencil I had gotten out of my bag. On top of the charred chunks of wood was a peculiar layer of filmy white ash that wafted like cobwebs at the slightest stirring. Beneath this was a lump of what looked like melted plastic.

* * *

"No offense, Doc," Marino said, backing his car out of the lot, "but you look like hell."

"Thanks a lot," I muttered.

"Like I said, no offense. Guess you didn't get much sleep."

When I didn't show up to take care of Cary Harper's autopsy in the morning, Marino wasted no time calling the Williamsburg police. Midmorning two sheepish officers showed up at the mansion, chains clanking and chewing tracks into the smooth, heavy snow. After the depressing rounds of questions about Sterling Harper's death, her body was loaded into an ambulance headed for Richmond, and the officers deposited me at headquarters in downtown Williamsburg, where I was plied with coffee and doughnuts until Marino picked me up.

"No way I would've stayed in that house all night," Marino went on. "I don't care if it was twenty below. I'd freeze my ass off before I'd spend the night with a stiff—"

"Do you know where Princess Street is?" I interrupted.

"What about it?" His mirrored shades turned toward me.

The snow was white fire in the sun, the streets fast turning to slush.

"I'm interested in a five-oh-seven Princess Street address," I replied in a tone indicating I expected him to take me there.

The address was at the edge of the historic district, tucked between other businesses in Merchants' Square. In the recently plowed parking lot were no more than a dozen cars, their roofs thatched with snow. I was relieved to see that The Village Frame Shoppe & Gallery was open.

Marino didn't ask questions as I got out. He probably sensed I wasn't in the mood to answer any at the moment. There was only one other customer inside the gallery, a young man in a black overcoat casually riffling through a rack of prints while a woman with long blond hair worked an adding machine behind the counter.

"May I help you?" the blond woman inquired, blandly looking up at me.

"That depends on how long you've worked here," I answered.

The cool, dubious way she looked me over made me realize I probably did look like hell. I'd slept in my coat. My hair was a god-awful mess. Self-consciously reaching up to smooth down a cowlick, I realized I had somehow managed to lose an earring. I told the woman who I was and drove home the point by producing the thin black wallet containing my brass medical examiner's shield.

"I've worked here two years," she said.

"I'm interested in a painting your shop framed probably before your time," I told her. "A portrait Cary Harper may have brought in."

"Oh, God. I heard about it on the radio this morning. About what happened to him. Oh, God, how awful." She was sputtering. "You'll need to speak to Mr. Hilgeman." She disappeared in back to fetch him.

Mr. Hilgeman was a tweedy, distinguished-looking gentleman who stated in no uncertain terms, "Cary Harper hasn't been in this shop in years, and no one here knew him well, at least not to my knowledge."

"Mr. Hilgeman," I said, "over the fireplace mantel in Cary Harper's library is a portrait of a blond girl. It was framed in your shop, possibly many years ago. Do you remember it?"

There wasn't the faintest spark of recognition in the gray eyes peering at me over reading glasses.

"It appears very old," I explained. "A good imitation but a rather unusual treatment of the subject. The girl is nine, ten, at the most twelve, but she's dressed more like a young woman, in white, and sitting on a small bench holding a silver hairbrush."

I could have kicked myself for not taking a Polaroid photograph of the painting. My camera was inside my medical bag and the thought had never occurred to me. I had been too distracted.

"You know," Mr. Hilgeman said, his eyes lighting up, "I think I might remember what you're talking about. A very pretty girl, but unusual. Yes. Rather suggestive, as I recall."

I didn't prod him.

"Must have been at least fifteen years ago. . . . Let me see." He touched an index finger to his lips. "No." He shook his head. "It wasn't me."

"It wasn't you? *What* wasn't you?" I asked.

"I didn't do the framing. That would have been Clara. An assistant who worked here then. I do believe—in fact I'm certain—Clara did the framing on that one. A rather expensive job and not really worth it, if you must know. The painting wasn't terribly good. Actually," he added with a frown, "it was one of her least successful efforts—"

"Her?" I interrupted. "Do you mean Clara?"

"I'm talking about Sterling Harper." He looked speculatively at me. "She's the artist." He paused. "That would have been years ago when she did a lot of painting. They had a studio in the house, as I understand it. I've never been there, of course. But she used to bring in a number of her works, most of them still lifes, landscapes. The painting you're interested in is the only portrait I recall."

"How long ago did she paint it?"

"At least fifteen years ago, as I've said."

"Did someone pose for it?" I asked.

"I suppose it could have been done from a photograph . . ." He frowned. "Actually, I really can't answer your question. But if someone posed for it, I don't know who that might have been."

I didn't show my surprise. Beryl would have been sixteen or seventeen and living at Cutler Grove then. Was it possible Mr. Hilgeman, the people in town, didn't know this?

"It's rather sad," he mused. "Such talented, intelligent people. No family, no children."

"What about friends?" I asked.

"I really don't know either of them personally," he said.

And you never will, I thought morbidly.

Marino was wiping off his windshield with a chamois cloth when I went back out into the parking lot. The melted snow and salt left by road crews had splotched and dulled his beautiful black car. He didn't look happy about it. On the pavement beneath the driver's door was an untidy collection of cigarette butts he had unceremoniously dumped from his ashtray.

"Two things," I began very seriously as we buckled up. "In the mansion's library is a portrait of a young blond girl that Miss Harper apparently had framed in this shop approximately fifteen years ago."

"Beryl Madison?" He got out his lighter.

"It may very well be a portrait of her," I replied. "But if so, it depicts her at an age much younger than she would have been when the Harpers met her. And the treatment of the subject is a little peculiar. Lolita-like . . ."

"Huh?"

"Sexy," I said bluntly. "A little girl painted to look sensual."

"Yo. So now you're going to tell me Cary Harper was a closet pedophile."

"In the first place, his sister painted the portrait," I said.

"Shit," he complained.

"Secondly," I went on, "I got the distinct impression the owner of the framing shop has no idea Beryl ever lived with the Harpers. It makes me wonder if other people know. And if not, I wonder how that's possible. She lived in the mansion for *years*, Marino. It's just a couple of miles from town. This is a *small* town."

He stared straight ahead as he drove and didn't say a word.

"Well," I decided, "it may all be idle speculation. They were reclusive. Perhaps Cary Harper did his best to hide Beryl from the world. Whatever the case, the situation doesn't sound exactly healthy. But it may have nothing to do with their deaths."

"Hell," he said shortly, "*healthy* ain't the word for it. Reclusive or not, it don't make sense for no one to know she was there. Not unless they had her locked up or chained to a bedpost. Damn perverts. I hate perverts. I hate people picking on kids. You know?" He glanced over at me again. "I really do hate that. I'm getting that feeling again."

"What feeling?"

"That Mr. Pulitzer Prize took Beryl out," Marino said. "She's going to spill the beans in her book, and he freaks, comes to see her and brings a knife."

"Then who killed him?" I asked.

"So maybe his batty sister did."

Whoever murdered Cary Harper was strong enough to inflict blows so forceful he was rendered unconscious almost immediately, and cutting someone's throat didn't fit with a female assailant. In fact, I had never had a case in which a woman did such a thing.

After a long silence, Marino asked, "Did Old Lady Harper strike you as senile?"

"Rather eccentric. But not senile," I said.

"Crazy?"

"No."

"Based on how you've described things, it don't sound to me like her response to her brother getting whacked was exactly appropriate," he answered.

"She was in shock, Marino. People who are in shock do not react appropriately to anything."

"You thinking she committed suicide?"

"Certainly that's possible," I replied.

"You find any drugs at the scene?"

"Some over-the-counter meds, none of them lethal," I said.

"No injuries?"

"None I could see."

"So, you know what the hell killed her?" he asked, looking over at me, his face hard.

"No," I answered. "At the moment I have absolutely no idea."

"I assume you're heading back to Cutler Grove," I said to Marino as he parked behind the OCME.

"Real thrilled about it, too," he grumbled. "Go home and get some decent sleep."

"Don't forget Cary Harper's typewriter."

Marino dug in a pocket for his lighter.

"The make and model, and any used ribbons," I reminded him.

He lit a cigarette.

"And any stationery or typing paper in the house. I suggest you collect the ashes in the fireplace yourself. It's going to be extremely difficult to preserve them—"

"No offense, Doc, but you're beginning to sound like my mother or something."

"Marino," I snapped, "I'm serious."

"Yeah, you're serious, all right—seriously in need of a good night's sleep," he said.

Marino was as frustrated as I and probably needed sleep, too.

The bay was locked and empty, the cement floor mottled with oil stains. Inside the morgue I was aware of the tedious humming of electricity and generators I hardly noticed during business hours. The rush of foul-smelling air seemed unusually loud as I entered the refrigerator.

Their bodies were on gurneys parked together against the left wall. Maybe it was because I was so tired. But when I pulled the sheet back from Sterling Harper, I went weak in the knees and dropped my medical bag to the floor. I recalled the keen beauty of her face, the terror in her eyes when the mansion's back door opened and she looked out as I attended to her dead brother, my gloved hands bright red with his blood. Brother and sister were present and accounted for. That was all I needed to know. I covered her gently, shrouding a face now as empty as a rubber mask. All around were tagged and protruding naked feet.

I had vaguely noticed the yellow film box beneath Sterling Harper's gurney when I had first walked into the refrigerator. But it wasn't until I reached down to pick up my medical bag that I took a good look and realized the significance. Kodak thirty-five millimeter, twenty-four exposure. The film on state contract for my office was Fuji, and we always ordered the thirty-six exposure. The paramedics who had transported Miss Harper's body would have been in and out many hours ago, and they wouldn't have taken any photographs.

I went back out into the hallway. The light over the elevator caught my attention, and I realized it was stopped on the second floor. Someone else was in the building! It was probably just the security guard making his rounds. Then, as my scalp began to prickle, I thought of the empty film box again. Gripping the strap of my medical bag tightly, I decided to take the stairs. On the second-floor landing I slowly opened the door and listened before stepping inside. The offices in the east wing were empty, the lights out. I turned right into the main hallway, passing the empty classroom, the library, and Fielding's office. I didn't hear or see anyone. Just to be sure, I decided as I turned into my office to call security.

When I saw him, I stopped breathing. For a terrible moment my mind wouldn't work. He was deftly and silently riffling through an open filing cabinet. The collar of a navy jacket was up around his ears, eyes masked by dark aviator glasses, hands sheathed in surgical gloves. Over a powerful shoulder was a leather strap attached to a camera. He looked as solid and hard as marble, and it wasn't possible for me to step out of sight fast enough. The gloved hands suddenly stilled.

When he lunged, it was a reflex, my medical bag looping back like an Olympic hammer. Momentum propelled it with such force between his legs the impact jarred the sunglasses from his face. He fell forward, doubling over in agony and knocked sufficiently off balance for me to send him sprawling with a kick to the ankles. He must not have felt any better when the hard metal lens of his camera was the only cushion between his ribs and the floor.

Medical impedimenta scattered as I frantically dug out of my bag the small canister of Mace I always carried, and he bellowed when the heavy stream hit him in the face. He clawed at his eyes, rolling around, screaming, while I grabbed the phone and called for help. I squirted him one more time for good measure just before the security guard hustled in. Then the cops arrived. My hysterical hostage begged to be taken to the hospital as an unsympathetic officer wrenched his arms behind his back, snapped on cuffs, and frisked him.

According to his driver's license, the intruder's name was Jeb Price, age thirty-four, address Washington, D.C. Wedged in the back of his corduroy trousers was a Smith & Wesson 9-millimeter automatic with fourteen rounds in the clip and one in the chamber.

* * *

I don't remember going into the morgue office and getting the keys off the pegboard for the other state car leased by the OCME. But I must have, because I was parking the dark blue station wagon in my driveway as night began to fall. Used to transport bodies, the car was oversize, the tailgate window discreetly covered with a screen, and in back was a removable plyboard floor that required hosing down several times a week. The car was a cross between a family wagon and a hearse, and the only thing harder to parallel park, in my opinion, was the *QE2*.

Like a zombie, I went straight upstairs without bothering to play back my telephone messages or turn off the answering machine. My right elbow and shoulder ached. The small bones in my hand hurt. Laying my clothes on a chair, I took a hot bath and numbly fell into bed. Deep, deep sleep. Sleep so deep it was like dying. Darkness was heavy and I was trying to swim through it, my body like lead, as the ringing telephone by my bed was abruptly cut off by my answering machine.

". . . don't know when I'll be able to call back, so listen. Please listen, Kay. I heard about Cary Harper . . ."

My heart was pounding as my eyes opened, Mark's urgent voice pulling me out of my torpor.

". . . Please stay out of it. Don't get involved. *Please.* I'll talk to you again as soon as I'm able . . ."

By the time I found the receiver I was listening to a dial tone. Replaying his message, I slumped against pillows and began to cry.

I don't remember going into the morgue office and getting the keys off the pegboard for the other state cars leased to the OCME. But I must have, because I was passing the dark blue station wagon in my driveway. It might have been [illegible] used to transport bodies, [illegible] the car was [illegible], its [illegible] window discreetly covered with a screen, and in back was a removable plywood floor that [illegible] down several times a week. The car was a cross between a family wagon and a hearse, and the only thing harder to parallel park, in my opinion, was the QE2.

Like a zombie, I went straight upstairs without bothering to play back my telephone messages or turn off the answering machine. My right elbow and shoulder ached. The small bones in my hand hurt. [illegible] my clothes on a chair, took a hot bath and [illegible]. [illegible] sleep. Sleep [illegible] was like dying. [illegible] and I was trying to swim through it, my body like lead, as the ringing telephone by my bed was abruptly cut off by my answering machine.

"... don't know when I'll be able to call back, [illegible]. Say, I heard about Cary Harper."

My heart was pounding as my eyes opened. [illegible] voice filling the room [illegible].

"[illegible] out of [illegible], got [illegible] worried. [illegible] I'll [illegible] try [illegible]."

By the time I found the receiver, I was listening to a dial tone. Replaying the message, I [illegible] against the pillows [illegible].

9

The next morning Marino arrived at the morgue as I was making a Y incision on Cary Harper's body.

I removed the breastplate of ribs and lifted the block of organs out of the chest cavity while Marino looked on mutely. Water drummed in sinks, surgical instruments clattered and clicked, and across the suite a long blade rasped against a whetstone as one of the morgue assistants sharpened a knife. We had four cases this morning, all of the stainless-steel autopsy tables occupied.

Since Marino didn't seem inclined to volunteer anything, I introduced the subject.

"What have you found out about Jeb Price?" I asked.

"His record check didn't come up with squat," he replied, staring off and restless. "No priors, no outstanding warrants, nothing. He ain't singing, either. If he was, it'd probably be soprano after the number you done on him. I stopped by ID right before I came down here. They're developing the film in his camera. I'll bring by a set of prints as soon as they're ready."

"Have you taken a look?"

"At the negatives," he answered.

"And?" I asked.

"Pictures he took inside the fridge. Of the Harpers' bodies," he said.

I had expected as much. "I don't suppose he's a journalist for some tabloid," I said in jest.

"Yo. Dream on."

I glanced up from what I was doing. Marino was not in a jovial mood. More disheveled than usual, he had nicked his jaw twice while shaving and his eyes were bloodshot.

"Most reporters I know don't pack nine mils loaded with Glasers," he said. "And they tend to whine when they get leaned on, ask for a quarter to call the paper's lawyer. This guy's not making a peep, a real pro. Must've picked a lock to get in. Makes his move on a Monday afternoon, a state holiday, when it's not likely anybody's going to be around. We found his ride parked about three blocks away in the Farm Fresh lot, a rental car with a cellular phone. Got enough ammo clips and magazines in the trunk to stop a small army, plus a Mac Ten machine pistol and a Kevlar vest. He ain't no reporter."

"I'm not so sure he's a *pro*, either," I commented, fitting a new blade in my scalpel. "It was sloppy to leave an empty film box inside the refrigerator. And if he really wanted to play it safe, he should have broken in at two or three in the morning, not in broad daylight."

"You're right. The film box was sloppy," Marino agreed. "But I can see why he broke in when he did. A funeral home or squad comes in to deliver a body while

Price's inside the fridge, right? In the middle of the day, maybe he's smooth enough to make it appear he works here, has a legit reason for being inside. But let's say he's surprised at two A.M. No way in hell he's going to be able to explain himself at that hour."

Whatever the case, I thought, Jeb Price meant business. Glaser Safety Slugs were one of the worst things out, the cartridges packed with small shot that disperse on impact and tear through flesh and organs like a lead hailstorm. Mac Tens are a favorite occupational tool of terrorists and drug lords, the machine pistols a dime a dozen in Central America, the Middle East, and my hometown of Miami.

"You might consider putting a lock on the fridge," Marino added.

"I've already alerted Buildings and Grounds," I said.

It was a precaution I had put off for years. Funeral homes and squads had to be able to get inside the refrigerator after hours. The security guards would have to be given keys. My local medical examiners on call would have to be given keys. There would be protests. There would be problems. Damn it, I was getting so tired of problems!

Marino had turned his attention to Harper's body. It didn't require an autopsy or a genius to determine the cause of death.

"He has multiple fractures of the skull and lacerations of the brain," I explained.

"His throat was cut last, like in Beryl's case?"

"The jugular veins and carotid arteries are transected, yet his organs aren't particularly pale," I answered. "He would have hemorrhaged to death in a matter of minutes if he'd had a blood pressure. In other words, he didn't bleed out enough to account for his death. He was dead or dying from his head injuries by the time his throat was cut."

"What about defense injuries?" Marino asked.

"None." I set down the scalpel to show him, one by one forcing open Harper's unwilling fingers. "No broken nails, cuts or contusions. He didn't attempt to ward off the blows of the weapon."

"Never knew what hit him," Marino commented. "He drives in after dark. The drone's waiting for him, probably hiding in the bushes. Harper parks, gets out of his Rolls. He's locking his door when the guy comes up behind him and hits him in the back of the head—"

"He has twenty percent stenosis of his LAD," I thought out loud, looking for my pencil.

"Harper goes down like a shot and the squirrel keeps swinging," Marino went on.

"Thirty percent of his right coronary." I scribbled notes on an empty glove packet. "No scarring from old infarcts. Heart's healthy but mildly enlarged, and he's got calcification of his aorta, moderate atherosclerosis."

"Then the guy slashes Harper's throat. Probably to make damn sure he's dead."

I looked up.

"Whoever did it wanted to make sure Harper was dead," Marino repeated.

"I don't know that I'd attribute such rational thinking to the assailant," I replied. "Look at him, Marino." I had deflected the scalp back from the skull, which was shattered like a hardboiled egg. Pointing out the fracture lines, I explained, "He was struck at least seven times with such force that none of the injuries was survivable. Then his throat was cut. It's overkill. Just as it was in Beryl's case."

"Okay. Overkill. I'm not arguing," he replied. "I'm just saying the killer wanted to make sure Beryl and Harper was dead. You nearly cut someone's damn head off, and you can walk away with the certainty your victim ain't going to be revived to tell the story."

Marino made a face as I began emptying the stomach contents into a cardboard container.

"Don't bother. I can tell you what he ate, was sitting right there. Beer nuts. And two martinis," he said.

The peanuts had barely begun clearing Harper's stomach when he died. There was nothing else but brownish fluid, and I could smell the alcohol.

I asked Marino, "What did you find out from him?"

"Not a damn thing."

I glanced at him as I labeled the container.

"I'm in the tavern drinking tonic and lime," he said. "I guess this was about quarter of. Harper walks in at five on the nose."

"How did you know it was him?" The kidneys were finely granular. I set them in the scale and jotted down the weights.

"Couldn't miss him with that mane of white hair," Marino replied. "He fit Poteat's description. I knew the second he walked in. He takes a table to himself and don't say nothing to nobody, just orders his 'usual' and eats beer nuts while he waits. I watch him for a while, then go over, pull up a chair and introduce myself. He says he's got nothing he can help me out with and he don't want to talk about it. I press him, tell him Beryl was being threatened for months, ask if he was aware of that. He looks annoyed, says he didn't know."

"Do you think he was telling the truth?" I was also wondering what the truth was about Harper's drinking. He had a fatty liver.

"No way for me to know," Marino said, flicking a cigarette ash on the floor. "Next I ask him where he was the night she was murdered, and he tells me he was in the tavern at his usual time, went home afterwards. When I ask if his sister can verify that, he tells me she wasn't home."

I looked up in surprise, the scalpel poised midair. "Where was she?"

"Out of town," he said.

"He didn't tell you where?"

"No. He said, and I quote, 'That's her business. Don't ask me.' " Marino's eyes fixed disdainfully on the sections of liver I was cutting. He added, "My favorite food used to be liver an' onions. You believe that? I don't know a single cop who's seen an autopsy and still eats liver . . ."

The Stryker saw drowned him out as I began work on the head. Marino gave up and backed away as bony dust drifted on the pungent air. Even when bodies are in good shape they smell bad when opened up. The visual experience isn't exactly Mary Poppins, either. I had to give Marino credit. No matter how awful the case, he always came to the morgue.

Harper's brain was soft, with numerous ragged lacerations. There was very little hemorrhage, verifying that he hadn't lived long after sustaining the injuries. At least his death was mercifully quick. Unlike Beryl, Harper had no time to register terror or pain or to beg for his life. His murder was different from hers in several other ways, as well. He had received no threats—at least none that we knew about. There were no sexual overtones. He had been beaten versus stabbed to death, and no articles of his clothing were missing.

"I counted one hundred and sixty-eight dollars in his wallet," I told Marino. "And his wristwatch and signet ring are present and accounted for."

"What about his necklace?" he asked.

I had no idea what he was talking about.

"He had on this thick gold chain with a medal on it, a shield, sort of like a coat of arms," he explained. "I noticed it at the tavern."

"It didn't come in with him, and I don't recall seeing it on him at the scene . . ." I started to say "last night." It wasn't last night. Harper had died early Sunday night. It was Tuesday now. I had lost all sense of time. The last two days seemed unreal, and had I not replayed Mark's message again this morning I would wonder if his call were real, too.

"So maybe the squirrel took it. Another souvenir," Marino said.

"That doesn't make sense," I answered. "I can understand the taking of a souvenir in Beryl's case, if her murder is the handiwork of a deranged individual who had an obsession with her. But why take something from Harper?"

"Trophies, maybe," Marino suggested. "Pelts from the hunt. Could be some hired gun who likes to keep little reminders of his jobs."

"I would think a hired gun would be too careful for that," I countered.

"Yeah, you'd think so. Just like you'd think Jeb Price

would be too careful to leave a film box in the fridge," he said ironically.

Peeling off my gloves, I finished labeling test tubes and other specimens I had collected. I gathered my paperwork and Marino followed me upstairs to my office.

Rose had left the afternoon newspaper on my blotter. Harper's murder and his sister's sudden death were the front-page headline. The accompanying sidebar was what ruined my day:

CHIEF MEDICAL EXAMINER ACCUSED OF
"LOSING" CONTROVERSIAL MANUSCRIPT

The dateline was New York, an Associated Press release, and the lead was followed by an account of my "incapacitating" a man named Jeb Price after catching him "ransacking" my office yesterday afternoon. The allegations about the manuscript had to have come from Sparacino, I thought angrily. The bit about Jeb Price must have come from the police report, and as I shuffled through message slips, I noted that the majority of them were from reporters.

"Did you ever check out her computer disks?" I asked, tossing the paper to Marino.

"Oh, yeah," he said. "I've been through 'em."

"And did you find this book everybody's in such a tizzy about?"

Perusing the front page, he muttered, "Nope."

"It's not there?" I broke out in frustration. "It's not on her disks? How can that be if she was writing it on her computer?"

"Don't ask me," he said. "I'm just telling you I looked

at maybe a dozen disks. Nothing recent on 'em. Looks like old stuff, you know, her novels. Nothing about herself, about Harper. Found a couple of old letters, including two business letters to Sparacino. They didn't excite me."

"Maybe she put the disks in a safe place before she left for Key West," I said.

"Maybe she did. But we ain't found 'em."

Just then Fielding walked in, his orangutan arms hanging out of the short sleeves of his surgical greens, his muscular hands lightly coated with the talc lining the latex gloves he had been wearing downstairs. Fielding was his own work of art. God knows how many hours each week he spent sculpting himself in some Nautilus room somewhere. It was my theory that his obsession with body building was inversely proportional to his obsession with his job. A competent deputy chief, he had been on board little more than a year and was already showing signs of burnout. The more disenchanted he got, the bigger he got. I gave him another two years before he retreated to the tidier, more lucrative world of hospital pathology, or became the heir apparent to the Incredible Hulk.

"I'm going to have to pend Sterling Harper," he said, hovering restlessly at the edge of my desk. "Her STAT alcohol's only point oh-three, nothing in her gastric that tells me much. No bleeding, no unusual odors. The heart's good, no evidence of old infarcts, her coronaries clear. Brain's normal. But something was going on with her. The liver's enlarged, around twenty-five hundred grams, and the spleen's about a thousand with thickening of the capsule. Some involvement of the lymph nodes, as well."

"Any metastases?" I asked.

"None on gross."

"Put a rush on the micros," I told him.

Fielding nodded and briskly left.

Marino looked questioningly at me.

"Could be a lot of things," I said. "Leukemia, lymphoma, or any one of a number of collagen diseases—some of which are benign, and some of which aren't. The spleen and lymph nodes react as a component of the immune system—in other words, the spleen is almost always involved in any blood disease. As for the big liver, that doesn't help us much diagnostically. I won't know anything until I can look at the histologic changes under the scope."

"You want to speak English for a change?" He lit a cigarette. "Tell me in simple terms what Doc-tor Schwarzenegger found."

"Her immune system was reacting to something," I said. "She was sick."

"Sick enough to account for her flaking out on her sofa?"

"That suddenly?" I said. "I doubt it."

"What about some sort of prescription drug?" he suggested. "You know, she takes all the pills and tosses the bottle in the fire, maybe explaining the melted plastic you found in the fireplace and the fact we didn't find no pill bottles or nothing in the house. Just over-the-counter crap."

A drug overdose was certainly high on my list, and there wasn't any point in my worrying about it at the moment. Despite my pleading, despite promises that her case would be a top priority, the toxicology results would take days, possibly weeks.

As for her brother, I had a theory.

"I think Cary Harper was struck with a homemade slapjack, Marino," I said. "Possibly a segment of metal pipe filled with bird shot for weight, the ends packed with something like Play-Doh to hold in the shot. After several blows, a wad of the Play-Doh flew out and the shot scattered."

He thoughtfully tapped an ash. "Don't exactly fit with the 'soldier of fortune' shit we found in Price's car. Not with anything Old Lady Harper might have thought up, either."

"I assume you didn't find anything like Play-Doh, modeling clay, or birdshot inside her house."

He shook his head and said, "Hell, no."

My phone did not stop ringing the rest of the day.

Accounts of my alleged role in the disappearance of a "mysterious and valuable manuscript," and exaggerated descriptions of my "disabling an attacker" who broke into my office, had made the wire services. Other reporters were trying to cash in on the scoop, some of them prowling the OCME's parking lot or appearing in the lobby, their microphones and cameras ready like rifles. One particularly irreverent local DJ was sending out over the airwaves that I was the only woman chief in the country who wore "golden gloves instead of rubber ones." The situation was quickly getting out of control, and I was beginning to take Mark's warnings a little more seriously. Sparacino was perfectly capable of making my life miserable.

Whenever Thomas Ethridge IV had something on his

mind, he dialed my direct line instead of going through Rose. I wasn't surprised when he called. I suppose I was relieved. It was late afternoon and we were sitting inside his office. He was old enough to be my father, one of those men whose homeliness in youth is gradually transformed by age into a monument of character. Ethridge had a Winston Churchill face that belonged in Parliament or a cigar smoke–filled drawing room. We had always gotten along extremely well.

"A publicity stunt? You think it likely anybody's going to believe that, Kay?" the attorney general asked as he absently fingered the rose-gold watch chain looped over his vest.

"I get the feeling *you* don't believe me," I said.

His response was to reach for a fat black Mont Blanc fountain pen and slowly unscrew the cap.

"I don't suppose anyone will get the chance to believe or disbelieve me," I added lamely. "My suspicions aren't founded on anything concrete, Tom. I make an accusation of this nature to counter what Sparacino's doing and he's going to have all the more fun."

"You're feeling very isolated, aren't you, Kay?"

"Yes. Because I am, Tom."

"Situations like this have a way of taking on a life of their own," he mused. "Problem's going to be nipping this one in the bud without generating more attention."

Rubbing his tired eyes behind horn-rimmed glasses, he turned to a fresh page in a legal pad and began making out one of his Nixonian lists, a line drawn down the center of the yellow page, advantages on one side, disadvantages on the other—advantages or disadvantages to what I had no idea. After filling half a page, one column dramatically longer than the other, he leaned back in his chair, looked up, and frowned.

"Kay," he said, "does it ever strike you that you seem to get more involved in your cases than your predecessors did?"

"I didn't know any of my predecessors," I replied.

He smiled a little. "That's not an answer to my question, Counselor."

"I honestly have never given the matter any thought," I said.

"Wouldn't expect you to," he surprised me by saying. "Wouldn't expect that at all because you're focused as hell, Kay. Which is just one of several reasons I solidly backed your appointment. The good side is you don't miss anything, are a damn good forensic pathologist in addition to being a fine administrator. The bad side is you tend to place yourself in jeopardy on occasion. Those strangling cases a year or so ago, for example. They might never have been solved and more women might have died were it not for you. But they almost cost you your life.

"Now this incident yesterday." He paused, then shook his head and laughed. "Though I have to admit I'm rather impressed. 'Decked him,' I believe I heard on the radio this morning. Did you *really*?"

"Not exactly," I replied uncomfortably.

"Do you know who he is, what he was looking for?"

"We're not sure," I said. "But he went inside the morgue refrigerator and took photographs. Photographs of Cary and Sterling Harper's bodies. The files he was looking through when I walked in on him didn't tell me anything."

"Alphabetized?"

"He was in the M through N drawer," I said.

"M as in Madison?"

"Possibly," I replied. "But her case is locked up in the front office. Nothing about her is in my filing cabinets."

After a long silence, he tapped the legal pad with his index finger and said, "I've been writing out what I know about these recent deaths. Beryl Madison, Cary Harper, Sterling Harper. Has all the trappings of a mystery novel, doesn't it? And now this intrigue over a missing manuscript that allegedly involves the medical examiner's office. What I have to say to you are a couple of things, Kay. First, if anybody else calls about the manuscript, I think it will make life easier if you refer the interested parties to my office. I fully expect some trumped-up lawsuit to follow. I'll get my staff involved now, see if we can head off the posse at the pass. Second, and I've been giving this a lot of careful consideration, I want you to be like an iceberg."

"What, exactly, is that supposed to mean?" I asked uneasily.

"What protrudes from the surface is but a fraction of what's really below," he answered. "This is not to be confused with keeping a low profile, even though you *will* be keeping a low profile for all practical purposes. Minimal statements to the press, making yourself as much a nonissue as possible." He began fingering his watch chain again. "Inversely proportional to your invisibility will be your level of activity, or involvement, if you will."

"My involvement?" I protested. "Is this your way of telling me to do my job, nothing but my job, and to keep the office out of the limelight?"

"Yes and no. Yes to doing your job. As for keeping the

medical examiner's office out of the limelight, I'm afraid that may be out of your control." He paused, folding his hands on top of his desk. "I'm quite familiar with Robert Sparacino."

"You've met him?" I asked.

"I had the distinct misfortune of making his acquaintance in law school," he said.

I looked at him in disbelief.

"Columbia, class of 'fifty-one," Ethridge went on. "An obese, arrogant young man with a serious character defect. He was also very bright and might have graduated top of the class and gone on to clerk for the chief justice had I not gotten compulsive." He paused. "I went to Washington and enjoyed the privilege of working for Hugo Black. Robert stayed in New York."

"Has he ever forgiven you?" I asked, a cloud of suspicion gathering. "I'm assuming there must have been a lot of rivalry. Has he ever forgiven you for beating him out, graduating at the top?"

"He never fails to send me a Christmas card," Ethridge said dryly. "Generated from a computer list, his signature stamped, my name misspelled. Just impersonal enough to be insulting."

It was beginning to make more sense why Ethridge wanted all battles with Sparacino routed through the AG's office. "You don't think it's possible he's causing this trouble with me to get to you," I offered hesitantly.

"What? That the missing manuscript is all a ruse and he knows it? That he's causing a stink in the Commonwealth to indirectly give me a black eye and a lot of headaches?" He smiled grimly. "I think it's unlikely this would be the whole of his motivation."

"But it might be added incentive," I commented. "He

would know that any legal snafus, any potential litigation involving my office would be handled by the state's attorney. What I hear you telling me is he's a vindictive man."

Ethridge began slowly tapping his fingertips together as he stared off and said, "Let me tell you something I heard about Robert Sparacino when we were at Columbia. He's from a broken home and lived with his mother while his estranged father made a lot of money on Wall Street. Apparently, the kid visited his father in New York several times a year, was precocious, a prolific reader quite taken with the literary world. On one such visit he managed to persuade his father to take him to lunch at the Algonquin on a day that Dorothy Parker and her Round Table were supposed to be there. Robert, no more than nine or ten at the time, had it all planned, according to the story, which he apparently told to several drinking buddies at Columbia. He would approach Dorothy Parker's table, offer his hand, and introduce himself by saying, 'Miss Parker, it's such a pleasure to meet you,' and so on. When he got to her table, what emerged instead was 'Miss Parker, it's such a meet to pleasure you.' Whereupon she quipped, as only she could, 'So many men have said, though none quite as young as you.' The laughter that followed mortified Sparacino, humiliated him. He never forgot it."

The image of the little fatso offering his sweaty hand and saying such a thing was so pathetic I didn't laugh. Had I been that embarrassed by a childhood hero, I never would have forgotten it, either.

"I tell you this," Ethridge said, "to demonstrate a point that has been corroborated by now, Kay. When Sparacino told this story at Columbia, he was drunk and bitter and loudly promising he would get his revenge, show Dorothy Parker and the rest of the elitist world he's not to be laughed at. And what's happened?" He looked appraisingly at me. "He's one of the most powerful book lawyers in the country, mingles freely with editors, agents, writers, all of whom may privately hate him but find it unwise not to fear him. Supposedly he regularly lunches at the Algonquin, and insists on signing all movie and book contracts there while he no doubt inwardly smirks at Dorothy Parker's ghost." He paused. "Sound farfetched?"

"No. One doesn't need to be a psychologist to figure it out," I said.

"Here's what I'm going to suggest," Ethridge said, his eyes fixed on mine. "Let me handle Sparacino. I want you to have no contact with him at all, if possible. You mustn't underestimate him, Kay. Even when you think you've told him very little, he's reading between the lines, is a master at making inferences that can be uncannily on the mark. I'm not sure what his involvement with Beryl Madison, the Harpers, really was or what his real agenda is. Perhaps a mixture of unsavory things. But I don't want him knowing any more details about these deaths than he already knows."

"He's already gotten a lot," I said. "Beryl Madison's police report, for example. Don't ask me how—"

"He's very resourceful," Ethridge interrupted. "I advise you to keep all reports out of circulation, send them only where you must. Tighten the lid on your office, beef up security, every file under lock and key. Make sure your staff releases no information about these cases to anyone unless you're absolutely certain the person calling in the request is who he says he is. Every crumb Sparacino will use to his advantage. It's a game to him. Many people could be hurt—including you. Not to mention what could happen to the cases come court time. After one of his typical publicity blitzes we'd have to change the damn venue to Antarctica."

"He may have anticipated that you'll do this," I said quietly.

"That I'd relegate myself to being the lightning rod? Step into the ring instead of letting an assistant handle it?"

I nodded.

"Well, perhaps so," he answered.

I was sure of it. I wasn't Sparacino's intended quarry. His old nemesis was. Sparacino couldn't pick on the attorney general directly. He would never get past the watchdogs, the aides, the secretaries. So Sparacino picked on me instead and was being rewarded with the desired result. The idea of being used this way only made me angrier, and Mark suddenly came to mind. What was his role in this?

"You're annoyed and I don't blame you," Ethridge said. "And you're just going to have to swallow your pride, your emotions, Kay. I need your help."

I just listened.

"The ticket that will get us out of Sparacino's amusement park, I strongly suspect, is this manuscript everyone's so interested in. Any possibility you might be able to track it down?"

I felt my face getting hot. "It never came through my office, Tom—"

"Kay," he said firmly, "that's not my question. A lot

of things never come through your office and the medical examiner manages to track them down. Prescription drugs, a complaint of chest pain overheard at some point before the decedent suddenly dropped dead, suicidal ideations you somehow manage to get a family member to divulge. You have no power of enforcement, but you can investigate. And sometimes you're going to find out details no one is ever going to tell the police."

"I don't want to be an ordinary witness, Tom."

"You're an expert witness. Of course you don't want to be ordinary. It's a waste," he said.

"And the cops are usually better interrogators," I added. "They don't expect people to tell the truth."

"Do you expect it?" he asked.

"Your local friendly doctor usually expects it, expects people to tell the truth as they perceive it. They do the best they can. Most docs don't expect the patient to lie."

"Kay, you're speaking in generalities," he said.

"I don't want to be in the position—"

"Kay, the Code reads that the medical examiner shall make an investigation into the cause and manner of death and reduce his findings to writing. This is very broad. It gives you full investigative powers. The only thing you can't do is actually arrest somebody. You know that. The police are never going to find that manuscript. You're the only person who can find it." He looked levelly at me. "It's *more important* to you, to your good name, than it is to them."

There was nothing I could do. Ethridge had declared war on Sparacino, and I had been drafted.

"Find that manuscript, Kay." The attorney general glanced at his watch. "I know you. You put your mind to it, you'll find it or at least discover what's become of it. Three people are dead. One of them a Pulitzer Prize-winner whose book happens to be a favorite of mine. We need to get to the bottom of this. In addition, everything you turn up that relates to Sparacino you report back to me. You'll try, won't you?"

"Yes, sir," I replied. "Of course I'll try."

I began by badgering the scientists.

Documents examination is one of very few scientific procedures that can supply answers right before your eyes. It is as concrete as paper and as tangible as ink. By late Wednesday afternoon the section chief, whose name was Will, and Marino and I had been at it for hours. What we were discovering was a vivid reminder that not one of us is above being driven to drink.

I wasn't sure what I was hoping. Maybe it would have been a simple solution had we determined right off that what Miss Harper had burned in her fireplace was Beryl's missing manuscript. Then we might conclude that Beryl had relegated it to the safekeeping of her friend. We might assume that the work contained indiscretions that Miss Harper chose not to share with the world. Most important, we could conclude that the manuscript really had not, after all, disappeared from the crime scene.

But the amount and type of paper we were examining were not consistent with these possibilities. There were very few unburned fragments, none bigger than a dime or worth placing under the infrared-filter-covered lens of the video comparator. No technical aids or chemical tests were going to assist us in examining the remaining tissuey white curls of ash. They were so fragile we didn't dare remove them from the shallow cardboard box Marino had collected them in, and we had shut the door and vents of the documents lab to keep the room as airless as possible.

What we were doing amounted to a frustrating, painstaking task of nudging weightless ashes aside with tweezers, picking here, picking there, for a word. So far we knew that Miss Harper had burned sheets of twenty-pound rag paper imprinted with characters typed with a carbon ribbon. We could be sure of this for several reasons. Paper produced from wood pulp turns black when incinerated, while paper made from cotton is incredibly clean, its ashes wispy white like the ones in Miss Harper's fireplace. The few unburned fragments we looked at were consistent with twenty-pound stock. Finally, carbon does not burn. The heat had shrunk the typed characters to what was comparable to fine print, or approximately twenty pitch. Some words were present in their entirety, standing out blackly against the filmy white ash. The rest were hopelessly fragmented and sullied like sooty bits of tiny paper fortunes from Chinese cookies.

"*A R R I V*," Will spelled out, eyes bloodshot behind unstylish black-framed glasses, his young face weary. He was having to work at being patient.

I added the partial word to the half-filled page of my notepad.

"Arrived, arriving, arrive," he added with a sigh. "Can't think of what else it could be."

"Arrival, arriviste," I thought out loud.

"*Arriviste?*" Marino asked sourly. "What the hell is that?"

"As in social climber," I replied.

"A little too esoteric for me," Will said humorlessly.

"Probably a little too esoteric for most people," I conceded, wishing for the bottle of Advil downstairs in my pocketbook and blaming my persistent headache on eyestrain.

"Jesus," Marino complained. "Words, words, words. Never seen so many words in my damn life. Never heard of half of 'em and not sorry about the fact, either."

He was leaning back in a swivel chair, his feet propped on a desk, as he continued reading the transcription of writings Will had deciphered from the ribbon removed from Cary Harper's typewriter. The ribbon wasn't carbon, meaning the pages Miss Harper burned could not have come from her brother's typewriter. It appeared that the novelist had been working in fits and starts on yet another book attempt. Most of what Marino was looking at didn't make much sense, and when I had perused it earlier I had wondered if Harper's inspiration had been of the bottled variety.

"Wonder if you could sell this shit," Marino said.

Will had fished another sentence fragment out of the god-awful sooty mess, and I was leaning close to inspect it.

"You know," Marino went on. "They're always coming out with stuff after a famous writer dies. Most of it crap the poor guy never wanted published to begin with."

"Yes. They could call it *Table Scraps from a Literary Banquet,*" I muttered.

"Huh?"

"Never mind. There's not even ten pages there, Marino," I said abstractedly. "Rather hard to get a book out of that."

"Yeah. So it gets published in *Esquire*, maybe *Playboy*, instead of a book. Probably still worth some bucks," Marino said.

"This word is definitely indicating a proper name of a place or company or something," Will mused, oblivious to the conversation around him. "*Co* is capitalized."

I said, "Interesting. Very interesting."

Marino got up to take a look.

"Be careful not to breathe," Will warned, the tweezers in his hand steady as a scalpel as he gingerly manipulated the wisp of white ash on which tiny black letters spelled out *bor Co.*

"County, company, country, college," I suggested. My blood was beginning to flow again, waking me up.

"Yeah, but what would have *bor* in it?" Marino puzzled.

"Ann Arbor?" Will suggested.

"What about a county in Virginia?" Marino asked.

We couldn't come up with any county in Virginia that ended with the letters *bor*.

"Harbor," I said.

"Okay. But followed by *Co*?" Will replied dubiously.

"Maybe something-Harbor Company," Marino said.

I looked in the telephone directory. There were five businesses with names beginning with Harbor: Harbor East, Harbor South, Harbor Village, Harbor Imports, and Harbor Square.

"Don't sound like we're in the right ball park," Marino said.

We didn't fare any better when I dialed directory assistance and asked for the names of any businesses in the Williamsburg area called Harbor-this or Harbor-that. Other than one apartment complex, there was nothing.

Next I called Detective Poteat of the Williamsburg Police, and other than that same apartment complex, he couldn't think of anything, either.

"Maybe we shouldn't get too hung up on this," Marino said testily.

Will was engrossed in the box of ashes again.

Marino looked over my shoulder at the list of words we had found so far.

You, your, I, my, we, and *well* were common. Other complete words included the mortar of everyday sentence constructions—*and, is, was, that, this, which, a,* and *an.* Some words were a bit more specific, such as *town, home, know, please, fear, work, think,* and *miss.* As for incomplete words, we could only guess at what they had been in their former life. A derivation of *terrible* apparently was used numerous times for lack of any other common word we could think of that began with *terri* or *terrib.* Nuance, of course, was forever lost on us. Did the person mean terrible, as in "It is so terrible"? Did the person mean terribly, as in "I am terribly upset" or "I miss you terribly"? Or was it as benign as "It is terribly nice of you"?

Significantly, we found several remnants of the name Sterling and just as many remnants of the name Cary.

"I'm fairly certain what she burned was personal letters," I decided. "The type of paper, the words used, make me think that."

Will agreed.

"Do you remember finding any stationery in Beryl Madison's house?" I asked Marino.

"Computer paper, typing paper. That's about it. None of this high-dollar rag you're talking about," he said.

"Her printer uses ink ribbons," Will reminded us as he anchored an ash with tweezers and added, "I think we may have another one."

I took a look.

This time all that was left was *or C.*

"Beryl had a Lanier computer and printer," I said to Marino. "I think it might be a good idea to find out if that's what she always had."

"I went through her receipts," he said.

"For how many years?" I asked.

"As many as she had. Five, six," he answered.

"Same computer?"

"No," he said. "But same damn printer, Doc. Something called a sixteen-hundred, with a daisy wheel. Always used the same kind of ribbons. Got no idea what she wrote with before that."

"I see."

"Yo, glad you do," Marino complained, kneading the small of his back. "Me, I'm not seeing a goddamn thing."

10

The FBI National Academy in Quantico, Virginia, is a brick and glass oasis in the midst of an artificial war. I would never forget my first stay there years ago. I went to bed and got up to the sound of semiautomatics going off, and when I took a wrong turn on the wooded fitness course one afternoon, I was almost flattened by a tank.

It was Friday morning. Benton Wesley had scheduled a meeting, and Marino perked up visibly as the Academy's fountain and flags came into view. I had to take two steps for his every one as I followed him inside the spacious sunny lobby of a new building that looked enough like a fine hotel to have earned the nickname Quantico Hilton. Checking his handgun at the front desk, Marino signed us in, and we clipped on visitor's passes while a receptionist buzzed Wesley to affirm our privileged clearance.

A maze of glass hyphens connect sections of offices, classrooms, and laboratories, and one can go from building to building without ever stepping outside. No matter how often I came here, I always got lost. Marino seemed to know where he was going, so I dutifully stayed on his heels and watched the parade of color-coded students pass. Red shirts and khaki trousers were police officers. Gray shirts with black fatigues tucked into spit-polished boots were new DEA agents, with the veterans dressed ominously in solid black. New FBI agents wore blue and khaki, while members of the elitist Hostage Teams wore solid white. Men and women were impeccably groomed and remarkably fit. They carried with them a mien of militaristic reserve as tangible as the odor of the gun-cleaning solvent they left in their wake.

We boarded a service elevator and Marino punched the button designated *LL* (for Low Low, so the joke goes). Hoover's secret bomb shelter is sixty feet under ground, two stories below the indoor firing range. It has always seemed appropriate to me that the Academy decided to locate its Behavioral Science Unit closer to hell than heaven. Titles change. The last I heard, the Bureau was calling profilers Criminal Investigative Agents, or CIAs (an acronym destined for confusion). The work doesn't change. There will always be pyschopaths, sociopaths, lust murderers—whatever one chooses to call evil people who find pleasure in causing unthinkable pain.

We got off the elevator and followed a drab hallway to a drab outer office. Wesley emerged and showed us into a small conference room, where Roy Hanowell was sitting at a long polished table. The fibers expert never seemed to remember me on sight from one meeting to the next. I always made a point of introducing myself when he offered his hand.

"Of course, of course, Dr. Scarpetta. How are you?" he inquired, just as he always did.

Wesley shut the door and Marino looked around, scowling when he couldn't find an ashtray. An empty Diet Coke can in a trash basket would have to do. I resisted the impulse to dig out my own pack. The Academy was about as smokeless as an intensive care unit.

Wesley's white shirt was wrinkled in back, his eyes tired and preoccupied as he began perusing paperwork inside a folder. He immediately got down to business.

"Anything new on Sterling Harper?" he asked.

I had reviewed her histology slides yesterday and wasn't unduly surprised by what I had found. Nor was I any closer to understanding her cause of sudden death.

"She had chronic myelocytic leukemia," I replied.

Wesley glanced up. "Cause of death?"

"No. In fact, I can't even be sure she knew she had it," I said.

"That's interesting," Hanowell commented. "You can have leukemia and not know it?"

"The onset of chronic leukemia is insidious," I explained. "Her symptoms could have been as mild as night sweats, fatigue, weight loss. On the other hand, it could have been diagnosed some time ago and was in remission. She wasn't in a blast crisis. There were no progressive leukemic infiltrations, and she wasn't suffering from any significant infections."

Hanowell looked perplexed. "Then what killed her?"

"I don't know," I admitted.

"Drugs?" Wesley asked, making notes.

"The tox lab is beginning its second round of testing," I answered. "Her preliminary report shows a blood alcohol of point zero-three. In addition, she had dextromethorphan on board, which is an antitussive found in numerous over-the-counter cough suppressants. At the scene we found a bottle of Robitussin on top of the sink inside her upstairs bathroom. It was more than half full."

"So that didn't do it," Wesley muttered to himself.

"The entire bottle wouldn't do it," I told him, adding, "It's puzzling, I agree."

"You'll keep me posted? Let me know what turns up on her," Wesley said. More pages turned, and he went to the next item on his agenda. "Roy's examined the fibers from Beryl Madison's case. We want to talk to you about that. And then, Pete, Kay"—he glanced up at us—"I have another matter to take up with both of you."

Wesley looked anything but happy, and I had the feeling that his reason for summoning us here wasn't going to make me happy, either. Hanowell, in contrast, was his usual unperturbed self. His hair, eyebrows, and eyes were gray. Even his suit was gray. Whenever I saw him, he always looked half asleep and gray, so colorless and calm I was tempted to wonder if he had a blood pressure.

"With one exception," Hanowell laconically began, "the fibers I was asked to look at, Dr. Scarpetta, reveal few surprises—no unusual dyes or shapes at cross sections to speak of. I have concluded that the six nylon fibers most likely came from six different origins, just as your examiner in Richmond and I discussed. Four of them are consistent with the fabrics used in automobile carpeting."

"How do you figure that?" Marino asked.

"Nylon upholstery and carpeting degrade very quickly in sunlight and heat, as you might imagine," Hanowell said. "If the fibers aren't treated with a premetalized dye, thereby adding UV and thermal stabilizers, car carpet will bleach out or rot in short order. By using X-ray fluorescence I was able to detect trace amounts of metals in four of the nylon fibers. Though I can't say with certainty the origin of these fibers is car carpeting, they are consistent with that."

"Any chance of tracing them back to a make and model?" Marino wanted to know.

"I'm afraid not," Hanowell replied. "Unless we're talking about a very unusual fiber with a patented modification ratio, tracing the darn thing back to a manufacturer is pretty futile, especially if the vehicles in question were manufactured in Japan. Let me give you an example. The precursor to the carpeting in a Toyota is plastic pellets, which are shipped from this country to Japan. There they are spun into fibers, the yarn shipped back here to be made into carpet. The carpet is then sent back to Japan to be placed inside the cars coming off the line."

He droned on. It only got more hopeless.

"We also have headaches with cars manufactured in the United States. Chrysler Corporation, for example, may procure a certain color for its carpeting from three different suppliers. Then halfway through the model year Chrysler may decide to change suppliers. Let's say you and I are both driving 'eighty-seven black LeBarons with burgundy interior, Lieutenant. Well, the suppliers for the burgundy carpet in mine may be different from the suppliers in yours. Point is, the only significance of the nylon fibers I've examined is the variety. Two may be from household carpeting. Four may be from automobile carpeting. The colors and cross sections vary. You add to this the finding of olefin, Dynel, acrylic fibers, and what you've got is a hodgepodge I find most peculiar."

"Obviously," Wesley interjected, "the killer has a profession or some other preoccupation that puts him in contact with many different types of carpeting. And when he murdered Beryl Madison, he was wearing something that caused numerous fibers to adhere to him."

Wool, corduroy or flannel could account for that, I thought. But no wool or dyed cotton fibers had been found that were thought to have come from the killer.

"What about Dynel?" I asked.

"Usually associated with women's dresses. With wigs, fake furs," Hanowell answered.

"Yes, but not exclusively," I said. "A shirt or pair of slacks made of Dynel would build up static electricity like polyester, causing everything to stick to it. This might explain why he was carrying so much trace."

"Possibly," Hanowell said.

"So maybe the squirrel was wearing a wig," Marino proposed. "We know Beryl let him in her house, translated into she didn't feel threatened. Most ladies ain't going to feel threatened by a woman at the door."

"A transvestite?" Wesley suggested.

"Could be," Marino replied. "Some of the best-looking babes you'll ever see. It's friggin' sickening. Even I can't tell with a few of 'em unless I get right up in their faces."

"If the assailant were in drag," I pointed out, "how do we account for the fibers adhering to him? If the origin of the fibers is his workplace, certainly he wouldn't have been dressed in drag at work."

"Unless he works the streets in drag," Marino said. "He's in and out of johns' rides all night long, maybe in and out of motel rooms with carpeted floors."

"Then his victim selection doesn't make any sense," I said.

"No, but the absence of seminal fluid might make sense," Marino argued. "Male transvestites, faggots, usually don't go around raping women."

"They usually don't go around murdering them, either," I answered.

"I mentioned an exception," Hanowell resumed, glancing at his watch. "This is the orange acrylic fiber you were so curious about." His gray eyes fixed impassively on me.

"The three-leaf clover shape," I recalled.

"Yes," Hanowell said, nodding. "The shape is very unusual, the purpose, as is true with other trilobals, to hide dirt and scatter light. Only place I know you'll find fibers with this shape is in Plymouths manufactured in the late seventies—the fibers are in the nylon carpeting. They're the same three-leaf clover shape at cross section as the orange fiber in Beryl Madison's case."

"But the orange fiber is acrylic," I reminded him. "Not nylon."

"That's correct, Dr. Scarpetta," he said. "I'm giving you background in order to demonstrate the unique properties of the fiber in question. The fact that it is acrylic versus nylon, the fact that bright colors such as orange are almost never used in automobile carpeting, assists us in excluding the fiber from a number of origins—including Plymouths manufactured in the late seventies. Or any other automobile you might think of."

"So you're never seen anything like this orange fiber before?" Marino asked.

"That's what I'm leading up to." Hanowell hesitated.

Wesley took over. "Last year we got in a fiber identical

to this orange one in every respect when Roy was asked to examine trace recovered from a Boeing seven forty-seven hijacked in Athens, Greece. I'm sure you recall the incident," he said.

Silence.

Even Marino was momentarily speechless.

Wesley went on, his eyes dark with trouble. "The hijackers murdered two American soldiers on board and dumped their bodies on the tarmac. Chet Ramsey was a twenty-four-year-old Marine, the first to be thrown out of the plane. The orange fiber was adhering to blood on his left ear."

"Could the fiber have come from the interior of the plane?" I asked.

"It doesn't appear so," Hanowell replied. "I compared it with exemplars of carpet, seat upholstery, the blankets stored in the overhead bins, and didn't come up with a match or even a near match. Either Ramsey picked up the fiber someplace else—and this doesn't seem likely since it was adhering to wet blood—or possibly it was the result of a passive transfer from one of the terrorists to him. The only other alternative I can think of is that the fiber came from one of the other passengers, but if so, this individual would have to have touched him at some point after he was injured. According to eyewitness accounts, none of the other passengers went near him. Ramsey was taken to the front of the plane, away from the other passengers, and beaten, shot, his body wrapped in one of the plane's blankets and thrown out onto the tarmac. The blanket, by the way, was tan."

Marino said it first, and he wasn't good humored about it, "You mind explaining how the hell a hijacking in

Greece is connected with two writers getting whacked in Virginia?"

"The fiber connects at least two of the incidences," Hanowell replied. "The hijacking and Beryl Madison's death. This isn't to say that the actual crimes are connected, Lieutenant. But this orange fiber is so unusual we have to consider the possibility there may be some common denominator in what happened in Athens and what is happening here now."

It was more than a possibility, it was a certainty. There was a common denominator. Person, place, or thing, I thought. It had to be one of the three, and the details were slowly materializing in my mind.

I said, "They were never able to question the terrorists. Two of them ended up dead. Another two managed to escape and have never been caught."

Wesley nodded.

"Are we even certain they *were* terrorists, Benton?" I asked.

After a pause, he answered, "We've never succeeded in tying them in with any terrorist group. But the assumption is they were making an anti-American statement. The plane was American, as were a third of its passengers."

"What were the hijackers wearing?" I asked.

"Civilian clothes. Slacks, open-neck shirts, nothing unusual," he said.

"And no orange fibers were found on the bodies of the two hijackers killed?" I asked.

"We don't know," Hanowell answered. "They were gunned down on the tarmac, and we weren't able to move fast enough to claim the bodies and fly them over here for examination along with the slain American soldiers. Unfortunately, I got only the fiber report from the Greek authorities. I never actually examined the hijackers' clothing or trace myself. Obviously, quite a lot could have been missed. But even if there had been an orange fiber or two recovered from one of the hijacker's bodies, this still wouldn't necessarily tell us the origin."

"Hey, what are you telling me?" Marino demanded. "What? I'm supposed to think we're looking for an escaped hijacker who's now killing people in Virginia?"

"We can't completely rule it out, Pete," Wesley said. "Bizarre as it may seem."

"The four men who hijacked that plane have never been associated with any group," I recalled. "We really don't know the whole of their purpose or who they were, except that two of them were Lebanese—if my memory serves me well—the other two who escaped possibly Greek. It seems to me there was some speculation at the time that the real target was an American ambassador on vacation who was scheduled to be on that flight with his family."

"This is true," Wesley said tensely. "After the American embassy in Paris was bombed several days earlier, the ambassador's travel plans were secretly changed even though the reservations weren't."

His eyes glanced past me, and he was tapping an ink pen against the knuckle of his left thumb.

He added, "We haven't ruled out the possibility the hijackers were a hit squad, professional guns hired by somebody."

"Okay, okay," Marino said impatiently. "And no one's ruled out that Beryl Madison and Cary Harper might have been murdered by a professional gun. You know, their crimes staged to look like a squirrel did 'em in."

"I suppose one place to start would be to see what else we can find out about this orange fiber, its possible origin." Then I came right out and said it. "And maybe someone ought to look a little harder at Sparacino, make sure he wasn't somehow connected with that ambassador who may have been the real target in the hijacking."

Wesley didn't respond.

Marino suddenly got interested in trimming a thumbnail with his pocketknife.

Hanowell looked around the table, and when it seemed apparent we had no more questions for him, he excused himself and left.

Marino fired up another cigarette.

"You ask me," he said, blowing out a stream of smoke, "this is turning into a damn wild goose chase. I mean, it don't add up. Why hire some international hit man to snuff a lady romance writer and a has-been novelist who ain't produced nothing in years?"

"I don't know," Wesley said. "It all depends on who had what connections. Hell, it depends on a lot of things, Pete. Everything does. All we can do is follow the evidence as best we're able. This brings me to the next item on the agenda. Jeb Price."

"He's back on the street," Marino said automatically.

I looked at him in disbelief.

"Since when?" Wesley inquired.

"Yesterday," Marino replied. "He posted bail. Fifty grand, to be exact."

"You mind telling me how he managed that?" I said, furious that Marino hadn't told me this before now.

"Don't mind at all, Doc," he said.

There were three ways to post bail, I knew. The first was on personal recognizance, the second with cash or property, the third through a bail bondsman who charged a ten percent fee and demanded a cosigner or some other sort of security to assure he wasn't left holding an empty bag if the accused decided to skip town. Jeb Price, Marino said, had opted for the latter.

"I want to know how he managed that," I said again, getting out my cigarettes and scooting the Coke can closer so we could share.

"Only one way I know of. He called his lawyer, who opened a bank escrow account and sent a passbook to Lucky's," Marino said.

"Lucky's?" I asked.

"Yo. Lucky Bonding Company on Seventeenth Street, conveniently located a block from the city jail," Marino answered. "Charlie Luck's pawnshop for prisoners. Also know as Hock & Walk. Charlie and me go back a long time, shoot the breeze, tell a few jokes. Sometimes he snitches a little, other times he zips his lip. This is one of those other times, unfortunately. Nothing I could pull on him succeeded in getting me the name of Price's lawyer, but I've got a suspicion he ain't local."

"Price obviously has connections in high places," I said.

"Obviously," Wesley agreed grimly.

"And he never talked?" I asked.

"Had the right to remain silent, and he sure as hell did," Marino answered.

"What did you find out about his arsenal?" Wesley was making notes to himself again. "You run it through ATF?"

Marino replied, "Comes back as registered to him, and he's got a license to carry a concealed weapon, issued six years ago by some senile judge up here in northern Virginia who's since retired and moved down south somewhere. According to the background check included in the record I got from the circuit court, Price was unmarried, was working in a D.C. gold and silver exchange called Finklestein's at the time he was issued the license. And guess what? Finklestein's ain't there no more."

"What about his DMV record?" Wesley continued to write.

"No tickets. An 'eighty-nine BMW is registered to him, his address in D.C., an apartment near Dupont Circle he apparently moved out of last winter. The rental office pulled his old lease, lists him as being self-employed. I'm still running it down, will get the IRS to pull records of his tax returns for the past five years."

"Possible he's a private eye?" I asked.

"Not in the District of Columbia," Marino answered.

Wesley looked up at me and said, "Someone hired him. For what purpose, we still don't know. Clearly, he failed in his mission. Whoever's behind it may try again. I don't want you walking in on the next one, Kay."

"Would it be stating the obvious to say I don't want that either?"

"I guess what I'm telling you," he went on like a no-nonsense father, "is I want you to avoid placing yourself in any situation where you might be vulnerable. For example, I don't think it's a good idea for you to be in your office when no one else is inside the building. I don't mean just on the weekends. If you work until six, seven at night, and everybody else has gone home, it's not a good idea for you to be walking out into a dark parking lot to get in your car. Possible you can leave at five when there are eyes and ears around?"

"I'll keep it in mind," I said.

"Or if you have to leave later, Kay, then call the security

guard and ask him to escort you to your car," Wesley went on.

"Hell, call me, for that matter," Marino was quick to volunteer. "You got my pager number. If I'm not available, ask the dispatcher to send a car by."

Fine, I thought. Maybe if I'm lucky I'll make it home by midnight.

"Just be extremely careful." Wesley looked hard at me. "All theories aside, two people have been murdered. The killer's still out there. The victimology, the motivation are sufficiently strange for me to believe anything's possible."

His words resurfaced more than once during the drive home. When anything is possible, nothing is impossible. One plus one does not equal three. Or does it? Sterling Harper's death did not seem to belong in the same equation as the deaths of her brother and Beryl. But what if it did?

"You told me Miss Harper was out of town the night Beryl was murdered," I said to Marino. "Have you learned anything more about that?"

"Nope."

"Wherever it was she went, do you suppose she drove?" I asked.

"Nope. Only car the Harpers had was the white Rolls, and her brother had it the night of Beryl's death."

"You know that?"

"Checked it out with Culpeper's Tavern," he said. "Harper came in his usual time that night. Drove up just like he always did and left around six-thirty."

* * *

In light of recent events, I doubted anybody thought it the least bit strange when I announced at staff conference the following Monday morning that I was taking annual leave.

The assumption was that my encounter with Jeb Price had stressed me to the point I needed to get away, regroup, bury my head in the sand for a while. I didn't tell anybody where I was going because I didn't know. I just walked out, leaving behind a secretly relieved secretary and an overwhelmed desk.

Returning home, I spent the entire morning on the phone, calling every airline that serviced Richmond's Byrd Airport, the airport most convenient for Sterling Harper.

"Yes, I know there's a twenty percent penalty," I said to the USAir ticket agent. "You misunderstand. I'm not trying to change the ticket. This was weeks ago. I'm trying to find out if she ever got on the flight at all."

"The ticket wasn't for you?"

"No," I said for the third time. "It was issued in *her* name."

"Then she really needs to contact us herself."

"Sterling Harper is dead," I said. "She can't contact you herself."

A startled pause.

"She died suddenly right around the time of a trip she was supposed to go on," I explained. "If you could just check your computer . . ."

This went on. It got to where I could recite the same lines without thinking. USAir had nothing, nor did the computers for Delta, United, American, or Eastern. As far as the agents could tell from their records, Miss Harper had not flown out of Richmond during the last week of October, when Beryl Madison was murdered. Miss Harper hadn't driven, either. I seriously doubted she had taken the bus. That left the train.

An Amtrak agent named John said his computer was down and asked if he could call me back. I hung up as someone rang my doorbell.

It was not quite noon. The day was as tart and crisp as a fall apple. Sunlight painted white rectangles in my living room and winked off the windshield of the unfamiliar silver Mazda sedan parked in my drive. The pasty, blond young man I observed through the peephole was standing back from my front door, head down, the collar of a leather jacket up around his ears. My Ruger was hard and heavy in my hand, and I stuffed it in the pocket of my warm-up jacket as I unfastened the dead bolt. I didn't recognize him until we were face-to-face.

"Dr. Scarpetta?" he asked nervously.

I made no move to let him inside, my right hand in my pocket and firm around the butt of the revolver.

"Please forgive me for appearing on your doorstep like this," he said. "I called your office and was told you're on vacation. I found your name in the book and the line was busy. So I concluded you were home. I, well, I really need to talk to you. May I come in?"

He looked even more innocuous in person than he had looked on the videotape Marino had shown me.

"What is this about?" I asked firmly.

"Beryl Madison, it's about her," he said. "Uh, my name's Al Hunt. I won't take much of your time. I promise."

I backed away from the door and he stepped inside. His face got as white as alabaster when he seated himself on my living room couch and his eyes fixed briefly on the butt of the revolver protruding from my pocket as I settled in a wing chair a safe distance away.

"Uh, you've got a gun?" he said.

"Yes, I do," I answered.

"I don't like them, like guns."

"They're not very likable," I agreed.

"No, ma'am," he said. "My father took me deer hunting once. When I was a boy. He hit a doe. She was crying. The doe, she was crying, lying on her side and crying. I never could shoot anything."

"Did you know Beryl Madison?" I asked.

"The police—The police have talked to me about her," he stammered. "A lieutenant. Marino, Lieutenant Marino. He came by the car wash where I work and talked to me, then asked me down to headquarters. We talked for a long time. She used to bring her car in. That's how I met her."

As he rambled on I couldn't help but wonder what "colors" were radiating from me. Steely blue? Maybe a hint of bright red because I was alarmed and doing my best not to show it? I contemplated ordering him to leave. I considered calling the police. I couldn't believe he was sitting inside my house, and perhaps the sheer audacity on his part and mystification on mine explains why I did nothing at all.

I interrupted him. "Mr. Hunt—"

"Please call me Al."

"Al, then," I said. "Why did you want to see me? If you have information, why aren't you talking to Lieutenant Marino?"

The color rose to his cheeks and he looked uncomfortably down at his hands.

"What I have to say doesn't really belong in the category of police information," he said. "I thought you might understand."

"Why would you think that? You don't know me," I answered.

"You took care of Beryl. As a rule, women are more intuitive, more compassionate than men," he said.

Perhaps it was that simple. Perhaps Hunt was here because he believed I would not humiliate him. He was staring at me now, a wounded, woebegone look in his eyes that was on the verge of becoming panic.

He asked, "Have you ever known something with certainty, Dr. Scarpetta, even though there is absolutely no evidence to support your belief?"

"I'm not clairvoyant, if that's what you're asking," I replied.

"You're being the scientist."

"I *am* a scientist."

"But you've had the feeling," he insisted, his eyes desperate now. "You know very well what I mean, don't you?"

"Yes," I said. "I think I know what you mean, Al."

He seemed relieved and took a deep breath. "I *know* things, Dr. Scarpetta. I know who murdered Beryl."

I didn't react at all.

"I *know* him, know what he thinks, feels, why he did it," he said with emotion. "If I tell you, will you promise to treat what I say with great care, consider it seriously and not— Well, I don't want you running to the police. They wouldn't understand. You see that, don't you?"

"I will very carefully consider what you have to say," I replied.

He leaned forward on the couch, his eyes luminous in

his wan El Greco face. I instinctively moved my right hand closer to my pocket. I could feel the rubber grip of the revolver against the side of my palm.

"The police already don't understand," he said. "They aren't capable of understanding me. Why I left psychology, for example. The police wouldn't understand that. I have a master's degree. And what? I worked as a nurse and now I'm working in a car wash? You don't really think the police are going to understand that, do you?"

I didn't respond.

"When I was a kid I dreamed of being a psychologist, a social worker, maybe even a psychiatrist," he went on. "It all came so naturally to me. It was what I should be, what my talents directed that I should be."

"But you're not," I reminded him. "Why?"

"Because it would have destroyed me," he said, averting his eyes. "It isn't something I have control over, what happens to me. I relate so completely to other people's problems and idiosyncrasies that the person who is me gets lost, suffocates. I didn't realize how dramatic this was until I spent time on a forensic unit. For the criminally insane. Uh, it was part of my research, my research for my thesis." He was getting increasingly distracted. "I'll never forget. Frankie. Frankie was a paranoid schizophrenic. He beat his mother to death with a stick of firewood. I got to know Frankie. I very gently walked him through his life until we reached that winter's afternoon.

"I said to him, 'Frankie, Frankie, what little thing was it? What pushed that button? Do you remember what was going through your mind, through your nerves?'

"He said he was sitting in the chair he always sat in before the fire, watching the flames burn down, when *they* began whispering to him. Whispering terrible, mocking things. When his mother walked in she looked at him the way she always did, but this time he saw it in her eyes. The voices got so loud he couldn't think and next thing he was wet and sticky and she didn't have a face anymore. He came to when the voices were still. I couldn't sleep for many nights after that. Every time I'd close my eyes I'd see Frankie crying, covered with his mother's blood. I understood him. I understood what he'd done. Whoever I talked to, whatever story I heard, it affected me the same way."

I was sitting calmly, my powers of imagination switched off, the scientist, the clinician deliberately donned like a suit of clothes.

I asked him, "Have you ever felt like killing anyone, Al?"

"Everybody's felt that way at some point," he said as our eyes met.

"Everybody? Do you really think so?"

"Yes. Every person has the capacity. Absolutely."

"Who have you felt like killing?" I asked.

"I don't own a gun or anything else, uh, dangerous," he answered. "Because I don't ever want to be vulnerable to an impulse. Once you can envision yourself doing something, once you can relate to the mechanism behind the deed, the door is cracked. It can happen. Virtually every heinous event that occurs in this world was first conceived in thought. We aren't good or bad, one or the other." His voice was trembling. "Even those classified as insane have their own reasons for why they do what they do."

"What was the reason behind what happened to Beryl?" I asked.

My thoughts were precise and clearly stated. And yet I was sick inside as I tried to block the images: the black stains on the walls, the stab wounds clustered over her breast, her books standing primly on the library shelf quietly waiting to be read.

"The person who did this loved her," he said.

"A rather brutal way to show it, don't you think?"

"Love can be brutal," he said.

"Did you love her?"

"We were very much alike."

"In what way?"

"Out of sync." He was studying his hands again. "Alone and sensitive and misunderstood. And this served to make her distant, very guarded and unapproachable. I know nothing about her—I'm saying, no one's ever told me anything about her. But I sensed the being inside her. I intuited that she was very aware of who she was, of her worth. But she was deeply angered by the price she paid for being different. She was wounded. I don't know by what. Something had hurt her. This made me care for her. I wanted to reach out because I knew I would have understood her."

"Why didn't you reach out to her?" I asked.

"The circumstances weren't right. Maybe if I'd met her somewhere else," he replied.

"Tell me about the person who did this to her, Al," I said. "Would he have reached out to her had the circumstances ever been right?"

"No."

"No?"

"The circumstances would never have been right because he is inadequate and knows it," Hunt said.

His sudden transformation was disconcerting. Now he

was the psychologist. His voice was calmer. He was concentrating very hard, tightly clasping his hands in his lap.

He was saying, "He has a very low opinion of himself and is unable to express feelings in a constructive manner. Attraction turns to obsession, love becomes pathological. When he loves, he has to possess because he feels so insecure and unworthy, is so easily threatened. When his secret love is not returned, he becomes increasingly obsessed. He becomes so fixated his ability to react and function becomes limited. It's like Frankie hearing the voices. Something else drives him. He no longer has control."

"Is he intelligent?" I asked.

"Reasonably so."

"What about education?"

"His problems are such that he isn't able to function in the capacity he is intellectually capable of."

"Why her?" I asked him. "Why did he select Beryl Madison?"

"She has freedom, fame, he doesn't have," Hunt replied, his eyes glazed. "He thinks he's attracted to her, but it's more than that. He wants to possess those qualities he lacks. He wants to possess her. In a sense, he wants to *be* her."

"Then you're saying he knew Beryl was a writer?" I asked.

"There is very little you can keep from him. One way or another, he would have found out she's a writer. He would know so much about her that when she began to pick up on it, she would have felt terribly violated and profoundly afraid."

"Tell me about that night," I said. "What happened the night she died, Al?"

"I know only what I've read in the papers."

"What have you pieced together from reading what has been in the papers?" I asked.

"She was home," he said, staring off. "And it was getting late in the evening when he appeared at her door. Most likely she let him in. At some point before midnight he left her house and the burglar alarm went off. She was stabbed to death. There was an implication of sexual assault. That's as much as I've read."

"Do you have any theories as to what might have gone on?" I asked blandly. "Speculations that go above and beyond what you've read?"

He leaned forward in the chair, his demeanor dramatically changing again. His eyes got hot with emotion. His lower lip began to quiver.

"I see scenes in my mind," he said.

"Such as?"

"Things I wouldn't want to tell the police."

"I'm not the police," I said.

"They wouldn't understand," he said. "These things I see and feel without having any reason to know them. It's like Frankie." He blinked back tears. "It's like the others. I could see what happened and understand it, even though I wasn't always given the details. But you don't always need the details. Nor are you likely to get them in most instances. You know why that is, don't you?"

"I'm not sure . . ."

"Because the Frankies in the world don't know the details, either! It's like a bad accident you can't remember. The awareness returns like waking up from a bad dream and you find yourself staring at the wreckage. The mother who no longer has a face. Or the Beryl who is bloody and dead. The Frankies *wake up* when they're running or a cop they don't remember calling pulls up in front of the house."

"Are you telling me Beryl's killer doesn't remember exactly what he did?" I asked carefully.

He nodded.

"You're quite sure of that?"

"Your most skilled psychiatrist could question him for a million years and there would never be an accurate replay," Hunt said. "The truth will never be known. It has to be re-created and, to an extent, inferred."

"Which is what you've done. Re-created and inferred." I said.

He wet his bottom lip, his breathing tremulous. "Do you want me to tell you what I see?"

"Yes," I answered.

"Much time had elapsed since his first contact with her," he began. "But she had no awareness of him as a person, though she may have seen him somewhere in the past—seen him without having any idea. His frustration, his obsessiveness had driven him to her doorstep. Something kicked that off, made it an overwhelming need to confront her."

"What?" I asked. "What kicked it off?"

"I don't know."

"What was he feeling when he decided to come after her?"

Hunt closed his eyes and said, "Anger. Anger because he couldn't make things work the way he wanted."

"Anger because he couldn't have a relationship with Beryl?" I asked.

Eyes still shut, Hunt slowly shook his head from side to side and said, "No. Maybe that's what was closest to the surface. But the root was much deeper. Anger because nothing worked the way he wanted it to in the beginning."

"When he was a child?" I asked.

"Yes."

"Was he abused?"

"He was emotionally," Hunt said.

"By whom?"

Eyes still shut, he answered, "His mother. When he killed Beryl he killed his mother."

"Do you study forensic psychiatry books, Al? Do you read about these things?" I asked.

He opened his eyes and stared at me as if he had not heard what I had said.

He went on, emotionally, "You have to appreciate how many times he had imagined the moment. It wasn't impulsive in the sense he simply rushed to her house without premeditation. The timing may have been impulsive, but his method had been planned with meticulous detail. He absolutely couldn't afford for her to be alarmed and refuse him entrance into her house. She'd call the police, give them a description. And even if he wasn't apprehended, his mask had been ripped off and he'd never be able to come near her again. He had created a scheme that was guaranteed not to fail, something that would not excite her suspicions. When he appeared at her door that night, he inspired trust. And she let him in."

In my mind I saw the man in Beryl's foyer, but I could not see his face or the color of his hair, just an indistinct figure and the glinting of the long steel blade as he introduced himself with the weapon he used to murder her.

"This is when it deteriorated for him," Hunt continued. "He won't remember what happened next. Her panic, her terror, are not pleasant for him. He had not completely thought out this part of his ritual. When she ran, tried to get away from him, when he saw the panic in her eyes, he fully realized her rejection of him. He realized the horrible thing he was doing, and his contempt for himself was acted out as contempt for her. Rage. He quickly lost control of her while he was reduced to the lowest form. A killer. A destroyer. A mindless savage tearing and cutting and inflicting pain. Her screams, her blood were awful for him. And the more he razed and defaced this temple where he had worshiped for so long, the more he couldn't bear the sight of it."

He looked at me and there was nobody home behind his eyes. His face was drained of all emotion when he asked, "Can you relate to this, Dr. Scarpetta?"

"I'm listening" was all I said.

"He is in all of us," he said.

"Does he feel remorse, Al?"

"He is beyond that," he said. "I don't think he feels good about what he did or even completely realizes what he did. He was left with confused emotions. In his mind he will not let her die. He wonders about her, relives his contacts with her, and fantasizes that his relationship with her was the deepest, most profound of all because she was thinking about him when she breathed her last and this is the ultimate closeness to another human being. In his fantasies he imagines she continues to think about him after death. But the rational part of him is unsatisfied and frustrated. No one can completely belong to another person, and this is what he begins to discover."

"What do you mean?" I asked.

"His deed could not possibly produce the desired effect," Hunt answered. "He is unsure of the closeness—just as he was never sure of his mother's closeness. The distrust again. And there are other people now who have a more legitimate reason to have a relationship with Beryl than he does."

"Like who?"

"The police." His eyes focused on me. "And you."

"Because we're investigating her murder?" I asked, a chill running up my spine.

"Yes."

"Because she has become a preoccupation for us, and our relationship with her is more public than his?" I said.

"Yes."

"Where does this lead?" I then asked.

"Cary Harper is dead."

"He killed Harper?"

"Yes."

"Why?" I nervously lit a cigarette.

"What he did to Beryl was a love thing," Hunt responded. "What he did to Harper was a hate thing. He is into hate things now. Anybody connected to Beryl is in danger. And this is what I wanted to tell Lieutenant Marino, the police. But I knew it wouldn't do any good. He— They would just think I have a loose screw."

"Who is he?" I asked. "Who killed Beryl?"

Al Hunt moved to the edge of the couch and rubbed his face in his hands. When he looked up, his cheeks were splotched red.

"Jim Jim," he whispered.

"Jim Jim?" I asked, mystified.

"I don't know." His voice broke. "I keep hearing that name in my head, hearing it and hearing it. . . ."

I sat very still.

"It was so long ago I was at Valhalla Hospital," he said.

"The forensic unit?" I broke out. "Was this Jim Jim a patient while you were there?"

"I'm not sure." The emotions were gathering in his eyes like a storm. "I hear his name and I see that place. My thoughts drift back to its dark memories. Like I'm being sucked down a drain. It was so long ago. So much blacked out now. Jim Jim. Jim Jim. Like a train chugging. The sound won't stop. I have headaches because of the sound."

"When was this?" I demanded.

"Ten years ago," he cried.

Hunt couldn't have been working on a master's thesis then, I realized. He would have been only in his late teens.

"Al," I said, "you weren't doing research in the forensic unit. You were a patient there, weren't you?"

He covered his face with his hands and wept. When he finally was in sufficient control, he refused to talk anymore. Obviously deeply distressed, he mumbled he was late for an appointment and practically ran out the door. My heart was racing and wouldn't slow down. I fixed myself a cup of coffee and paced the kitchen, trying to figure out what to do next. I jumped when the telephone rang.

"Kay Scarpetta, please."

"Speaking."

"This is John with Amtrak. I've finally got your information, ma'am. Let's see . . . Sterling Harper had a round-trip ticket on The Virginian for October twenty-seventh, returning on the thirty-first. According to my records, she was on the train, or at least somebody with her tickets was. You want the times?"

"Yes, please," I said, and I wrote them down. "What stations?"

He answered, "Originating in Fredericksburg, destination Baltimore."

I tried to call Marino. He was on the street. It was evening when he returned my call with news of his own.

"Do you want me to come?" I asked, stunned.

"Don't see no point in it," Marino's voice came over the line. "No question what he did. He wrote a note and pinned it to his undershorts. Said he was sorry, he couldn't take it no more. That's pretty much it. Nothing suspicious about the scene. We're about to clear on out. And Doc Coleman's here," he added, referring to one of my local medical examiners.

Shortly after Al Hunt left my house he drove to his own, a brick colonial in Ginter Park where he lived with his parents. He took a pad of paper and a pen from his father's study. He descended the stairs leading to the basement and removed his narrow black-leather belt. He left his shoes and trousers on the floor. When his mother went down later to put in a load of wash, she found her only son hanging from a pipe inside the laundry room.

11

A freezing rain began to fall past midnight, and by morning the world was glass. I stayed in my house Saturday, my conversation with Al Hunt replaying in my mind, startling the solitude of my private thoughts like the thawing ice suddenly crackling to the earth beyond my window. I felt guilty. Like every other mortal who has ever been touched by suicide, I had the fallacious belief that I could have done something to stop it.

Numbly, I added him to the list. Four people were dead. Two deaths were blatant, vicious homicides, two of them were not, and yet all of the cases were somehow connected. Perhaps connected by a bright orange thread. Saturday and Sunday I worked in my home office because my downtown office would only remind me that I no longer felt in charge—for that matter, I no longer felt needed. The work went on without me. People reached out to me and then were dead. Respected colleagues like the attorney general asked for answers, and I did not have anything to offer.

I fought back in the only feeble way I knew how. I stayed in front of my home computer typing out notes about the cases and poring over reference books. And I made a lot of phone calls.

I did not see Marino again until we met at the Amtrak station on Staples Mill Road Monday morning. We passed between two waiting trains, the dark, wintry air warmed by engines and smelling of oil. We found seats in the back of our train and resumed a conversation we had started inside the station.

"Dr. Masterson wasn't exactly chatty," I said about Hunt's psychiatrist as I carefully set down the shopping bag I was carrying. "But I'm suspicious he remembers Hunt a lot more clearly than he's letting on." Why was it I always got a seat with a footrest that didn't work?

Marino yawned voraciously as he pulled down his, which worked just fine. He didn't offer to exchange seats with me. If he had, I would have accepted.

He answered, "So Hunt would've been eighteen, nineteen when he was in the bin."

"Yes. He was treated for severe depression," I said.

"Yeah, well, I guess so."

"And what's that supposed to mean?" I asked.

"His type's always depressed."

"What is his *type*, Marino?"

"Let's just say the word *fag* went through my mind more'n once when I talked to him," he said.

The word *fag* went through Marino's mind more than once when he talked to anybody who was different.

The train glided forward, silently, like a boat from a pier.

"I wish you'd taped that conversation," Marino went on, yawning again.

"With Dr. Masterson?"

"No, the one with Hunt. When he dropped by your crib," he said.

"It's moot and it doesn't matter," I replied uncomfortably.

"I don't know. Seems to me like the squirrel knew an awful lot. Wish like hell he'd hung around a little longer, so to speak."

What Hunt had said in my living room would have been significant were he still alive and not armored in alibis. The police had taken apart his parents' house. Nothing was found that might have linked Hunt to the murders of Beryl Madison and Cary Harper. More to the point, Hunt was eating dinner with his parents at their country club the night of Beryl's death, and he was with his parents at the opera when Harper was murdered. The stories had been checked out. Hunt's parents were telling the truth.

We bumped, swayed, and rumbled northbound, the train whistle hooting balefully.

"The stuff with Beryl pushed him over the edge," Marino was saying. "You want my opinion, he related to her killer to the point he freaked, took himself out of circulation, kissed off before he cracked."

"I think it's more likely Beryl reopened the old wound," I answered. "It reminded him of his inability to have relationships."

"Sounds like he and the killer are cut from the same cloth. Both of them unable to relate to women. Both of them losers."

"Hunt wasn't violent."

"Maybe he was leaning that way and couldn't live with it," Marino said.

"We don't know who killed Beryl and Harper," I reminded him. "We don't know if it was someone like Hunt. We don't know that at all, and we still have no idea about the motive. The killer could just as easily be someone like Jeb Price. Or someone called Jim Jim."

"Jim Jim my ass," he said snidely.

"I don't think we should dismiss anything at this point, Marino."

"Be my guest. You run across a Jim Jim who graduated from Valhalla Hospital and now's a part-time terrorist carrying around orange acrylic fibers on his person, give me a buzz." Settling down in his seat and shutting his eyes, he mumbled, "I need a vacation."

"So do I," I said. "I need a vacation from you."

Last night Benton Wesley had called to talk about Hunt, and I mentioned where I was going and why. He was adamant that it was unwise for me to go alone, visions of terrorists, Uzis, and Glasers dancing in his head. He wanted Marino with me, and I might not have minded had it not turned out to be such an ordeal. There were no other seats available on the six-thirty-five morning train, so Marino had booked both of us on the one leaving at four-forty-eight A.M. I ventured into my downtown office at three A.M. to pick up the Styrofoam box now inside my shopping bag. I was feeling physically punished, my sleep deficit climbing out of sight. The Jeb Prices of the world wouldn't need to do me in. My guardian angel Marino would spare them the trouble.

Other passengers were dozing, their overhead lamps switched off. Soon we were creaking slowly through the middle of Ashland and I wondered about the people living in the prim white frame homes facing the tracks. Windows were dark, bare flagpoles greeting us with stark salutes from porches. We passed sleepy storefronts—a barbershop, a stationery store, a bank—then picked up speed as we curved around the campus of Randolph-Macon College with its Georgian buildings and its frosted athletic field peopled at this early moonlit hour by a row of varicolored football sleds. Beyond the town were woods and raw red clay banks. I was leaning back in the seat, entranced by the rhythm of the train. The farther we got from Richmond the more I relaxed, and quite without intending to I drifted off to sleep.

I did not dream but was unconscious for an hour, and when I opened my eyes the dawn was blue beyond the glass and we were passing over Quantico Creek. The water was polished pewter catching light in laps and ruffles, and there were boats out. I thought of Mark. I thought of our night in New York and of times long past. I had not heard a word from him since the last cryptic message on my answering machine. I wondered what he was doing, and yet I was afraid to know.

Marino sat up, squinting groggily at me. It was time for breakfast and cigarettes, not necessarily in that order.

The dining car was half filled with semicomatose clientele who could have been sitting in any bus station in America and looked very much at home. A young man dozed to the beat of whatever was playing inside the headphones he wore. A tired woman held a squirming baby. An older couple was playing cards. We found an empty table in a corner, and I lit up while Marino went to see about food. The only positive thing I could say about the prepackaged ham and egg sandwich he came back with was that it was hot. The coffee wasn't bad.

He tore open cellophane with his teeth and eyed the shopping bag I had placed next to me on the seat. Inside it was the Styrofoam box containing samples of Sterling Harper's liver, tubes of her blood, and her gastric contents, packed in dry ice.

"How long before it thaws?" he asked.

"We'll get there in plenty of time, providing we don't make any detours," I replied.

"Speaking of plenty of time, that's exactly what we got on our hands. You mind going over it again, the bit about this cough syrup shit? I was half asleep when you were rattling on about it last night."

"Yes, half asleep just like you are this morning."

"Don't you ever get tired?"

"I'm so tired, Marino, I'm not sure I'm going to live."

"Well, you better live. I sure as hell ain't delivering those pieces an' parts by myself," he said, reaching for his coffee.

I explained with the deliberation of a taped lecture. "The active ingredient in the cough suppressant we found in Miss Harper's bathroom is dextromethorphan, an analogue of codeine. Dextromethorphan is benign unless you ingest a tremendous dose. It's the d-isomer of a compound, the name of which won't mean anything to you—"

"Oh, yeah? How do you know it won't mean nothing to me?"

"Three-methoxy-N-methylmorphinan."

"You're right. Don't mean a damn thing to me."

I went on, "There's another drug which is the l-isomer of this same compound that dextromethorphan is the d-isomer of. The l-isomer compound is levomethorphan, a potent narcotic about five times stronger than morphine. And the only difference between the two drugs as far as detection goes is that, when viewed through an optical rotatory device called a polarimeter, dextromethorphan rotates light to the right, and levomethorphan rotates light to the left."

"In other words, without this contraption you can't tell the difference between the two drugs," Marino concluded.

"Not in tox tests routinely done," I answered. "Levomethorphan comes up as dextromethorphan because the compounds are the same. The only discernible difference is they bend light in opposite directions, just as d-sucrose and l-sucrose bend light in opposite directions even though they're both structurally the same disaccharide. D-sucrose is table sugar. L-sucrose has no nutritional value to humans."

"I'm not sure I get it," Marino said, rubbing his eyes. "How can compounds be the same but different?"

"Think of dextromethorphan and levomethorphan as identical twins," I said. "They're not the same people, so to speak, but they *look* the same—except one is right-handed, the other left-handed. One is benign, the other strong enough to kill. Does that help?"

"Yeah, I guess. So how much of this levomethorphan stuff would it take for Miss Harper to snuff herself?"

"Thirty milligrams would probably do it. Fifteen two-milligram tablets, in other words," I answered.

"What then, saying she did?"

"She would very quickly slip into a deep narcosis and die."

"You think she would've known about this isomer stuff?"

"She might have," I replied. "We know she had cancer, and we also suspect she wanted to disguise her suicide, perhaps explaining the melted plastic in the fireplace and the ashes of whatever else it was she burned right before she died. It's possible she deliberately left the bottle of cough syrup out to throw us off track. After seeing that, I wasn't surprised when dextromethorphan came up in her tox."

Miss Harper had no living relatives, very few friends—if any—and she didn't strike me as someone who traveled very often. After discovering she had recently made a trip to Baltimore, the first thing that came to mind was Johns Hopkins, which has one of the finest oncology clinics in the world. A couple of quick calls confirmed that Miss Harper had made periodic visits to Hopkins for blood and bone marrow workups, a routine relating to a disease she obviously had been quite secretive about. When I was informed of her medication, the pieces suddenly snapped together in my mind. The labs in my building did not have a polarimeter or any way to test for levomethorphan. Dr. Ismail at Hopkins had promised to assist if I could supply him with the necessary samples.

It was not quite seven now, and we were on the outer fringes of D.C. Woods and swamps streamed past until the city was suddenly there, the Jefferson Memorial flashing white through a break in the trees. Tall office buildings were so close I could see plants and lampshades through spotless windows before the train plunged underground like a mole and burrowed blindly beneath the Mall.

We found Dr. Ismail inside the pharmacology lab of the oncology clinic. Opening the shopping bag, I set the small Styrofoam box on his desk.

"Are these the samples we talked about?" he asked with a smile.

"Yes," I replied. "They should still be frozen. We came here straight from the train station."

"If the concentrations are good, I can have an answer for you in a day or so," he said.

"What exactly will you do with the stuff?" Marino inquired as he looked around the lab, which looked like every lab I have ever seen.

"It's very simple, really," Dr. Ismail replied patiently. "First I will make an extract of the gastric sample. That will be the longest, most painstaking part of the test. When that is done I place the extract into the polarimeter, which looks very much like a telescope. But it has rotatory lenses. I look through the eyepiece and rotate the lenses to the left and right. If the drug in question is dextromethorphan, then it will bend light to the right, meaning the light in my field will get brighter as I rotate the lenses to the right. For levomethorphan the opposite is true."

He went on to explain that levomethorphan is a very effective pain reliever prescribed almost exclusively for people terminally ill with cancer. Because the drug had been developed here, he kept a list of all Hopkins patients who were on it. The purpose was to establish the therapeutic range. The bonus for us was he had a record of Miss Harper's treatments.

"She would come in every two months for her blood and bone marrow workups and on each visit was given a supply, about two hundred fifty two-milligram tablets," Dr. Ismail was saying as he smoothed open the pages of a thick monitoring book. "Let's see . . . Her last visit was October twenty-eighth. She should have had at least seventy-five, if not a hundred tablets left."

"We didn't find them," I said.

"A shame." He lifted dark, saddened eyes. "She was doing so well. A very lovely woman. I was always pleased to see her and her daughter."

After a moment of startled silence, I asked, "Her daughter?"

"I assume so. A young woman. Blond . . ."

Marino cut in, "She with Miss Harper last time, the last weekend in October?"

Dr. Ismail frowned and said, "No. I don't recall seeing her then. Miss Harper was alone."

"How many years had Miss Harper been coming here?" I asked.

"I'll have to pull her chart. But I know it has been several. At least two years."

"Was her daughter, the young blond woman, always with her?" I asked.

"Not so often in the early days," he answered. "But during the past year she was with Miss Harper on every visit, except for this last one in October, and possibly the one before that. I was impressed. Being so ill, well, it is nice when one has the support of family."

"Where did Miss Harper stay when she was here?" Marino's jaw muscles were flexing again.

"Most of the patients stay in hotels located nearby. But Miss Harper was fond of the harbor," Dr. Ismail said.

My reactions were slowed by tension and lack of sleep.

"You don't know what hotel?" Marino persisted.

"No. I have no idea . . ."

Suddenly I began seeing images of the fragmented typed words on filmy white ash.

I interrupted both of them. "May I see your telephone directory, please?"

Fifteen minutes later Marino and I were standing out on the street looking for a cab. The sun was bright, but it was quite cold.

"Damn," he said again. "I hope you're right."

"We'll find out soon enough," I said tensely.

In the business listings of the telephone directory was a hotel called Harbor Court. *bor Co, bor C.* I kept seeing the miniature black letters on the wisps of burned paper. The hotel was one of the most luxurious in the city, and it was directly across the street from Harbor Place.

"I tell you what I can't figure," Marino went on as another taxi passed us by. "Why all the bother? So Miss Harper kills herself, right? Why go to all the trouble to do it in such a mysterious way? Make any sense to you?"

"She was a proud woman. Suicide was probably a shameful act to her. She may not have wanted anyone to figure it out, and she may have chosen to take her life while I was inside her house."

"Why?"

"Perhaps because she didn't want her body found a week later." Traffic was terrible, and I was beginning to wonder if we were going to have to walk to the harbor.

"And you really think she knew about this isomer business?"

"I think she did," I said.

"How come?"

"Because she would wish for death with dignity, Marino. It's possible she'd premeditated suicide for quite a long time, in the event her leukemia became acute and she didn't want to suffer or make others suffer any longer. Levomethorphan was a perfect choice. In most instances, it never would have been detected—providing a cough suppressant containing dextromethorphan was found inside her house."

"No shit?" he marveled as a taxi, thank God, pulled out of traffic and headed our way. "I'm impressed. You know, I really am."

"It's tragic."

"I don't know." He peeled open a stick of gum and began to chew with vigor. "Me, I wouldn't want to be tied down to no hospital bed with tubes in my nose. Maybe I would've thought like she did."

"She didn't kill herself because of her cancer."

"I know," he said as we ventured off the curb. "But it's related. Gotta be. She's not long for this world anyway. Then Beryl gets whacked. Next, her brother gets whacked." He shrugged. "Why hang around?"

We got into the taxi and I gave the driver the address. For ten minutes we rode in silence. Then the taxi crept almost to a stop and threaded through a narrow arch leading into a brick courtyard bright with beds of ornamental cabbages and small trees. A doorman dressed in tails and a top hat was immediately at my elbow, and I found myself escorted inside a splendid light-filled lobby of rose and cream. Everything was new and clean and highly polished, with fresh flowers arranged on fine furniture, and crisp members of the hotel staff alighting where needed but not obtrusive.

We were shown to a well-appointed office, where the well-dressed manager was talking on the telephone. T. M. Bland, according to the brass nameplate on his desk, glanced up at us and quickly completed his call. Marino wasted no time telling him what we wanted.

"The list of our guests is confidential," Mr. Bland replied, smiling benignly.

Marino helped himself to a leather chair and lit a cigarette, despite the THANK YOU FOR NOT SMOKING sign in plain view on the wall, then reached for his wallet and flashed his badge.

"Name's Pete Marino," he said laconically. "Richmond P.D., Homicide. This here's Dr. Kay Scarpetta, Chief Medical Examiner of Virginia. We sure as hell understand your insistence on confidentiality, and respect your hotel for that, Mr. Bland. But you see, Sterling Harper's dead. Her brother Cary Harper's dead. And Beryl Madison's dead, too. Cary Harper and Beryl was murdered. We're not too sure yet what happened to Miss Harper. That's what we're here for."

"I read the newspapers, Detective Marino," Mr. Bland said, his composure beginning to waver. "Certainly the hotel will cooperate with the authorities in any way possible."

"Then you're telling me they was guests here," Marino said.

"Cary Harper was never a guest here."

"But his sister and Beryl Madison was."

"That is correct," Mr. Bland said.

"How often, and when was the last time?"

"I'll have to pull Miss Harper's account," Mr. Bland answered. "Will you please excuse me for a moment?"

He left us for no more than fifteen minutes, and when he returned he handed us a computer printout.

"As you can see," he said, reseating himself, "Miss Harper and Beryl Madison stayed with us six times during the past year and a half."

"Approximately every two months," I thought out loud, scanning the dates on the printout, "except for the last week in August and the last few days of October. Then it appears Miss Harper stayed here alone."

He nodded.

"What was the purpose of their visits?" Marino asked.

"Business, possibly. Shopping. Simply relaxation. I really don't know. It isn't the practice of the hotel to monitor our guests."

"And it ain't my practice to care about what your guests is up to unless they turn up dead," Marino said. "Tell me what you observed when the two ladies was here."

Mr. Bland's smile disappeared, and he nervously plucked a gold ballpoint pen off a notepad and then seemed at a loss as to what purpose the action served. Tucking the pen in the breast pocket of his starched pink shirt, he cleared his throat.

"I can only tell you what I noted," he said.

"Please do," Marino said.

"The two women made separate travel arrangements. Usually Miss Harper checked in the night before Beryl Madison did, and they often didn't leave at the same time, or, uh, together."

"What do you mean, they didn't *leave* at the same time?"

"I mean that they may have checked out on the same day, but not necessarily at the same time, and they didn't necessarily choose the same means of transportation. Not in the same cab, for example."

"Were they both headed for the train station?" I inquired.

"It seems to me Miss Madison frequently took the limo to the airport," Mr. Bland replied. "But yes. I think Miss Harper's habit was to take the train."

"What about their accommodations?" I asked, studying the printout.

"Yeah," Marino butted in. "It don't say nothing about their room on this thing." He tapped the printout with his index finger. "They stay in a double or a single? You know, one bed or two?"

His cheeks coloring at the implication, Mr. Bland replied, "They always stayed in a double room facing the water. They were guests of the hotel, Detective Marino, if you really need to know that detail, and certainly it isn't for publication."

"Hey, what do I look like, a damn reporter?"

"You're saying they stayed in your hotel free of charge?" I asked, confused.

"Yes, ma'am."

"You mind explaining that?" Marino said.

"It was the desire of Joseph McTigue," Mr. Bland answered.

"I beg your pardon?" I leaned forward and stared hard at him. "The contractor from Richmond? You're referring to *that* Joseph McTigue?"

"The late Mr. McTigue was one of the developers of much of the waterfront. His holdings include substantial interests in this hotel," Mr. Bland replied. "It was his request that we accommodate Miss Harper in any way possible, and we continued to honor this after his death."

Minutes later I was slipping a dollar bill to the doorman and Marino and I were getting into a cab.

"You mind telling me who the hell Joseph McTigue is?" Marino asked as we took off into traffic. "I got a feeling you know."

"I visited his wife in Richmond. At Chamberlayne Gardens. I told you about it."

"Ho-ly shit."

"Yes, it's rather thrown me for a loop, too," I agreed.

"You want to tell me what the hell you make of that?"

I didn't know, but I was beginning to formulate a suspicion about it.

"Sounds pretty weird to me," he went on. "For starters, the bit about Miss Harper's taking the train while Beryl usually flew, when both of them was heading in the same direction."

"It's not so strange," I said. "Certainly they couldn't travel together, Marino. Miss Harper, Beryl, couldn't risk that. They weren't supposed to have anything to do with each other, remember? If Cary Harper routinely picked up his sister at the train station, there wouldn't be a way for Beryl to suddenly disappear if she and Miss Harper were traveling together." I paused as it came to mind. "It may also be that Miss Harper was assisting with Beryl's book, giving her background information about the Harper family."

Marino was staring out his side window.

He said, "You want my opinion, I think the two ladies was closet lesbians."

I saw the driver's curious eyes in the rearview mirror.

"I think they loved each other," I said simply.

"So maybe the two of them was having a little affair, getting together every two months here in Baltimore where nobody knew 'em or paid 'em any mind.

"You know," Marino persisted, "maybe that's why Beryl decided to run to Key West. She was a fag-ette, would've felt at home there."

"Your homophobia really is rabid, not to mention tiresome, Marino. You should be careful. People might wonder about *you*."

"Yeah, right," he said, not the least bit amused.

I was silent.

He went on, "Point is, maybe Beryl found herself a little girlfriend while she was down there."

"Maybe you ought to check into that."

"No way, José. No way I'm getting bit by no goddamn mosquito in the AIDS capital of America. And talking to a bunch of queers ain't my idea of a good time."

"Have you gotten the Florida police to check out her contacts down there?" I asked seriously.

"A couple of them said they poked around. Talk about a sorry assignment. They was afraid to eat anything, drink the water. One of the queerbaits from the restaurant she wrote about in her letters is dying of AIDS even as we speak. The cops had to wear gloves the entire time."

"During the interviews?"

"Oh, yeah. Surgical masks, too—at least when they was talking to the guy dying. Didn't come up with nothing helpful, none of the information worth a damn."

"I guess not," I commented. "You treat people like lepers and they're not likely to open up to you."

"You ask me, they ought to saw off that part of Florida and send it drifting out to sea."

"Well, fortunately," I said, "nobody asked you."

There were numerous messages waiting on my answering machine when I returned home midevening.

I hoped one would be from Mark. I sat on the edge of my bed drinking a glass of wine and half-heartedly listening to the voices drifting out of the machine.

Bertha, my housekeeper, had the flu and announced she would not be able to come the next day. The attorney general wanted to meet me for breakfast tomorrow morning and went on to report that Beryl Madison's estate was suing over the missing manuscript. Three reporters had called demanding comment, and my mother wanted to know if I would prefer turkey or ham for Christmas—her not-so-subtle way of finding out if she could count on me for at least one holiday this year.

I did not recognize the breathy voice that followed.

". . . You have such pretty blond hair. Is it real or do you bleach it, Kay?"

I rewound the tape. I frantically opened the drawer of my bedside table.

". . . Is it real or do you bleach it, Kay? I left a little gift for you on your back porch."

Stunned and with Ruger in hand, I rewound the tape one more time. The voice was almost a whisper, very quiet and deliberate. A white male. I could determine no accent, sense no emotion in the tone. The sound of my feet on the stairs unnerved me, and I turned on the lights in each room I passed through. The back porch was off the kitchen, and my heart was pounding as I stepped to one side of the picture window overlooking the bird feeder and barely parted the curtains, the revolver held high, barrel pointed at the ceiling.

Light seeped from the porch, pushing back the darkness from the lawn and etching the shapes of trees in the wooded blackness at the edge of my property. The brick stoop was bare. I saw nothing on it or the steps. I curled my fingers around the doorknob and stood very still, my heart hammering as I unfastened the dead bolt.

A scraping against the wooden exterior of the door was barely perceptible as it opened, and when I saw what was looped over the outer knob I slammed the door so hard the windows shook.

Marino sounded as if I had gotten him out of bed.

"Get here now!" I exclaimed into the phone, my voice an octave higher than usual.

"Stay put," he said firmly. "Don't open the door for nobody until I get there. You got that? I'm on my way."

Four cruisers lined the street in front of my house, and in the darkness officers probed the woods and shrubbery with long fingers of light.

"The K-nine unit's on the way," Marino said, setting his portable radio upright on my kitchen table. "Seriously doubt the drone hung around, but we'll make damn sure he didn't before we book on out of here."

It was the first time I had ever seen Marino in jeans, and he might have looked casually stylish were it not for the pair of white athletic socks and penny loafers, and the gray sweatshirt one size too small. The smell of fresh coffee filled the kitchen. I was percolating a pot big enough to accommodate half the neighborhood. My eyes were darting around, looking for things to do.

"Tell it to me again real slow," Marino said as he lit a cigarette.

"I was playing back the messages on my answering machine," I repeated. "When I got to the last one it was this voice, a white male, young. You'll have to hear it for yourself. He said something about my hair, wanting to know whether I bleach it." Marino's eyes annoyingly shifted to my roots. "Then he said he'd left a present on my back porch. I came down here, looked out the window and didn't see anything. I don't know what I was expecting. I don't know. Something awful in a box, gift wrapped. When I opened the door, I heard something scraping against the wood. It was looped over the outer knob."

Inside a plastic evidence envelope in the center of the table was an unusual gold medallion attached to a thick gold chain.

"You're sure it's what Harper was wearing at the tavern?" I asked again.

"Oh, yeah," Marino replied, his face tight. "No question about it. No question where the thing's been all this time either. The squirrel took it from Harper's body and now you're getting an early Christmas present. Looks like our friend's gotten sweet on you."

"Please," I said impatiently.

"Hey. I'm taking it serious, okay?" He wasn't smiling as he slid the envelope closer and examined the necklace through the plastic. "You notice the clasp's bent, so's the little ring at the end. Looks to me like maybe it got broke when he yanked it off Harper's neck. Then he maybe fixes it with pliers. He's probably been wearin' it. Shit." He tapped an ash. "Find any injury on Harper's neck from the chain?"

"There wasn't much of his neck left," I said dully.

"Ever seen a medallion like this before?"

"No."

It looked like a coat of arms in eighteen-karat gold, but there was nothing engraved on it except the date 1906 on the back.

"Based on the four jeweler's marks stamped on the back, I think its origin is English," I said. "The marks are a universal code indicating when the medallion was made, where, and by whom. A jeweler could interpret them. I know it's not Italian—"

"Doc—"

"It would have a seven-fifty stamped on the back for eighteen-karat gold, five hundred for the equivalent of fourteen-karat—"

"Doc . . ."

"I have a jeweler consultant at Schwarzschild's—"

"Hey," Marino said loudly. "It don't matter, all right?"

I was prattling on like a hysterical old woman.

"A friggin' family tree of everybody who ever owned this necklace ain't going to tell us the most important thing—the name of the squirrel who hung it on your door." His eyes softened a little and he lowered his voice. "What you got to drink in this crib? Brandy. You got any brandy?"

"You're on the job."

"Not for me," he said, laughing. "For you. Go pour yourself this much." Touching his thumb to the middle knuckle of his index finger, he marked off two inches. "Then we'll talk."

I went to the bar and returned with a small snifter. The brandy burned going down and instantly began to spread warmth through my blood. I stopped shivering inside. I stopped shaking. Marino eyed me curiously. His attentiveness began to make me conscious of many things. I was wearing the same rumpled suit I had worn on the train back from Baltimore. My pantyhose were biting into my waist and bagging around my knees. I was aware of a maddening compulsion to wash my face and brush my teeth. My scalp itched. I was certain I looked awful.

"This guy ain't into empty threats," Marino said quietly as I sipped.

"He's probably just jerking me around because I'm involved in the case. Taunting. It's not unusual for psychopaths to taunt investigators or even send them souvenirs." I didn't really believe it. Certainly Marino didn't.

"I'm going to keep a unit or two staked out. We'll watch your house," he said. "And I got a couple rules for you. Follow them to the letter. No fooling around." He met my eyes. "For starters, whatever your normal routines are, I want you to scramble them up as much as possible. If you usually go to the grocery store on Friday afternoon, go on Wednesday next time and pick a different store. Don't ever set foot outside your house or car without looking around. You see anything that catches your eye, like a strange car parked on the street or evidence anybody's been on your property, you haul ass out of there or keep yourself locked up tight in here and call the police. When you walk inside your house, if you sense anything—I mean if you so much as get a creepy feeling—get out of here, find a phone and call the police, ask an officer to accompany you inside to make sure everything's okay."

"I've got a burglar alarm," I said.

"So did Beryl."

"She let the bastard in."

"You don't let nobody in you're not sure about."

"What's he going to do, bypass my alarm system?" I persisted.

"Anything's possible."

I remembered Wesley saying that.

"No leaving your office after dark or when nobody else is around. The same applies to your coming in. If you usually come in when it's still pretty dark, the parking lot empty, start coming in a little later. Keep your answering machine on. Tape everything. You get another call, get hold of me immediately. A couple more and we'll put a trap on your line—"

"Like you did with Beryl?" I was beginning to get angry.

He didn't respond.

"What, Marino? Will my rights be honored in the breach, too? When it's too damn late to do me any damn good?"

"You want me to sleep on your couch tonight?" he asked calmly.

Facing the morning was hard enough. I envisioned Marino in boxer shorts, a T-shirt stretched taut over his big belly as he padded barefooted in the general direction of the bathroom. He probably still left the seat up.

"I'll be fine," I said.

"You've got a license for carrying a gun, don't you?"

"Carrying a concealed weapon?" I asked. "No."

He pushed back his chair, deciding. "I'll have a little chat with Judge Reinhard in the morning. We'll get you one."

That was all. It was almost midnight.

Moments later I was alone and unable to sleep. I downed another shot of brandy, then one more, and lay in bed staring up at the dark ceiling. If you have enough bad things happen to you in life, others begin to privately question if you invite them, are a magnet that attracts misfortune or danger or dysfunction. I was beginning to wonder. Maybe Ethridge was right, I got too involved in my cases and placed myself at risk. I'd had close calls before that could have sent me spinning off into eternity.

When I finally faded into sleep, I dreamed nonsensical things. Ethridge burned a hole in his vest with a cigar ash. Fielding was working on a body that was beginning to look like a pin cushion because he couldn't find an artery that had any blood. Marino was riding a pogo stick up a steep hill and I knew he was going to fall.

12

In the early morning I stood inside my dark living room, staring out at the shadows and shapes of my property.

My Plymouth wasn't back from the state garage. As I looked out at the oversize station wagon I was stuck with, I found myself wondering how difficult it would be for a grown man to hide under it and grab my foot as I unlocked the driver's door. He wouldn't need to kill me. I would die of a heart attack first. The street beyond was empty, street lights burning dimly. Peering through the barely parted draperies, I saw nothing. I heard nothing. Nothing seemed out of the ordinary. Probably nothing had seemed out of the ordinary when Cary Harper had driven home from the tavern, either.

My breakfast appointment with the attorney general was in less than an hour. I was going to be late if I didn't muster up the courage to step outside my own front door and negotiate the thirty feet of sidewalk that would lead me to my car. I studied the shrubbery and small dogwoods bordering my front lawn, scrutinizing their quiet silhouettes as the sky lightened by degrees. The moon was roundly iridescent like a white morning glory, grass silver with frost.

How had he gotten to their houses, to *my* house? He had to have some means of transportation. There had been little speculation about the killer's ability to move around. Type of vehicle is as much a part of criminal profiling as age and race are, and yet no one was commenting, not even Wesley. I wondered why as I stared at the vacant street. And Wesley's grim demeanor in Quantico still bothered me.

I voiced my concern as Ethridge and I were eating breakfast.

"It may be, simply, that there are things Wesley chooses not to tell you," he suggested.

"He's always been very open with me in the past."

"The Bureau tends to be very closemouthed, Kay."

"Wesley is a profiler," I replied. "He's always been generous with his theories and opinions. But in this instance he's not talking. He's barely profiling these cases at all. His personality has changed. He's humorless, and he scarcely looks me in the eyes. It's weird and incredibly unnerving."

I took a deep breath.

Then Ethridge said, "You're still feeling isolated, aren't you, Kay?"

"Yes, Tom."

"And just a little paranoid."

"That, too," I said.

"Do you trust me, Kay? Do you believe I'm on your side and have your best interests in mind?" he asked.

I nodded and took another deep breath.

We were talking in quiet voices inside the dining room of the Capitol Hotel, a favorite watering hole for politicians and plutocrats. Three tables away sat Senator Partin, his well-known face more wrinkled than I remembered as he talked seriously to a young man I had seen somewhere before.

"Most of us feel isolated and paranoid during stressful times. We feel alone in the wilderness." Ethridge's eyes were kind on me, his face troubled.

"I am alone in the wilderness," I replied. "I feel that way because it's true."

"I can see why Wesley is worried."

"Of course."

"What worries me about you, Kay, is you're basing your theories on intuition, going on instinct. Sometimes that can be very dangerous."

"Sometimes it can be. But it can also be very dangerous when people begin to make things too complicated. Murder is usually depressingly simple."

"Not always, though."

"Almost always, Tom."

"You don't think Sparacino's machinations are related to these deaths?" the attorney general queried.

"I think it would be all too easy to be distracted by his machinations. What he's doing and what the killer is doing could be trains running on parallel tracks. Both of them dangerous, even deadly. But not the same. Not connected. Not driven by the same forces."

"You don't think the missing manuscript is connected?"

"I don't know."

"You're no closer to knowing?"

The interrogation made me feel as if I hadn't done my homework. I wished he hadn't asked.

"No, Tom," I admitted. "I have no idea where it is."

"Is it possible it could be what Sterling Harper burned in her fireplace right before she died?"

"I don't think so. The documents examiner looked at charred bits of paper, identified them as twenty-pound, high-quality rag. They're consistent with fine stationery or the paper lawyers use for legal documents. It's very unlikely someone would write a book draft on paper like that. It's more likely Miss Harper burned letters, personal papers."

"Letters from Beryl Madison?"

"We can't rule it out," I replied, even though I had pretty much ruled it out.

"Or perhaps Cary Harper's letters?"

"There was quite a collection of his private papers found inside the house," I said. "There's no evidence that any of it had been disturbed or recently gone through."

"If the letters were from Beryl Madison, why would Miss Harper burn them?"

"I don't know," I replied, and I knew Ethridge was thinking about his nemesis Sparacino again.

Sparacino had moved quickly. I had seen the lawsuit, all thirty-three pages of it. Sparacino was suing me, the police, the governor. The last time I had checked in with Rose, she had informed me that *People* magazine had called, and one of its photographers was out front taking pictures of my building the other day after being refused entrance beyond the lobby. I was becoming notorious. I was also becoming expert at refusing comment and making myself scarce.

"You think we're dealing with a psycho, don't you?" Ethridge asked me point-blank.

Orange acrylic fiber connected with hijackers or not, that was what I thought, and I told him so.

He looked down at his half-eaten food and when he lifted his eyes I was undone by what I saw in them. Sadness, disappointment. A terrible reluctance.

"Kay," he began, "there's no easy way to say this to you."

I reached for a biscuit.

"You need to know. No matter what is really going on or why, no matter your beliefs and private opinions, you need to hear this."

I decided I would rather smoke than eat, and got out my cigarettes.

"I have a contact. Suffice it to say he is privy to Justice Department activities—"

"This is about Sparacino," I interrupted.

"It's about Mark James," he said.

I couldn't have been more unnerved had the attorney general just sworn at me.

I asked, "What about Mark?"

"I'm wondering if I should ask *you* that, Kay."

"What do you mean, exactly?"

"The two of you were seen together in New York several weeks ago. At Gallagher's." An awkward pause as he coughed and added inanely, "I haven't been there in years."

I stared at the smoke drifting up from my cigarette.

"As I remember it, the steaks are pretty good. . . ."

"Stop it, Tom," I said quietly.

"A lot of good-hearted Irishmen in that place who don't hold back on the booze or the banter—"

"Stop it, goddamn it," I said a little too loudly.

Senator Partin stared straight at our table, his eyes mildly curious as they briefly alighted on Ethridge, then me. Our waiter was suddenly pouring more coffee and inquiring if we needed anything. I was uncomfortably warm.

"Don't bullshit me, Tom," I said. "Who saw me?"

He waved it off. "What matters is how you know him."

"I've known him for a very long time."

"That's not an answer."

"Since law school."

"You were close?"

"Yes."

"Lovers?"

"Jesus, Tom."

"I'm sorry, Kay. It's important." Dabbing his lips with his napkin, he reached for his coffee, his eyes drifting around the dining room. Ethridge was very ill at ease. "Let's just say that the two of you were together most of the night in New York. At the Omni."

My cheeks were burning.

"I don't give a damn about your personal life, Kay. I doubt anybody else does, either. Except in this one instance. You see, I'm very sorry." He cleared his throat, finally giving me his eyes again. "Dammit. Mark's pal, Sparacino, is being investigated by the Justice Department—"

"His *pal*?"

"It's very serious, Kay," Ethridge went on. "I don't know what Mark James was like when you knew him in law school, but I do know what's become of him since. I know his record. After you were spotted with him, I did some investigating. He got in serious trouble in Tallahassee seven years ago. Racketeering. Fraud. Crimes for which he was convicted and for which he actually spent time in prison. It was after all this that he ended up with Sparacino, who is suspected of being tied in with organized crime."

I felt as if a vise were rapidly squeezing the blood from my heart, and I must have become pale because Ethridge quickly handed me my glass of water and waited patiently until I composed myself. But when I met his eyes again, he picked up where he had interrupted his damaging testimony.

"Mark has never worked for Orndorff & Berger, Kay. The firm has never even heard of him. Which doesn't surprise me. Mark James couldn't possibly practice law. He was disbarred. It appears he is simply Sparacino's personal aide."

"Does Sparacino work for Orndorff & Berger?" I managed to ask.

"He's their entertainment lawyer. That much is true," he answered.

I said nothing, tears fighting to break out.

"Stay away from him, Kay," Ethridge said, his voice a rough caress in its attempt to be tender. "For God's sake, break it off. Whatever you've got going with him, break it off."

"I don't have anything going with him," I said shakily.

"When's the last time you had contact with him?"

"Several weeks ago. He called. We talked no more than thirty seconds."

He nodded as if he had expected as much. "The paranoid life. One of the poisonous fruits of criminal activity.

I doubt Mark James is given to long telephone conversations, and I doubt he'll approach you at all unless there is something he wants. Tell me how it is you were with him in New York."

"He wanted to see me. He wanted to warn me about Sparacino." I added lamely, "Or this is what he said."

"And did he warn you about him?"

"Yes."

"What did he say?"

"The very sorts of things you've already mentioned about Sparacino."

"Why did Mark tell you this?"

"He said he wanted to protect me."

"Do you believe that?"

"I don't know what the hell I believe," I said.

"Are you in love with this man?"

I stared mutely at the attorney general, my eyes turning to stone.

He said very quietly, "I need to know how vulnerable you are. Please don't think I'm enjoying this, Kay."

"Please don't think I'm enjoying this either, Tom," I said, an edge to my voice.

Ethridge removed his napkin from his lap and folded it neatly, deliberately, before tucking it under the rim of his plate.

"I have reason to fear," he said, so softly I had to lean forward to hear him, "that Mark James could do you terrible damage, Kay. There is reason to suspect he's behind the break-in at your office—"

"*What* reason?" I cut him off, my voice rising. "What are you talking about? What proof—" The words caught in my throat, as Senator Partin and his young companion were suddenly at our table. I hadn't noticed them get up and head toward us. I could tell by the look on their faces they realized they had intruded upon a tense conversation.

"John, good to see you." Ethridge was pushing back his chair. "You know the chief medical examiner, Kay Scarpetta, don't you?"

"Of course, of course. Yes, how are you, Dr. Scarpetta?" The senator was shaking my hand, smiling, his eyes distant. "And this is my son, Scott."

I noticed that Scott had not inherited his father's rugged, rather coarse features or short, stocky build. The young man was incredibly handsome, tall, fit, his fine face framed by a crown of magnificent black hair. He was in his twenties, with a quiet burning insolence in his eyes that bothered me. The cordial conversation did not ease my disconcertedness, nor did I feel any better when father and son finally left us alone again.

"I've seen him somewhere before," I said to Ethridge after the waiter refilled our coffees.

"Who? John?"

"No, no—of course I've seen the senator before. I'm talking about his son. Scott. He looks very familiar."

"You've probably seen him on TV," he replied, stealing a distracted glance at his watch. "He's an actor, or trying to be one, at any rate. I think he's had a few minor roles in a couple of the soaps."

"Oh, my God," I muttered.

"Maybe a couple of bit parts in movies, too. He was out in California, now lives in New York."

"No," I said, stunned.

Ethridge put down his coffee cup and fixed calm eyes on me.

"How did he know we were having breakfast here this

morning, Tom?" I asked, working hard to keep my voice steady as the images came back to me. Gallagher's. The lone young man drinking beer several tables away from where Mark and I had been sitting.

"I don't know how he knew," Ethridge replied, his eyes glinting with a secret satisfaction. "Suffice it to say that I'm not surprised, Kay. Young Partin's been shadowing me for days."

"He's not your Justice Department contact . . ."

"Good God, no," Ethridge said flatly.

"Sparacino?"

"I would think so. That would make the most sense, wouldn't it, Kay?"

"Why?"

He began studying the check, then said, "To make sure he knows what's going on. To spy. To intimidate." He glanced up at me. "Take your choice."

Scott Partin had struck me as one of these self-contained young men often a study in sullen splendor. I remembered he had been reading the *New York Times* and gloomily drinking a beer. I had been vaguely aware of him only because extremely beautiful people, like gorgeous arrangements of flowers, are difficult not to notice.

I felt a compulsion to tell Marino all about it as we rode the elevator down to the first floor of my building later that morning.

"I'm certain," I repeated. "He was sitting two tables over from us at Gallagher's."

"And he wasn't with nobody?"

"Correct. He was reading, drinking a beer. I don't think he was eating, but I really don't remember," I replied as we cut through a large storage room smelling of cardboard and dust.

My mind and heart were racing, trying to outrun yet another one of Mark's lies. Mark had said that Sparacino didn't know I was coming to New York, that it was coincidence when Sparacino appeared at the steak house. That couldn't be true. Young Partin had been sent to spy on me that night, and that could have happened only if Sparacino knew I was there with Mark.

"Well, there's another way to look at it," Marino said as we walked through the dusty bowels of my building. "Let's say one of the ways he stays alive in the Big Apple is he does some part-time snitching for Sparacino, okay? Could be Partin was sent to tail Mark, not you. Remember, Sparacino recommended the steak house to Mark—or at least this is what Mark told you. So Sparacino had reason to know Mark was going to eat there that night. Sparacino tells Partin to be there, check out what Mark's up to. Partin does, is sitting alone drinking a brew when the two of you walk in. Maybe at some point he slips out to call Sparacino, give him the scoop. Bingo! Next thing you know, Sparacino's walking in."

I wanted to believe it.

"Just a theory," Marino added.

I knew I could not believe it. The truth, I harshly reminded myself, was that Mark had betrayed me, that he was the criminal Ethridge had described.

"You got to consider all the possibilities," Marino concluded.

"Of course," I muttered.

Down another narrow corridor, we stopped before a heavy metal door. Finding the right key, I let us inside the range where the firearms examiners conducted test fires on virtually every weapon known to man. It was a drab, lead-contaminated cinderblock room, one entire wall covered by a pegboard and lined with scores of handguns and machine pistols confiscated by the courts and eventually released to the lab. Propped up in racks were shotguns and rifles. The far wall was heavy steel reinforced in the center and pitted by thousands of rounds fired over the years. Marino headed for a corner where nude manikin torsos, hips, heads, and legs were commingled in a heap ghoulishly reminiscent of an Auschwitz common grave.

"You prefer light meat, don't you?" he asked, selecting a pale flesh-colored male chest.

I ignored him as I opened my carrying case and got out the stainless-steel Ruger. Plastic clacked as he rummaged, finally selecting a Caucasian head with brown-painted hair and eyes. This went on top of the chest, both of which Marino set on top of a cardboard box against the steel wall some thirty paces away.

"You get one clip to make him history," Marino said.

Loading wadcutters into my revolver, I glanced up as Marino withdrew a 9-millimeter pistol out of the back of his trousers. Cocking back the slide, he pulled out the clip, then snapped it back in place.

"Merry Christmas," he said, offering it to me, safety on, butt first.

"No, thank you," I said as politely as possible.

"Five pops with your piece and you're out of business."

"If I miss."

"Shit, Doc. Everybody misses a few. Problem is, with your Ruger there, a few's all you got."

"I'd rather have a few well-placed shots with mine. All that thing does is spray lead."

"It's a hell of a lot more firepower," he said.

"I know. About a hundred foot-pounds more at fifty feet than I've got with mine if I'm using Silvertips Plus ammo."

"Not to mention three times as many shots," Marino added.

I had fired 9-millimeters before and didn't like them. They weren't as accurate as my .38 special. They weren't as safe, and they could jam. I had never been one to substitute quantity for quality, and there was no substitution for being informed and practiced.

"You need only one shot," I said, placing a set of hearing protectors over my ears.

"Yeah. If it's between the damn eyes."

Steadying the revolver with my left hand, I repeatedly squeezed the trigger and shot the manikin in the head once, the chest three times, the fifth bullet grazing the left shoulder—all of it happening in a matter of seconds as head and torso flew off the box and clattered dully against the steel wall.

Wordlessly, Marino set the 9-millimeter on top of a table and slipped his .357 out of his shoulder holster. I could tell I had hurt his feelings. No doubt he had gone to a lot of trouble to find the automatic for me. He had thought I would be pleased.

"Thank you, Marino," I said.

Clicking the cylinder back in place, he slowly raised his revolver.

I started to add that I appreciated his thoughtfulness, but I knew either he couldn't hear me or he wasn't listening.

I backed away as he unloaded six rounds, the manikin head jumping crazily on the floor. Slapping in a speed loader, he started in on the torso. When he was finished, gun smoke was acrid on the air and I knew I would never want him murderously angry with me.

"Nothing like shooting a man while he's down," I said.

"You're right." He removed his earplugs. "Nothing like it."

We slid a wooden frame along an overhead track and attached to it a Score Keeper paper target. When the box of cartridges was empty and I was satisfied that I could still hit the broad side of a barn, I fired a couple of Silvertips to clean out the bore before I took a patch cloth of Hoppe's No. 9 to it. The solvent always reminded me of Quantico.

"You want my opinion?" Marino said, cleaning his gun as well. "What you need at home's a shotgun."

I said nothing as I returned the Ruger to its carrying case.

"You know, something like an autoloading Remington, three-inch magnum double-aught buck. Be like hitting the fool with fifteen thirty-two-caliber bullets—three times that you hit him with all three rounds. We're talking forty-five friggin' pieces of lead. He ain't gonna come back for more."

"Marino," I said quietly. "I'm fine, all right? I really don't need an arsenal."

He looked up to me, his eyes hard. "You got any idea what it's like to shoot a guy and he keeps on coming?"

"No, I don't," I said.

"Well, I do. Back in New York I emptied my gun on this animal who's freaked out on PCP. Hit the bastard four times in the upper body and it didn't even slow him down. It was like something out of Stephen King, the guy coming at me like the friggin' living dead."

I found some tissues in the pockets of my lab coat and began wiping gun oil and solvent off my hands.

"The squirrel who was chasing Beryl through her house, Doc, he was like that, like that lunatic I'm telling you about. Whatever his gig is, he ain't gonna slow down once he's in gear."

"The man in New York," I ventured, "did he die?"

"Oh, yeah. In the ER. We both rode to the hospital in the back of the same ambulance. That was a trip."

"You were badly hurt?"

Marino's face was unreadable as he replied, "Naw. Seventy-eight stitches. Flesh wounds. You've never seen me with my shirt off. The guy had a knife."

"How awful," I muttered.

"I don't like knives, Doc."

"I don't either," I agreed.

We headed out. I felt grimy with gun oil and gunshot residue. Shooting is much dirtier than most people might imagine.

Marino was reaching back for his wallet as we walked. Next he was handing me a small white card.

"I didn't fill out an application," I said, staring, rather dazed, at the license authorizing me to carry a concealed weapon.

"Yeah, well, Judge Reinhard owed me a favor."

"Thank you, Marino," I said.

He smiled as he held open the door for me.

Despite the directives of Wesley and Marino and my own good sense, I stayed inside my building until it was dark out, the parking lot empty. I had given up on my desk, and a glance at my calendar had about done me in.

Rose had been systematically reorganizing my life. Appointments had been pushed weeks ahead or canceled, and lectures and demonstration autopsies had been rerouted to Fielding. The health commissioner, my immediate boss, had tried to reach me three times, finally inquiring if I were ill.

Fielding was becoming quite adept at filling in for me. Rose was typing his autopsy protocols and micro-dictations. She was doing his work instead of mine. The sun continued to rise and set, and the office was running without a hitch because I had selected and trained my staff very well. I wondered how God had felt after He created a world that thought it did not need Him.

I did not go home right away, but drove to Chamberlayne Farms. The same outdated notices were still taped to the elevator walls. I rode up with an emaciated little woman who never took her lonely eyes off me as she clutched her walker like a bird clinging to its branch.

I had not told Mrs. McTigue I was coming. When the door to 378 finally opened after several loud knocks, she peered quizzically out from her lair of crowded furniture and loud television noise.

"Mrs. McTigue?" I introduced myself again, not at all sure she would remember me.

The door opened wider as her face lit up. "Yes. Why, of course! How grand of you to stop by. Won't you please come in?"

She was dressed in a pink quilted housecoat and matching slippers, and when I followed her into the living room she turned off the television set and removed a lap robe from the couch, where she evidently had been sitting as she snacked on nutbread and juice and watched the evening news.

"Please forgive me," I said. "I've interrupted your dinner."

"Oh, no. I was just nibbling. May I offer you some refreshment?" she was quick to say.

I politely declined, seating myself while she moved about, tidying up. My heart was tugged by memories of my own grandmother, whose humor was unflagging even as she watched her flesh fall to ruin around her ears. I would never forget her visit to Miami the summer before she died when I took her shopping, and her improvised "diaper" of men's briefs and Kotex pads sprung a safety pin and ended up around her knees in the middle of Woolworth's. She held herself together as we hurried off to find a ladies' room, both of us laughing so hard I nearly lost control of my bladder, too.

"They say we may get snow tonight," Mrs. McTigue commented when she seated herself.

"It's very damp out," I replied abstractedly. "And it certainly feels cold enough to snow."

"I don't believe they're predicting any accumulation, though."

"I don't like driving in the snow." I said, my mind working on weighty, unpleasant things.

"Perhaps we'll have a white Christmas this year. Wouldn't that be special?"

"It would be special." I was looking in vain for any evidence of a typewriter in the apartment.

"I can't remember the last time we had a white Christmas."

Her nervous conversation tried to overcome her uneasiness. She knew I had come to see her for a reason and sensed it wasn't good news.

"Are you quite sure I can't get you something? A glass of port?"

"No, thank you," I said.

Silence.

"Mrs. McTigue," I ventured. Her eyes were as vulnerable and uncertain as a child's. "I wonder if I might see that photograph again? The one you showed me last time I was here."

She blinked several times, her smile thin and pale like a scar.

"The one of Beryl Madison," I added.

"Why, certainly," she said, slowly getting up, an air of resignation about her as she went to the secretary to fetch it. Fear, or maybe it was merely confusion, registered on her face when she handed me the photograph and I also asked to see the envelope and sheet of creamy folded paper.

I knew instantly by the feel of it that the paper was twenty-pound weight, and when I tilted it toward the lamp I saw the Crane's watermark, translucent in the high-quality rag. I briefly glanced at the photograph, and by now Mrs. McTigue looked thoroughly bewildered.

"I'm sorry," I said. "I know you must be wondering what on earth I'm doing."

She was at a loss for words.

"I'm curious. The photograph looks much older than the stationery."

"It is," she replied, her frightened eyes not leaving me. "I found the photograph among Joe's papers and tucked it in the envelope for safekeeping."

"This is your stationery?" I asked as benignly as possible.

"Oh, no." She reached for her juice and carefully sipped. "It was my husband's, but I did pick it out for him. A very nice engraved stationery for his business, you see. After he passed on, I kept only the blank second sheets and envelopes. I have more than I'll ever use."

There was no way to ask her without being direct.

"Mrs. McTigue, did your husband have a typewriter?"

"Why, yes. I gave it to my daughter. She lives in Falls Church. I always write my letters out in longhand. Not so many anymore, because of my arthritis."

"What kind of typewriter?"

"Dear me. I don't recall except that it's electric and fairly new," she stammered. "Joe would trade it in on a new one every few years. You know, even when these computers came out, he insisted on handling his correspondence the way he always had. Burt—that was his office manager—urged Joe for years to start using the computer, but Joe always had to have his typewriter."

"At home or in his office?" I asked.

"Why, both. He often stayed up late working on things in his office at home."

"Did he correspond with the Harpers, Mrs. McTigue?"

She had slipped a tissue out of a pocket of her robe and was twisting it in her fingers.

"I'm sorry to ask you so many questions," I persisted gently.

She stared down at her gnarled, thin-skinned hands and said nothing.

"Please," I said quietly. "It's important or I wouldn't ask."

"It's about her, isn't it?" The tissue was shredding and she wouldn't look up.

"Sterling Harper."

"Yes."

"Please tell me, Mrs. McTigue."

"She was very lovely. And so gracious. A very fine lady," Mrs. McTigue said.

"Did your husband correspond with Miss Harper?" I asked.

"I'm quite sure he did."

"What makes you think that?"

"I came in on him once or twice when he was writing a letter. He always said it was business."

I said nothing.

"Yes. My Joe." She smiled, her eyes dead. "Such a ladies' man. You know, he always kissed a lady's hand and made her feel the queen."

"Did Miss Harper write to him as well?" I asked hesitantly, for I did not enjoy irritating an old wound.

"Not that I'm aware."

"He wrote her but she never returned his letters?"

"Joe was a man of letters. He always said he would write a book someday. He was always reading something, don't you know."

"I can see why he would enjoy Cary Harper so much," I commented.

"Quite often when Mr. Harper was frustrated, he would call. I suppose writer's block is the term. He would call Joe and they would talk about the most interesting things. Literature and whatnot." The tissue was little bits of twisted paper in her lap. "Joe's favorite was Faulkner, if you can imagine. He was also quite fond of Hemingway and Dostoyevski. When we were courting, I lived in Arlington and he was here. He would write me the most beautiful letters you can imagine."

Letters like the ones he began to write his love in later life, I thought. Letters like the ones he began to write the gorgeous, unmarried Sterling Harper. Letters she was kind enough to burn before she committed suicide, because she did not wish to shatter the heart and memories of his widow.

"You found them, then," she barely said.

"Found letters to her?"

"Yes. His letters."

"No." It was, perhaps, the most merciful half truth I had ever told. "No, I can't say that we found anything like that, Mrs. McTigue. The police found no correspondence from your husband among the Harpers' personal effects, no stationery with your husband's letterhead, nothing of an intimate nature addressed to Sterling Harper."

Her face relaxed as denial was blessedly reinforced.

"Did you ever spend any time with the Harpers? Socially, for example?" I asked.

"Why, yes. Twice that I remember. Once Mr. Harper came for a dinner party. And on one other occasion the Harpers and Beryl Madison were overnight guests."

This piqued my interest. "When were they your overnight guests?"

"Mere months before Joe passed on. I 'spect that would have been the first of the year, just a month or two after Beryl spoke to our group. In fact, I'm sure it was because the Christmas tree was still up. I remember that. It was such a treat to have her."

"To have Beryl?"

"Oh, yes! I was so pleased. It seems the three of them had been in New York on business. They were seeing Beryl's agent, I believe. They flew into Richmond on their way home and were generous enough to stay the night with us. Or at least the Harpers stayed the night. Beryl lived here, you see. Late in the evening Joe gave her a ride back to her home. Then he took the Harpers back to Williamsburg the following morning."

"What do you remember about that night?" I asked.

"Let me see . . . I remember I fixed leg of lamb and they were late coming in from the airport because the airline lost Mr. Harper's bags."

Almost a year ago, I considered. This would have been before Beryl had begun receiving the threats—based on the information we had gotten.

"They were rather tired from the trip," Mrs. McTigue continued. "But Joe was so good. He was the most charming host you'd ever want to meet."

Could Mrs. McTigue tell? Did she know by the way her husband looked at Miss Harper that he was in love with her?

I remembered the distant look in Mark's eyes during those final days so long ago when we were together. When I knew. It was instinct. I knew he was not thinking about me, and yet I would not believe he was in love with someone else until he finally told me.

"Kay, I'm sorry," he said as we drank Irish coffee for the last time in our favorite bar in Georgetown while tiny flakes of snow spiraled down from gray skies and beautiful couples walked by bundled in winter coats and brightly knitted scarves. "You know I love you, Kay."

"But not the same way I love you," I said, my heart gripped by the worst pain I ever remember feeling.

He looked down at the table. "I never intended to hurt you."

"Of course you didn't."

"I'm sorry. I'm so sorry."

I knew he was. He really and truly was. And it didn't change a goddamn thing.

I never knew her name because I did not want to know it, and she was not the woman he said he had later married. Janet, who had died. But then, maybe that was a lie, too.

". . . he had quite a temper."

"Who did?" I asked, my eyes focusing on Mrs. McTigue again.

"Mr. Harper," she replied, and she was beginning to look very tired. "He was so irritable about his luggage. Fortunately, it came in on the very next flight." She paused. "Goodness. That seems so long ago, and it really wasn't that long ago a'tall."

"What about Beryl?" I asked. "What do you remember about her that night?"

"All of them gone, now." Her hands went still in her lap as she faced that dark, empty mirror. Everyone was dead but her, the guests from that cherished and frightful dinner party, ghosts.

"We are talking about them, Mrs. McTigue. They are still with us."

"I 'spect that's so," she said, her eyes bright with tears.

"We need their help and they need ours."

She nodded.

"Tell me about that night," I said again. "About Beryl."

"She was very quiet. I remember her watching the fire."

"What else?"

"Something happened."

"What? What happened, Mrs. McTigue?"

"She and Mr. Harper seemed to be unhappy with each other," she said.

"Why? Did they have an argument?"

"It was after the boy delivered the luggage. Mr. Harper opened one of the bags and pulled out an envelope that had papers in it. I don't really know. But he was drinking too much."

"Then what happened?"

"He exchanged some rather harsh words with his sister and Beryl. Then he took the papers and just flung them into the fire. He said, 'That's what I think of that! Trash, trash!' Or words to that effect."

"Do you know what it was he burned? A contract, perhaps?"

"I don't think so," she replied, staring off. "I remember getting the impression it was something Beryl had written. They looked like typed pages, and his anger seemed directed at her."

The autobiography she was writing, I thought. Or perhaps it was an outline that Miss Harper, Beryl, and Sparacino had discussed in New York with an increasingly enraged and out-of-control Cary Harper.

"Joe intervened," she said, lacing her misshapen fingers together, holding in her pain.

"What did he do?"

"He drove her home," she said. "He drove Beryl Madison home." She stopped, staring at me in abject fear. "It's why it happened. I know it."

"It's why *what* happened?" I asked.

"It's why they're dead," she said. "I know it. I had this feeling at the time. It was such a frightful feeling."

"Describe it to me. Can you describe it?"

"It's why they're dead," she repeated. "There was so much hate in the room that night."

13

Valhalla Hospital was situated on a rise in the genteel world of Albemarle County, where my faculty ties with the University of Virginia brought me periodically throughout the year. Though I had often noticed the formidable brick edifice rising from a distant foothill visible from the Interstate, I had never visited the hospital for either personal or professional reasons.

Once a grand hotel frequented by the wealthy and well-known, it went bankrupt during the depression and was bought by three brothers who were psychiatrists. They systematically set about to turn Valhalla into a Freudian factory, a rich man's psychiatric resort where families with means could tuck away their genetic inconveniences and embarrassments, their senile elders and poorly programmed kids.

It didn't really surprise me that Al Hunt had been farmed out here as a teenager. What did surprise me was that his psychiatrist seemed so reluctant to discuss him. Beneath Dr. Warner Masterson's professional cordiality was a bedrock of secrecy hard enough to break the drill bits of the most tenacious inquisitors. I knew he did not want to talk to me. He knew he had no choice.

Parking in the gravel lot designated for visitors, I went into a lobby of Victorian furnishings, Oriental rugs, and heavy draperies with ornate cornices well along their way to being threadbare. I was about to announce myself to the receptionist when I heard someone behind me speak.

"Dr. Scarpetta?"

I turned to face a tall, slender black man dressed in a European-cut navy suit. His hair was a sandy sprinkle, his cheekbones and forehead aristocratically high.

"I'm Warner Masterson," he said, and smiling broadly, he offered his hand.

I was about to wonder if I had forgotten him from some former encounter when he explained that he recognized me from pictures he had seen in the papers and on the television news, reminders I could do without.

"We'll go back to my office," he added pleasantly. "I trust your drive up wasn't too tiring? May I offer you something? Coffee? A soda?"

All this as he continued to walk, and I did my best to keep up with his long strides. A significant portion of the human race has no idea what it is like to be attached to short legs, and I am forever finding myself indignantly pumping along like a handcar in a world of express trains. Dr. Masterson was at the other end of a long, carpeted corridor when he finally had the presence of mind to look around. Pausing at a doorway, he waited until I caught up with him, then ushered me inside. I helped myself to a chair while he took his position behind his desk and automatically began tamping tobacco into an expensive briar pipe.

"Needless to say, Dr. Scarpetta," Dr. Masterson began in his slow, precise way as he opened a thick file folder, "I am dismayed by Al Hunt's death."

"Are you surprised by it?" I asked.

"Not entirely."

"I'd like to review his case as we talk," I said.

He hesitated long enough for me to consider reminding him of my statutory rights to the record. Then he smiled again and said, "Certainly," as he handed it over.

I opened the manila folder and began to peruse its contents as blue pipe smoke drifted over me like aromatic wood shavings. Al Hunt's admission history and physical examination were fairly routine. He was in good physical health when he was admitted on the morning of April tenth, eleven years ago. The details of his mental status examination told another story.

"He was catatonic when he was admitted?" I asked.

"Extremely depressed and unresponsive," Dr. Masterson replied. "He couldn't tell us why he was here. He wasn't able to tell us anything. He didn't have the emotional energy to answer questions. You'll note from the record that we were unable to administer the Stanford-Binet or the MMPI, and had to repeat these tests at a later date."

The results were in the file. Al Hunt's score on the Stanford-Binet intelligence test was in the 130 range, a lack of smarts certainly not his problem, not that I'd had any question. As for the Minnesota Multiphasic Personality Inventory, he did not meet the criteria for schizophrenia or organic mental disorder. According to Dr. Masterson's evaluation, what Al Hunt suffered from was "a schizotypal personality disorder with features of borderline personality, which presented as a brief reactive psychosis when he cut his wrists with a steak knife after locking himself in the bathroom." It was a suicidal gesture, the superficial wounds a cry for help versus a serious attempt to end his life. His mother rushed him to a nearby hospital emergency room, where he was stitched up and released. The next morning he was admitted at Valhalla. An interview with Mrs. Hunt revealed that the incident was precipitated by her "husband losing his temper" with Al during dinner.

"Initially," Dr. Masterson went on, "Al would not participate in any of the group or occupational therapy sessions or social functions the patients are required to attend. His response to antidepressant medication was poor, and during our sessions I could barely get a word out of him."

When there was no improvement after the first week, Dr. Masterson continued to explain, he considered electroconvulsive treatment, or ECT, which is the equivalent of rebooting a computer versus determining the reason for the errors. Though the end result may be a healthy reconnecting of brain pathways, a realignment of sorts, the formatting "bugs" causing the problem will inevitably be forgotten and, possibly, forever lost. As a rule, ECT is not the treatment of choice in the young.

"Was ECT administered?" I asked, for I was finding no record of it in the file.

"No. Just at the point when I was deciding I had no

other viable alternative, a small miracle occurred during psychodrama one morning."

He paused to relight his pipe.

"Explain psychodrama as it was conducted in this instance," I said.

"Some of the routines are done by rote and are warm-ups, you might say. During this particular session, the patients were lined up and asked to imitate flowers. Tulips, daffodils, daisies, whatever came to mind, each person contorting himself into a flower of his private choosing. Obviously, there is much one can infer from the patient's choice. This was the first time Al had participated in anything at all. He made loops with his arms and bent his head." He demonstrated, looking more like an elephant than a flower. "When the therapist asked what flower he was, he replied, 'A pansy.' "

I said nothing, experiencing a mounting wave of pity for this lost boy we had conjured up before us.

"Of course, one's first reaction was to assume this was a reference to what Al's father thought of him," Dr. Masterson explained, cleaning his glasses with a handkerchief. "Harsh, mocking references to young Al's effeminate traits, his fragility. But it was more than that." Slipping his glasses back on, he looked steadily at me. "Are you aware of Al's color associations?"

"Remotely."

"Pansy is also a color."

"Yes. A very deep violet," I agreed.

"It is what you get if you blend the blue of depression with the red of rage. The color of bruises, the color of pain. Al's color. It is the color he said radiated from his soul."

"It is a passionate color," I said. "Very intense."

"Al Hunt was a very intense young man, Dr. Scarpetta. Are you aware that he believed he was clairvoyant?"

"Not exactly," I replied uneasily.

"His magical thinking included clairvoyance, telepathy, superstitiousness. Needless to say, these characteristics became much more pronounced during times of extreme stress, when he believed he had the ability to read other people's minds."

"Could he?"

"He was very intuitive." His lighter was out again. "I have to say there was often validity in his perceptions, and this was one of his problems. He sensed what others thought or felt and sometimes seemed to possess an inexplicable *a priori* knowledge of what they would do or what they had already done. The difficulty came, as I briefly mentioned during our telephone conversation, in that Al would project, run too far with his perceptions. He would lose himself in others, become agitated, paranoid, in part because his ego was so weak. Like water, he tended to take the shape of whatever he filled. To use a cliché, he personalized the universe."

"A dangerous way to be," I observed.

"To say the least. He's dead."

"You're saying he considered himself empathic?"

"Definitely."

"That strikes me as inconsistent with his diagnosis," I said. "People with borderline personality disorders generally feel nothing for others."

"Ah, but this was part of his magical thinking, Dr. Scarpetta. Al blamed his social and occupational dysfunction on what he believed was his overwhelming empathy for others. He truly believed he sensed and even experienced other people's pain, that he knew their minds, as I've already mentioned. In fact, Al Hunt was socially isolated."

"The staff at Metropolitan Hospital described him as having a very good bedside manner when he worked there as a nurse," I pointed out.

"Unsurprisingly," Dr. Masterson countered. "He was a nurse in the ER. He would never have survived in a long-term care unit. Al could be very attentive providing he didn't have to get close to anyone, providing he wasn't forced to truly relate to that person."

"Explaining why he could get his master's degree but then be unable to function in the setting of a psychotherapy practice," I conjectured.

"Exactly."

"What about his relationship with his father?"

"It was dysfunctional, abusive," he replied. "Mr. Hunt is a hard, overbearing man. His idea of raising a son was to beat him into manhood. Al simply did not have the emotional makeup to withstand the bullying, the manhandling, the mental boot camp that was supposed to prepare him for life. It sent him fleeing to his mother's camp, where his image of himself became increasingly confused. I'm sure it comes as no surprise to you, Dr. Scarpetta, that many homosexual males are the sons of big brutes who drive pickups with gun racks and Confederate flag bumper stickers."

Marino came to mind. I knew he had a grown son. It had never occurred to me before this moment that Marino never talked about this only son, who lived out west somewhere.

I asked, "Are you suggesting that Al was homosexual?"

"I'm suggesting he was too insecure, his feelings of inadequacy too great, for him to respond to anyone, for him to form intimate relationships of any nature. To my knowledge, he never had a homosexual encounter." His face was unreadable as he gazed over my head and sucked on his pipe.

"What happened in psychodrama that day, Dr. Masterson? What was the small miracle you mentioned? His imitation of a pansy? Was that it?"

"It cracked the lid," he said. "But the miracle, if you will, was an intense and volatile dialogue he got into with his father, who was imagined to be sitting in an empty chair in the center of the room. As this dialogue intensified, the therapist sensed what was happening and slipped into the chair and began playing the part of Al's father. By now Al was so involved he was almost in a trance. He could not distinguish the real from the imagined, and finally his rage broke."

"How did it manifest itself? Did he become violent?"

"He began to weep uncontrollably," Dr. Masterson replied.

"What was his 'father' saying to him?"

"He was assaulting him with the usual brickbats, being critical, telling him how worthless he was as a man, as a human being. Al was hypersensitive to criticism, Dr. Scarpetta. This was, in part, the root of his confusion. He thought he was sensitive to others, when, in truth, he was sensitive only to himself."

"Was Al assigned a social worker?" I asked, continuing to flip through pages and finding no entries made by any therapists.

"Of course."

"Who was it?" There appeared to be pages missing from the record.

"The therapist I just mentioned," he replied blandly.

"The therapist from psychodrama?"

He nodded.

"Is he still employed by this hospital?"

"No," Dr. Masterson said. "Jim is no longer with us—"

"Jim?" I interrupted.

He began knocking burnt tobacco out of his pipe.

"What is his last name and where is he now?" I asked.

"I regret to say that Jim Barnes died in a car accident many years ago."

"How many years ago?"

Dr. Masterson began cleaning his glasses again. "I suppose it was eight, nine years ago."

"How did it happen, and where?"

"I don't recall the details."

"How tragic," I said, as if the matter were no longer of any interest to me.

"Am I to assume you are considering Al Hunt a suspect in your case?" he asked.

"There are two cases. Two homicides," I said.

"Very well. Two cases."

"To answer your question, Dr. Masterson, it isn't my business to consider anyone a suspect in anything. That's up to the police. My interest is in gathering information about Al Hunt that might assist me in verifying that he had a history of suicidal ideations."

"Is there any question about that, Dr. Scarpetta? He hanged himself, didn't he? Could that be anything other than a suicide?"

"He was dressed oddly. A shirt and his boxer shorts," I responded matter-of-factly. "Such things often lead to speculations."

"Are you suggesting autoerotic asphyxiation?" He raised his eyebrows in surprise. "An accidental death that occurred while he was masturbating?"

"I'm doing my best to obviate that question, should it ever be asked."

"I see. For insurance reasons. In the event his family might contest what you put down on the death certificate."

"For any reason," I said.

"Are you really in doubt as to what happened?" He frowned.

"No," I replied. "I think he took his own life, Dr. Masterson. I think this was his intention when he went down to the basement, and that he may have taken his pants off when he removed his belt. The belt he used to hang himself."

"Very well. And perhaps I can clear up another matter for you, Dr. Scarpetta. Al never demonstrated violent tendencies. The only individual he ever inflicted harm upon, to my knowledge, was himself."

I believed him. I also believed there was much he wasn't telling me, that his memory lapses and vagueness were patently deliberate. Jim Barnes, I thought. *Jim Jim.*

"How long was Al's stay here?" I changed the subject.

"Four months, I believe."

"Did he ever spend time in your forensic unit?"

"Valhalla doesn't have a forensic unit per se. We have a ward called Backhall for patients who are psychotic, suffering the DTs, a danger to themselve. We don't warehouse the criminally insane."

"Was Al ever on this ward?" I asked again.

"It was never necessary."

"Thank you for your time," I said, getting up. "If you would simply mail a photocopy of this record to me, that will be fine."

"It will be my pleasure." He smiled his broad smile again, but he would not look at me. "Don't hesitate to call if there's anything further I can do."

It nagged at me as I followed the long, empty corridor to the lobby, but my instinct was not to ask about Frankie or even mention the name. Backhall. Patients who are psychotic or suffering the DTs. Al Hunt had mentioned interviewing patients confined to the forensic unit. Was this a figment of his imagination or confusion? There was no forensic unit at Valhalla. Yet there very well may have been someone named Frankie locked up on Backhall. Maybe Frankie had improved and was later moved to a different ward while Al was a patient at Valhalla? Maybe Frankie had imagined he had murdered his mother, or maybe he had wished he could?

Frankie beat his mother to death with a stick of firewood. The killer beat Cary Harper to death with a segment of metal pipe.

By the time I got to my office it was dark out and the custodians had come and gone.

Seating myself at my desk, I swiveled around to face the computer terminal. After several commands, the amber screen was before me, and moments later I was staring at Jim Barnes's case. Nine years ago on April twenty-first, he had been in a single-car accident in Albemarle County, the cause of death "closed head injuries." His blood alcohol was .18, almost twice the legal limit, and he had nortriptyline and amitriptyline on board. Jim Barnes was a man with a problem.

In the computer analyst's office down the hall, the archaic, boxy microfilm machine sat squarely on a back table like a Buddha. My audiovisual skills have never been extraordinary. After an impatient search through the film library, I found the roll I was looking for and somehow managed to thread it properly into the machine. With lights out, I watched an endless stream of fuzzy black-on-white print flow by. My eyes were beginning to ache by the time I found the case. Film quietly creaked as I worked a knob and centered the handwritten police report on the screen. At approximately ten forty-five on a Friday night, Barnes's 1973 BMW was traveling east on I-64 at a high rate of speed. When his right wheel left the pavement, he overcorrected, hit the median strip, and became airborne. Advancing the film, I found the medical examiner's initial report of investigation. In the comments section a Dr. Brown had written that the decedent was fired that afternoon from Valhalla Hospital, where he had been employed as a social worker. When he left Valhalla at approximately five P.M. that day, he was noted to be extremely agitated and angry. Barnes was unmarried when he died, and he was only thirty-one years old.

There were two witnesses listed on the medical examiner's report, individuals Dr. Brown must have interviewed. One was Dr. Masterson, the other an employee at the hospital named Miss Jeanie Sample.

* * *

Sometimes working a homicide case is like being lost. Whatever street seems even remotely promising, you follow it. Maybe, if you're lucky, a back road will eventually steer you toward the main drag. How could a therapist dead nine years have anything to do with the recent murders of Beryl Madison and Cary Harper? Yet I felt there was something, a link.

I was not looking forward to quizzing Dr. Masterson's staff, and was willing to bet he would already have warned those who counted that if I called, they were to be polite—and silent. The next morning, Saturday, I continued to let my subconscious work on this problem while I rang up Johns Hopkins, hoping Dr. Ismail might be in. He was, and he confirmed my theory. Samples derived from Sterling Harper's gastric contents and blood showed she had ingested levomethorphan shortly before death, her level eight milligrams per liter of blood, which was too high to be either survivable or accidental. She had taken her own life, and had done so in a manner that under ordinary circumstances would have gone undetected.

"Did she know that dextromethorphan and levomethorphan both come up as dextromethorphan in routine tox tests?" I asked Dr. Ismail.

"I don't recall ever discussing such a thing with her," he said. "But she was very interested in the details of her treatments and medications, Dr. Scarpetta. It is possible she could have researched the subject in our medical library. I do recall her asking numerous questions when I first prescribed levomethorphan. This was several years ago. Since it is experimental, she was curious, perhaps somewhat concerned . . ."

I was barely listening as he continued explaining and

defending. I would never be able to prove Miss Harper had deliberately left the bottle of cough suppressant out where I would find it. But I was reasonably certain this was what she had done. She was determined to die with dignity and without reproach, but she did not want to die alone.

After I hung up, I fixed a cup of hot tea and paced the kitchen, pausing every so often to gaze out at the bright December day. Sammy, one of Richmond's few albino squirrels, was plundering my bird feeder again. For an instant we were eye to eye, his furry cheeks frantically working, seeds flying out from under his paws, his scrawny white tail a twitching question mark against the blue sky. We had become acquainted last winter as I stood before my window and watched his repeated attempts at leaping from a branch only to slide slowly off the coned top of the feeder, his paws grabbing wildly at thin air on his way down. After a remarkable number of tumbles to terra firma, Sammy finally got the hang of it. Every so often I would go out and throw him a handful of peanuts, and it had gotten to the point where if I didn't see him for a while, I experienced a tug of anxiety followed by joyous relief when he reappeared to clean me out again.

Sitting down at the kitchen table, a pad of paper and pen in hand, I dialed the number for Valhalla.

"Jeanie Sample, please." I did not identify myself.

"Is she a patient, ma'am?" the desk clerk asked without pause.

"No. She's an employee . . ." I acted addled. "I think so, at any rate. I haven't seen Jeanie in years."

"One moment, please."

The woman came back on the line. "We have no record of anybody by that name."

Damn. How could that be? I wondered. The telephone number listed with her name on the medical examiner's report was Valhalla's number. Had Dr. Brown made a mistake? Nine years ago, I thought. A lot could happen in nine years. Miss Sample could have moved. She could have gotten married.

"I'm sorry," I said. "Sample is her maiden name."

"Do you know her married name?"

"How awful. I should know—"

"Jean Wilson?"

I paused with uncertainty.

"We have a Jean Wilson," the voice went on. "One of our occupational therapists. Can you hold, please?" Then she was back very quickly. "Yes, her middle name is listed as Sample, ma'am. But she doesn't work on the weekend. She'll be back Monday morning at eight o'clock. Would you like to leave a message?"

"Any possibility you could tell me how to get in touch with her?"

"We're not allowed to give out home numbers." She was beginning to sound suspicious. "If you'll give me your name and number, I can try to get hold of her and ask her to call you."

"I'm afraid I won't be at this number long." I thought for a moment, then sounded dismally disappointed when I added, "I'll try again—next time I'm in the area. And I suppose I can write her at Valhalla, at your address."

"Yes, ma'am. You can do that."

"And that address is?"

She gave it to me.

"And her husband's name?"

A pause. "Skip, I believe."

Sometimes a nickname for Leslie, I thought. "Mrs. Skip

or Leslie Wilson," I muttered, as if I were writing it down. "Thank you so much."

There was one Leslie Wilson in Charlottesville, directory assistance informed me, and one L. P. Wilson and one L. T. Wilson. I started dialing. The man who answered when I tried the number for L. T. Wilson told me "Jeanie" was running errands and would be home within the hour.

I knew that a strange voice asking questions over the phone wasn't going to work. Jeanie Wilson would insist on conferring with Dr. Masterson first, and that would end the matter. It is, however, a little more difficult to refuse someone who unexpectedly appears in the flesh at your door, expecially if this individual introduces herself as the chief medical examiner and has a badge to prove it.

Jeanie Sample Wilson didn't look a day over thirty in her jeans and red pullover sweater. She was a perky brunette with friendly eyes and a smattering of freckles over her nose, her long hair tied back in a ponytail. In the living room beyond the open door, two small boys were sitting on the carpet, watching cartoons on television.

"How long have you been working at Valhalla?" I asked.

She hesitated. "Uh, about twelve years."

I was so relieved I almost sighed out loud. Jeanie Wilson would have been employed there not only when Jim Barnes was fired nine years ago, but also when Al Hunt was a patient two years before that.

She was planted squarely in the doorway. There was one car in the drive, in addition to mine. It appeared her husband had gone out. Good.

"I'm investigating the homicides of Beryl Madison and Cary Harper," I said.

Her eyes widened. "What do you want from me? I didn't know them—"

"May I come inside?"

"Of course. I'm sorry. Please."

We sat inside her small kitchen of linoleum and white Formica and pine cabinets. It was impeccably clean, with boxes of cereal neatly lined on top of the refrigerator, and counters arranged with big glass jars filled with cookies, rice and pasta. The dishwasher was running, and I could smell a cake baking in the oven.

I intended to beat down any lingering resistance with bluntness. "Mrs. Wilson, Al Hunt was a patient at Valhalla eleven years ago, and for a while was a suspect in the cases in question. He was acquainted with Beryl Madison."

"Al Hunt?" She looked bewildered.

"Do you remember him?" I asked.

She shook her head.

"And you say you've worked at Valhalla twelve years?"

"Eleven and a half, actually."

"Al Hunt was a patient there eleven years ago, as I've already said."

"The name isn't familiar . . ."

"He committed suicide last week," I said.

Now she was very bewildered.

"I talked to him shortly before his death, Mrs. Wilson. His social worker died in a motor vehicle accident nine years ago. Jim Barnes. I need to ask you about him."

A flush was creeping up her neck. "Are you thinking his suicide was related, had something to do with Jim?"

It was a question impossible to answer. "Apparently,

Jim Barnes was fired from Valhalla just hours before his death," I went on. "Your name—or at least your maiden name—is listed on the medical examiner's report, Mrs. Wilson."

"There was— Well, there was some question," she stammered. "You know, whether it was a suicide or an accident. I was questioned. A doctor, coroner, I don't remember. But some man called me."

"Dr. Brown?"

"I don't remember his name," she said.

"Why did he want to talk to you, Mrs. Wilson?"

"I suppose because I was one of the last people to see Jim alive. I guess the doctor called the front desk, and Betty referred him to me."

"Betty?"

"She was the receptionist back then."

"I need you to tell me everything you can remember about Jim Barnes's being fired," I said as she got up to check on the cake.

When she returned, she was a little more composed. She no longer looked unnerved. Instead, she looked angry.

She said, "Maybe it's not right to say bad things about the dead, Dr. Scarpetta, but Jim was not a nice person. He was a very big problem at Valhalla, and he should have been fired long before he was."

"Exactly how was he a problem?"

"Patients say a lot of things. They're often not very, well, credible. It's hard to know what's true and what isn't. Dr. Masterson, other therapists, would get complaints from time to time, but nothing could be proven until there was a witnessed event one morning, the morning of that day. The day Jim was fired and had the accident."

"This event was something you witnessed?" I asked.

"Yes." She stared off across the kitchen, her mouth firmly set.

"What happened?"

"I was walking through the lobby, on my way to see Dr. Masterson about something, when Betty called out to me. She was working the front desk, the switchboard, like I said— Tommy, Clay, now you keep it down in there!"

The shrieking in the other room only got louder, television channels switching like mad.

Mrs. Wilson got up wearily to see about her sons. I heard muffled smacks of hand against bottoms, after which the channel stayed put. Cartoon characters were shooting each other with what sounded like machine guns.

"Where was I?" she asked, returning to the kitchen table.

"You were talking about Betty," I reminded her.

"Oh, yes. She motioned me over and said Jim's mother was on the line, long distance, and it seemed important. I never did know what it was about, the call. But Betty asked if I could find Jim. He was in psychodrama, which is held in the ballroom. You know, Valhalla has a ballroom we use for various functions. The Saturday night dances, parties. There's a stage, an orchestra stage. From when Valhalla was a hotel. I slipped into the back, and when I saw what was going on, I couldn't believe it." Jeanie Wilson's eyes were bright with anger. She started fidgeting with the edge of a place mat. "I just stood there and watched. Jim's back was to me, and he was up on the stage with, I don't know, five or six patients. They were in chairs turned in such a way that they couldn't see what he was doing with this one patient. A young girl. Her name was Rita. Rita was maybe thirteen. Rita had been raped by her stepfather. She never talked, was functionally mute. Jim was forcing her to reenact it."

"The rape?" I asked calmly.

"The damn bastard. Excuse me. But it still upsets me."

"Understandably."

"He later claimed he wasn't doing anything inappropriate. Damn, he was such a liar. He denied everything. But I'd seen it. I knew exactly what he was doing. He was playing the role of the stepfather, and Rita was so terrified she didn't move. She was frozen in the chair. He was in her face, leaning over her, talking in a low voice. Sound carries inside the ballroom. I could hear everything. Rita was very mature, developed, for thirteen. Jim was asking her, 'Is this what he did, Rita?' He kept asking her that as he touched her. Fondled her, just as her stepfather had done, I suppose. I slipped out. He never knew I'd seen it until both Dr. Masterson and I confronted him minutes later."

I was beginning to understand why Dr. Masterson had refused to discuss Jim Barnes with me, and possibly why pages of Al Hunt's case file were absent. If something like this was ever made public, even though it had happened long ago, the hospital's reputation would take it on the nose.

"And you were suspicious Jim Barnes had done this before?" I asked.

"Some of the early complaints would indicate he had," Jeanie Wilson replied, her eyes flashing.

"Always females?"

"Not always."

"You received complaints from male patients?"

"From one of the young men. Yes. But no one took it seriously at the time. He had sexual problems anyway, supposedly had been molested or something. The very type someone like Jim would fix on because who would believe anything the poor kid said?"

"Do you remember this patient's name?"

"God." She frowned. "It was so long ago." She thought. "Frank . . . Frankie. That's it. I remember some of the patients called him Frankie. I don't recall his last name."

"How old was he?" I could feel my heart beating.

"I don't know. Seventeen, eighteen."

"What do you remember about Frankie?" I asked. "It's important. Very important."

A timer went off, and she pushed back her chair to take the cake out of the oven. While she was up, she checked on her boys again. When she returned, she was frowning.

She said, "I vaguely remember he was on Backhall for a while, right after he was admitted. Then he was moved downstairs to the second-floor ward where the men are. I had him in occupational therapy." She was thinking, an index finger touching her chin. "He was very industrious, I remember that. Made a lot of leather belts, brass rubbings. And he loved to knit, which was a little unusual. Most of the male patients won't knit, don't want to. They'll stick with leather work, make ashtrays and so on. He was very creative and really pretty skilled. And something else stands out. His neatness. He was obsessively neat, always cleaning off his work space, picking bits and pieces of whatever off the floor. Like it really bothered him if everything wasn't just right, clean." She paused, lifting her eyes to mine.

"When did he make the complaint about Jim Barnes?" I asked.

"Not too long after I started working at Valhalla." She hesitated, thinking hard. "I think Frankie had only been at Valhalla a month or so when he said something about Jim. I think he said it to another patient. In fact"—she paused, her prettily arched brows moving together in a frown—"it was actually this other patient who complained to Dr. Masterson."

"Do you remember who the patient was? The patient Frankie told this to?"

"No."

"Could it have been Al Hunt? You mentioned you hadn't been working at Valhalla long. Hunt would have been a patient eleven years ago during the spring and summer."

"I don't remember Al Hunt . . ."

"They would have been close to the same age," I added.

"That's interesting." Her eyes filled with innocent wonder as they fixed on mine. "Frankie had a friend, another teen-age boy. I do remember that. Blond. The boy was blond, very shy, quiet. I don't recall his name."

"Al Hunt was blond," I said.

Silence.

"Oh, my God."

I prodded her. "He was quiet, shy . . ."

"Oh, my God," she said again. "I bet it was him, then! And he committed suicide last week?"

"Yes."

"Did he mention Jim to you?"

"He mentioned someone he called Jim Jim."

"*Jim Jim*," she repeated. "Jeez. I don't know . . ."

"Whatever happened to Frankie?"

"He wasn't there long, two or three months."

"He went back home?" I asked.

"I would imagine so," she said. "There was something about his mother. I think he lived with his father. Frankie's mother deserted him when he was small—it was something like that, anyway. All I really remember is his family situation was sad. But then, I suppose you could say the same thing about most all the patients at Valhalla." She sighed. "God. This is something. I haven't thought about all this in years. Frankie." She shook her head. "I wonder what ever became of him."

"You have no idea?"

"Absolutely none." She looked a long time at me, and it was coming to her. I could see the fear gathering behind her eyes. "The two people murdered. You don't think Frankie . . ."

I said nothing.

"He never was violent, not when I was working with him. He was very gentle, actually."

She waited. I did not respond.

"I mean, he was very sweet and polite to me, would watch me very closely, do everything I told him to do."

"He liked you, then," I said.

"He knitted a scarf for me. I just remembered. Red, white, and blue. I'd completely forgotten. I wonder what happened to it?" Her voice trailed off. "I must have given it to the Salvation Army or something. I don't know. Frankie, well, I think he sort of had a crush on me." She laughed nervously.

"Mrs. Wilson, what did Frankie look like?"

"Tall, thin, with dark hair." She briefly shut her eyes.

"It was so long ago." She was looking at me again. "He doesn't stand out. But I don't remember him as being particularly nice looking. You know, I would remember him better, maybe, if he had been really nice looking or really ugly. So I think he was kind of plain."

"Would your hospital have any photographs of him on file?"

"No."

Silence again. Then she looked at me with surprise.

"He stuttered," she said slowly, then again with conviction.

"Pardon?"

"Sometimes he stuttered. I remember. When Frankie got extremely excited or nervous, he stuttered."

Jim Jim.

Al Hunt had meant exactly what he had said. When Frankie was telling Hunt what Barnes had done or tried to do, Frankie would have been upset, agitated. He would have stuttered. He would have stuttered whenever he talked to Hunt about Jim Barnes. Jim Jim!

I hit the first pay phone after leaving Jeanie Wilson's house. Marino, the dope, had gone bowling.

14

Monday rolled in on a tide of clouds marbled an ominous gray that shrouded the Blue Ridge foothills and obscured Valhalla from view. Wind buffeted Marino's car, and by the time he parked at the hospital tiny flakes of snow were clicking against the windshield.

"Shit," he complained as we got out. "That's all we need."

"It's not supposed to amount to anything," I reassured him, flinching as icy flakes stung my cheeks. We bent our heads against the wind and hurried in frigid silence toward the front entrance.

Dr. Masterson was waiting for us in the lobby, his face as hard as stone behind his forced smile. When the two men shook hands, they eyed each other like unfriendly cats, and I did nothing to ease the tension, for I was frankly sick of the psychiatrist's games. He had information we wanted, and he would give it to us unvarnished and in its entirety by virtue of cooperation or a court order. He could take his pick. Without delay we accompanied him to his office, and this time he shut the door.

"Now, what may I help you with?" he asked right off as he took his chair.

"More information," I replied.

"Of course. But I must confess, Dr. Scarpetta," he went on as if Marino were not in the room, "I fail to see what else I can tell you about Al Hunt that might assist you in your cases. You've reviewed his record, and I've told you as much as I remember—"

Marino cut him off. "Yeah, well, we're here to massage that memory of yours," he said, getting out his cigarettes. "And it ain't Al Hunt we're all that interested in."

"I don't understand."

"We're more interested in his pal," Marino said.

"What *pal*?" Dr. Masterson appraised him coldly.

"The name Frankie ring a bell?"

Dr. Masterson began cleaning his glasses, and I decided this was a favorite ploy of his for buying time to think.

"There was a patient here when Al Hunt was, a kid named Frankie," Marino added.

"I'm afraid I'm drawing a blank."

"Draw all the blanks you want, Doc. Just tell us who Frankie is."

"We have three hundred patients at Valhalla at any given time, Lieutenant," he answered. "It isn't possible for me to remember everybody who's been here, particularly those whose stay was of a brief duration."

"So, you're telling me this Frankie character didn't stay very long?" Marino said.

Dr. Masterson reached for his pipe. He had made a slip, and I could see the anger in his eyes. "I'm not *telling* you anything of the sort, Lieutenant." He began slowly tamping tobacco into the bowl. "But perhaps if you could give me a little more information about this patient, the young man you refer to as Frankie, I might at least have a glimmer. Can you tell me something about him other than that he was a 'kid'?"

I intervened. "Apparently, Al Hunt had a friend while he was here, someone he referred to as Frankie. Al mentioned him to me during our conversation. We believe this individual may have been restricted to Backhall after he was admitted, and then transferred to a different floor where he may have become acquainted with Al. Frankie has been described as tall, dark, slender. He also liked to knit, a hobby rather atypical among male patients, I should think."

"This is what Al Hunt told you?" Dr. Masterson asked unemphatically.

"Frankie was also obsessively neat," I said, evading the question.

"I'm afraid a patient's enjoyment of knitting isn't likely to be something brought to my attention," he commented, relighting his pipe.

"It's also possible he had a tendency to stutter when he was under stress," I added, controlling my impatience.

"Hmm. Perhaps someone with spastic dysphonia in his differential diagnosis. That might be a place to start—"

"The place to start is for you to cut the shit," Marino said rudely.

"Really, Lieutenant." Dr. Masterson gave him a condescending smile. "Your hostility is unwarranted."

"Yeah, yeah, and you're *unwarranted* at the moment, too. But I just might get the itch to change that in a minute, slap you with a warrant and haul your ass off to lockup for accessory to murder. How's that sound?" Marino glared at him.

"I think I've about had enough of your impertinence," he replied with maddening calm. "I don't respond well to threats, Lieutenant."

"And I don't respond well to someone jerking me around," Marino retorted.

"Who is Frankie?" I tried again.

"I assure you I don't know, offhand," Dr. Masterson replied. "But if you'll be so kind as to wait a few minutes, I'll go see what we can pull up on our computer."

"Thank you," I said. "We'll be right here."

The psychiatrist had barely gotten out the door before Marino started in.

"What a dirt bag."

"Marino," I said wearily.

"It ain't like this joint's overrun with kids. I'm willing to bet seventy-five percent of the patients here's over the age of sixty. You know, young people would stand out in your memory, right? He knows damn well who Frankie is, probably could tell us what size shoes the drone wears."

"Perhaps."

"There's nothing *perhaps* about it. I'm telling you the guy's jerking us around."

"And he'll continue to do so as long as you antagonize him, Marino."

"Shit." He got up and went to the window behind Dr. Masterson's desk. Parting the curtains, he stared out into the bleak late morning. "I hate like shit when someone lies to me. Swear to God I'll pop 'im if I have to, nail his ass. That's the thing about shrinks that frosts me so bad. They can have Jack the Ripper for a patient and they don't care. They'll still lie to you, tuck the animal in bed and spoon-feed him chicken soup like he's Mr. Apple Pie America." He paused, mumbling inanely, "At least the snow's stopped."

Waiting until he sat back down, I said, "I think threatening to charge him with accessory to murder was a bit much."

"Got his attention, didn't I?"

"Give him a chance to save face, Marino."

He stared sullenly at the curtained window as he smoked.

"I think by now he's realizing it's in his best interest to help us," I said.

"Yeah, well, it's not in my best interest to sit around playing cat and mouse with him. Even as we speak, Frankie Fruitcake's on the street thinking his screwy thoughts, ticking away like a damn bomb about to go off."

I thought of my quiet house in my quiet neighborhood, of Cary Harper's necklace looped over the knob of my back door, and the whispery voice on my answering machine. *Is your hair naturally blond, or do you bleach it. . . .* How odd. I puzzled over the significance of that question. Why did it matter to him?

"If Frankie is our killer," I said quietly, taking a deep breath, "I can't imagine how there can be any connection between Sparacino and these homicides."

"We'll see," he muttered, lighting up another cigarette and staring sourly at the empty doorway.

"What do you mean, 'we'll see'?"

"Never ceases to surprise me how one thing leads to another," he replied cryptically.

"What? What things lead to other things, Marino?"

He glanced at his watch and cursed. "Where the hell is he, anyhow? He go out to lunch?"

"Hopefully he's tracking down Frankie's record."

"Yeah. Hopefully."

"What things lead to other things?" I asked him again. "What are you thinking about? You mind being a little more specific?"

"Let's just put it this way," Marino said. "I got a real strong feeling if it wasn't for that damn book Beryl was writing, all three of 'em would still be alive. In fact, Hunt would probably still be alive, too."

"I can't say that with certainty."

"Course you can't. You're always so goddamn objective. So I'm saying it, okay?" He looked over at me and rubbed his tired eyes, his face flushed. "I got this feeling, all right? It's telling me Sparacino, the book, is the connection. It's what initially linked the killer to Beryl, and then one thing led to another. Next, the squirrel whacks Harper. After that Miss Harper takes enough pills to kill a damn horse so she don't have to rattle around in that big crib of hers all alone while cancer eats her alive. Then Hunt's swinging from the rafters in his fuckin' undershorts."

The orange fiber with its peculiar three-leaf clover shape drifted through my mind, as did Beryl's manuscript, Sparacino, Jeb Price, Senator Partin's Hollywood son, Mrs. McTigue, and Mark. They were limbs and ligaments of a body I could not piece together. In some inexplicable way, they were the alchemy by which seemingly unrelated people and events had been fashioned into Frankie.

Marino was right. One thing always leads to another. Murder never emerges full blown from a vacuum. Nothing evil ever does.

"Do you have any theories as to just what *exactly* this link might be?" I asked Marino.

"Nope, not a goddamn one," he replied with a yawn at the exact moment Dr. Masterson walked into the office and shut the door.

I noticed with satisfaction that he had a stack of case files in hand.

"Now then," he said coolly and without looking at either of us, "I found no one with the name Frankie, which I'm assuming may be a nickname. Therefore, I pulled cases by date of treatment, age, and race. What I have here are the records of six white males, excluding Al Hunt, who were patients at Valhalla during the interval you're interested in. All of them are between the ages of thirteen and twenty-four."

"How about you just let us go through them while you sit back and smoke your pipe." Marino was a little less combative, but not much.

"I would prefer to give you only their histories, for confidentiality reasons, Lieutenant. If one is of keen interest, we'll go through his record in detail. Fair enough?"

"Fair enough," I said before Marino could argue.

"The first case," Dr. Masterson began, opening the top file, "is a nineteen-year-old from Highland Park, Illinois, admitted in December of 1978 with a history of substance abuse—heroin, specifically." He flipped a page. "He was five-foot-eight, weighed one-seventy, brown eyes, brown hair. His treatment was three months in duration."

"Al Hunt wasn't admitted until that following April," I reminded the psychiatrist. "They wouldn't have been patients at the same time."

"Yes, I believe you're right. An oversight on my part. So we can strike him." He set the file on his ink blotter as I gave Marino a warning glance. I knew he was about to explode, his face as red as Christmas.

Opening a second file, Dr. Masterson resumed, "Next we have a fourteen-year-old male, blond, blue-eyed, five-foot-three, one-fifteen pounds. He was admitted in February 1979, discharged six months later. He had a history of withdrawal and fragmentary delusions, and was diagnosed as schizophrenic of the disorganized or hebephrenic type."

"You mind explaining what the hell that means?" Marino asked.

"It presented as incoherence, bizarre mannerisms, extreme social withdrawal, and other oddities of behavior. For example"—he paused to look over a page—"he would leave for the bus stop in the morning but fail to show up at school, and on one occasion was found sitting under a tree drawing peculiar, nonsensical designs in his notebook."

"Yeah. And now he's a famous artist living in New York," Marino mumbled sardonically. "His name Frank, Franklin, or begin with an *F*?"

"No. Nothing close."

"So, who's next?"

"Next is a twenty-two-year-old male from Delaware. Red hair, gray eyes, uhhhh, five-foot-ten, one-fifty pounds. He was admitted in March of 1979, discharged in June. He was diagnosed as suffering from organic delusional syndrome. Contributing factors were temporal lobe epilepsy and a history of cannabis abuse. Complications included dysphoric mood and his attempting to castrate himself while reacting to a delusion."

"What's dysphoric mean?" Marino asked.

"Anxious, restless, depressed."

"This before or after he tried to turn himself into a soprano?"

Dr. Masterson was beginning to register annoyance, and I really couldn't blame him.

"Next," Marino said like a drill sergeant.

"The fourth case is an eighteen-year-old male, black hair, brown eyes, five-foot-nine, one-forty-two pounds. He was admitted in May of 1979, was diagnosed as schizophrenic of the paranoid type. His history"—he flipped a page, then reached for his pipe—"includes unfocused anger and anxiety, with doubts about gender identity and a marked fear of being thought of as homosexual. The onset of his psychosis apparently was related to his being approached by a homosexual in a men's room—"

"Hold it right there." If Marino hadn't stopped him, I would have. "We need to talk about this one. How long was he at Valhalla?"

Dr. Masterson was lighting his pipe. Taking his time glancing through the record, he replied, "Ten weeks."

"Which would have been while Hunt was here," Marino said.

"That's correct."

"So he was approached in a men's room and lost his cookies? What happened? *What* psychosis?" Marino asked.

Dr. Masterson was turning pages. Pushing up his

glasses, he replied, "An episode of delusional thinking of a grandiose nature. He believed God was telling him to do things."

"What things?" Marino asked, leaning forward in his chair.

"There's nothing specific, nothing written here except that he was talking in rather bizarre ways."

"And he was paranoid schizophrenic?" Marino asked.

"Yes."

"You want to define that? Like, what are the other symptoms?"

"Classically speaking," Dr. Masterson replied, "there are associated features which include grandiose delusions or hallucinations with a grandiose content. There may be delusional jealousy, extreme intensity in interpersonal interactions, argumentativeness, and in some instances violence."

"Where was he from?" I asked.

"Maryland."

"Shit," Marino muttered. "He lived with both parents?"

"He lived with his father."

I said, "You're sure he was paranoid versus undifferentiated?"

The distinction was important. Schizophrenics of the undifferentiated type often exhibit grossly disorganized behavior. They generally don't have the wherewithal to premeditate crimes and successfully evade apprehension. The person we were looking for was organized enough to successfully plan and execute his crimes and escape detection.

"I'm quite sure," Dr. Masterson answered. After a

pause, he added blandly, "The patient's first name, interestingly enough, is Frank." Then he handed me the file, and Marino and I briefly looked it over.

Frank Ethan Aims, or Frank E., and thus "Frankie" I could only conclude, had left Valhalla in late July of 1979 and soon after, according to a note Dr. Masterson had made at the time, Aims ran away from his home in Maryland.

"How do you know he ran away from home?" Marino asked, looking up at the psychiatrist. "How do you know what happened to him after he left this joint?"

"His father called me. He was very upset," Dr. Masterson said.

"Then what?"

"I'm afraid there was nothing I or anyone else could do. Frank was of legal age, Lieutenant."

"Do you recall anyone ever referring to him by the nickname Frankie?" I asked.

He shook his head.

"What about Jim Barnes? Was he Frank Aims's social worker?" I asked.

"Yes," Dr. Masterson said reluctantly.

"Did Frank Aims have a bad encounter with Jim Barnes?" I asked.

He hesitated. "Allegedly."

"Of what nature?"

"Allegedly of a sexual nature, Dr. Scarpetta. And for God's sake, I'm trying to help. I hope you'll be mindful of that."

"Hey," Marino said, "we're mindful of it, all right? I mean, we ain't planning on sending out press releases."

"Then Frank knew Al Hunt," I said.

Dr. Masterson hesitated again, his face tight. "Yes. It was Al who came forward with the accusations."

"Bingo," Marino mumbled.

"What do you mean by saying Al Hunt came forth with the accusations?" I asked.

"I mean that he complained to one of our therapists," Dr. Masterson replied, his tone beginning to sound defensive. "He also said something to me during one of our sessions. Frank was questioned and he refused to say anything. He was a very angry, withdrawn young man. It wasn't possible for me to act on what Al had said. Without Frank's corroboration, the accusations were hearsay."

Marino and I were silent.

"I'm sorry," Dr. Masterson said, and by now he was thoroughly unnerved. "I can't help you with Frank's whereabouts. I know nothing further. The last time I heard from his father must have been seven, eight years ago."

"What was the occasion of that conversation?" I queried.

"Mr. Aims called me."

"For what reason?"

"He wondered if I'd heard from Frank."

"Well, had you?" Marino asked.

"No," Dr. Masterson answered. "I've never heard a word from Frank, I'm sorry to say."

"Why did Mr. Aims want to know if you'd heard from Frank?" I put forth the critical question.

"He wanted to find him, hoped that perhaps I might have a clue as to his whereabouts. Because his mother had died. Frank's mother, that is."

"Where did she die and what happened?" I asked.

"Freeport, Maine. I'm really not clear on the circumstances."

"A natural death?" I asked.

"No," Dr. Masterson said, refusing to meet our eyes. "I'm fairly certain it wasn't."

It didn't take Marino long to track it down. He called the Freeport, Maine, police. According to their records, on the late afternoon of January 15, 1983, Mrs. Wilma Aims was beaten to death by a "burglar" who was apparently inside her house when she returned from grocery shopping. She was forty-two when she died, a petite woman with blue eyes and bleached blond hair. The case remained unsolved.

I had no doubts about who the so-called burglar was. Marino didn't either.

He said, "So maybe Hunt really was clairvoyant, huh? He knew about Frankie's taking out his mother. That sure as hell happened a long time after the two fruitcakes was in the bin together."

We were idly watching Sammy Squirrel's antics around the bird feeder. After Marino had driven me back from the hospital and let me out at my house, I invited him in for coffee.

"You're certain Frankie wasn't employed at Hunt's car wash at any point during the past few years?" I asked.

"I don't remember any Frank or Frankie Aims on their books," he said.

"He very well may have changed his name," I said.

"Probably did if he whacked his old lady. Figured the cops might look for him." He reached for his coffee.

"Problem is we don't have a recent description, and joints like Masterwash are a damn revolving door. Guys in and out all the time. Work a couple of days, a week, a month. You got any idea how many white guys are tall, thin, and dark? I'm running down names and running out of road."

We were so close but so far away. It was maddening. "The fibers are consistent with a car wash," I said in frustration. "Hunt worked in the car wash Beryl patronized, and he possibly knew her killer. Do you understand what I'm saying, Marino? Hunt knew about Frankie's killing his mother because Hunt and Frankie may have had contact after Valhalla. Frankie may have worked at Hunt's car wash, perhaps even recently. It's possible Frankie may have first fixed on Beryl when she brought her car in to be cleaned."

"They've got thirty-six employees. All but eleven of them are black, Doc, and out of that eleven honkies, six of them are women. That leaves, what? Five? Three of them is under twenty, meaning they were eight, nine, back when Frankie was at Valhalla. So we know that ain't right. The other three don't fit, either, for various other reasons."

"What various other reasons?" I asked.

"Like they was just hired during the last couple of months, weren't even working there when Beryl would have been bringing in her ride. Not to mention their physical descriptions aren't even close. One guy's got red hair, another one's a munchkin, almost as short as you are."

"Thanks a lot."

"I'll keep checking," he said, turning away from the bird feeder as Sammy Squirrel watched us with pink-rimmed eyes. "What about you?"

"What *about* me?"

"Your office downtown know you still work there?" Marino asked.

He was looking strangely at me.

"Everything's under control," I added.

"I'm not so sure about that, Doc."

"I'm quite sure of it."

"Me"—Marino wouldn't give it a rest—"I think you ain't doing so hot."

"I'm going to stay out of the office for a couple more days," I explained firmly. "I've got to track down Beryl's manuscript. Ethridge is on my case about it. And we need to see what's there. Maybe the link you were talking about."

"Just so long as you remember my rules." He pushed back from the table.

"I'm being quite careful," I assured him.

"And nothing more from him, right?"

"That's right," I said. "No calls. Not a sign of him. Nothing."

"Well, let me just remind you his style wasn't to call Beryl every day, either."

I didn't need the reminder. I didn't want him starting in again. "If he calls, I'll simply say, 'Hello, *Frankie*. What's going on?' "

"Hey. It ain't a joke." He stopped in the foyer and turned around. "You *were* kidding, right?"

"Of course." I smiled, patting his back.

"I mean, really, Doc. Don't do nothing like that. You hear him on your machine, don't pick up the damn phone—"

Marino froze as I opened the door, his eyes widening in horror.

"Holy shiiiiit . . ." He stepped out on my porch, idi-

otically reaching for his revolver, casting about like a madman.

I was too stunned to speak as I stared past him, the winter air alive with the crackle and roar of heat.

Marino's LTD was an inferno against the black night, flames dancing, licking up toward the quarter moon. Grabbing Marino's sleeve, I yanked him back inside the house just as the wailing of a siren sounded in the distance and the gas tank exploded. The living room windows lit up as a ball of fire shot into the sky and ignited the small dogwood trees at the edge of my yard.

"Oh, God," I cried as the power went out.

Marino's big shape paced the carpet in the dark like a crazed bull about to charge as he fumbled with his portable radio and swore.

"The fucking bastard! The fucking bastard!"

I sent Marino away shortly after the incinerated heap that was left of his beloved new car was hauled off in a flatbed truck. He had insisted on staying the night. I had insisted that the several patrol units staking out my house would suffice. He had insisted I check into a hotel, and I had refused to budge. He had his wreckage to deal with and I had mine. My street and yard were a sooty swamp, the downstairs hazy with vile-smelling smoke. The mailbox at the end of my drive looked like a blackened matchstick, and I had lost at least half a dozen boxwoods and just as many trees. More to the point, though I appreciated Marino's concern, I needed to be alone.

It was well past midnight and I was undressing in candlelight when the telephone rang. Frankie's voice seeped like a noxious vapor into my bedroom, poisoning the air I breathed, fouling the privileged refuge of my home.

Sitting on the edge of the bed, I stared blindly at the answering machine as bile crept up my throat and my heart thudded sickly against my ribs.

". . . I wish I could have stayed around to watch. Was it impre-pre-pressive, Kay? Wasn't it something? I don't like it when you have other me-me-men in your house. Now you know. Now you know."

The answering machine stopped and the message light began to blink. Shutting my eyes, I took slow, deep breaths as my heart raced, shadows from the candle flame wavering silently on the walls. How could this be happening to me?

I knew what I had to do. It was the same thing Beryl Madison had done. I wondered if I was experiencing the same fear she had felt when fleeing the car wash, the ragged heart scratched on her car door. My hands trembled violently as I opened the drawer in the bedside table and pulled out the Yellow Pages. After I made the reservations, I called Benton Wesley.

"I don't advise that, Kay," he said, instantly wide awake. "No. Under no circumstances. Listen to me, Kay—"

"I have no choice, Benton. I just wanted someone to know. You can inform Marino, if you wish. But don't interfere. Please. The manuscript—"

"Kay—"

"I've got to find it. I think that's where it is."

"Kay! You're not thinking right!"

"Look." My voice rose. "What am I supposed to do? Wait here until the bastard decides to kick in my door or blow up my car? I stay here, I'm dead. Haven't you figured that out yet, Benton?"

"You've got an alarm system. You've got a gun. He can't blow up your car with you in it. Uh, Marino called. He told me what happened. They're pretty sure someone doused a rag with gasoline, stuffed it into the gas tank. They found pry marks. He pried open the—"

"Jesus, Benton. You're not even listening to me."

"Listen. *You* listen. Please listen to me, Kay. I'll get cover for you, get someone to move in with you, all right? One of our female agents—"

"Good night, Benton."

"Kay!"

I hung up and didn't answer when he immediately called back. I listened numbly to his protests on the machine, blood pounding in my neck as the images rushed back at me, images of Marino's car hissing as flames snarled at arching blasts of water from tumescent fire hoses snaking over my street. When I had discovered the charred little corpse at the end of my driveway, something inside me snapped. The gas tank in Marino's car must have exploded at the very instant Sammy Squirrel was frantically hopping along the power line. Crazily, he leapt for safety. For a split second, his paws simultaneously made contact with the grounded transformer and primary line. Twenty thousand volts of electricity surged through his tiny body, burning him to a crisp and blowing the fuse.

I had scooped him into a shoe box and buried him in my rose garden, the idea of seeing his blackened shape in the light of morning more than I could bear.

The electricity was still out when I finished packing. I went downstairs and nursed brandy and smoked until

I stopped shaking, my Ruger on top of the bar glinting in the light of hurricane lanterns. I did not go to bed. I did not look at the wreckage of my yard when I bolted out my door, my suitcase thumping against my leg and filthy water splashing my ankles as I ran to my car. I did not see a single patrol unit as I drove swiftly along my silent street. When I got to the airport shortly after five A.M., I headed straight for the ladies' room and took my handgun out of my pocketbock. Unloading it, I packed it inside my suitcase.

15

Passing through the boarding bridge, I deplaned at noon into the sun-drenched concourse of Miami International Airport.

I stopped to buy the Miami *Herald* and a cup of coffee. Finding a small table halfway hidden by a potted palm, I took off my winter blazer and pushed up my sleeves. I was soaking wet, perspiration trickling down my sides and back. My eyes burned from lack of sleep, my head ached, and what I discovered when I spread open the paper did nothing to improve my condition. In the lower left-hand corner of the front page was a spectacular photograph of firefighters hosing down Marino's flaming car. Accompanying the dramatic tableau of arching water, billowing smoke, and trees igniting at the edge of my yard was the following caption:

POLICE CAR EXPLODES

Richmond firefighters work on a city homicide detective's car engulfed in flames on a quiet residential street. The Ford LTD was unoccupied when it exploded last night. There were no injuries. Arson is suspected.

At least there was no reference to whose house Marino's car had been parked in front of or why, thank God. All the same, my mother would see the photograph and she would try to call. "I wish you'd move back to Miami, Kay. Richmond sounds so awful. And the new medical examiner's office is so lovely down here, Kay—looks like something out of the movies," she would say. Oddly, it never seemed to occur to my mother that there were more homicides, shoot-outs, drug busts, race riots, rapes, and robberies in my Spanish-speaking hometown in any given year than in Virginia and the entire British Commonwealth combined.

I would call my mother later. Forgive me, Lord, but I don't have it in me to talk to her now.

Gathering my belongings, I crushed out a cigarette and immersed myself in the tide of tropical clothes, duty-free shopping bags and foreign tongues flowing toward the baggage area, my handbag pressed protectively against my side.

I didn't begin to relax until several hours later as I sped along the Seven Mile Bridge in my rental car. As I drove deeper south, the Gulf of Mexico on one side and the Atlantic on the other, I tried to remember the last time I had been to Key West. Of all the times Tony and I had visited my family in Miami, this was one outing we had never considered. I was fairly certain the last time I had made this drive, I had made it with Mark.

His passion for the beaches and the water and the sun

was a devotion returned in kind. If it is possible for nature to favor one creature over another, nature favored Mark. I could scarely remember the year, much less where we had gone, on the occasion he had spent a week with my family. What I remembered with clarity were his baggy white swim trunks and the firm warmth of his hand in mine during our strolls across cool, wet sand. I remembered the startling whiteness of his teeth against his coppery skin, the health and unsuppressed joy in his eyes as he looked for shark's teeth and shells while I smiled in the shade of a wide-brimmed hat. Most of all, what I could not forget was loving a young man named Mark James more than I had thought it was possible to love anything on this earth.

What had changed him? It was hard for me to fathom that he had crossed over into enemy camps, as Ethridge believed and I had no choice but to accept. Mark was always spoiled. He carried about him a sense of entitlement that comes from being the beautiful son of beautiful people. The fruits of the world were his to enjoy, but he had never been dishonest. He had never been cruel. I couldn't even say that he had ever been condescending to those less fortunate than himself, or manipulative with those vulnerable to his charms. His only real sin was that he had not loved me enough. From the distant perch of my midlife perspective, I could forgive him for that. What I could not forgive him for was his dishonesty. I could not forgive him for deteriorating into a lesser man than the one I had once respected and adored. I could not forgive him for no longer being *Mark*.

Passing the U.S. Naval Hospital on U.S. 1, I followed the gentle shoreline curve of North Roosevelt Boulevard.

Soon enough I was threading my way through a maze of Key West streets in search of Duval. Sunlight painted the narrow streets white as shadows of tropical foliage stirred by the breeze danced across the pavement. Beneath a blue sky that went on forever, huge palms and mahogany trees cradled houses and shops in spreading arms of vivid green as bougainvillea and hibiscus wooed sidewalks and porches with bright gifts of purple and red. Slowly, I passed people in sandals and shorts, and an endless parade of mopeds. There were very few children and a disproportionate number of men.

The La Concha was a tall, pink Holiday Inn of open spaces and gaudy tropical plants. I'd had no problem making reservations, ostensibly because the tourist season did not begin until the third week of December. But as I left my car in the half-empty parking lot and walked into the somewhat deserted lobby, I couldn't help but think about what Marino had said. Never in my life had I seen so many same-sex couples, and it was patently clear that running deep beneath the robust health of this tiny offshore island was a mother lode of disease. Wherever I looked, it seemed, I saw men dying. I had no phobia of catching hepatitis or AIDS, having learned long ago to cope with the theoretical danger of disease endemic to my work. Nor was I bothered by homosexuals. The older I got, the more I was of the opinion that love can be experienced in many different ways. There is no right or wrong way to love, only in how it is expressed.

As the desk clerk returned my credit card, I asked him to steer me in the general direction of the elevators, and I foggily headed up to my room on the fifth floor. Stripping down to my underwear, I crawled in bed, where I slept for the next fourteen hours.

* * *

The following day was just as glorious as the one before, and I was outfitted like any other tourist, except for the loaded Ruger in my pocketbook. My self-imposed mission was to search this island of some thirty thousand people and find two men known to me only as PJ and Walt. I knew from the letters Beryl had written in late August that they were her friends and lived in the rooming house where she had stayed. I had not the slightest clue as to the location or name of this rooming house, and it was my prayer that someone at Louie's could tell me.

I walked, a map that I had bought in the hotel gift shop in hand. Following Duval, I passed rows of shops and restaurants with balustraded balconies that brought to mind New Orleans's French Quarter. I passed sidewalk art displays and boutiques selling exotic plants, silks, and Perugina chocolates, then waited at a crossing to watch the bright yellow cars of the Conch Tour Train rattle by. I began to understand why Beryl Madison had not wanted to leave Key West. With each step I took, Frankie's threatening presence began to fade. By the time I turned left on South Street, he was as remote as Richmond's raw December weather.

Louie's was a white-frame restaurant that had once been a house, on the corner of Vernon and Waddell. Its hardwood floors were spotless, its pale-peach linen-covered tables impeccably set and arranged with exquisite fresh flowers. I followed my host through the air-conditioned dining room, to be seated on the porch where I was dazzled by the variegated blues of water meeting sky, and palms and hanging baskets of blooming plants stirring in air perfumed by the sea. The Atlantic Ocean was nearly under my feet, a bright spattering of sailboats anchored a short swim away. Ordering a rum and tonic, I thought of Beryl's letters and wondered if I were sitting where she had written them.

Most of the tables were occupied. I felt removed from the crowd, my table in a corner against the railing. To my left were four steps leading down to a wide deck, where a small group of young men and women were lounging in bathing suits near a chikee bar. I watched a sinewy Latin boy in a yellow bikini flick a cigarette butt into the water, then get up and languidly stretch. He padded off to buy another round of beers from the bearded bartender, who moved about with the ennui of one tired of his job and no longer young.

Long after I finished my salad and bowl of conch chowder, the group of young people finally clambered down back steps and waded noisily out into the water. Soon they were swimming in the direction of the anchored boats. I paid my bill and approached the bartender. He was leaning back in a chair beneath his thatched canopy, reading a novel.

"What will it be?" he drawled as he rose unenthusiastically to his feet and tucked the book under the bar.

"I was wondering if you sold cigarettes," I said. "I didn't see a machine inside."

"That's it," he said, gesturing toward a limited display behind him. I made a selection.

Slapping the pack on the bar, he charged me the outrageous sum of two dollars, and wasn't particularly gracious when I threw in another fifty cents for a tip. His eyes were a very unfriendly green, his face weathered by years of the sun, his thick, dark beard flecked with gray. He looked hostile and hardened, and I had a suspicion he had lived in Key West for quite a while.

"Do you mind if I ask you a question?" I said.

"Doesn't matter because you just did, ma'am," he answered.

I smiled. "You're right. I just did. And now I'm going to ask you another one. How long have you worked at Louie's?"

"Going on five years." He reached for a towel and began polishing the bar.

"Then you must have known a young woman who went by the name Straw," I asked, recalling from Beryl's letters that she had not used her proper name while here.

"Straw?" he repeated, frowning as he continued to polish.

"A nickname. She was blond, slender, very pretty, and came to Louie's almost every afternoon during this past summer. She would sit out at one of your tables and write."

He stopped polishing and fixed those hard eyes on me. "What's it to you? She a friend of yours?"

"She's a patient of mine." I said the only thing I could think of that was neither off-putting nor a bald-faced lie.

"Huh?" His thick eyebrows shot up. "A patient? What? You're her *doctor*?"

"That's correct."

"Well, there's not a whole lot of good you're going to do her now, *Doc*, I'm sorry to tell you." He plopped down in his chair and leaned back, waiting.

"I'm aware of that," I said. "I know she's dead."

"Yeah, I was pretty shocked when I heard about it. The

cops stormed in a couple weeks back with their rubber hoses and thumbscrews. I'll tell you what my buddies told them, nobody here knows shit about what happened to Straw. She was real quiet, a real fine lady. Used to sit right over there." He pointed at an empty table not far from where I was standing. "Used to sit there all the time, just minding her own business."

"Did any of you get to know her?"

"Sure." He shrugged. "We all drank a few brews together. She was partial to Coronas and lime. But I wouldn't say the people here knew her *personally*. I mean, I'm not sure anybody could even tell you where she was from, except that it was from the land of snowbirds."

"Richmond, Virginia," I said.

"You know," he went on, "a lot of people come and go around here. Key West's a live-and-let-live place. A lot of starving artists here, too. Straw wasn't any different from a lot of people I meet—except most people I meet don't end up murdered. Damn." He scratched his beard and slowly shook his head from side to side. "It's really hard to imagine. Kind of blows your mind."

"There are a lot of unanswered questions," I said, lighting a cigarette.

"Yeah, like why the hell do you smoke? I thought doctors are supposed to know better."

"It's a filthy, unhealthy habit. And I do know better. And I think you may as well fix me a rum and tonic because I like to drink, too. Barbancourt with a twist, please."

"Four, eight, what's your pleasure?" He challenged my repertoire of fine booze.

"Twenty-five, if you've got it."

"Nope. Can only get the twenty-five-year-old stuff in the islands. So smooth it will make you cry."

"The best you've got, then," I said.

He shot his finger at a bottle behind him, familiar with its amber glass and five stars on the label. Barbancourt Rhum, aged in barrels for fifteen years, just like the bottle I had discovered in Beryl's kitchen cabinet.

"That would be wonderful," I said.

Grinning and suddenly energized, he got up from his chair, his hands moving with the dexterity of a juggler as he snapped up bottles, measuring a long stream of liquid Haitian gold without benefit of a jigger, which was followed by sparkling splashes of tonic. For the grand finale, he deftly sliced a perfect sliver of a Key lime that looked as if it had just been plucked from the tree, squeezed it into my drink and ran a bruised lemon peel around the rim of the glass. Wiping his hands on the towel he had tucked into the waistband of his faded Levi's, he slid a paper napkin across the bar and presented me with his art. It was, without question, the best rum and tonic I had ever raised to my lips, and I told him so.

"This one's on the house," he said, waving off the ten-dollar bill I extended to him. "Any doctor who smokes and knows her rum's all right by me." Reaching under the bar, he got out his own pack.

"I tell ya," he went on, shaking out the match, "I get so damn tired of hearing all this self-righteous shit about smoking and all the rest of it. You know what I mean? People make you feel like a damn criminal. Me, I say live and let live. That's my motto."

"Yes. I know exactly what you mean," I said as we took long, hungry drags.

"Always something they got to judge you for. You know, what you eat, what you drink, who you date."

"People certainly can be extremely judgmental and unkind," I answered.

"Amen to that."

He sat back down in the shade of his bottle-lined shelter while the sun baked the top of my head. "Okay," he said, "so you're Straw's doctor. What is it you're trying to find out, if you don't mind my asking?"

"There are various circumstances that occurred prior to her death that are very confusing," I said. "I'm hoping her friends might be able to clarify a few points for me—"

"Wait a minute," he interrupted, sitting up straighter in his chair. "When you say *doctor*, like what kind of doctor do you mean?"

"I examined her . . ."

"When?"

"After her death."

"Oh, shit. You telling me you're a *mortician*?" he asked in disbelief.

"I'm a forensic pathologist."

"A *coroner*?"

"More or less."

"Well, I'll be damned." He looked me up and down. "I sure as hell never would've guessed that one."

I didn't know if I had just been paid a compliment or not.

"Do they always send—what did you call it?—a forensic pathologist like you around, you know, tracking down information like you're doing?"

"Nobody sent me. I came of my own accord."

"Why?" he asked, his eyes dark with suspicion again. "You came one hell of a long way."

"I care about what happened to her. I care very much."

"You're telling me the cops didn't send you?"

"The cops don't have the authority to *send* me anywhere."

"Good." He laughed. "I like that."

I reached for my drink.

"Bunch of bullies. Think they're all junior Rambos." He stubbed out his cigarette. "Came in here with their damn rubber gloves on. Jesus Christ. Just how do you think *that* looked to our customers? Went to see Brent—he was one of our waiters. He's dying, man, and what do they do? The assholes wear surgical masks and stand back ten feet from his bed like he's Typhoid Mary while they're asking him shit. I swear to God, even if I'd known a thing about what happened to Beryl, I wouldn't have given them the time of day."

The name hit me like a two-by-four, and when our eyes met, I knew he realized the significance of what he had just said.

"Beryl?" I asked.

He leaned back silently in his chair.

I pressed him. "You knew her name was Beryl?"

"Like I said, the cops were here asking questions, talking about her." Uncomfortably, he lit another cigarette, unable to meet my eyes. My bartender friend was a very poor liar.

"Did they talk to you?"

"Nope. I made myself scarce when I saw what was going on."

"Why?"

"I told you. I don't like cops. I've got a Barracuda, a beat-up piece of shit I've had since I was a kid. For some reason, they've always got to pop me. Always giving me tickets for one thing or another, throwing their weight around with their big guns and Ray Bans, like they think they're stars in their own TV series or something."

"You knew her name when she was here," I said quietly. "You knew her name was Beryl Madison long before the police came."

"So what if I did? What's the big deal?"

"She was very secretive about it," I replied with feeling. "She didn't want people down here to know who she was. She didn't tell people who she was. She paid for everything in cash so she wouldn't have to use credit cards, checks, anything that might identify her. She was terrified. She was running. She didn't want to die."

He was staring wide-eyed at me.

"Please tell me what you know. Please. I have a feeling you were her friend."

He got up, saying nothing, and stepped out from behind the bar. His back to me, he began collecting the empty bottles and other trash the young people had scattered over the deck.

I sipped my drink in silence and stared past him at the water. In the distance a bronzed young man was unfurling a deep blue sail as he prepared to set out to sea. Palm fronds whispered in the breeze and a black Labrador retriever danced along the shore, darting in and out of the surf.

"Zulu," I muttered, staring numbly at the dog.

The bartender stopped what he was doing and looked up at me. "What did you say?"

"Zulu," I repeated. "Beryl mentioned Zulu and your cats in one of her letters. She said Louie's stray animals eat better than any human."

"What letters?"

"She wrote several letters while she was here. We found them in her bedroom after she was murdered. She said the people here had become like family. She thought this was the most beautiful place in the world. I wish she'd never returned to Richmond. I wish she'd stayed right here."

The voice drifting out of me sounded as if it were coming from somebody else, and my vision was blurring. Poor sleep habits, accumulated stress, and the rum were ganging up on me. The sun seemed to dry up what little blood I had left flowing to my brain.

When the bartender finally returned to his chikee hut, he spoke with quiet emotion. "I don't know what to tell you. But yeah, I was Beryl's friend."

Turning to him, I replied, "Thank you. I'd like to think I was her friend, too. That I *am* her friend."

He looked down awkwardly, but not before I detected a softening of his face.

"You can never be real sure who's all right and who ain't," he commented. "It's real hard to know these days, that's for damn sure."

His meaning slowly penetrated my fatigue. "Have there been people asking about Beryl who *aren't* all right? People other than the police? People other than me?"

He poured himself a Coke.

"Have there been? Who?" I repeated, suddenly alarmed.

"Don't know his name." He took a big swallow of his drink. "Some good-looking guy. Young, maybe in his twenties. Dark. Fancy clothes, designer shades. Looked like he just stepped out of *GQ*. I guess this was a couple weeks ago. He said he was a private investigator, shit like that."

Senator Partin's son.

"He wanted to know where Beryl lived while she was here," he went on.

"Did you tell him?"

"Hell, I didn't even talk to him."

"Did *anybody* tell him?" I persisted.

"Not likely."

"Why isn't it likely, and are you ever going to tell me your name?"

"It's not likely because nobody knew except me and a buddy," he said. "And I'll tell you my name if you tell me yours."

"Kay Scarpetta."

"Pleased to meet you. My name's Peter. Peter Jones. My friends call me PJ."

PJ lived two blocks from Louie's in a tiny house completely overcome by a tropical jungle. The foliage was so dense I'm not sure I would have known the paint-eroded frame house was there had it not been for the Barracuda parked in front. One look at the car told me exactly why the police continually hassled its owner. The thing was a piece of subway graffiti on oversize wheels, with spoilers, headers, a rear end jacked up high, and a homemade paint job of hallucinatory shapes and designs in the psychedelic colors of the sixties.

"That's my baby," PJ said, affectionately thumping the hood.

"It's something else, all right," I said.

"Had her since I was sixteen."

"And you should keep her forever," I said sincerely as I ducked under branches and followed him into the cool, dark shade.

"It's not much," he apologized, unlocking the door. "Just one extra bedroom and john upstairs where Beryl stayed. One of these days, I guess I'll rent it out again. But I'm pretty picky about my tenants."

The living room was a hodgepodge of junkyard furniture: a couch and overstuffed chair in ugly shades of pink and green, several mismatched lamps fashioned from odd things like conch shells and coral, and a coffee table constructed from what appeared to have been an oak door in a former life. Scattered about were painted coconuts, starfish, newspapers, shoes, and beer cans, the damp air sour with decay.

"How did Beryl find out about the room you were renting?" I asked, sitting on the couch.

"At Louie's," he replied, switching on several lamps. "Her first few nights here she was staying at Ocean Key, a pretty nice hotel on Duval. I guess she figured out in a hurry that was going to cost her some bucks if she planned to stick around a while." He sat down in the overstuffed chair. "It was maybe the third time she'd come to Louie's for lunch. She would just get a salad and sit there and stare out at the water. She wasn't working on anything then. She would just sit. It was kind of weird the way she would hang around. I mean we're talking hours, like most of the afternoon. Finally, and like I said, I think it was the third time she'd come to Louie's, she wandered down to the bar and was leaning against the railing, looking out at the view. I guess I felt sorry for her."

"Why?" I asked.

He shrugged. "She looked so damn lost, I guess. Depressed or something. I could tell. So I started talking to her. She wasn't what I'd call easy, that's for sure."

"She wasn't easy to get to know," I agreed.

"She was hard as hell to hold a friendly conversation with. I asked her a couple of simple questions, like 'This your first visit here?' Or 'Where are you from?' That sort of thing. And sometimes she wouldn't even answer me. It's like I wasn't there. But it was funny. Something told me to hang in there with her. I asked her what she liked to drink. We started talking about different kinds. It sort of loosened her up, caught her interest. Next thing, I'm letting her try out a few favorites on the house. First a Corona with a twist of lime, which she went nuts over. Then the Barbancourt, like I fixed you. That was real special."

"No doubt that loosened her up quite a bit," I remarked.

He smiled. "Yeah, you got that straight. I mixed it pretty strong. We started shooting the breeze about other things, and next thing you know she's asking me about places to stay in the area. That's when I told her I had a room, and I invited her to come see it, told her to stop by later if she wanted. It was a Sunday, and I'm always off early on Sundays."

"And she came by that night?" I inquired.

"It really surprised me. I sort of figured she wouldn't show. But she did, found the place without a hitch. By then Walt was home. He used to stay at the Square selling his shit until dark. He'd just come in, and the three of us started talking and hitting it off. Next thing, we're walking around Old Town, and end up in Sloppy Joe's. Being a writer and all, she really flipped out, went on and on about Hemingway. She was one smart lady, I'll tell you that."

"Walt was selling silver jewelry," I said. "In Mallory Square."

"How'd you know that?" PJ asked, surprised.

"The letters Beryl wrote," I reminded him.

He stared off in sadness for a moment.

"She also mentioned Sloppy Joe's. I got the impression she was very fond of you and Walt."

"Yeah, the three of us could put away some beer." He picked a magazine off the floor and tossed it on the coffee table.

"You both may have been the only friends she had."

"Beryl was something." He looked at me. "She was something. I'd never met anybody like her before, and probably won't again. Once you got past that wall of hers, she was some fine lady. Smart as shit," he said again, resting his head on the back of the chair and staring up at the paint-peeled ceiling. "I used to love to hear her talk. She could say things just like that." He snapped his fingers. "In a way I couldn't if I had ten years to think about it. My sister's the same way. She teaches school in Denver. English. I've never been real quick with words. Before I bartended I did a lot of things with my hands. Construction, bricklaying, carpentry. Dabbled a little in pottery until I about starved to death. I came here because of Walt. Met him in Mississippi, of all places. In a bus station, if you can fucking believe that. We started talking, rode all the way to Louisiana together. A couple months later, we're both down here. It's so weird." He looked at me. "I mean, that was almost ten years ago. And all I got left is this dump."

"Your life is far from over, PJ," I said gently.

"Yeah." His face turned up to the ceiling, he shut his eyes.

"Where is Walt now?"

"Lauderdale, last I heard."

"I'm very sorry," I said.

"It happens. What can I say?"

There was a moment of silence and I decided it was time to take a chance.

"Beryl was writing a book while she was here."

"You got that straight. When she wasn't frapping around with the two of us, she was working on that damn book."

"It's disappeared," I said.

He didn't respond.

"The so-called private investigator you mentioned and various other people are keenly interested in it. You know that already. I believe you do."

He remained silent, his eyes shut.

"You have no good reason to trust me, PJ, but I hope you'll listen," I went on in a low voice. "I've got to find that manuscript, the manuscript Beryl was working on while she was here. I think she didn't take it back to Richmond with her when she left Key West. Can you help me?"

Opening his eyes, he peered over at me. "With all due respect, Dr. Scarpetta, saying I did know, why should I? Why should I break a promise?"

"Did you promise her you'd never tell where it is?" I asked.

"Doesn't matter, and I asked you first," he answered.

Taking a deep breath, I looked down at the dirty gold shag carpet beneath my feet as I leaned forward on the couch.

"I know of no good reason for you to break a promise to a friend, PJ," I said.

"Bullshit. You wouldn't ask me if you didn't know of a good reason."

"Did Beryl tell you about him?" I asked.

"You mean the asshole hassling her?"

"Yes."

"Yeah. I knew about it." He suddenly got up. "I don't know about you, but I'm ready for a beer."

"Please," I said, believing it was important I accept his hospitality despite my better judgment. I was still woozy from the rum.

Returning from the kitchen, he handed me a sweating bottle of ice-cold Corona, a wedge of lime floating in the long neck. It tasted wonderful.

PJ sat down and began talking again. "Straw, I mean Beryl, I guess I may as well call her Beryl, was scared shitless. To be honest, when I heard about what happened, I wasn't really surprised. I mean, it freaked me. But I wasn't really surprised. I told her to stay here. I told her to screw the rent, that she could stay. Walt and me, well, I guess it was funny, but it got to where she was sort of like our sister. The fuckhead screwed me, too."

"I beg your pardon?" I asked, startled by his sudden anger.

"That's when Walt left. It was after we heard about it. I don't know. He changed, Walt did. I can't say that what happened to her was the only reason. We had our problems. But it did something to him. He got distant and wouldn't talk anymore. Then, one morning, he left. He just left."

"This was when? Several weeks ago, when you found out from the police, when they came to Louie's?"

He nodded.

"It's screwed me, too, PJ," I said. "It's totally screwed me, too."

"What do you mean? How the hell's it screwed you, other than causing you a lot of trouble?"

"I'm living Beryl's nightmare." I was barely able to say it.

He took a swallow of beer, his eyes intense on me.

"Right now I suppose I'm running, too—for the same reason she was."

"Man, you're making my brain bleed," he said, shaking his head. "What are you talking about?"

"Did you see the photograph on the front page of this morning's *Herald*?" I asked. "A photograph of a police car burning in Richmond."

"Yeah," he said, puzzled. "I sort of remember it."

"That was in front of my house, PJ. The detective was inside my living room talking to me when his car was torched. It's not the first thing that's happened. You see, he's after me, too."

"Who is, for Christ's sake?" he asked, even though I could tell he knew.

"The man who murdered Beryl," I said with great difficulty. "The man who then butchered Beryl's mentor, Cary Harper, whom you may have heard her mention."

"Lots of times. Shit. I'm not believing this."

"Please help me, PJ."

"I don't know how I can." He became so upset he jumped out of the chair and started pacing. "Why would the pig come after you?"

"He suffers delusional jealousy. He's obsessive. He's a paranoid schizophrenic. He seems to hate anyone connected with Beryl. *I don't know why, PJ.* But I have to find out who he is. I have to find *him*," I said.

"I don't know who the hell he is. Or where the hell he is. If I did, I'd find him and tear his fucking head off!"

"I need that manuscript, PJ," I said.

"What the fuck does her manuscript have to do with it?" he protested.

So I told him. I told him about Cary Harper and his necklace. I told him about the phone calls and the fibers, and the autobiographical work Beryl was writing that I had been accused of stealing. I revealed everything I could think of about the cases while my soul withered in fear. I had never, not even once, discussed the details of a case with anyone other than the investigators or attorneys involved. When I was finished, PJ silently left the room. When he returned, he was carrying an army knapsack, which he placed in my lap.

"There," he said. "I swore to God I would never do this. I'm sorry, Beryl," he muttered. "I'm sorry."

Opening the canvas flap, I carefully pulled out what must have been close to a thousand typed pages scribbled with handwritten notes, and four computer diskettes, all of it bound in thick rubber bands.

"She told us never to let anybody have it should something happen to her. I promised."

"Thank you, Peter. God bless you," I said, and then I asked of him one last thing.

"Did Beryl ever mention anyone she referred to as 'M'?"

He stood very still and stared at his beer.

"Do you know who this person is?" I asked.

"Myself," he said.

"I don't understand."

" 'M' for 'Myself.' She wrote letters to herself," he said.

"The two letters we found," I said to him. "The ones we found on the floor of her bedroom after she was murdered, the ones that mentioned you and Walt, were addressed to 'M.' "

"I know," he said, shutting his eyes.

"How do you know?"

"I knew it when you mentioned Zulu and the cats. I knew you'd read those letters. That's when I decided you were all right, that you were who you said you were."

"Then you've read the letters, too?" I asked, stunned.

He nodded.

"We never found the originals," I muttered. "The two we found are photocopies."

"That's because she burned everything," he said, taking a deep breath, steadying himself.

"But she didn't burn her book."

"No. She told me she didn't know where she'd go next or what she'd do if he was still there, still after her. That she'd call me later on and tell me where to mail the book. And if I didn't hear from her, to hold on to it, never give it up to anyone. She never called, you know. She never fucking called." He wiped his eyes, averting his face from me. "The book was her hope, you know. Her hope of being alive." His voice caught when he added, "She never stopped hoping things would turn out all right."

"What exactly was it that she burned, PJ?"

"Her diary," he replied. "I guess you could call it that. Letters she'd been writing to herself. She said it was her therapy and that she didn't want anyone to see them. They were very private, her most private thoughts. The day before she left, she burned all her letters except two."

"The two I saw," I almost whispered. "Why? Why didn't she burn those two letters?"

"Because she wanted me and Walt to have them."

"As a remembrance?"

"Yeah," he said, reaching for his beer and roughly rubbing tears from his eyes. "A piece of herself, a record of thoughts she had while she was here. The day before she left, the day she burned the stuff, she went out and photocopied just those two. She kept the copies and gave us the originals, said it sort of made us *indentured* to each other—that was the word she used. The three of us would always be together in our thoughts as long as we had the letters."

When he walked me out, I turned around, throwing my arms around him in a hug of thanks.

I headed back to my hotel as the sun settled, palms etched against a spreading band of fire. Throngs of people clambered noisily toward the bars along Duval, and the enchanted air was alive with music, laughter, and lights. I walked with a spring in my step, the army knapsack slung over my shoulder. For the first time in weeks I was happy, almost euphoric. I was completely unprepared for what awaited me in my room.

16

I did not recall leaving any lamps on and just assumed the housekeeping staff must have neglected to switch them off after changing the linen and emptying the ashtrays. I had already locked the door and was humming to myself as I passed the bath when I realized I was not alone.

Mark was sitting near the window, an open briefcase on the carpet beside his chair. In that moment's hesitation when my feet didn't know which way to move, his eyes met mine in speechless communication, thrilling my heart and seizing it with terror.

Pale and dressed in a winter gray suit, he looked as if he had just arrived from the airport, his suit bag propped against the bed. If he had a mental geiger counter, I was sure my knapsack was making it click like mad. Sparacino had sent him. I thought of the Ruger in my handbag, but I knew I could never turn a gun on Mark James and squeeze the trigger if it came to that.

"How did you get in?" I asked dully, standing very still.

"I'm your husband," he said, and reaching in his pocket, he displayed a hotel key to my room.

"You bastard," I whispered, my heart pounding harder.

His face blanched. He averted his eyes. "Kay—"

"Oh, God. You bastard!"

"Kay. I'm here because Benton Wesley sent me. Please." Then he got up from the chair.

I watched him in stunned silence as he produced a fifth of whiskey from his suit bag. Walking past me to the bar, he began filling glasses with ice. His motions were slow and deliberate, as if he was doing his best not to further unnerve me. He also seemed very tired.

"Have you eaten?" he asked, handing me a drink.

Moving past him, I unceremoniously dropped the knapsack and my pocketbook on top of the dresser.

"I'm starved," he said, loosening his shirt collar and yanking off his tie. "Damn, I must have changed planes four times. Don't think I've had anything to eat but peanuts since breakfast."

I said nothing.

"I've already ordered for us," he went on quietly. "You'll be ready to eat by the time it gets here."

Moving to the window, I gazed out at the purple-gray clouds over the lights of Key West's Old Town streets. Mark pulled up a chair, slipped off his shoes, and propped his feet up on the edge of the bed.

"Let me know when you're ready for me to explain," he said, swirling ice in his glass.

"I wouldn't believe anything you said, Mark," I answered coldly.

"Fair enough. I'm paid to live a lie. I've gotten unbelievably good at it."

"Yes," I echoed, "you've gotten unbelievably good at it. How did you find me? I don't believe Benton told you. He doesn't know where I'm staying, and there must be fifty hotels on this island and just as many guesthouses."

"You're right. I'm sure there are, and it took me exactly one phone call to find you," he said.

Defeated, I sat down on the bed.

Reaching inside his suit jacket, he pulled out a folded brochure and handed it to me. "Look familiar?"

It was the same visitor's information guide Marino had found inside Beryl Madison's bedroom, a photocopy of which was included in her case file. It was the same guide I had studied countless times and then recalled two nights before when I had decided to flee to Key West. One side of it listed restaurants and places to sightsee and shop, the other was a street map bordered by advertisements, including one for this hotel, which was where I had gotten the idea to stay here.

"Benton finally got hold of me yesterday after repeated attempts," he went on. "He was pretty upset, said you'd taken off, headed here, and then we went about the business of trying to track you down. Apparently there's a photocopy of Beryl's brochure in the file he has. He assumed you would have seen it, too, and possibly even made a copy for your own record. We decided it might occur to you to use it as a guide."

"Where did you get this?" I returned the brochure to him.

"At the airport. It just so happens this hotel is the only one listed. It was the first place I called. They had a reservation in your name."

"All right. So I wouldn't make a very good fugitive."

"A damn poor one."

"It *is* where I got the idea, if you must know," I admitted angrily. "I've been through Beryl's paperwork so many times, I remembered the brochure, remembered seeing the ad for a Holiday Inn on Duval. I suppose it stood out to me because I wondered if she might have stayed here when she first arrived in Key West."

"Had she?" He lifted his glass.

"No."

As he got up to refresh our drinks, there was a knock on the door and my heart jumped as Mark casually reached around and withdrew a 9-millimeter pistol from under the back of his suit jacket. Holding it up, he looked through the peephole and returned the gun to the back of his trousers as he opened the door. Our dinner had arrived, and when Mark paid the young woman in cash, she smiled brightly and said, "Thank you, Mr. Scarpetta. I hope you enjoy your steaks."

"Why did you check in as my husband?" I demanded.

"I'll sleep on the floor. But you're not staying alone," he answered, setting covered dishes on the table near the window and uncorking the bottle of wine. Slipping out of his suit jacket and tossing it on the bed, he set the pistol on top of the dresser not far from my knapsack and within easy reach.

I waited until he had sat down to eat before asking him about the gun.

"An ugly little monster, but maybe my only friend," he replied, cutting into his steak. "And for that matter, I presume you have your thirty-eight with you, probably in your knapsack." He glanced at the knapsack on the dresser.

"It's in my pocketbook, for your information," I blurted

out ridiculously. "And how in God's name did you know I have a thirty-eight?"

"Benton told me. He also said you'd recently gotten a license to carry it concealed, and he figured you weren't going many places without your piece these days." He sipped his wine, adding, "Not bad."

"Has Benton told you my dress size, too?" I asked, forcing myself to eat as my stomach begged me not to.

"Now, that he doesn't need to tell me. You still wear an eight, look just as good as you did when we were in Georgetown. Better, in fact."

"I'd greatly appreciate it if you'd stop acting like a cavalier son of a bitch and tell me how the hell you even know Benton Wesley's name, much less merit the privilege of enjoying so many little tête-à-têtes with him about me."

"Kay." He set down his fork as he met my angry gaze. "I've known Benton longer than you have. Haven't you figured it out yet? Do I have to spell it in neon lights?"

"Yes. Write it in big letters across the sky, Mark. Because I don't know what to believe. I have no idea who you are anymore. I don't trust you. In fact, at this moment I'm scared to death of you."

Leaning back in the chair, his face as serious as I had ever seen it, he said, "Kay, I'm sorry you're afraid of me. I'm sorry you don't trust me. And it makes perfect sense because very few people in this world have any idea who I am, and there are times when I'm not so sure myself. I couldn't tell you this before, but it's over." He paused. "Benton taught me in the Academy long before you got to know him."

"You're an *agent*?" I asked in disbelief.

"Yes."

"No," I said, my mind reeling. "No! *I'm not going to believe you this time, goddammit!*"

Getting up without a word, he went to the phone by the bed and dialed.

"Come here," he said, glancing over at me.

Then he handed me the receiver.

"Hello?" I recognized the voice immediately.

"Benton?" I said.

"Kay? Are you all right?"

"Mark's here," I replied. "He found me. Yes, Benton. I'm all right."

"Thank God. You're in good hands. I'm sure he'll explain."

"I'm sure he will. Thank you, Benton. Good-bye."

Mark took the receiver from me and hung up. When we returned to the table he looked at me for a long time before he spoke again.

"I left my law practice after Janet was killed. I'm still not sure why, Kay, but it doesn't matter. I worked in the field, in Detroit for a while, then went under deep cover. The bit about my working for Orndorff & Berger was all a ruse."

"You're not going to tell me Sparacino's working for the Feds, too," I said, and I was trembling.

"Hell, no," he replied, looking away from me.

"What's he involved in, Mark?"

"His minor infractions included his cheating Beryl Madison, tampering with her royalty statements like he's done with a number of his clients. And as I've already told you, he was manipulating her, playing her against Cary Harper and cooking up a big publicity scam—again, like he's done a number of times before."

"Then what you told me in New York is true."

"Certainly not everything. I couldn't tell you everything."

"Did Sparacino know I was coming to New York?" It was a question that had been tormenting me for weeks.

"Yes. I set it up, ostensibly so I could get more information from you and manipulate you into talking to him. He knew you would never agree to a discussion. So I volunteered to bring you to him."

"Jesus," I muttered.

"I thought everything was under control. I thought he wasn't on to me until we got to the restaurant. That's when I realized everything was going to hell," Mark went on.

"Why?"

"Because he had me tailed. I've known for a long time that the Partin brat's one of his snitches. It's how he pays the rent while he's waiting for bit parts in soaps, TV commercials, and underwear ads. Obviously, Sparacino was getting suspicious of me."

"Why would he send Partin? Wouldn't he realize you'd recognize him?"

"Sparacino isn't aware that I know about Partin," he said. "Point is, when I saw Partin in the restaurant, I knew Sparacino had sent him to make sure I was really meeting with you, to see what I was up to, just like he sent the so-called Jeb Price to ransack your office."

"Are you going to tell me Jeb Price is a starving actor, too?"

"No. We arrested him in New Jersey last week. He won't be bothering anybody for a while."

"And I suppose your knowing Diesner in Chicago was also a lie," I said.

"He lives in legend. But I've never met the man."

"And I suppose your coming to see me in Richmond was a setup, too, wasn't it?" I fought back tears.

Refilling our wineglasses, he replied, "I wasn't really driving in from D.C. I'd just flown in from New York. Sparacino sent me to pick your brain, find out everything he could about Beryl's murder."

I sipped my wine, silent for a moment as I tried to regain my composure.

Then I asked, "Is he somehow involved in her murder, Mark?"

"At first that worried me," he answered. "If nothing else, I wondered if Sparacino's games with Harper had gone too far, if Harper had gone haywire and murdered Beryl. But then Harper was murdered, and as time went by, I failed to pick up on anything that would make me think Sparacino was connected with their deaths. I think he wanted me to find out everything I could about Beryl's murder because he was paranoid."

"Was he worried the police would have gone through her office, that maybe it would come out that her royalty statements were fraudulent?" I asked.

"Maybe. I do know he wants her manuscript. No question of its value. But beyond that, I'm not sure."

"What about his lawsuit, his vendetta against the attorney general?"

"It's generated a lot of publicity," Mark replied. "And Sparacino despises Ethridge, would be delighted if he could humiliate him or even run him out of office."

"Scott Partin has been down here," I informed him. "He was down here not long ago asking questions about Beryl."

"Interesting" was all he said, taking another bite of steak.

"How long have you been connected with Sparacino?"

"More than two years."

"Lord," I said.

"The Bureau set it up very carefully. I was sent in as a lawyer named Paul Barker looking for work, looking to get rich quick. I went through the moves necessary to make him hook into me. Of course he checked me out, and when certain details didn't add up, he finally confronted me. I admitted I was living under an assumed name, that I was part of the Federal Protected Witness Program. It's convoluted and difficult to explain, but Sparacino believed I had been involved in illegal activities in a former life in Tallahassee, had gotten nailed, and that the Feds had rewarded me for my testimony by fictionalizing my identity and my past."

"Had you been involved in illegal activities?" I asked.

"No."

"Ethridge is of the opinion that you have been," I said. "That you've also served time in prison."

"I'm not surprised, Kay. The federal marshals tend to be very cooperative with the Bureau. On paper, the Mark James you once knew looks pretty bad. A lawyer who crossed over, was disbarred, and spent two years in the pen."

"Am I to assume that Sparacino's connection with Orndorff & Berger is a front?" I asked.

"Yes."

"For what, Mark? There must be more to it than his publicity scams."

"We are convinced he has been laundering money for

the mob, Kay. Money from narcotics trafficking. We also believed he is tied in with organized crime in the casinos. Politicians are involved, judges, other attorneys. The network is unbelievable. We've known it for quite a while, but it's dangerous business when one part of the criminal justice system attacks another. We had to have admissible evidence of guilt. That's why I was sent in. The more I uncovered, the more there was. Three months turned into six, and then it became years."

"I don't understand. His firm is legitimate, Mark."

"New York is Sparacino's own little country. He has power. Orndorff & Berger knows very little about what he does. I've never worked for the firm. They don't even know my name."

"But Sparacino does," I pressed him. "I heard him refer to you as Mark."

"Yes, he knows my real name. As I've said, the Bureau was very careful. They did quite a good job of rewriting my life, of creating a paper trail that makes the Mark James you once knew someone you wouldn't recognize, much less like." He paused, his face grim. "Sparacino and I agreed that he would refer to me as Mark in your presence. The rest of the time I was Paul. I worked for him. For a while I lived with his family. I was his loyal son, or at least this is what he thought."

"I know Orndorff & Berger never heard of you," I confessed. "I tried to call you in New York and Chicago, and they didn't know who I was talking about. I called Diesner. He didn't know who you were, either. I may not make a good fugitive, but you make an equally poor spy."

He was silent for a moment.

Then he said, "The Bureau had to bring me in, Kay. You came on the scene, and I took a lot of chances. I got emotionally involved because you were involved. I was stupid."

"I don't know how I'm suppose to respond to that."

"Drink your wine and watch the moon rise over Key West. That's the best way to respond."

"But, Mark," I said, and by now I was hopelessly caught up in him, "there's one very important point I don't understand."

"I'm quite sure there are any number of points you don't understand and may never understand, Kay. We have a lot of life between us that can't be spanned in an evening."

"You said Sparacino sicced you on me to pick my brain. How did he know you were acquainted with me? Did you tell him?"

"He introduced you into a conversation right after we heard about Beryl's murder. He said you were the medical examiner, the chief in Virginia. I panicked. I didn't want him messing with you. I decided it would be better if I did it instead."

"I appreciate the chivalry," I said ironically.

"And you should." His eyes were on mine. "I told him we had dated in a former life. I wanted him to turn you over to me. And he did."

"And that's the whole of it?" I said.

"I would like to think so, but I'm afraid my motives may have been mixed."

"Mixed?"

"I think I was enticed by the possibility of seeing you again."

"So you've said."

"I wasn't lying."

"Are you lying to me now?"

"I swear to God I'm not lying to you now," he said.

I suddenly realized I was still dressed in a polo shirt and shorts, my skin sticky, my hair a mess. I excused myself from the table and went into the bathroom. Half an hour later, I was swathed in my favorite terrycloth robe, and Mark was sound asleep on top of my bed.

He groaned and opened his eyes when I sat down beside him.

"Sparacino's a very dangerous man," I said, slowly running my fingers through his hair.

"No question about it," Mark said sleepily.

"He sent Partin. I'm not sure I understand how he knew that Beryl was ever down here."

"Because she called him from down here, Kay. He's known it all along."

I nodded, not really surprised. Beryl may have depended on Sparacino to the bitter end, but she must have begun to distrust him. Otherwise she would have left her manuscript with him and not in the hands of a bartender named PJ.

"What would he do if he knew you were here?" I asked quietly. "What would Sparacino do if he knew you and I were together in this room having this conversation?"

"Be jealous as hell."

"Seriously."

"Probably kill us if he thought he could get away with it."

"Could he get away with it, Mark?"

Pulling me close, he said into my neck, "Shit, no."

* * *

We were awakened the next morning by the sun, and after making love again we slept entangled in each other's arms until ten.

While Mark showered and shaved, I stared out at the day, and never had colors been so bright or the sun shone so magnificently on the tiny offshore island of Key West. I would buy a condo where Mark and I would make love for the rest of our lives. I would ride a bicycle for the first time since I was a child, take up tennis again, and quit smoking. I would work harder at getting along with my family, and Lucy would be our frequent guest. I would visit Louie's often and adopt PJ as our friend. I would watch sunlight dance over the sea and say prayers to a woman named Beryl Madison whose terrible death had given new meaning to my life and taught me to love again.

After brunch, which we ate in the room, I pulled Beryl's manuscript out of the knapsack while Mark looked on in disbelief.

"Is that what I think it is?" he asked.

"Yes. It's exactly what you think it is," I said.

"Where in God's name did you find it, Kay?" He got up from the table.

"She left it with a friend," I answered, and next we were propping pillows behind us, the manuscript between us on the bed as I told Mark all about my conversations with PJ.

Morning turned into afternoon, and we did not step outside the room except to place dirty dishes in the hall and replace them with sandwiches and snacks we ordered sent up as the spirit moved. For hours we said very little to each other as we turned through the pages of Beryl's Madison's life. The book was incredible, and more than once it brought tears to my eyes.

Beryl was a songbird born in a storm, a ragged bit of beautiful color clinging to the branches of a terrible life. Her mother had died, and her father had replaced her with a woman who treated Beryl with scorn. Unable to endure the world she lived in, she learned the art of creating one of her own. Writing was her way of coping, and it was a talent enhanced like artistry by the deaf and music by the blind. She could fashion from words a world I could taste, smell, and feel.

Her relationship with the Harpers was as intense as it was deranged. They were three volatile elements forming a thunderhead of unbelievable destruction when they finally lived together in that storybook mansion on its river of timeless dreams. Cary Harper bought and restored the great house for Beryl, and it was in the upstairs bedroom where I had slept that he robbed her one night of her virginity when she was only sixteen.

When she did not come down to breakfast the following morning, Sterling Harper went upstairs to check and found Beryl in a fetal position, crying. Unable to face that her famous brother had raped their surrogate daughter, Miss Harper battled the demons of her house with troops of denial. She never said a word to Beryl or attempted to intervene, but softly shut her door at night and slept her fitful sleep.

The molestation of Beryl continued, week after week, less frequently as she got older and finally ending with the Pulitzer Prize–winner's impotence, brought on by long evenings of hard drinking and other excesses, including drugs. When the interest from his accumulated book earnings and family inheritance could no longer support his vices, he turned to his friend, Joseph McTigue, who focused his kindly attentions and skills on Harper's precarious finances, eventually making the author "not only solvent again, but wealthy enough to afford the finest whiskey by the case and cocaine binges whenever he pleased."

According to Beryl, after she moved out Miss Harper painted the portrait over the library mantel, a portrait of a child robbed of innocence, intended unconsciously or not to torment Harper forever. He drank more, wrote less, and began suffering from insomnia. He began frequenting Culpeper's Tavern, a ritual encouraged by his sister, who used those hours to conspire against him with Beryl on the phone. The final blow came in a dramatic act of defiance when Beryl, encouraged by Sparacino, violated her contract.

It was her way of reclaiming her life and, in her words, "preserving the beauty of my friend, Sterling, by pressing the memory of her between these pages like wildflowers." Beryl began her book very shortly after Miss Harper was diagnosed as having cancer. Their bond was inviolable, their love for each other immense.

Naturally, there were lengthy digressions about the books Beryl had written and the sources of her ideas. Excerpts from earlier works were included, and I suspected this might have explained the partial manuscript we found on her bedroom dresser after she was dead. It was hard to say. It was hard to know what had gone on in Beryl's mind. But I could see that her work was extraordinary, and sufficiently scandalous to have frightened Cary Harper and caused Sparacino to lust after it.

What I failed to see as the afternoon wore on was anything that raised the specter of Frankie. There was no mention in her manuscript of the ordeal that would eventually end her life. I supposed it was too much for her to contemplate. Perhaps, she hoped, it would pass with time.

I was nearing the end of Beryl's book when Mark suddenly put his hand on my arm.

"What?" I could barely tear my eyes away.

"Kay. Take a look at this," he said, lightly placing a page on top of the one I was reading.

It was the opening of Chapter Twenty-five, a page I had previously read. It took me a moment to see what I had missed. It was a very clean photocopy, and not an original typed page like all of the others.

"I thought you said this was the only copy," Mark quizzed me.

"I was under the impression that it was," I replied, mystified.

"I wonder if she made a copy and mixed up two of the pages."

"That's the way it looks," I considered. "But where is the copy, then? It hasn't turned up."

"Got no idea."

"You sure Sparacino doesn't have it?"

"I'm pretty sure I would know if he did. I've turned his office inside out during his absences and I've done the same to his house. Besides, I think he would have told me, at least when he thought we were buddies."

"I think we'd better go see PJ."

It was, we discovered, PJ's day off. He was not at Louie's or at home. Dusk was settling over the island before we finally caught up with him at Sloppy Joe's, by which time he was three sheets to the wind. I grabbed him at the bar and led him by the hand to a table.

I hastily made introductions. "This is Mark James, a friend of mine."

PJ nodded and lifted his longnecked bottle of beer in a drunken toast. He blinked several times, as if trying to clear his vision, while he openly admired my attractive masculine companion. Mark seemed oblivious.

Raising my voice above the din of the crowd and band, I said to PJ, "Beryl's manuscript. Did she make a copy of it while she was here?"

Taking a swig of beer and rocking to the music, he replied, "Don't know. She never said anything about it to me, if she did."

"But is it possible?" I persisted. "Might she have done this when she photocopied the letters she gave to you?"

He shrugged, beads of perspiration rolling down his temples, face flushed. PJ was more than drunk, he was stoned.

While Mark looked on impassively, I tried again. "Well, did she carry the manuscript with her when she went out to photocopy the letters?"

". . . Just like Bogie and Bacall . . ." PJ sang along in a hoarse baritone, slapping the edge of the table in rhythm with the mob.

"PJ!" I cried loudly.

"Man," he protested, his eyes riveted to the stage, "it's my favorite song."

So I sank back in my chair and let PJ sing his favorite song. During a brief break in the performance, I repeated my question. PJ drained his bottle of beer, then replied with surprising clarity, "All I remember is Beryl had the knapsack with her that day, okay? I gave it to her, you know. Something she could use down here to haul her shit around in. She headed off to Copy Cat or somewhere, and she sure as hell had the knapsack with her. So, yeah." He got out his cigarettes. "She might've had the book in the knapsack. And she might've made a copy of it when she copied the letters. All I know is she left me the one I handed over to you whenever it was."

"Yesterday," I said.

"Yeah, man. Yesterday." Shutting his eyes, he started slapping the edge of the table again.

"Thank you, PJ," I said.

He didn't pay any attention as we left, pushing our way out of the bar to escape into the fresh night air.

"That's what's known as an exercise in futility," Mark said as we began walking back to the hotel.

"I don't know," I answered. "But it makes sense to me that Beryl would have copied the manuscript when she copied the letters. I can't imagine her leaving her book with PJ unless she had a copy."

"After having met him, I can't imagine her doing so, either. PJ's not exactly what I'd call a reliable custodian."

"Actually he is, Mark. He's just a little carried away tonight."

"Fried is the word."

"Maybe that's what my appearance did to him."

"If Beryl copied her manuscript and carried it back to Richmond with her," Mark continued, "then whoever killed her must have stolen it."

"Frankie," I said.

"Which may explain why he next went after Cary Harper. Our friend Frankie got jealous, the thought of Harper in Beryl's bedroom driving him crazy—crazier. Harper's habit of going to Culpeper's every afternoon is in Beryl's book."

"I know."

"Frankie could have read about that, known how to find him, figured it was the best time to catch him by surprise."

"What better time than when you're half crocked and getting out of your car on a dark driveway in the middle of nowhere?" I said.

"Just surprises me he didn't go after Sterling Harper, too."

"Maybe he would have."

"You're right. He never had the chance," Mark said. "She spared him the trouble."

Reaching for each other's hands, we fell silent, our shoes quietly scuffing along the sidewalk as the breeze stirred the trees. I wanted the moment to go on forever. I dreaded the truths we had to face. It wasn't until Mark and I were in our room, drinking wine together, that I asked the question.

"What next, Mark?"

"Washington," he said, turning away to look out the window. "In fact, tomorrow. I'll be debriefed, reprogrammed." He took a deep breath. "Hell, I don't know what I'll do after that."

"What do you want to do after that?" I asked.

"I don't know, Kay. Who knows where they'll send me?" He continued staring out at the night. "And I know you're not going to leave Richmond."

"No, I can't leave Richmond. Not now. My work is my life, Mark."

"It's always been your life," he said. "My work is my life, too. That leaves very little room for diplomacy."

His words, his face were breaking my heart. I knew he was right. When I tried to speak again, the tears came.

We held each other tightly until he fell asleep in my arms. Gently disengaging myself, I got up and returned to the window, where I sat smoking, my mind obsessively turning over many things until dawn began to pink the sky.

I took a long shower. The hot water soothed me and reinforced my resolve. Refreshed and robed, I left the humid bathroom to find Mark up and ordering breakfast.

"I'm returning to Richmond," I announced firmly, sitting next to him on the bed.

He frowned. "Not a good idea, Kay."

"I've found the manuscript, you're leaving, and I don't want to wait here alone expecting Frankie, Scott Partin, or even Sparacino himself to show up," I explained.

"They haven't found Frankie. It's too risky. I'll arrange for your protection here," he protested. "Or in Miami. That's probably better. You could stay with your family for a while."

"No."

"Kay—"

"Mark, Frankie may already have left Richmond. They may not find him for weeks. They may never find him. What am I supposed to do, hide in Florida forever?"

Leaning back into the pillows, he didn't respond.

I reached for his hand. "I won't allow my life, my career to be disrupted like this, and I refuse to be intimidated any longer. I'll call Marino and arrange for him to meet me at the airport."

He wrapped both of his hands around mine. Looking into my eyes, he said, "Come back with me to D.C. Or you can stay at Quantico for a while."

I shook my head. "Nothing's going to happen to me, Mark."

He pulled me close. "I can't stop thinking about what happened to Beryl."

Neither could I.

We kissed good-bye at the Miami airport, and I walked quickly away from him and did not look back. I was awake only during the interval when I changed planes in Atlanta. The rest of the time I slept in my seat, physically and emotionally drained.

Marino met me at the gate. For once he seemed to sense my mood and followed me patiently and in silence through the terminal. The Christmas decorations and merchandise in the airport's shop windows only fed my depression. I wasn't looking forward to the holidays. I wasn't sure how or when Mark and I would see each other again. To make matters worse, when Marino and I got to the baggage area we spent an hour watching luggage make its lazy rounds on a carousel. It gave Marino an opportunity to debrief me while I got increasingly out of sorts. Finally, I reported my suitcase missing. After the tedium of filling out a detailed multiple-part form, I retrieved my car and, with Marino once again tailing me, drove home.

The dark, rainy night blessedly obscured the damage to the front yard as we parked in my driveway. Marino had reminded me earlier that they'd had no luck locating Frankie while I was away. He wasn't taking any chances.

After shining his flashlight over my property in search of broken windows or anything else hinting of an intruder, he took me through my house, turning on lights in each room, checking closets and even looking under the beds.

We were heading to the kitchen and thinking about coffee when we both recognized the code blaring out of his portable radio.

"Two-fifteen, ten-thirty-three—"

"Shit!" Marino exclaimed, snatching the radio out of his jacket pocket.

Ten-thirty-three was the code for "Mayday." Radio broadcasts were ricocheting like bullets through the air. Patrol cars were responding like jets taking off. An officer was down at a convenience store not far from where I lived. Apparently he had been shot.

"Seven-oh-seven, ten-thirty-three," Marino barked to the dispatcher that he was responding as he hurried to my front door.

"Goddamm it! Walters! He's just a fuckin' kid!" He ran out cursing into the rain, calling back to me, "Lock up tight, Doc. I'll have a couple uniform men over here right away!"

I paced the kitchen, finally sitting at the table nursing straight Scotch while a hard rain drummed the roof and beat against windowpanes. My suitcase was lost and my .38 was inside it. It was a detail I had neglected to mention to Marino, my mind dulled by exhaustion. Too jittery to go to bed, I flipped through Beryl's manuscript, which I had been wise enough to hand-carry on the plane, and sipped my drink waiting for the police to arrive.

Just before midnight my doorbell rang, startling me out of my chair.

Looking through my front door peephole and expecting the officers Marino had promised, I saw a pale young man wearing a dark slicker and some sort of uniform cap. He looked cold and wet as he hunched against the blowing rain, a clipboard held against his chest.

"Who is it?" I called out.

"Omega Courier Service from Byrd Airport," he answered. "I've got your suitcase, ma'am."

"Thank God," I said with feeling, deactivating the alarm and unlocking the door.

Incapacitating terror seized me as he put down my suitcase inside the foyer and I suddenly remembered. I had written my office address on the lost baggage claim I had filled out at the airport, not my home address!

17

Dark hair was a stringy fringe beneath his cap, and he did not look me in the eye as he said, "If you'll just sign this, ma'am." He handed me the clipboard as voices played madly in my mind.

"They were late coming in from the airport because the airline lost Mr. Harper's bag."

"Is your hair naturally blond, Kay, or do you bleach it?"

"It was after the boy delivered the luggage . . ."

"All of them gone, now."

"Last year we got in a fiber identical to this orange one in every respect when Roy was asked to examine trace recovered from a Boeing seven forty-seven . . ."

"It was after the boy delivered the luggage!"

Slowly I took the offered pen and clipboard from the outstretched brown leather–gloved hand.

In a voice I did not recognize, I instructed, "Would you

please be so kind as to open my suitcase. I can't possibly sign anything until I make sure my belongings are present and accounted for."

For an instant his hard pale face registered confusion. His eyes widened a little as they dropped down to my upright bag, and I struck so fast he didn't have time to raise his hands to ward off the blow. The edge of the clipboard caught him in the throat, then I bolted like a wild animal.

I got as far as my dining room before I heard his footsteps coming after me. My heart was hammering against my ribs as I raced into the kitchen, my feet nearly going out from under me on the smooth linoleum as I wheeled around the butcher block and jerked the fire extinguisher off the wall near the refrigerator. The instant he burst into the kitchen I blasted him in the face with a choking storm of dry powder. A long-bladed knife clattered dully to the floor as he clutched his face with his hands and gasped. Snatching a cast-iron skillet off the stove, I swung it like a tennis racket, hitting him solidly in the belly. Struggling for breath, he doubled over and I swung again, this time at his head. My aim was off. I felt cartilage crunch beneath the flat iron bottom. I knew I had broken his nose and probably knocked out several teeth. It barely slowed him down. Dropping to his knees, coughing and partially blinded by the powder, he grabbed at my ankles with one hand, his other hand groping for the knife. Throwing the skillet at him, I kicked the knife out of the way and fled from the kitchen, slamming my hip into the sharp edge of the table and knocking my shoulder against the doorframe.

Disoriented and sobbing, I somehow managed to dig

my Ruger out of my suitcase and jam two cartridges into the cylinder. By then he was almost on top of me. I was aware of the sound of the rain and his wheezing breath. The knife was inches from my throat when the third squeeze of the trigger finally struck firing pin against primer. In a deafening explosion of gas and flame, a Silvertip ripped through his abdomen, knocking him back several feet and down to the floor. He fought to sit up, glassy eyes staring at me, his face a gory mass of blood. He tried to say something as he feebly raised the knife. My ears were ringing. Steadying the gun in my shaking hands, I put the second bullet through his chest. I smelled acrid gunpowder tainted by the sweet odor of blood as I watched the light fade from Frankie Aims's eyes.

Then I fell apart, wailing as the wind and rain bore down hard against the house and Frankie's blood seeped over polished oak. My body shook as I wept, and I did not move until the telephone rang a fifth time.

All I could say was "Marino. *Oh God, Marino!*"

I did not return to my office until Frankie Aims's body had been released from the morgue, his blood rinsed off the stainless-steel table, washed out pipes, and diffused into the fetid waters of the city's sewers. I was not sorry I had killed him. I was sorry he had ever been born.

"The way it's looking," Marino said as he regarded me over the depressing mountain of paperwork on top of my office desk, "is Frankie hit Richmond a year ago October. Least, that's how long he'd been renting his crib on Redd Street. A couple weeks later he got himself a job delivering lost bags. Omega's got a contract with the airport."

I said nothing, my letter opener slitting through another item of mail destined for my wastepaper basket.

"The guys who work for Omega drive their personal cars. And that's the problem Frankie run into long about last January. His 'eighty-one Mercury Lynx blew the transmission, and he didn't have the dough to fix it. No car, no job. That's when he asked Al Hunt for a favor, I think."

"Had the two of them been in contact before this?" I asked, feeling, and I'm sure sounding, burned out and distracted.

"Oh, yeah," Marino answered. "No doubt in my mind, or Benton's, either."

"What are you basing your assumptions on?"

"For starters," he said, "Frankie, it turns out, was living in Butler, Pennsylvania, a year and a half ago. We been going through Old Man Hunt's phone bills for the past five years—saves all the shit in case he gets audited, right? Turns out that during the time Frankie was in Pennsylvania, the Hunts received five collect calls from Butler. The year before that it was collect calls from Dover, Delaware, the year before that there was half a dozen or so from Hagerstown, Maryland."

"The calls were from Frankie?" I asked.

"We're still running it down. But me, I got a strong suspicion Frankie was calling Al Hunt from time to time, probably told him all about what he done to his mother. That's how Al knew so much when he talked to you. Hell, he wasn't no mind reader. He was reciting what he knew from conversations with his sicko pal. It's like the crazier Frankie got, the closer he moved to Richmond. Then, boom! A year ago he hits our lovely city and the rest's history."

"What about Hunt's car wash?" I asked. "Was Frankie a regular visitor?"

"According to a couple of guys working there," Marino said, "someone fitting Frankie's description was down there from time to time, apparently going back to last January. The first week in February, based on receipts we found in his house, he had the engine in his Mercury overhauled to the tune of five hundred bucks, which he probably got from Al Hunt."

"Do you know if Frankie happened to be at the car wash on a day when Beryl might have brought her car in?"

"I'm guessing that's what happened. You know, he spots her for the first time when he delivers Harper's bags to the McTigues' house last January. Then what? He spots her again maybe a couple weeks later when he's hanging out at Al Hunt's car wash begging for a loan. Bingo. It's like a message to him. Then maybe he spots her again at the airport—he was in and out all the time picking up lost bags, doing who knows what. Maybe he sees Beryl this third time when she's at the airport catching a plane for Baltimore, where she's going to meet Miss Harper."

"Do you think Frankie talked to Hunt about Beryl, too?"

"No way to know. But I wouldn't be surprised. It would sure help explain why Hunt hung himself. He saw it coming—what his squirrelly pal finally did to Beryl. Then, next thing, Harper gets whacked. Hunt probably felt guilty as shit."

I shifted painfully in my chair as I shoved paper around in search of the date stamp I'd had in hand but a second ago. I ached all over and was seriously contemplating having my right shoulder X-rayed. As for my psyche, I wasn't sure what anyone could do about that. I didn't feel like myself. I wasn't sure what I felt except that it was very hard for me to sit still. It was impossible for me to relax.

I commented, "Part of Frankie's delusional thinking would be to personalize his encounters with Beryl and ascribe profound significance to them. He sees Beryl at the McTigues' house. He sees her at the car wash. He sees her in the airport. It would really set him off."

"Yeah. Now the schizo knows God's talking to him, telling him he has some connection with this pretty blond lady."

Just then Rose walked in. Taking the pink telephone message she offered to me, I added it to the pile.

"What color was his car?" I slit open another envelope. Frankie's car had been parked in my drive. I had seen it when the police arrived, when my property was pulsing with red strobe lights. But nothing had penetrated. I remembered very few details.

"Dark blue."

"And no one remembers seeing a blue Mercury Lynx in Beryl's neighborhood?"

Marino shook his head. "After dark, if he had his headlights off, the car wouldn't exactly be conspicuous."

"True."

"As for when he hit Harper, he probably pulled his ride off the road somewhere and went the rest of the way on foot." He paused. "The upholstery of the driver's seat was rotted out."

"I beg your pardon?" I asked, looking up from the letter I was glancing over.

"He had it covered with a blanket he must have swiped from one of the planes."

"The source of the orange fiber?" I inquired.

"They got to run some tests. But we're thinking that's the case. The blanket's got orangish-red pinstripes running through it, and Frankie would have been sitting on it when he drove to Beryl's house. Probably explains the terrorist shit. Some passenger was using a blanket like Frankie's during an overseas flight. The guy changes planes and it just so happens an orange fiber ends up on the one that gets hijacked in Greece. Bingo! Some poor Marine ends up with this same type of fiber stuck to his blood after he's whacked. Got any idea how many fibers must get transferred from plane to plane?"

"It's hard to imagine," I agreed, wondering why I merited being on every junk mailer's list in the United States. "And it probably also explains why Frankie carried so many fibers on his clothes. He was working in the baggage area. He was all over the airport and may even have gone inside the planes. Who knows what he did or what debris he picked up on his clothes?"

"Omega wears uniform shirts," Marino remarked. "Tan. They're made of Dynel."

"That's interesting."

"You should know that, Doc," he said, watching me closely. "He was wearing one when you shot him."

I didn't remember. I remembered only his dark rain slicker, and his face bloody and covered with the white powder from my fire extinguisher.

"Okay," I said. "So far I'm following you, Marino. But what I don't understand is how Frankie got Beryl's telephone number. It was unlisted. And how did he know she was flying in from Key West the night of October twenty-ninth, the night she returned to Richmond? And how the hell did he know when I flew in, too?"

"The computers," he said. "All passenger info, including flight schedules, phone numbers, and home addresses, is in the computers. All we can figure is Frankie sometimes played around with the computers when one of the counters was unattended, maybe late at night or early in the morning. The airport was like his damn crib. No telling what all he was into without anybody paying him any mind. He wasn't much of a talker, a real low-profile kind of guy, the sort who slips around quiet as a cat."

"According to his Stanford-Binet," I mused, grinding the date stamp into its dried-out ink pad, "he was well above average in intelligence."

Marino said nothing.

I mumbled, "His IQ was in the upper one-twenty range."

"Yeah, yeah," Marino said somewhat impatiently.

"I'm just telling you."

"Shit. You really take those tests seriously, don't you?"

"They're a good indicator."

"They ain't gospel."

"No, I won't say that Intelligence Quotient tests are gospel," I agreed.

"Maybe I'm glad I don't know what mine is."

"You could have your IQ tested, Marino. It's never too late."

"Hope it's higher than my damn bowling score. That's all I got to say."

"Not likely. Not unless you're a pretty sorry bowler."

"I was last time I went."

I slipped off my glasses and gingerly rubbed my eyes. I had a headache that I was sure would never go away.

Marino went on, "All me and Benton can figure is

Frankie got Beryl's phone number out of the computer, and after a while was monitoring her flights. I'm figuring he knew from the computer that she'd taken a plane to Miami back in July when she ran off after finding that heart scratched on her car door—"

"Any theories as to when he might have done this?" I interrupted, pulling the wastepaper basket closer.

"When she'd fly to Baltimore she'd leave her car at the airport, and the last time she met Miss Harper up there was in early July, less than a week before Beryl found that heart scratched on her door," he said.

"So he may have done it while her car was parked at the airport."

"What do you think?"

"I think that seems very plausible."

"Ditto."

"Then Beryl flees to Key West." I continued attacking my mail. "And Frankie keeps checking the computer for her return reservation. That's how he knew exactly when she'd be back."

"The night of October twenty-ninth," Marino said. "And Frankie had it all figured out. A piece of cake. He had legitimate access to the passengers' baggage, and I figure he probably checked out the bags from her flight as they were being loaded on the conveyor belt. When he finds a bag with Beryl's name tag on it, he snatches it. A little later, she's complaining that her brown leather tote bag is missing."

He didn't need to add that this was exactly the same maneuver Frankie used on me. He monitored my return from Florida. He snatched my suitcase. Then he appeared at my door, and I let him in.

The governor had invited me to a reception I had missed by a week. I supposed Fielding had gone in my place. The invitation went into the trash.

Marino went on to supply more details about what the police had discovered inside Frankie Aims's Northside apartment.

Inside his bedroom was Beryl's tote bag, containing her bloody blouse and underclothes. Inside a trunk that served as a table next to his bed was an assortment of violent pornographic magazines and a bag of small-gauge pellets that Frankie had used to fill the section of pipe he bashed against Cary Harper's head. Out of this same trunk came an envelope containing a second set of Beryl's computer disks, still taped between two stiff squares of cardboard, and the photocopy of Beryl's manuscript, including the opening page of Chapter Twenty-five that she had gotten mixed up with the original Mark and I had read. Benton Wesley's theory was that Frankie's habit was to sit up in bed reading Beryl's book while he fondled the clothes she was wearing when he murdered her. Perhaps so. What I did know with certainty was that Beryl never had a chance. When Frankie arrived at her door, he was carrying her leather tote bag and identifying himself as a courier. Even if she recognized him from that night when he had delivered Cary Harper's bags to the McTigues' house, there was no reason for her to give it a second thought—just as I had not given it a second thought until I had already opened my door.

"If only she hadn't invited him in," I muttered. My letter opener had disappeared. Where the hell had it gone?

"It made sense that she would," Marino replied. "Frankie's all official and smiling and wearing an Omega uniform shirt and cap. He's got the bag, meaning he's also got her manuscript. She's relieved. She's grateful. She opens the door, deactivates the alarm, and invites him in—"

"But why did she *reset* the alarm, Marino? I have a burglar alarm system, too. And I have delivery men arrive occasionally, too. If my alarm is on when UPS pulls up to the house, I deactivate it and open the door. If I'm trusting enough to invite the person in, I'm certainly not going to reset the alarm only to have to deactivate it and reset it again a minute later when the person leaves."

"You ever locked your keys in your car?" Marino looked thoughtfully at me.

"What's that got to do with anything?"

"Just answer my question."

"Of course I have." I found my letter opener. It was in my lap.

"How does it happen? In new cars, they got all kinds of safety devices to prevent it, Doc."

"Right. And I learn them all so well I go through the motions without a thought, and next thing my doors are locked, my keys dangling from the ignition."

"I have a feeling that's exactly what Beryl did," Marino went on. "I think she was obsessive about that damn alarm system she had installed after she started getting the threats. I think she kept it on all the time, that it was a reflex for her to punch those buttons the minute she shut her front door." He hesitated, staring off at my bookcase. "Kind of weird. She leaves her damn gun in the kitchen and then resets her alarms after letting the drone inside her house. Shows how screwy her mind was, how nervous the whole ordeal made her."

I straightened up a stack of toxicology reports and moved them and a pile of death certificates out of my way. Glancing around at the tower of micro-dictations next to my microscope, I instantly felt depressed again.

"Jesus Christ," Marino finally complained. "You mind sitting still, at least until I leave? You're making me crazy."

"It's my first day back," I reminded him. "I can't help it. Look at this mess." I swept a hand over my desk. "You'd think I'd been gone a year. It will take me a month to catch up."

"I give you until eight o'clock tonight. By then everything will be back to normal, back exactly like it was."

"Thanks a lot," I said rather sharply.

"You got a good staff. They know how to keep things running when you're not here. So, what's wrong with that?"

"Not a thing." I lit a cigarette and shoved more papers aside in search of the ashtray.

Marino picked it up from the edge of the desk and moved it closer.

"Hey, it's not like you ain't needed around here," he said.

"No one is indispensable."

"Yeah, right. I knew that's what you were thinking."

"I'm not thinking anything. I'm simply distracted," I said, reaching up to the shelf to my left and fetching my datebook. Rose had crossed everything out through the end of next week. After that it was Christmas. I felt on the verge of tears, and I didn't know why.

Leaning forward to tap an ash, Marino asked quietly, "What was Beryl's book like, Doc?"

"It will break your heart and fill you with joy," I said, my eyes welling. "It's incredible."

"Yeah, well, I hope it ends up published. It will sort of keep her alive, if you know what I mean."

"I know exactly what you mean." I took a deep breath. "Mark's going to see what he can do. I suppose new arrangements will have to be made. Sparacino certainly won't be handling Beryl's business anymore."

"Not unless he does it behind bars. I guess Mark told you about the letter."

"Yes," I said. "He did."

One of the business letters from Sparacino to Beryl that Marino had found inside her house shortly after her death took on new meaning when Mark looked at it after having read her manuscript:

> How interesting, Beryl, that Joe helped Cary out—makes me all the happier I originally got the two of them together when Cary bought that magnificent house. No, I don't find it curious, at all. Joe was one of the most generous men I've ever had the pleasure of knowing. I look forward to hearing more.

That simple paragraph hinted at quite a lot, though it was unlikely Beryl had a clue. I seriously doubted Beryl had any idea that when she mentioned Joseph McTigue, she was stepping dangerously close to the forbidden turf of Sparacino's own illicit domain, which included numerous dummy corporations the lawyer had formulated to facilitate his money laundering. Mark believed that McTigue, with his tremendous assets and real estate holdings, was no stranger to Sparacino's illegal ways, and that, finally, the assistance McTigue had offered a financially desperate Harper had been something less than legitimate. Because Sparacino had never seen Beryl's manuscript, he was paranoid about what she may have unwittingly revealed. When the manuscript disappeared, his incentive for getting his hands on it was more than just greed.

"He probably thought it was his lucky day when Beryl turned up dead," Marino was saying. "You know, she's not around to argue when he doctors her book, takes out anything that might point a finger at what he's really into. Then he turns around, sells the damn thing, and makes a killing. I mean, who wouldn't be interested after all the publicity he's generated? No telling where it was going to end, either—probably with pictures of the Harpers' dead bodies showing up in some tabloid. . . ."

"Sparacino never got the photographs Jeb Price took," I reminded him. "Thank God."

"Well, whatever. Point is, after all the noise, even I'd rush out to get the damn thing, and I bet I haven't bought a book in twenty years."

"A shame," I muttered. "Reading is wonderful. You should try it sometime."

We both looked up as Rose walked in again, this time carrying a long white box tied with a luxurious red bow. Perplexed, she looked around for a clear area on my desk to set it down, then finally gave up and placed it in my hands.

"What on earth . . . ?" I muttered, my mind going blank.

Pushing back my chair, I set the unexpected gift in my lap and began to untie the satin ribbon while Rose and Marino looked on. Inside the box were two dozen long-stemmed beauties shining like red jewels swathed in green tissue paper. Bending over, I shut my eyes and enjoyed their fragrance; then I opened the small white envelope tucked inside.

"When the going gets tough, the tough go skiing. In Aspen after Christmas. Break a leg and join me," the card read. "I love you, Mark."

POSTMORTEM

Patricia D. Cornwell

Winner of the Crime Writers' Association John Creasey Award for best first novel, 1990.

Introducing Dr Kay Scarpetta

A serial killer is on the loose in Richmond, Virginia. Three women have died, brutalised and strangled in their own bedrooms. There is no pattern: the killer appears to strike at random – but always early on Saturday mornings.

So when Dr Kay Scarpetta, chief medical examiner, is awakened at 2.33 a.m., she knows the news is bad: there is a fourth victim, and she fears now for those that will follow unless she can dig up new forensic evidence to aid the police.

But not everyone is pleased to see a woman in this powerful job. Someone may even want to ruin her career and reputation . . .

'Terrific first novel, full of suspense, in which even the scientific bits grip' *The Times*

'An excellent chiller with pace and tension' *Sunday Telegraph*

'Dazzling . . . first-rate' *Los Angeles Times*

'Cornwell makes looking through a microscope as exciting as a hot-pursuit chase' *Washington Post*

FICTION
0 7088 4851 6

WHEN THE BOUGH BREAKS

Jonathan Kellerman

It began with a double murder: particularly vicious, particularly gruesome. There was only one witness: but little Melody Quinn can't or won't say a word. Which is where child psychologist Alex Delaware comes in – and takes the first step into a maelstrom of atrocities . . .

A stunning debut, a breathtaking novel of the sewer of perversion and corruption lying below the glittering surface of California cool.

'A gruesome psychodrama of depravity and organised vice . . . assured skill and horripilating effect' *Observer*

'Exceptionally exciting' *New York Times*

FICTION/THRILLER
0 7088 3141 9

OVER THE EDGE

Jonathan Kellerman

A deeply troubled young man . . . a series of vicious crimes . . . and a trail that leads to shattering revelations and murderous passions . . .

The case against Jamey Cadmus is open and shut. Found clutching a bloody knife at the scene of a horrifying double murder, he's the prime suspect in a series of killings that have rocked Los Angeles. Even his lawyer won't do more than plead diminished responsibility. No one – not the police, not the family, not the lawyers – wants Alex Delaware lifting up stones. But under those stones lies something unspeakable . . .

'OVER THE EDGE is a compulsive page-turner . . . filled with insight, charged with suspense, and laced with just enough humour to make the whole thing sparkle. This one is simply too good to miss' Stephen King

'As sleek and high-powered a performance as its predecessors' *New York Times*

'The first two Alex Delaware books were very good indeed. This one, more complexly plotted, more richly psychological . . . is the best yet' *Publishers Weekly*

'He writes with the sharpness of Chandler and the compassion of Macdonald' *Sunday Tribune*

'Impales the reader . . . worth a four-star rating' *Guardian*

FICTION
0 7088 3585 6

What horrifying secret lies within . . .

THE VIOLET CLOSET

Gary Gottesfeld

A terrified young voice cries out from the dark.

"Da hurt . . . Da kill . . . Help me!"

These are the panic-stricken words of a little girl phoning in to Dr Rena Halbrook's radio show. But who is little Alice – and where is she?

As Charles Halleran, veteran reporter, hears the child's plea over his car radio, he recalls another little girl named Alice who died in New York 18 years before. Can there possibly be a connection?

As the anniversary of that shocking death approaches, Charles teams up with Rena in a desperate search to uncover dark secrets from the past and prevent almost certain tragedy from striking again.

Their race against time will lead them on a spine-tingling chase from the placid streets of Beverly Hills to the burnt-out tenements of the South Bronx. And the more they discover, the surer they become that what they still don't know could definitely hurt them . . .

FICTION
0 7088 4550 1

BLOOD HARVEST

Gary Gottesfeld

"The scalpel rests near her lifeless head. I then do what is needed . . ."

These words of Gustave de Montret, an insane nobleman responsible for a string of hideous murders in Bordeaux in 1772, have come back to haunt beautiful Maura McKinney. A successful New York lawyer, Maura has long left behind a tormented childhood in California's Napa Valley. Now she is drawn back to the wine country of her youth . . . and to a reunion with her dearest friend, Rena Halbrook.

But then Maura disappears – and a migrant worker is found mutilated and crucified on her land. Rena is horrified, for everything points to her friend as the killer. And as Rena and reporter Charlie Halleran pursue this bloody trail, they come ever closer to uncovering Maura's shocking secret – and to meeting a grisly fate of their own . . .

FICTION
0 7088 4931 8

A TWIST OF THE KNIFE

Stephen Solomita

Detective Stanley Moodrow is a bit of a dinosaur – too sharp to be a street cop, but too devoted to life on the streets to ever fit comfortably behind a desk. He works Manhattan block by block, door by door, operating by the book when he can, and by his own rules when he can't.

And now he's got an enemy: a sick genius named Johnny Katanos, nicknamed Zorba the Creep, who is as addicted to violence as any junkie to drugs. With an almost erotic savagery, Katanos is dedicated to bringing terror to the streets of New York in a series of ever-escalating atrocities.

Until, in one explosive act, he goes too far . . . and this time he has made it personal.

'Pulsates with the vitality of New York's street life'
Publishers Weekly

'Raw truth'
New York Times

FICTION/CRIME
0 7088 4536 3